OF RUIN & SILK

THE SKY PIRATE CHRONICLES

ANTOINE BANDELE

EDITED BY

CALLAN BROWN

BANDELE
BOOKS

Interior Design: Vellum
Publisher: Bandele Books
Editors: Fiona McLaren, Callan Brown, Seth Hansen
Cover Artist: Sutthiwat Dekachamphu
Cartographer: Maria Gandolfo | RenflowerGrapx
Character Art: Sarayu Ruangvesh

ISBN: 978-1-951905-01-9 (eBook)

ISBN: 978-1-951905-39-2 (Paperback)

ISBN: 978-1-951905-15-6 (Hardback)

First Edition | April 1, 2024

CONTENTS

What are The Sky Pirate Chronicles?   v
Pronunciation Guide   vii

Chapter 1   1
Chapter 2   10
Chapter 3   17
Chapter 4   21
Chapter 5   30
Chapter 6   41
Chapter 7   50
Chapter 8   58
Chapter 9   69
Chapter 10   74
Chapter 11   88
Chapter 12   99
Chapter 13   110
Chapter 14   119
Chapter 15   132
Chapter 16   143
Chapter 17   156
Chapter 18   162
Chapter 19   171
Chapter 20   180
Chapter 21   190
Chapter 22   198
Chapter 23   209
Chapter 24   221
Chapter 25   228
Chapter 26   240
Chapter 27   250
Chapter 28   258
Chapter 29   269
Chapter 30   279
Chapter 31   288
Chapter 32   295
Chapter 33   307
Chapter 34   314

Chapter 35   322
Chapter 36   329
Chapter 37   335
Chapter 38   340
Chapter 39   345
Chapter 40   356
Chapter 41   364
Chapter 42   372
Chapter 43   375
Chapter 44   387
Chapter 45   392
Chapter 46   403
Chapter 47   408
Chapter 48   416
Chapter 49   423
Chapter 50   433
Chapter 51   440
Chapter 52   444
Chapter 53   454
Chapter 54   460
Chapter 55   462
Chapter 56   474
Chapter 57   476
Chapter 58   481

A Note From The Author   491
More to Read   492
Also by Antoine Bandele   493
About the Author   494
Glossary   497

Of Ruin & Silk is the second book in
The Sky Pirate Chronicles, a pirate fantasy.

The series is inspired by the culture and mythos of
the West Indies, East Africa, and the Middle East.

For suggested and chronological reading order visit:
antoinebandele.com/esowon-timeline

If you enjoy this story and are interested in the rest of its world,
you can join Antoine Bandele's e-mail alerts list.
He'll send you notifications for new book releases,
exclusive updates, and behind-the-page content.
antoinebandele.com/stay-in-touch

PRONUNCIATION GUIDE

<u>Characters</u>

    Za·la - zah'lah

    Je·lani - je'lah'knee

    Fon - fon

    Sho·ma·ri - show'mah'ree

    Man·tu - mon'two

    Nu·bi·a - new'bee'ah

    Ka·rim El·Say·yed - kah'reem el'sah'yed

    Is·sa A·kif - ee'sah ah'keef

    Ta·laat Sha·moun - tah'laht sha'moon

    Has·san Ma·louf - hah'sahn mah'loof

<u>Terms & Titles</u>

    A·zi·za - ah'zee'zah

    Cha·na - chah'nah

    Di·ka·la - dee'kah'lah

    Jan·bi·ya - jan'bee'yah

    Kaf·fi·yeh - kah'fee'yay

    Ki·ja·na - kee'jah'nah

    Pak·ka - pah'kah

<u>Locations</u>

    Al A·nim - al ah'kneem

    Al Ha·ru - al hah'rue

    I·ba·bi Isles - ee'bah'bee eye'ls

    Jul·ti·a - jew'tee'ah

    Ki·do·go - kee'doe'go

    Kho·pesh - koh'pesh

    Na·li·be·la - nah'lee'bell'lah

    Py·rus - pie'rus

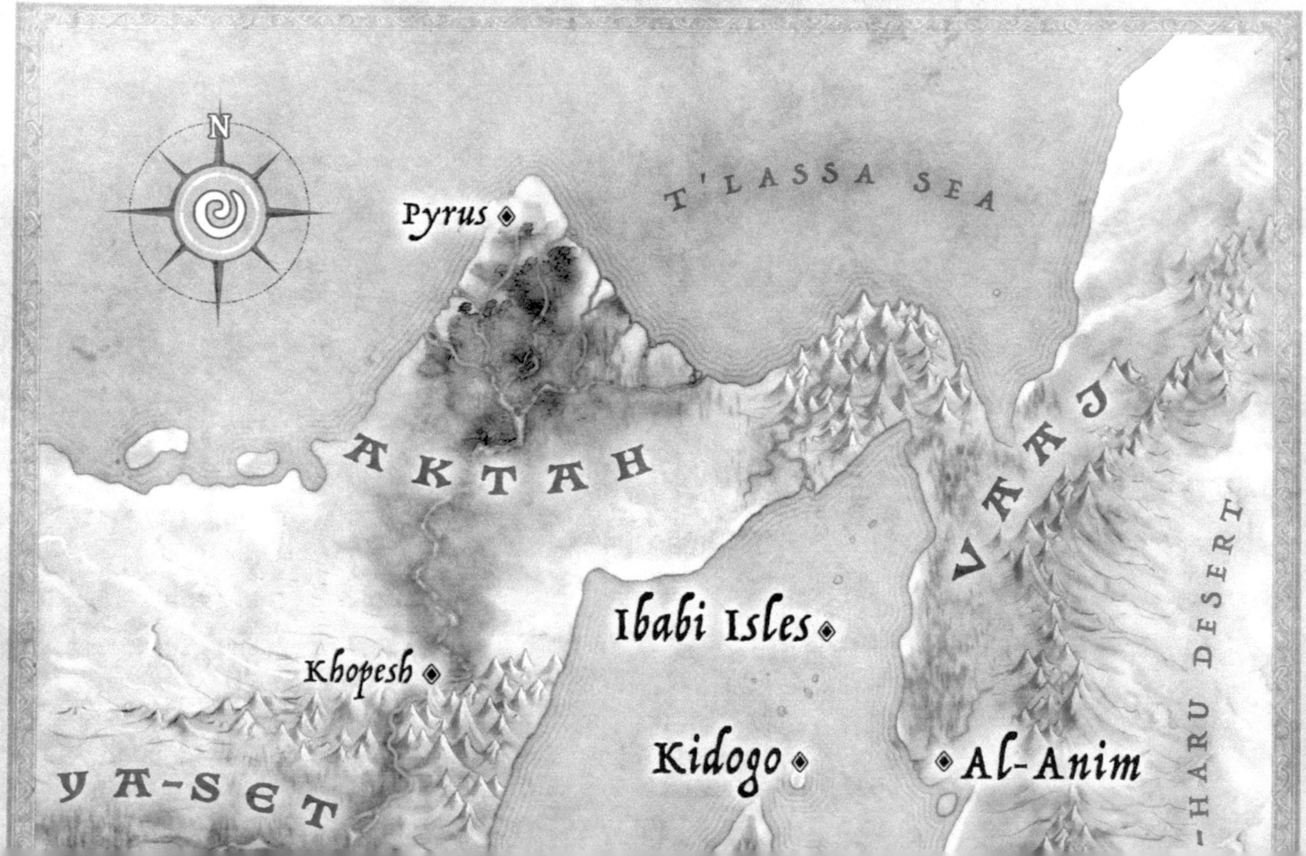

HARU DESERT
Al-Anim
Ibabi Isles
Kidogo
Khopesh
AKTAH
YA-SET
T'LASSA SEA
Pyrus
N

ESOWON
ESTERLANDS
The SAPPHIRE Isles
THE SAPPHIRE SEAS
JULTIA
Nalibela

KIDOGO

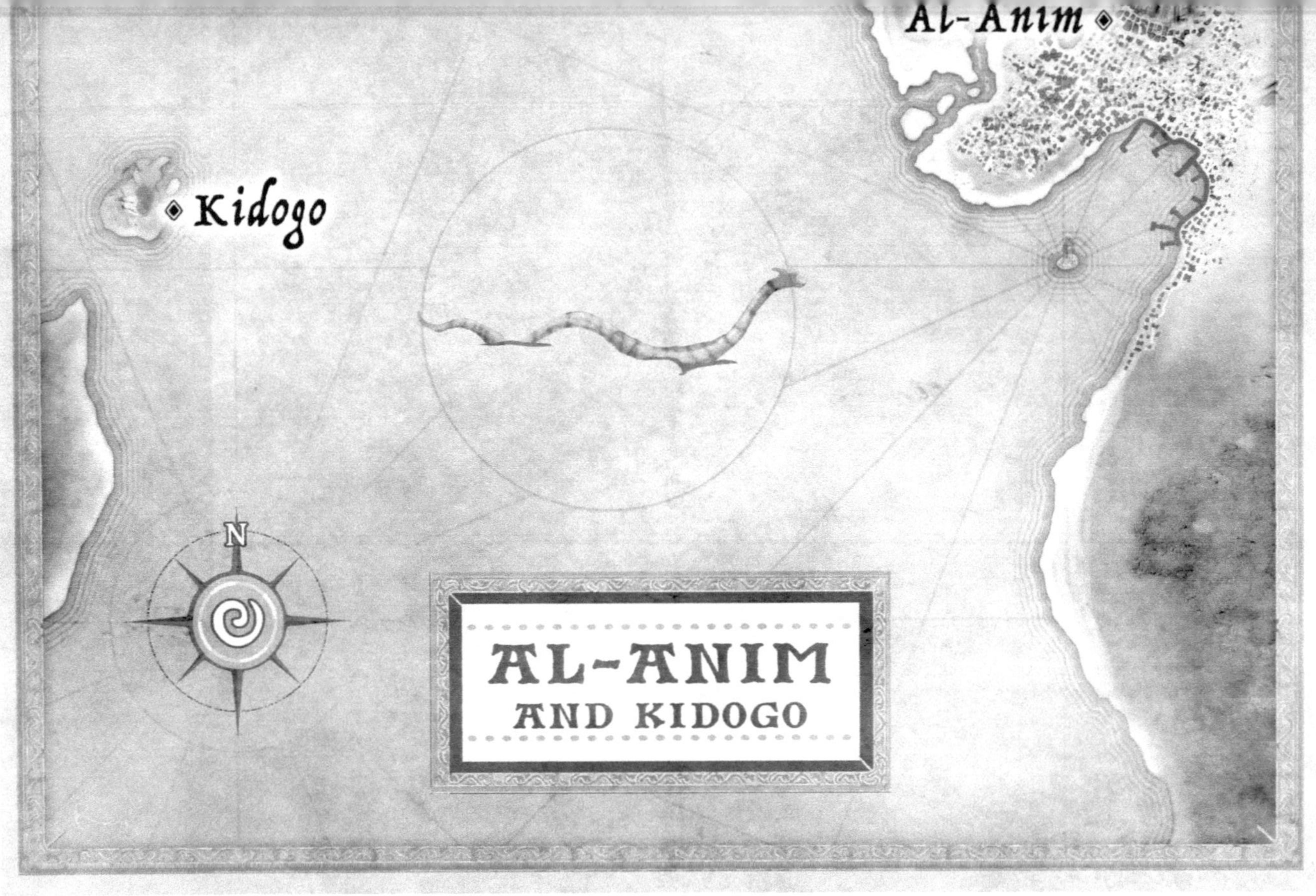

Kidogo
N
AL-ANIM
AND KIDOGO

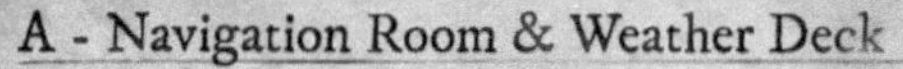

A - Navigation Room & Weather Deck
B - Captain's Quarters & Bridge
C - Crew Quarters & Engine Room
D - Supply, Brig, Communication, Infirmary, & Galley
E - Gunnery, Longboat Davits & Undercarriage
A
B
C
D
E
The Piper
Year 3582 AC

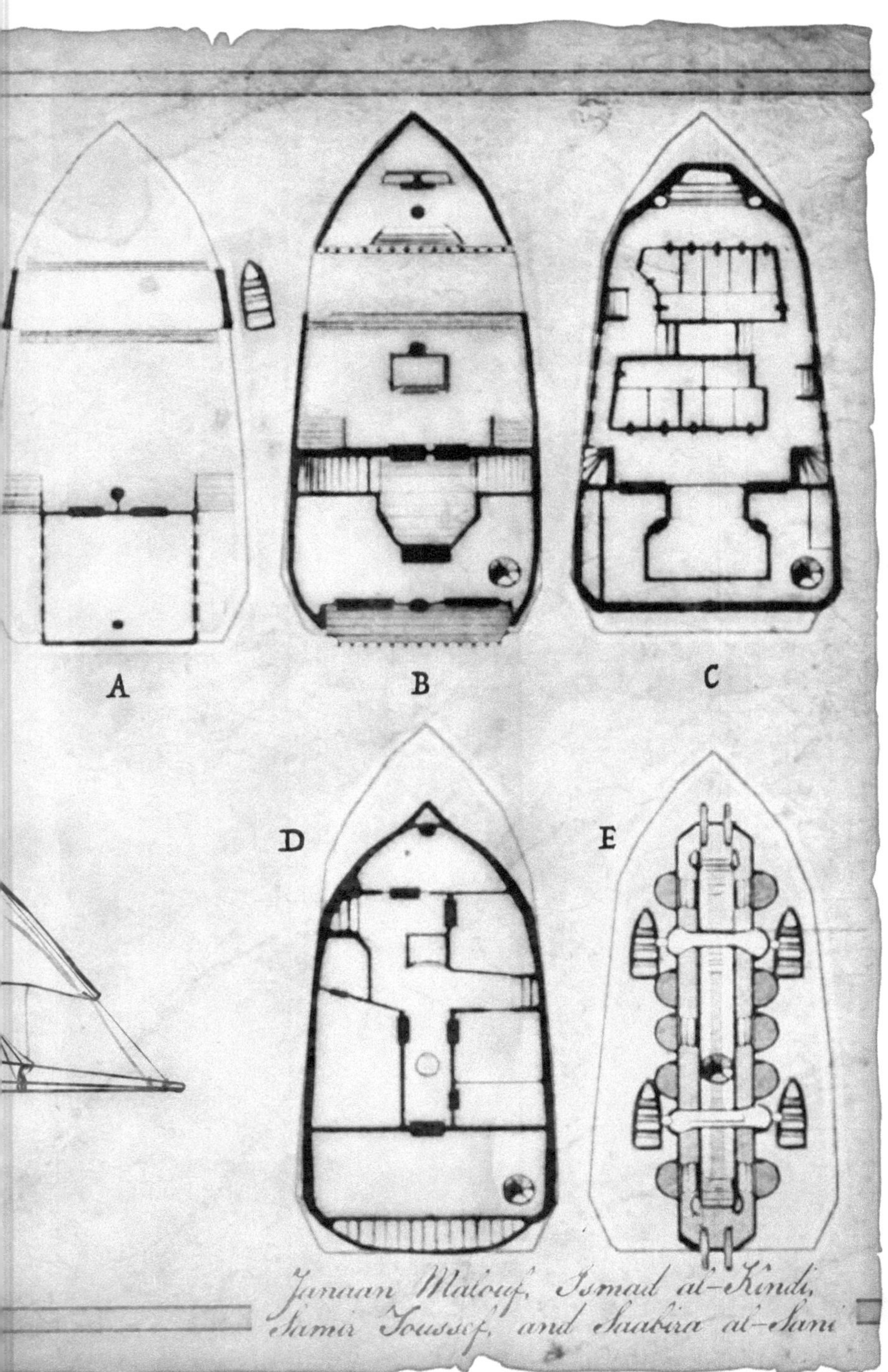
A
B
C
D
E
Janaan Malouf, Ismael al-Kindi,
Samir Youssef, and Saabira al-Sani

"'And now she is sailing the skies of Esowon.' I suppose that was all nonsense then."

"I never said this was the end of the story, wageni. The woman was persistent. Merely failing to steal an airship once wasn't going to stop her. She spent a mere few days licking her wounds before she set off for al-Anim."

"And what about that el-Sayyed fellow, the acting captain? I am thinking I have heard of the name when I made my own run from these wretched hairless. Bet those humans were chewing him out good for getting most of his crew killed."

"He was just as assiduous as the pirate... perhaps more so. But —"

"Stand back. Stand back. We got another delinquent joinin' ya."

"Well, well, one is surprised. Did not think I see you here, Limp-Tongue."

"Hang on, you two are knowing each other?"

"This one comes up toward the end of this tale. But not quite yet. I believe we left off somewhere near the twilight of the eleventh moon. Listen up, and I'll tell you our story..."

CHAPTER 1
ZALA

Even in her dreams, Zala always got it wrong.

It was what kept her awake throughout the night. Sleeping would only bring her back into her nightmares: images of her stone-skinned husband along with her bloody and bruised friends.

All dead.

All gone.

Reality was no better, however—the fear of it is what kept her eyelids pinched. To open them meant she had to face the day, face another failure. But she knew she couldn't lay around like she did, pretending to sleep.

The song of morning seagulls crashed against waves, and, finally, Zala opened her eyes to the moldy wood ceiling of the Seaborne Inn. The visage of Jelani's deadened eyes were still plastered across her vision, somewhere between dream and reality.

At least it was Jelani's face this time.

Though all of her moments of rest—if she could call them that —culminated in nightmares, each ending was different. Sometimes she saved her crew, sometimes her husband, other times Captain Nubia and the Rovers. Yet each time, no matter who she rescued, she found herself dying alongside them in the end anyway, in one gruesome fashion or another — Shomari bleeding out from a thousand stab wounds, Fon with bloodshot eyes and a look of shock.

Despite the horror of it, she always preferred to see Jelani. At least then she could see him one last time, knowing it was the end. With things as they were, she couldn't say for certain she'd ever get to see those tender brown eyes again.

At least in her dreams she knew it was the last time.

After her heartbeat had finally steadied to something resembling a normal rhythm, she drew from her damp blankets, doing her best not to press her heel into the floorboards with too much weight. Zala tilted her head to the sleeping aziza in the cot beside her; she had been on enough raids to know that even cannon blasts couldn't stir her little friend from her dreams.

Zala lifted the blanket slumped around Fon's bare shoulder. She shuddered when her hand came around the bruised and damaged wing at Fon's back, which was still black and blue at the shoulder blade where it had once been properly attached. Now it was hanging by the barest of threads. Even a tiny gnat could've zipped by and snapped her wing apart.

That had been Zala's doing, if not directly by her hand. Another mistake. Fon had made it clear she had forgiven Zala, that Zala going after her husband instead of leading the crew was a decision anyone would have struggled with. Zala, however, didn't see it that way. She only saw her failings, what she could —*should*—have done better.

She might still be getting it wrong in her dreams, but in reality, she had another chance. In reality, she could still do it *right*.

Brushing a loose hair from Fon's face and tucking it behind her pointed ear, Zala turned her heel to the single window in their cramped room. They were set to leave soon, so dawn couldn't be long off.

When she drew the moth-eaten curtain away, a gentle red-orange light painted the sky just beyond the port and along the horizon of the Sapphire Seas. Yet the brightness of the sun hadn't yet graced the base of the sky's edge — in fact, it seemed as though the sun had been rising from the west, just behind Zala and her view.

It was sun*set*, not sun*rise*.

Zala sucked her teeth when she realized she must've only been between sleep and waking a handful of minutes, no more than an hour.

Slumber had been intermittent for her the past few days, but she had hoped that she could've slept longer. She edged her chin over her shoulder to look back at her cot. But she knew what awaited her if she tried sleeping again. Besides, she wasn't all that tired to begin with.

Zala turned to the cauldron at the edge of the room, pressed between the door and a cobwebbed corner. Her stonesbane potion had long since been completed, corked and vialed. There was nothing else to be done, nothing more to do in the room besides sleep or wait in silence.

Zala never did well in silence.

So, pulling on a shawl and head wrap to warm her against the night's cold, taking up her dagger to protect against the night's dangers, and writing a note so Fon wouldn't worry if she woke, Zala set out into the Kidogon night.

SHE KEPT TO THE WELL LIT STREETS. HER WALK WAS AIMLESS, just a means to stave off dark thoughts she didn't mean to dwell in.

Most of the islanders knew her by name now, or at least by face, and she knew which paths meant the difference between a rough night and a leisurely stroll. Had this been even a few moons ago, she would've found herself skulking down the dark alleyways of the tiny port town in search of easy thieving. Hells, if it had been just one moon ago, she might've been caught throwing up signs of her pirate crew to others trying to act tough.

As she approached a group of one-eyed and peg-legged scoundrels glaring at her from a darkened corner, Zala wasn't even sure what signs she could raise up. Officially, she didn't have a crew. Captain Kobi's *Titan* was sunk, and her association with the *Redtide* was a loose one at best. She decided to avoid eye contact and take a different route. It didn't help that she could barely understand what they were saying since they spoke on her left side, where her charred ear had been deafened.

Her thoughts turned to her future plan, or what little there was of one. It had become clear to her in these last moons that her best work came by way of whims—hence the aimless walks she took then. Things needed to change; *she* needed to change. It wouldn't hurt her to figure out what exactly that was ahead of time. But she couldn't even begin to form a coherent idea of the how at that moment. For the time being, getting to al-Anim across the Sapphire Sea was good enough for her. Then, maybe, she could speak to the only person Jelani knew in the city, as much as she didn't want to converse with *that* certain someone in question.

Zala's wandering hike eventually brought her back to a familiar collection of dwellings. She wondered then if her stroll was truly without aim; perhaps some inner voice had brought her there, some instinctive draw to the one district she was most familiar with.

To most, the buildings lining its edge might've looked like nothing more than shanty homes, with their slapped-together wood panelling of mismatched hues and semi-finished roofs of thatch. To Zala, however, it had once been home, and each domicile held its own story. They had been built by the hands of those who lived within, quite unlike the town proper, with its uniform inns and identically crafted squared buildings of smooth sandstone. At least here there was personality. At least here things were never quite the same with each visit.

And Zala couldn't help staring at the changes of one shanty in particular.

When she had last seen it, there had been a rug hanging from its front, the twin-image of Yemàyá and their two moons sewn across it. Now there were nothing but wet dresses and a few pairs of damp trousers pegged along a line. And where before there had been a small garden of impala lilies, now the flowers were wilting and overgrown by weeds. But most of all, where before one might've caught the glimpse of a husband singing to his wife, both swaying peacefully in rocking chairs, now there was a new couple playing a game of wood and marbles with their newborn bundled in wool.

That couple could have been Zala and Jelani.

It *should* have been.

The woman, whose hair fell in thick curls atop her shoulder made a triumphant move that seemed to put her in a winning position in the board game. Her bright eyes came up to her disgruntled partner and she looked away to save his pride, small smiles lighting both their faces. Her gaze landed on Zala, her expression turning curious and on the border of recognition. Surely the woman would remember Zala, who sold the shanty to her only a little under a year ago.

Before the woman could call Zala over or make a beckoning wave, Zala was already peeling away, shuffling through the cramped space between two shanties. She didn't need all the pleasantries and the questions that would come of *that* encounter right now.

How have you been?

Not so great.

Where's that lovely husband of yours?

Captured by the Vaaji, dying of stoneskin. How about you?

No. She wouldn't have it. So she continued her wayward stride toward the pier.

Zala eventually settled for the harbor. In the Sapphire Isles, Kidogo—and by extension Kidogo's port—was the smallest. Many of the dhows and sloops could fit in and share moorings, occasionally a pair or trio of carracks were squeezed in too—if the pirates, sailors, and fishers were kind enough to let them all coexist. But that was not often the case.

Tonight, however, there were two large ships in the harbor surrounded by many smaller boats. The tiny dhows' single-sailed masts rose and gave way like flags, leading to the floating fortresses that were the *Redtide* and the Tide Lord's own *Seabreaker,* where it was usually anchored.

Zala strolled the boardwalk, watching as the last ships and

boats came in. Guards took up their night posts while townsfolk sat along wooden struts or unused barrels as they shared in their day's stories.

Just off the harbor, where the sand spit drew into the cove, a quartet of boys seemed to dance around a fire pit. Except, as Zala got a better look, she realized they weren't dancing, not exactly. They were playing a game of flips. One of them did a cartwheel, his feet kicking up sand like fireflies shooting through the young night.

A second boy waved him off, kissing his teeth. "Bet you can't do a backflip though!"

"Get outta here," came the reply. "I was doin' these back when I was a babe."

"Backflip?" Another voice purred. Zala hadn't noticed the pakka youth among them at first. "Can you do *this* though?"

Though silhouetted against the fire pit, Zala could make out the distinct cat ears of the feline figure as the youngster rocked back on one foot and flipped not once, but twice in the air, twisting like a pinwheel and landing on his feet with impossible grace.

"No one asked you, Rafi."

The boys shared in a bout of laughter. Zala couldn't remember the last time she had had as much fun, the last time she had let out a genuine guffaw. Not even in her own adolescence was she ever so carefree.

As the boys came down from their latest bid of chuckling, rearing up for another round of who-can-flip-the-highest, Zala closed her eyes in an attempt to capture the moment. The sound of their cheers played around her ear, fire snapped and crackled around pounding feet, and it all mixed with the high tide crashing along the shore. But every time the pakka laughed or purred, she couldn't help her mind being drawn back to her own friend, still healing in his bed.

Shomari loved his acrobatic tricks too. It seemed like every pakka got a kick out of them. Zala wondered if he'd still be able to do so moving forward. The brewmaster had said the cat would make a full recovery, physically. But his mind... that had taken a hit. Imagining a muted version of her feline friend just didn't sit right in her heart.

Wanting to get away once more from her inner thoughts, she opened her eyes.

A shadow passed at the corner of Zala's gaze, pulling her attention from the beach and the youths and farther down the pier. Squinting, she couldn't see anything against the stretch of lanterns lining the boardwalk. It must've been her imagination, or else a dog or some critter that had passed into the ocean.

But then she saw something again.

A dark figure raised its head from behind a bundle of netting. It took a few steps and then, suddenly, vaulted off the pier and out of view just behind where the *Seabreaker* was docked. Zala followed its path—more out of curiosity than anything else. Surely no thief would be so bold as to try and plunder the Tide Lord's own ship. Zala recalled how brazen she had been when she first came to Kidogo Isle. She would've loved it if someone had told *her* where the best spots were. And which to steer clear of.

As Zala approached the far end of the pier, she realized whoever had made the jump was likely alone; there had been no other shadows following its wake. And when she arrived at the *Seabreaker's* stern, a faint orange light spilled onto the pier from the lantern hanging at the captain's quarters' balcony.

Zala found no one.

It was ghostly quiet, save for the lapping tide coming high against the ship's hull. After a moment more of nothing, Zala decided the thief must've already found a way in, or perhaps it was just a crew member who was late for a shift.

A few times a guard would peek her head over the *Seabreaker's* port rail, scanning with the nonchalance of someone ready to be replaced. The guard's languid expression halted Zala. It was the *perfect* time for someone to try and make their way onto the ship.

Yet she didn't see anyone in the light or shadows. She squinted again and scanned for the slightest movement in the dark.

Then she asked herself, what was she doing? This wasn't any of her business. She should have turned on her heel, headed back to the tavern to buy a flagon of wine and drink herself to sleep. She'd been out long enough as it was, her head had long since cleared.

"You're late, dikala," came the woman guard's voice from above. "Who was it tonight? Kamaria? Etenesh?"

"Makena, actually," came a male's voice gruff and labored. "I couldn't get away. You know how it goes."

"Don't come late again."

"Ah, don't be jealous just 'cause you never get called on by no lovers."

"Oh, don't you worry none. I get mine."

"That right?" The man chuckled. "How many bodies you get this week?"

The woman took a moment too long to answer but she stammered, "W-week? Shit, kijana… I-I get multiple daily."

"Your brother doesn't count."

Zala felt a smile crease her cheeks as she stepped forward for a better listen. She couldn't quite catch what the woman said in return though as the pair drifted farther down the deck.

Then, suddenly, something else had drawn her attention. A clawed hand had risen over the railing at the stern, mere paces away from where the bickering crew members were. A head with short-cropped hair slid around the edge of the ship's hull. Orange light bathed a face. A face Zala knew: Mantu's.

That damn fool of a pirate.

"Stop frontin', chana," the male guard went on, entirely oblivious. "You ain't laid with Kirabo. I asked 'im."

What in the Sapphire Hells was Mantu thinking?

He couldn't possibly think he could steal from the Tide Lord's own ship and get away with it. Then a second thought struck Zala: The idiot wasn't trying to take the ship *alone*, was he? Surely there would have been a guard posted at stern and bow, more still belowdecks.

Before Zala could lift her arms to grab his attention, Mantu grabbed one of the balusters. His footing was awkward. He seemed too eager to make that final leap.

And then he slipped, losing purchase with the hull beneath him.

His arms hung as his massive body weighed him down. He was going to fall. Zala couldn't say anything, couldn't call out or else the guards would've seen Mantu flailing just on the other side of the railing.

Come on, Mantu. What's the point of all those muscles if you can't use them?

Mantu's foot kept sliding in and out of nooks but none of them could hold his large feet. This is why they had Shomari do these sorts of things. Mantu was the muscle, not the acrobat.

Zala jerked her head from left to right to find something that would help, but there was only a bundle of rope. She was halfway to working at a plan when she heard a scrape and then a tumble. Eyes lifting just in time, she watched as Mantu fell back and away from the ship, his arms reaching desperately for anything to hold.

There was nothing for him to grab.

The splash that came soon after sounded like a cannonball crashing into the sea.

CHAPTER 2
ZALA

Mantu didn't come up straight away. The impact from his lopsided dive was still ebbing with ripples.

Good, stay down there as long as you can, Zala thought. *Swim under the pier if you can.*

But she wasn't certain of how good a swimmer Mantu was. He had to be at least halfway decent—he was a pirate for tide's sake—but that fall looked nasty.

"What in the Sapphire Hells was that?" came the male guard's voice from above.

Bubbles floated to the black water's surface. Mantu must've been panicking, losing air. The harbor was shallow and he might've hit his head against some rocks below. He'd be too disoriented to swim away. So that meant he was going to shoot straight up—right in the line of sight of the guards who were already peering over their railings.

"Heru! Heru!" Zala cried out, springing forward in a flash and kneeling at the pier's edge. "Heru! Heru! Take my hand, you drunk fool."

"Hey, what's going on down there?" the female guard called from above. Zala lifted her head with a hand over her brow to shield against the hanging lantern's light. The guardswoman was nothing more than a shadowed outline.

Zala grinned feebly. As Mantu's head broke the water's surface, she gritted her teeth through her smile and grunted down to him, "Swim to me and play along." To the guard, she called up, "I'm sorry. My husband had some of Bulwa's special brew tonight. He took a bad fall."

The male guard chuckled. "Ain't nothin' like a bit o' Bulwa Bliss to put you flat on your ass." He smacked his comrade against the shoulder. "Hey, maybe next time you see your brother you could give him —"

The female guard punched him in the gut. Staggering and pressing down around on his abdomen, the man coughed for breath. And with a satisfied little smirk, the guardswoman turned her nose back below to say, "All right, well... get him out of here. Townsfolk ain't 'posed to buoy 'round this part of the pier after sundown."

"Yes, ma'am." Zala nodded, still struggling to pull Mantu from the water. "I've got something that'll sober him up real good."

After a few tense heaves that brought strain to Zala's back, she pulled Mantu up. As suspected, he did hit the bottom. His eyes had trouble focusing on Zala's face and blood leaked out of his ear. Zala led him away down the pier and back toward the port town. Behind them, Zala could hear the coughing male guard struggling to mumble, "Ain't that Jelani's woman?"

"Yeah, I think so. But you didn't hear? They've been gone for moons, he's probably kicked it by now."

"Damn. Chana moves on fast." Zala had half a mind to turn round and face them, but then the guard said, "You can learn a thing or two from her, ya?"

Another thud and cough rang out, and Zala knew the woman had punched her fellow crewmate. Again.

***

Zala didn't stop her and Mantu's little charade until they were far away from the pier, well into the better-lit town square. She hadn't noticed until then, but there were more than a few of the Tide Lord's guards out on patrol tonight. Then again,

Zala hadn't been out and about much since her return. Maybe this was normal now.

Eyeing a bench, Zala moved to settle Mantu down on it, but the man shrugged her loose and broke away. He rubbed at his shoulder with a scowl. "All right, enough of that, enough of that. Your husband? *Really?*"

Zala scoffed. "You know, it wouldn't kill you to say thanks."

"I ain't need no help."

"Oh, really. What would your plan have been?"

"Get out and run off into the shadows," he said matter-of-factly. "It woulda taken them forever to get down and chase me."

Zala eyed a pair of passing guards, whose bandanas of gold trim over black shined with each passing lamp post they drifted under. Once they were out of earshot, Zala said, "They don't have to pursue you when they can just call out to their friends."

"Yeah, well…" Mantu waved her off and sat himself on a bench.

A silence fell between them as it so often had since their return. Both pretended to watch the passersby coming in for the night, pretended to listen to the chatter in the streets, pretended to take interest in the jubilation of a hard day's work being drunk away within the various bustling taverns.

In truth, Zala hadn't seen Mantu's face properly since they had been back. His beard had always been unruly, but now it looked no better than a bird's nest. Even his hair, which he usually kept shaved down to near-baldness, was growing out into the makings of tiny curls she never knew he had.

"That was pretty smart what you did back there, though," Zala said first, filling the quiet between them. Mantu answered her with a questioning brow. So she went on. "Making your move on the ship between guard shifts like that, especially choosing *those* two. If you hadn't slipped, they would've been bickering as you snuck past them."

He glanced her way. "What can I say? Maybe you're rubbing off on me."

She wanted to hear a smile creeping from beneath that tangled mess of a beard, but Mantu was deadpan, his voice as indifferent as the sea breeze.

"Well, perhaps I should have rubbed a little better." Zala took a seat next to him. "You couldn't possibly have thought you were gonna make off with that ship alone?"

Mantu drew back with a scowl. "I weren't tryin' for the ship. You really think me that dim? I was just gonna hide away in their supply room."

"Oh, I didn't know the *Seabreaker* was making a visit to al-Anim."

"They ain't. But I heard one of them guards say they was goin' back to the Big Isle. If I got there, I could find at least one ship going out that way. Ain't enough traffic in this shitty port."

"Hey, this is my home you're talking about."

"Just 'cause it's your home don't make it any less shit."

Zala peered around the town square, to the bakery where Old Nani made the best *vitumbua*, to the alleyway between the market ward and the Temple of Yem where Jelani had saved her from some bandits with a horde of crabs. That was a good night. One of the last good nights they had, she thought sadly.

Taking a breath of air though, she couldn't deny the truth of Mantu's words. Kidogo, particularly the town square, had a real stink to it—if you let yourself inhale deep enough. But she had sort of gotten used to it. And it *was* her home. She loved it. Sure, it may not be where she had come from originally, but for her entire adult life, this had been it for her. For her and Jelani both.

She turned to Mantu again. "Hey, I may know of a ship that's heading to al-Anim."

"No." His answer came immediately.

"Come on, you didn't even let me start. I had this whole spiel. First, I was gonna be sly about the 'ship heading to al-Anim.' Then I was going to try a guilt-trip—"

"No, Zala."

She sighed, throwing up her arms. "What other choice do you have right now? You've been trying to get on a crew for days and no one's taking you on. You want to know why?" Zala waited for a retort, but it didn't come. Mantu looked half ready to leave her there on the bench alone. "Because you're a fucking mess, Mantu. They can smell it on you a league away. No one needs," she gestured to all of him, "*this*, on their ship."

"So is this meant to be the guilt-trip?"

"Nope. I'm changing tack. Improvising."

"Right…" Mantu dipped his chin into his hand and rubbed at his beard. "Whatever it is you want to say or offer, the answer's still gonna be no. I'm not gettin' on that ship with them crazy Meroé Rovers again. And don't you promise me no watertight plan or scheme. Look at all the good that did for Dum—" He stopped short on the name. His lips disappeared between the burrow of his beard, but Zala knew they were pursed tight.

She knew what feeling was running through the man.

She didn't like saying Jelani's name either, when she didn't have to. Especially when it meant acknowledging that he was so far away, his disease growing every day. What was worse, she couldn't say for certain if Mantu's own partner was alive or dead. A big guy like Sniffs wasn't often captured, but put down. It was always easier that way. But still, until you knew, you never *really* knew. Somewhere deep in Mantu, Zala was certain, he held onto a sliver of hope that his lover was still alive. Not only alive, but that Mantu would be the one to save him.

Just as Zala would save Jelani.

Mantu didn't know the whole truth of it though. He didn't know it was Zala's fault that Sniffs was captured in the first place. She planned on telling him at some point. But only after she convinced him to come along, not before.

"I'm sorry about Duma, Mantu. I really am."

Mantu stirred at that. "What?" He rubbed at his ears, then banged the side of his head. "Hold on, I got to hear that again. I ain't never thought I'd hear those words from *your* mouth, chana."

"Don't push it," she gritted. "But yes… I mean it. Sniffs— Duma put his faith in me on the back of Illopa's Bond. It's only fair that I do the same for you and yours with him."

Mantu waved a dismissive hand and sneered. "Don't give me

that shit again. You don't give a damn 'bout the Gods and Their Blessings. It's the Ibabi Isles all over again."

"No, Mantu, I mean it." She placed her hand on his bicep, his shirt still damp from his dip in the water, and gave him a light squeeze. "Okay, so I'm not all the way behind the Gods myself, but I can understand other people's way of things. Believe me." She knew her next words couldn't be left lightly. *"I know your heart.* And you may deny it, but you know mine too. You won't find that with just any crew. That's what I can offer you. I don't have a plan right now, but you know I'll fight any fight I have to to get another chance at getting them back. And when my plan shows us the door, I'm going to need someone to help kick it down. And not just anyone will do." She thumbed behind her. "I could find the muscle at any ol' tavern. But I can't find someone like you. Not someone I know who is *truly* motivated." She took a break for a beat, letting it settle.

Then Mantu shot up and started walking away. He didn't want to hear her, but Zala wasn't done with him.

She bolted up too and called out, "You need my mind; I need your brawn. And together we have our mutual love bonds to bind us."

That halted Mantu's march. The next hush that came didn't feel as stiff as the ones before it. Even as Mantu's beard rustled from what she assumed was him grinding his teeth, she knew she had convinced him.

Hells, she had convinced herself.

"Ugh!" Mantu bellowed, spinning around on Zala, then stomping in a circle. "How do you do that? It's bloody maddening! I swear," he pointed a finger between her eyes, "if you mess this up, I'm gonna kill you. For real this time. I'll actually kill you."

"Keep your voice down," Zala said, standing to settle him down. "Someone's gonna come over here and wonder what the fuss is about."

Mantu slumped back into the bench and interlocked his fingers tightly behind his head as he surveyed the stars above. "I need a drink—No, I need *all* the drinks."

"Where are you staying?"

"Nowhere. You did just see me try to stow away, didn't you?"

Zala stood up and offered Mantu her hand. "I can't promise it'll be comfortable—and Fon tends to snore when she gets to dreamin'… but I got a spot with a fair few drinks on hand. Maybe we can *actually* take a dive into Bulwa's Bliss."

CHAPTER 3
KARIM

IT HAD BEEN THREE DAYS SINCE THEY HAD ARRIVED BACK IN the capital, yet still Karim could not enter the city to see his father.

His office felt more like a prison than a workspace. Neither he nor his crew were allowed to speak to anyone outside Jasmiin Towers and its grounds until the debrief began that afternoon.

On the first day, he understood why. He and his crew were being made to speak with priests and priestesses to ensure their mission had not harmed their minds, that they remained resolute as soldiers of Vaaj. Karim had been dismissed almost instantly, his current drive for vengeance far too great to be pulled down by depression or madness.

He couldn't say the same for the rest of his crew.

The morning sun glinted at the edge of his window, shining against the rounded golden cap on his desk. The blood ruby at its center cast a deep, reddish glow. The object signified the position of a senior officer; for Karim, it was for his role as the chief officer of Vaaj's very first airship. But the object brought with it the images of his crew.

Just the day before he had received reports of Communications Officer Tahan being held an additional day due to bouts of anxiety—the late Deck Officer Ahmad's name on her lips. Karim had done his best to make himself numb to the name. Even now picturing the patchy beard of the deck officer made his stomach twist; he stood up quickly to cease its fresh churning.

Keeping busy had been his greatest defense against guilt, shame, and grief. But there was only so much one could do in a room fifteen paces by five. The official debrief was hours away yet, but he could start preparing. That'd keep his mind clear, he hoped.

Shuffling to his wardrobe—a feature of the room set for high-ranking officers—he pulled its doors away to reveal a mirror. He almost didn't recognize the man staring back at him, hair disheveled and falling over his brows, bloodshot eyes that had not seen rest since he had returned, and a scar splitting his lip under an increasingly unruly beard.

He could admit that the thought of Officer Ahmad's corpse and all the others who perished under his command still brought a clench from his fist, but he knew far too well that dwelling on the dead, even those he had led, would do him no good. He had to keep his shoulders back and his face forward. He would honor them; sulking just insulted their memory, belied their sacrifice.

Forcing his eyes away from his own twisted visage, he started with the formal uniform. It was a tight thing, laced with the symbol of the blood lily—the Royal Family's sigil. Several minutes passed and he still couldn't get his arms through the damn thing. He'd been told the stitching had been intentional, a design to represent the ironclad prestige of the military. Karim just called it poor tailoring, and someone trying to save face.

After almost half an hour, finally, he managed to put on the whole of his outfit. He moved to lift his arms, but the sound of tearing threads brought him up short.

Great, now how am I going to shave? he thought through a clenched jaw.

In snapping his arms down, his hand caught the sharp edge of a storage chest, which urged a small yelp from his mouth. He sucked at his knuckle, and his eyes passed over the little oak box. It had weighed almost as heavily on his mind as everything else, its contents the reason he had been so keen to see to his father.

Within it lay a letter: A message detailing the hardships his father had gone through, while Karim had been away facing down pirates and losing damn near half his crew for the effort.

My Son,

Collector Vaziri returned. He's asking — insisting — that we pay double this coming moon, and he wants our share ready by next sundown. I know you're away someplace, and I know you can't say where, but please — if you can, our people need your help.

— Your Father

Karim recalled that central part of the letter. That had been *weeks* ago, the new moon only days away then.

On the second day of their return, and after being deemed mentally stable, Karim thought he'd surely be able to venture out at his leisure. His father had sent him yet another letter about this imposing tax collector, and he was eager to get out into the city again.

Karim had hoped he could send out Runner Nabila with a message. The Admiralty wouldn't have noticed a gull-shifter among the other messenger birds in the city, would they? But alas, Nabila was put on fortress arrest.

Like the rest of them.

It took a while to appreciate the reason why, but Karim understood it. He and his crew had just come back from a particularly important mission, one that saw the first combat of Vaaji's latest creation: an airship. They couldn't have anyone — especially officers — recovering from not one but two battles out among the civilian population without being looked at.

"Chief Officer el-Sayyed," came a small voice at the door a few moments later. Karim knew it to belong to Nabila.

"Enter."

The door swung inward as Karim started on the combing of his hair before the wrapping of his turban. He gave the messenger a sidelong glance. The wounds on the young woman's arm were healing well. The perfume wafting from her shoulders was doing its job. It made Karim stop the combing to take in the scent. Today's aroma was some spice, maybe cinnamon. Yesterday it had been something floral.

"Aw," Nabila said once she got a look at him. "I like your curls; don't comb them out. What's the point anyway if you're going to wear a—"

Karim gave her a look that had become customary between the two of them. She wore her perfumes; he ignored them. She attempted small talk; he shut her down. Karim had to give it to her though. She was persistent in trying to win his attention—outside of military protocol.

"Sir," Nabila cleared her throat, "Vice Admiral Shamoun has invited you to the war room at your earliest convenience."

Karim flitted a look to the sundial at the edge of his window's perch. Then he turned a curious expression Nabila's way. "Are you certain? The debriefing isn't due to start for another hour."

"Yes, sir. The Vice Admiral said some of the senior officers are meeting earlier, you included."

Wrapping the first of his turban around his head, Karim asked, "How many?"

Nabila shrugged one shoulder. "Most, if not all the crew of the *Viper*, sir, save Officer Tahan, of course."

"And it has nothing to do with the debrief?" Karim questioned again.

The messenger shook her head.

It sounded more like a social gathering—not something Karim particularly fancied. But he couldn't decline an invitation from the Vice Admiral himself.

"Tell Vice Admiral Shamoun I'll be there shortly, then," he answered, placing his golden cap atop his head. At least now he'd be free from his stuffy quarters, even if it meant having to schmooze with the nobles.

CHAPTER 4
KARIM

AS KARIM SAT THERE IN THE WAR ROOM AND ITS GRAND TABLE, his mind kept pulling back to the letter his father had sent him. He could almost smell the incense of his father's small home, the familiar laughter of the old man's deep and weathered voice against his ears. His father's shanty might've been a bit dirty and tad cramped, but Karim would rather visit him than be with the audience that sat about him now. Any day.

Before the meeting had even begun, conversation awashed the large room. Karim, while not engaged in any of these splices of chit-chat, kept his attention on each discussion — trying to discern if anyone knew why they had been gathered so early. Then he quickly realized the invitation was simply for rubbing shoulders. Despite being invited, Karim held his tongue and hoped no one engaged him.

Issa sat nearest to him on his left, ever the exception. She was deep in conversation with another senior officer named Abaza, who seemed to be sharing old war stories. Though Karim was almost certain Issa hadn't ever met the elderly woman before, their conversation sounded like they were two old comrades.

Issa always had a way of making anyone feel like an old friend.

It was good to see at least a few of his crew members were doing well, at least. Especially one as close as Issa was to him.

Karim kept to himself as the other senior and junior officers awaited the last of the nobles. Some of the Admiralty were there too, all huddled around the head of the grand table. The difference between the nobles and military officials was small, but present. Though everyone wore similarly tight uniforms, those of the noble class seemed to sloop their shoulders a bit more casually, while the military folk still held to straight backs and alert expressions.

Karim couldn't help but feel the weight of the war room bearing down on him, its ceiling stretching the length of five or six men high. Three pillared arches lined one side of the room, each painted green, red, and white.

How many great men and women had swept through those arches to write the history of this nation, Karim wondered. So much work had been done for his people within these walls, work that Karim realized only now he would embark on himself. The thought brought a shiver down his spine as his neck tightened.

A cool sea breeze brushed at the back of Karim's turban from the large windows behind him. The brief draft helped quell his nerves for a moment, but only just. He turned his attention to the open view at his back. Light winds drifted up from the bustling markets of al-Anim—and the Sapphire Sea that lay beyond it. If Karim squinted, he could just make out the area he grew up in, hidden beneath the thick density of the renewed city. From this height, it looked almost as if the capital had begun to swallow the old districts below.

Karim adjusted himself in his seat, his movement restricted by the damn formal garb required for such meetings. He would've preferred his looser officer's clothes—at least he could breathe easier in them. Perhaps then his nerves wouldn't be running amok, each of his heartbeats pounding against the rigid threading tight around his chest.

His restlessness couldn't be helped. Karim had never been in the war room before, and he'd been with the military his entire adult life. The splendor of the room had taken him aback. Each surface, wall, pillar, floor, and ceiling was covered in elaborate designs, designs that were inscribed with Jo'baran and Qibasi poetry and prayers alike, a respect of the old and the new... or perhaps a transition that the monarchy had simply felt did not need redesigning. Thanks to his father and Issa, Karim knew the old religion as well as he did the new, though he shouldn't have if he considered himself a "good" Vaaji. The old religion was deemed taboo, yet still some of his old friends and family clung to the Old Way.

Karim turned a look on Issa who continued her laughter at her partner's unfunny jokes.

"Oh, no," Issa said with her hand to her chest. "I've never had the honor of meeting the Grand Admiral." Her voice lowered. "Anything I should be privy to?"

Karim peered down to the end of the table, where the most notable officer sat in attendance: Grand Admiral Awad, the very man who recruited him all those years ago. The man, who was decked in the most expensive silks—and, even while sitting, dwarfed those around him with his thin neck and slender shoulders—was surrounded by the rest of the Admiralty. The Small Council, however, seemed to be missing one particular member...

"Karim," a voice mumbled from behind Karim's chair. "Just the man I wanted to see."

It was Shamoun, the dark-skinned Vice Admiral. Even as he smiled, the deep wrinkle lines about his eyes told a story of years spent scowling at the crews he led.

The elderly man pulled up a chair alongside Karim. "Is this your first time here, in this room?" Karim nodded, still not wanting to speak "And... what do you think?"

Karim hesitated as his eyes ran across the familiar prayers carved on the table. "It's more beautiful than I imagined it would be. The recruits in the academy always talked of fire pits and sabers strung up on walls. If I didn't know any better, I'd think we were in a temple."

"Yes, it's a little different from what one might expect." Shamoun gazed up at the high ceilings. "Have you spoken to anyone else on the Council? Now would be the best time to get your name out there."

"Well, sir, I thought making *our* familiarity known might serve as a dramatic start." Karim smirked. Clearly he was being primed for a lesson against the silence he committed to since coming into the war room.

"Ah, I see. Well, that'll get your foot in the door, I'll give you that." Shamoun inclined his head to his fellow admirals. "But you'll need to make more of an impression than that if you want to garner the attention of *these* officers."

Karim clasped his hands together tightly beneath the table as he looked to the leading heads.

"Tell me," Shamoun said, nodding slightly down the table. "What do you know of Vice Admiral Bashar?"

Karim looked to the middle-aged, frog-faced woman who sat at the Grand Admiral's left. "She's renowned for her victory in the River War. 'The True Heir of Àyá' they call her. No one has ever used elementals in battle better than she."

"And she'd be the first to tell you that it's because she can't turn a wave with her own mystical power to save her life." Shamoun smiled and waved a hand in the Admiral's direction as she noticed him looking her way. "Oh, she trained tirelessly, but she could never muster the magic herself, not properly, at least. But all that practice though... it earned her a greater under-standing of the art than anyone alive. Regardless, that's not what I mean, Young Officer. What do you know about *her*."

Karim looked at the woman again. She wore the same outfit all the others did with no jewelry or anything that would distin-guish herself. All Karim could recall was her military prowess... So he simply shrugged.

Shamoun gave Karim a light pat on the back. "I'll have you know that she was brought up in the old port, not far from the Old Temple Ward you yourself grew up in. Did you know that?"

"I didn't."

Karim looked to Bashar again with fresh eyes. He would never have guessed it. But he supposed those lines on her face weren't all wrinkles. His own hand drifted along the scar through his beard. Though officially his home district had been known to the Empire as the Old Temple Ward, anyone who actually lived there referred to it as the Scars.

"Or how about Kassab there?" Shamoun nodded to a stout man with a lumpy turban. "What do you know of him?"

Now that Karim knew what kind of answer his senior officer was looking for, he simply shrugged.

"He has a particular fascination for birds," Shamoun continued. "He's got himself an extensive collection, actually. I try my best to brush up on my knowledge before engaging with him. And Gammill, just to the right of the Grand Admiral there, has a great talent with the flute. I try to make it a habit to visit him once a moon with my *riqq*, though my own ear is less musically inclined." He nodded further up the table. "I know little about al-Sulayhi, she's new to the council. I think I shall use today's debriefing to remedy that myself. And of course, Grand Admiral Awad. Did you know his family was once enslaved? His father and mother worked the mines of al-Haru."

Karim raised an eyebrow. "The Grand Admiral can't have more than fifty years, no?"

"He tells me he's no more than forty, but who can tell? The man never ages."

"I thought we disbanded slavers and their practices hundreds of years ago?"

Shamoun's already soft voice dropped lower. "East of the Red Pass, no. It's still illegal, officially, but there are still pockets of our own within the desert who disagree with the current laws."

"I see…" Karim trailed off. How had Shamoun learned of these more personal stories, he wondered.

"A child of slaves," the Vice Admiral continued, "to the top of Vaaj's military fleet in a single generation. Now he's trying to wed his only daughter to the Prince. And rumors have it, the Monarchy is seriously entertaining the notion. That's the sort of man you want to speak to. Don't you think so, Officer el-Sayyed?"

Karim nodded slowly. "Yes, sir."

Shamoun gave him a small smile. "Follow me. I'd like you to meet the Grand Admiral."

The Vice Admiral pushed his chair back, waiting for Karim to follow. Karim felt stuck to his seat, his nerves getting the better of him once more. Surely Shamoun wasn't expecting him to speak with the Grand Admiral just then? Karim thought maybe he'd start by speaking with some of the junior officers, perhaps even Bashar, who must've had a similar story to his own, but speaking to one of two military heads was too much to ask from him. And not Awad in particular, a nobleman he'd had a less than ceremonious introduction to years prior. Karim knew he'd only end up making a fool of himself.

Karim's chair jerked violently under him. He looked to the source of the disturbance at his left. He only barely caught the retreating line of Issa's leg as it flashed back beneath the table when he looked down to his side. A too-wide smile creased her face as she listened to Officer Abaza's latest anecdote. Then she took an innocuous sip from her goblet, her pinky finger pointing toward the Grand Admiral. Karim took the *subtle* prompt, swallowing hard and standing to follow Shamoun to the far end of the table.

"Shati'ala be with you, Grand Admiral Awad," Shamoun greeted.

Awad's figure gave Karim the first impression of being literally stretched thin. His dark complexion was taut over sharp etched edges in his face, his gaze measured and his focus like flint. A cream-colored head wrap of the capital's latest fashion covered his head. In defiance of the current trend toward beards though, his cheeks were bare, a sharp goatee outlining his mouth instead. He wore a peach tunic with a floral design, which was wrapped with a large fuchsia belt around his waist, a janbiya tucked between the fabric. His flamboyant clothing was matched by the smile stretched across his mouth.

"Shati'ala be with *you*, Brother Shamoun." His was voice steady and deep, the kind of voice one could feel rumbling through their own chest.

Shamoun stretched a hand to Karim. "I'd like to introduce you to Chief Officer el-Sayyed."

"It's an honor, Grand Admiral." Karim offered his superior a military salute.

"The honor is all mine, so I've heard." Awad angled his head to Shamoun with a sliver of a smile that shone bright against his dark skin. When his gaze returned to Karim, Karim thought he saw his eyes change subtly. "Have we met before, Brother?"

"Y-you recruited me years ago, sir," Karim stammered, thankful his turban covered what must have been reddening ears. "Back when you still taught at the academy, of course. You found me near the markets near the Scars and—"

"Ah, yes, the slummer who tried to steal one of my boats. I remember." Awad sat up in his seat. "My, oh my. Look how far you've come."

Karim held his head low. "Thank you, Grand Admiral. The Empire has taught me many valuable lessons."

"And respect for Her citizens' property, I hope," Awad said with an amused little chuckle. Karim smirked inwardly, holding his posture and his face firm.

Shamoun cleared his throat. "I was just telling Karim here that he should speak to a few of the council members. He had a few issues with Malouf during our time in the clouds."

"Ah, yes, Malouf." Awad's eyes drifted down the table to where Malouf spoke with his personal group of advisors. "I apologize for that one. The decision was out of my hands."

"I would never question the Council's orders, sir," Karim said evenly.

"Of course. Is this your first time in the palace proper?"

"It is, sir. I've only ever seen it from the outside—or from the bay, rather."

Awad folded his hands on top of the table. "And what do you think?"

"It's exquisite, sir."

"And the people in it? What do you think of *them*?"

"I—don't know what you mean, sir." Karim turned an eye to Shamoun for help, but none was offered.

"I've heard from Shamoun here that you are an excellent sailor, and all told an even better sky pilot. But you take issue with some ways of the nobility."

Karim tried his best not to shift his gaze to Malouf. He tried even harder not to think back on the Purser, Umar Jad, and his undercutting compliments on the airship. *"You've come a long way from street ratting, el-Sayyed. Ismail will be proud."*

"Apologies, sir," Karim said. "I'm just not used to the way some of our great nobles interact."

"I understand. But you must keep up with the tongue of the capital if you ever want to climb the ranks higher than a chief officer or captain." Awad gestured for Karim to come closer. "And I don't mean the dialect. The noble traditions are just as important —perhaps even more so after a point—as your abilities as an officer."

Karim bowed his head into the Vaaji salute again. "I'll keep that in mind, sir."

"I look forward to hearing more from you on your mission during this meeting," Awad said. "May Her Will be yours." He had a way about him, something that made clear exactly when he was done with a conversation with very few words.

"Yes, of course. I'll heed your advice, Grand Admiral. And may Her Will be yours."

Karim turned on his heel and returned to his seat. As he sat, he caught Malouf's eye.

The fool had seen Karim talking to the Admirals then.

Good, he thought.

Issa looked to Karim from her chair beside him. "And here I thought *I* was rubbing the right shoulder."

Karim leaned toward her and murmured into his fist, "I'll tell you later."

The sound of clinking chainmail filled the room, drawing Karim's attention away from Issa and to the three archways leading into the chamber. Past the threshold and deep in the hall, a procession of guards dressed in red cloth and golden armor pushed forward.

The visage of the group was obscured by Awad, who rose to

his feet and clapped his long hands together. "Good day everyone, good day. Please join me in rising to welcome our final and most esteemed guests of the day."

A dozen guards, each adorned in pristine golden armor and topped with red turbans, marched into the large room. Both their pauldrons and a silver mark that latched centerfold in their head wraps bore the family symbol of al-Nasir: two crossed sabers over a blood lily.

These were the Monarchy's guard.

Awad outstretched a hand, his robes falling gently like sands down a dune. "May we welcome Their Majesties and The Prince."

CHAPTER 5

KARIM

KARIM COULDN'T BELIEVE IT AT FIRST, BUT HIS EYES DID NOT deceive him. Among the throng of guards came Emperor and Empress al-Nasir. Everyone at the table stood up at once, lifting their pointed hands to their chests and leaning forward in salute until the pair took their seats. Karim kept his eyes fixed on the floral design cut around the prayers in the wooden table, not wanting to offend either with unwarranted eye contact.

"Announcing Their Majesties' presence in the war room," one of the royal family's advisors decked in red lily robes said. "All parties may now be seated."

The room had grown brighter with the gold of the guard and the red of the retinue, yet at the same time, seemed to darken under the weight Their Majesties brought with them. Every breath came carefully, every movement measured.

A hiss sounded from somewhere close to the marble floor. Karim tilted his chin down to see a trio of carpet vipers, each one trailing one of the Royals. Anyone in the palace was familiar with them and their infamous name: the Triplets of Death. Many assassins foolish enough to make attempts against Their Majesties' lives were met with poisoned fangs followed by slow and agonizing deaths.

When the Royal Family finally sat, Karim stole a look the

Emperor's way. He had never seen the man before, at least not this close. Emperor al-Nasir was smaller and thinner than he imagined, draped in ceremonial purple robes with gold ornate trim that must have fit him at one point, but now drowned him in its flowing grace. Loose-fitting clothes aside, all other features spoke of His Majesty's power: a crisp and sharp beard, high cheekbones and a squared jaw, and his pointed and intense stare which commanded absolute respect.

To his right sat his wife and paired monarch, Empress al-Nasir, who carried a gentler but no less intimidating presence. She dressed in stark red robes that flowed like wine over her sloped shoulders. Though Karim knew her to be an older woman, her features did nothing to betray her age.

On the Empress' right sat their son in matching robes with his father, a menacing stare of his own. Unlike his father, however, his own clothing was far more fitted. Odd that he would be present for the military meeting, Karim mused. He was still just a child, no more than nine or ten if Karim had tracked the boy's years correctly.

"If it please, Your Majesties," Awad said, standing just to the left of the Emperor and Empress. "Now that everyone is gathered, I would begin the meeting by ceding the table to Captain Hassan Malouf of the Twelfth Fleet."

Captain Malouf waited with what seemed a bated breath for Their Majesties' nod of acquiescence. When it came, he lifted himself from his seat and held his chest in pain. The wound he acquired when they faced the pirates looked to still be pestering him.

"Thank you, Grand Admiral Awad," he began. "And thank you, Your Majesties, for gracing us with your presence today."

"Tell us, Malouf, how did your mission go?" Awad asked as he took his seat again while straightening his stylish tunic. "You've brought back quite a few pirates it seems. Can we assume the *Viper* is combat-ready?"

Malouf gave sidelong glances to his crew before he spoke. "It was… perfect, sir. The pirates had no chance against the *Viper*."

"Is that so?" Awad steepled his fingers atop the table. "The

Viper took some damage, did it not? And casualties, if I have read my reports right."

"Well, yes. You see—"

"How did you acquire your own injuries?"

Karim scratched at his beard to hide his smile. *Awad doesn't like Malouf anymore than I do.*

And here he thought it was he who was going to get reprimanded.

Malouf indicated the bandages around his chest, frowning from the interruption. "This happened while we were boarding."

"Is this true?" Awad asked the other senior officers of the *Viper*. "Why was your Captain so exposed to danger?"

They said nothing at first—Malouf's advisors finding an acute interest in their twiddling thumbs—so Shamoun spoke for their silence. "To be precise, Captain Malouf was injured prior to leaving the undercarriage of the *Viper*. Had he already boarded the enemy's vessel, I am certain his guard would have been well established. They are good men and women, all of them. Isn't that right, Captain?"

The knot in Malouf's throat bounced dubiously. "Well... you see," he fumbled. "When I say we were boarding..." Malouf's eyes darted to the *Viper's* crew again, looking for support in their expressions. But it seemed no one was about to die on that hill. "Y-you see..."

"One of the pirates boarded our ship. An assassin, we suspect," Karim spoke up. In the navy they always taught you to throw your comrades a rope when they went overboard. Plus, it was too painful to just sit and watch Malouf drown like this—no matter how much he disliked the man. "As we were approaching the enemy vessel for boarding, one of those feral pakka creatures crept up the hull of our ship, and attacked without warning. Even after having already surrendered—"

"You are Karim el-Sayyed, are you not?" Karim turned at the unexpected interruption. It took him a moment to realize that it was the Young Prince that had asked the question. His boyish timbre matched his small frame, yet his cadence was nothing like any child Karim had ever known.

Too serious for one so young, he thought.

Karim, finally, nodded the affirmative.

"Please, explain something to me," the boy continued. "You were flying an *air*ship, were you not?"

"Yes..." Karim turned from the Prince to his father. "But you have to understand, Your Majesty—"

"*I* asked the question el-Sayyed, not my father." Despite the interruption, the Prince didn't raise his voice—that was the worst part. He cut Karim's words short with cool calm alone. Karim was suddenly regretting stepping into the fire. What was worse, the Prince's carpet viper came slithering against Karim's ankle. A chill shot up his calf as he shot a side-eye Malouf's way and desperately fought the urge to tug at his collar.

"Just answer the question, Officer el-Sayyed," Empress al-Nasir added, her tone almost soothing. "My son is quite astute with these matters."

"Of course. Please, forgive me, Your Highness." Karim angled to the Prince. "I am not accustomed to such an esteemed audience as yourself." He was not at all sure how he should speak to the child. "We were in the process of boarding their ship when we incurred severe damage."

The Prince left Karim barely a breath's pause before asking his next question. "How?"

Because someone *mucked it all up.*

"Because we lowered the Viper for boarding."

"Why?" The quiet, almost bored expression on the Prince's face unsettled Karim. He felt like a puppet on strings. He would've given anything to have someone silence the hissing of the carpet viper at his feet.

"I believe the Captain can answer that, Your Highness," Karim said, conceding to Malouf.

Time for you to retake the stage. I've danced on these coals for you long enough.

The Prince leveled his young eyes on Malouf, his look repeating the question without so much as a flicker.

"Well, Your Highness, so that... we could... take their ship?"

Malouf's words rang more as a question than a statement. Karim flinched.

The Prince gave them a heavy sigh as his shoulders dropped back into his chair. He cast a look of despair on Grand Admiral Awad.

Awad rubbed tiredly at the edge of his brow before speaking. "Would it not have made more sense to board the enemy's ship with your *sea*faring vessels while the *Viper* provided cover from above? I believe that's why we kept the longboats in the first place, after all."

"It would, sir." Malouf gulped. It had been exactly what Karim had suggested before.

Shamoun interjected again. "Officer el-Sayyed advised as much at the time, Grand Admiral. But ultimately it was decided to take the pirates directly—in light of their apparent surrender."

"I see…" Awad said, eyeing Malouf who had lowered his gaze. "While I understand your point of view at the time Captain Malouf, I must say I stand with your Chief Officer's assessment of the situation. Your trust in honor is to be commended, but it is not a sentiment shared by many pirates I have met."

One of Malouf's chief advisors, Umar Jad, cleared his throat. Another, Priestess Dahlia Fahyad, seemed like she had sat on something uncomfortable. Karim couldn't help feeling gratitude for the comfort of Shamoun's words and Awad's compliments as a brief and awkward silence hung in the room.

"Tell us more about how you overtook the pirates, Brother el-Sayyed," the Empress said. Karim was getting the impression Her Majesty had a lot of experience smoothing over tense situations such as these.

Karim explained his tactics against the pirates, how he used the longboats to close the distance while the airship gave support from above. With Malouf sat down and out of the picture, it was an easy and honest retelling. Shortly into his debrief, Karim noticed he seemed to have recaptured the attention of the Young Prince. He saw what looked halfway like approval in the boy's eyes—approval and contemplation. It helped that the carpet viper had finally left his feet as well.

"Impressive," Awad said with pursed lips. "And by your assessment did the *Viper* perform to the best of her abilities?"

"No, sir, she did not," Karim admitted.

A subtle hush cut through the room. Karim felt everyone's eyes on him as heat flushed his cheeks.

The Prince leaned forward, his tiny eyes curious. "What do you propose be done to improve the vessel?"

Karim turned to his captain before saying, "Captain Malouf was correct in his thinking. It would have taken us too long to board the pirate's ship under normal circumstances. And the *Viper* was too slow to give pursuit."

"We'll have that figured out in time," another woman, one of the red-robed advisors at the table, said. She had been writing notes on a scroll. Karim didn't recognize her, yet something about her face was familiar.

"Forgive me, but I do not believe we've met," he said.

"I am Janaan Malouf," she said. "One of the original engineers of the *Viper*."

"I was not aware the Captain had a wife." Karim thought back to the maidens he often found lying with the Captain.

"He doesn't. I am his sister."

"I... see." Karim gulped, trading an awkward glance with the Captain. Now that he knew what to look for, her long, thin nose did seem just like her brother's. He must've been staring too long because Janaan started tapping her reed pen impatiently across her scroll.

Karim gave a short cough. "During the battle, Vice Admiral Shamoun suggested we use the exhaust cast from the Skyglass. It cloaked us when we approached the pirates."

Janaan's lips thinned in thought and turned her head to Shamoun, who tilted his head in affirmation.

"I would like to take that a step further," she said. "Until we can give our airships more speed, it may be our best option to cloak our approach through a fabricated storm."

"And in terms of boarding," Karim added. "If we can get the airship in position before our enemy is aware, we can use ballista grapples to attach ourselves to their ship. If they try to escape, we'll still be pulled with them, or slow them down at the very least."

Janaan thought it over for only a moment. "That… should be possible."

"Very good, el-Sayyed," Emperor al-Nasir said, his voice as grave and low as his facade. Karim's heart thrummed with the satisfaction of earning a compliment from the Emperor himself.

The Prince cleared his throat. "Father, if it's not too much to ask. I do have a few additional questions with regards to these reports."

"Very well."

The boy thumbed through the set of parchment before him. "Scribe Asfour," he called. "These reports are all in order, yes?"

"Y-yes, Your Highness." One of the juniors bowed in salute at the far end of the table.

"Interesting. Because I'm seeing two conflicting reports here, or perhaps the dates were mixed up. Right here, on the Seventeenth Day of the Eleventh Moon, it says you incurred two casualties—which aligns with what Captain Malouf and Chief Officer el-Sayyed are saying now. But a few days later," he wet his thumb and pulled out another sheet, "it says here that you incurred twenty-two *additional* casualties. Or did you perhaps miswrite this section here by adding a two?"

The scribe's eyes flitted between Malouf and Karim, and sweat came down his brow as he stuttered, "Y-yes, Prince."

"Yes, you wrote it incorrectly?"

"I-I mean, no. No, Your Highness." The lump at the junior's throat seemed to dance. "T-the writings are accurate, sir. Twenty-two is correct."

"So that would mean that nearly *half* the crew perished during your away mission, then?" The Prince had flung his voice to Malouf, who sat stiff in his chair.

"N-not mine, Your Highness," he said. And then the slow turn of his head started. Karim didn't have to guess where his chin would settle next. "As you know, I was injured during our first attack." He indicated his still-healing injury. "I was under the impression we were to return to al-Anim at that point."

Karim had been pressing his fingers together so hard under the table, he almost lost feeling in his palm. His heart pounded in his ears. Surely everyone else could hear it too. He knew where this line of conversation was leading. It was just a matter of time before Malouf said a "it was the boy's fault" or a "had I been in command at the time, this wouldn't have happened."

A gentle hand came at the tip of Karim's knuckles. Issa didn't look at him, still watching as Malouf fumbled through his explanation, but he knew what the touch had meant. She was there with him. She'd have his back.

"There was a second attack," Karim cut into Maloufs' roundabout excuse-making. "Under my lead, we took a... longer way back to al-Anim. You see, we had the sea speaker who stopped us at Kidogo. I thought it was in our best interest to secure the island's cove, and its Skyglass deposit."

"Why couldn't this wait until you returned to the capital?" the Empress asked.

Karim did his best to look away from Surgeon Abadi's hawk's gaze. "Because I went against my surgeon's advice. We had a prisoner with a disease I thought might kill him before the Empire had all the information it needed. If we hadn't been delayed in our return, then those casualties—"

"The Chief Officer is too modest," Shamoun cut in, placing a hand to Karim's knee to hush him. It was strange having two military officials at his side coddling him like some babe. "He is omitting that were it not for his astute leadership, we would not have turned the tides to our favor."

"Turned the tides?" The Prince lifted an eyebrow. "Apologies if I am misunderstanding something here, Admiral, but what happened with this attack exactly? What force could bring down an airship? These officers need more explanation than that," he lifted a page to his face and read, "Mutasim al-Dar. Faraj Zakari. Haakima Masri. Shahla Fayez. Tahir Ahmad." The last line did it for Karim. He couldn't let the list go on. Each word was a stake in his heart.

"All of those names are my burden to bear, Your Highness," Karim spoke up. Shamoun clenched his jaw, and Karim would've sworn he heard Issa release a tight breath. "It was my own pride, my own miscalculation that put our people in such a position. We were attacked by pirates. The same ones we assaulted on the Seventh of the Eleventh Moon. I expect they laid in wait for us. They had an illusionist—a powerful one. The mystic held us in a perception well as they brought the ship down with elementals. I tried to secure the bridge, but I should have met them head-on. Maybe then I could have saved—"

"El-Sayyed isn't telling it right," Issa butted in with a sharp tone. "None of us would have known what was even happening were it not for him. He identified the illusion we were stuck in. It was such astute attention to detail that saved us. Were it not for him, I daresay, I wouldn't be speaking with you now. Yes, many were lost. Yes, Chief Officer el-Sayyed shares some responsibility for that. But he saved twenty-six *other* lives that day."

The Prince peered over another set of reports, his expression betraying nothing of his thoughts. "You are Akif, Chief Gunner, yes?"

"I am, Your Highness." She nodded shortly.

"Is it true that you've been with Chief Officer el-Sayyed since your days in the academies? If I'm reading this correctly, the pair of you haven't parted since you signed on. That's curious for naval posting, is it not?" His carpet viper, which had returned to his shoulders, hissed.

Issa didn't have an answer for the boy. Instead, she slothed back in her seat and made a tight line of her lips. Karim had half a mind to set his *own* hand to her knee. It was worth a shot, but with this prince and his stern parents, nothing was going to get by them. It was best she just kept her mouth shut and waited for whatever was to come.

"It is rare, in truth, Your Highness," Shamoun spoke up, interlacing his fingers over the table, "but a relationship like el-Sayyed and Akif's is not unheard of. The Navy knows winning combinations when it sees them, as the Grand Admiral could attest." Awad inclined his head sagely. "Why, my own sailing unit back in my days with the *Nadia* followed me up all the way from my first vessel. I wouldn't have had it any other way."

Malouf cleared his throat, his voice coming with a fair bit more confidence than it had before. "As my Chief Officer says, these deaths could have been avoided were he not at the helm. Were it me, we would've been heading home immediately."

"With all due respect, Captain," Shamoun said, "with you at the helm, we were nearly taken by pirates *without* an illusion well to help them." Malouf looked like he wanted to bark back in his rage, but Shamoun seemed to choose not to see it. The Vice Admiral shifted his attention to his senior at the head of the table. "Sir, were it not for this young man's direction and capacity to work under pressure, we would not have the notorious pirate, Captain Nubia, in our possession now."

A few rumblings came from the group around the table, the first stir since the Prince started laying into Malouf and Karim.

"I thought it was you yourself who brought her in, Shamoun," Vice Admiral Bashar, the elemental, asked.

"If it had been up to me, I might've shoved her off the *Viper* altogether. It was young el-Sayyed who corralled us all to make it happen."

Bashar pursed her lips and nodded approvingly. "Very well done, el-Sayyed. We've had her marked for years now."

It didn't feel right. Any of it. What Karim said next could've earned him demerit at the least, execution at the worst. But it's what needed to be done.

"Please, stop," he told them all. The gratitude was nice, but the anguish, the grief roiling through him won out. It didn't help that Malouf's grin was sickening to look at. What was Karim thinking trying to cover for the man? But he couldn't blame the Captain. Not really. Karim's gaze traveled to the Emperor, the Empress, and the Prince. "Your Majesties, Your Highness, I take *full* responsibility for each of the names on that list."

"El-Sayyed," Shamoun hissed.

"*Every* single one, sir. A captain, acting or not, should take credit for his successes and failures both. Yes, I conducted the counteroffensive that led to Captain Nubia's capture. And yes, I subdued the Kidogon pirates on our initial assault. But my decision to take matters into my own hands exposed us over the

Sapphire Seas. It is what put ink to the names on that paper." He pointed to the reports ahead of the Prince, then listed off every name by memory. "Whatever it is my Monarchs decide—whatever *you* decide, Grand Admiral—I will accept it with no rebuttal at all."

A heavy silence sat atop the room. The gentle ocean breeze that came from the balcony before seemed now to still to the tension hanging over them all.

"Captain Malouf," the Emperor finally said, clearing his throat. "You and your crew are still weary from your travels, I'm sure. We have enough to be getting on with for now. You and your men take a brief reprieve. I'll have refreshments brought to you at once."

Grand Admiral Awad nodded his agreement. "I agree, Your Majesty. Captain Malouf, you and your crew are dismissed for a brief recess."

CHAPTER 6

KARIM

"CAN YOU BELIEVE THAT, *DIKALA*?" KARIM SPAT AS HE PACED the courtyard outside the war room.

The Emperor and Empress' guard had ushered them out to where the rest of the *Viper* crew awaited. Now that the weight of the room and all the scrutiny was off his shoulders, his true emotions seemed to billow out all at once.

"Since when did you start using the pirate's curses?" Issa asked incredulously as the soft winds from the open courtyard fluttered through her delicate blue tarha.

Karim shook his head, frustrated. "It fits." He continued his pacing after a brief pause. "To think I was going to stick up for the Captain when he was going to just let me take the fall." He turned dark eyes to Malouf, who had done well to keep his distance at the other end of the courtyard near an out-facing veranda. "Do you think they'll kick me out of the Navy? They probably should. I practically told them to."

"Unlikely. You're one of our best," Issa said through a mouthful of fig served to her by a kitchen servant. She pulled the rest of the fig from her mouth and wagged it in front of Karim as an exclamation to her next point. "But the way the Prince was looking at you... it was a bit strange, wasn't it?"

The kitchen servant seemed to hover too near, as though she

was expecting something. "Would you like anything, sir?" she asked in a meek tone. But Karim was too inside his head to be polite.

"That'll be all for now, thank you," Issa said for him. The server turned on her heel sadly with slumped shoulders.

"Why was he even there?" Karim asked as he watched Malouf deliberately avoiding eye contact. "I didn't know they allowed children into the war room."

"The rumors must be true about him."

"What rumors?" Karim never let himself get caught up in military gossip, but Issa had always been good at laying her ear to the ground.

"The Prince is supposed to be... special," she said as she sat on a nearby bench covered in auburn leaves.

"A mystic?" Karim asked with parted lips.

Issa brushed the crunchy red leaves from the bench and tapped the open space next to her. "No, nothing like that. He's just smart. *Really* smart."

"To think my career rests beneath the heel of a child," Karim huffed as he lumped down next to her, his shoulders stiff and rigid. What he would give to be rid of this formal garb. More than ever, he needed to breathe freely.

"You know, you would've been fine if you let Shamoun and me just say what we were going to —"

"You were sugarcoating it all. I can't let you do that."

"Stop worrying," Issa whispered, smacking him lightly with her fig. She turned and crossed her legs on the bench beside him. "If they try anything, the rest of my unit and I will back you up. You're the only reason we took those pirates down, and everyone knows it."

Karim sighed, releasing the tension in his shoulders. "I hope you're right."

"Besides," Issa started, peering over Karim's shoulder for any eavesdroppers. "Even if they do kick you out, we've served the mandated five years. We could've left a year ago. What more do we need from the military? We always said we'd get our education and move back to the Scars, help rebuild the slums."

Karim felt an uncomfortable heat simmer through him. That *had* been his desire at one time. At the start. Now with his chief officer title on the line, he felt oddly... possessive. He wasn't even sure why he wanted it so badly. But it was one thing to leave on his own terms and another to be pushed out because of Malouf's incompetent leadership. Now, when he thought of leaving—potential clean break or not—he was unsure. The only problem was how to tell Issa that he didn't want it anymore.

How could you tell your closest friend—your *only* friend—something like that?

His thoughts must have been playing across his face, because Issa placed a gentle hand on his shoulder. "Whatever happens, happens. I'm with you all the way, you hear me?"

Karim tried for a smile, but he could feel it coming out as little more than an awkward grimace. He really didn't know what he'd do without her.

<hr>

DESPITE MUCH PRODDING FROM ISSA, KARIM DRANK LITTLE and ate less for the duration of the reprieve, too nervous to stomach the refreshment. When the red-robed Janaan Malouf came to retrieve them a few moments later, the pounding in Karim's chest grew all the more harsh. Taking a deep breath, he lifted himself from the bench and followed the advisor.

Once he crossed the threshold into the war room, almost immediately, he felt a change. Somehow the air hung more thick. The large windows that had let in the cool ocean breeze were now covered by red silks, shrouding the room in an ominous crimson shadow. Karim tried to read the faces in the room, the Emperor's, the Empress', even the Prince's, but nothing was given, save for a handful of nods at the group as they entered.

What had they discussed? Why did the room feel so grave?

Karim didn't like it one bit.

He took his seat at the far end of the table—as far from Captain Malouf as he could get—as Grand Admiral Awad stood to his full slender height. "So we've come to an agreement on a few matters. First…" He turned his attention to the captain. "Captain Talaat Malouf. You have served this council very well for many years. Your family has been instrumental in developing our plans for the proposed air fleet."

Karim couldn't help but feel lighter as he released his rigid grip against his chair. Awad's words were the softening that came before a great blow. The Council was *actually* going to get rid of Malouf… Karim would *finally* see the Captain get what he deserved.

"For these achievements and more," Awad continued. "Captain Malouf of the Twelfth Fleet and field officer for *The Flying Viper Project*, we are promoting you to overseer of all airship acquisition operations here in al-Anim. Your logistics and supply experience will serve the nation well in the wars to come. Congratulations, Overseer."

A light smattering of congratulations echoed around the room. Malouf looked absolutely stunned. Karim almost forgot himself, stiff in his seat. Issa had to give him a second kick before he realized that he too should have joined in the adulations. His "praise" was barely above a stilted whisper.

A promotion? Karim thought with a clenched jaw.

He couldn't believe it. They heard the report. How could they give such an important role to a man so undeserving, so reprehensible? Then his thoughts turn inward to himself.

If Malouf got a promotion, then Karim was as good as gone.

"I am honored. And I thank the Council, truly," Malouf let out a great sigh.

Karim wondered if Malouf had thought he'd get kicked out from the military or reprimanded in some way. He was likely just as surprised as Karim. The Captain was never a fan of his Chief Officer, he made that plain on the *Viper,* and now that he had greater influence, he would no doubt make good use of it—at Karim's expense.

Karim ground down on his teeth harshly. He had made the title of chief officer his. *He* had earned it, worked tirelessly to attain the position that so many said a "street rat" like him could never acquire. He'd given the Empire nearly a decade of his life, and now they would have him thrown away as though he were the same slummer they had found before his first day at the academy.

He could accept being chucked out. It wouldn't be ideal, but that's what he deserved. But to be kicked out *and* have Malouf climb higher in the ranks felt like an injustice even in the eyes of these nobles. Whatever was about to happen, Karim knew damn well he wasn't going back to sit there and take it, despite his previous proclamations.

Karim looked to Issa, his cold and angry eyes asking the obvious question: *what the hell is this?*

Issa shrugged solemnly.

"And to Officer el-Sayyed." Awad turned to Karim with eyes of stone, all his earlier warmth gone from his smile. Karim swallowed, ready for the worst. "You are one of our youngest officers. You came to us with very little and have grown immensely since. You may have struggled from time to time with some of our procedures..."

That was it, wasn't it? Because I can't speak to pompous nobles? Not even the people who were killed because of me, but because I don't like kissing ass?

"But rough edges aside," Awad went on. "You are a great talent. You have proven this time and again. The Navy has recognized this before and it does so now. Effective immediately, I name you Captain, assigned vessel: the *Viper.* Your ship shall be the first of the coming Vaaji Air Fleet, the first step on our nation's great journey towards supremacy of the sky. Congratulations, *Captain* el-Sayyed."

The shock coursing through Karim had him stiff in his seat in complete stillness. He had to have misheard that, right?

"I... don't know what to say," Karim said, mouth agape. It felt as though all feeling had rushed away from his body. He clearly must've misheard. "A-are you sure? I-I mean, thank you, Grand Admiral."

"Well first things first," Awad said—now that he saw him in a new light, Karim could have sworn the man was suppressing a grin. "Do you accept your new rank?"

"Accept it? I was born for it, sir."

A bout of congratulations came from the rest in attendance. Karim was still in shock, his senses shot to pieces even as Issa celebrated him the loudest. When the fervor died down though, it became clear that one man had not joined the rest. When they all had quieted, he cleared his throat.

"You have something to say, Umar Jad?" Awad acknowledged.

"Permission to speak freely, Grand Admiral?" the hooked-nose man said.

"That is what such meetings as these are for, Purser Jad."

Jad cleared his throat again. "Correct me if I am wrong, but we've never had a captain who has served less than ten years within our ranks, is that so?"

"You are correct..." Awad said, his voice leading.

Karim's eyes grew dark. Jad had often hit him with back-handed compliments to be cheeky. This, however, was something else entirely, far more forward than Jad's usual. For whatever reason, the man did not seem to like Karim altogether. What was the point of bringing up his age at all but to shame the Council's decision?

"Officer el-Sayyed is talented," Jad said, "to be sure."

Captain el-Sayyed, Karim thought.

"But there is a reason we've not accepted a captain so young, sir." Despite Jad's undermining words, his tone was even, almost indifferent. It made Karim go mad. If the old man didn't like him, why was he being so even-tempered about it all?

"You are right, Purser Jad," Awad said. "Much of our discussion stemmed around Karim's youth, Janaan Malouf primary among the dissenters." Awad gestured to the former Captain's sister. "But Vice Admiral Shamoun made a very persuasive point. And seeing as he had the closest relationship with our Young Captain, we sided with his counsel."

Karim couldn't help but notice that Awad's gaze panned the table to all points but the Prince when he spoke of youth. Did the boy speak on Karim's behalf? Karim tried his best to decipher the stoic expression on the Prince's face, but, as always, there was nothing, just that slate stare.

"May I ask what that point was?" Jad intoned.

Shamoun spoke for himself in his faint voice. "My point was that since these proposed airships are mere babes climbing from their cribs, it stands to reason we should helm them with such."

A ripple of laughter ran around the room, and Karim fought down a blush.

Shamoun smiled at his peers and continued. "New weapons should be wielded by new minds. Besides, the value of age is experience, and none has more with the *Viper* than *Captain* el-Sayyed."

Jad sat back in his seat subtly. "Then I have no more to say. The council has once again shown me its wisdom." Jad turned to Karim. "Let me take this moment to congratulate you personally, Captain el-Sayyed."

Karim nodded wordlessly, though with apprehension. Jad had given up too quickly in his rebuttal. What did the man want? Or was he just biding his time for another opportunity to undercut Karim?

Grand Admiral Awad clapped his hands together once more. "Very good, then. Captain, do you know who you would have for your chief officer?"

Karim gave a token display of examining the men and women at the table. As far as he was concerned, there was only one choice. The first chance he got, he'd be ridding himself of Malouf's advisors. Umar Jad chief among the cuts. None of them had contributed much more than kissing Malouf's ass.

He gave a nod, feigning a hard-fought conclusion. "I would have Chief Gunner Akif, sir, if she is willing."

Awad tilted his head. "Officer Akif is younger even than you, is she not?"

"Only by a year and a half, sir. But she is just as able, just as determined to serve the Empire."

"It is unusual... I would argue you should have an older mind to balance your own." Awad glanced at the Vice Admiral, who seemed to give an approving nod. "But if you are sure of your decision, I have no objection. Gunner Chief, what say you?"

"With respect, sir, I must decline," Issa said.

A swift chill ran through Karim as he furrowed his brow. He whipped his head to her.

"I am not ready to take on such a task," she said. "I've only just now got a handle on my gunners." She turned to face Karim. "I appreciate your offer, Captain el-Sayyed, but it may do you better to choose another."

Why had she declined? She was the only one he trusted. Together they could lead the Empire's new air fleet. It would only take a year, maybe two, under Karim, and Issa would have a ship of her own. Karim did his best not to break face, but his insides ran amok with utter confusion.

"I agree," Awad said. "Take some time to think further on your second choice, el-Sayyed. We don't need names straight away. We have other business to attend to, after all."

"The Skyglass at Kidogo chief among them..." Emperor al-Nasir suggested, sitting forward slightly. "Were you able to uncover their location?"

"We weren't, Your Majesty," Malouf said, speaking for Karim. "But..." The former Captain's eyes fell on the new one's. "Captain el-Sayyed was able to secure a person of interest who might be able to tell us where we can find it."

Karim gave Malouf a look he had never given him before, something that surprised even himself as he did. It was a look of respect.

"Who is this person?" The Emperor's steady voice was directed toward Karim.

Adjusting the tight fabric around his chest, Karim said, "A mystic from the island. He goes by 'Jelani'."

"Any family name?"

"Not that we are aware of."

"Very well, we'll bring him into the palace for further questioning."

"Your Majesty, if I may?" Karim asked cautiously.

The Emperor lifted a slow eyebrow that pushed against his

wrinkled forehead, his carpet viper at his shoulder rocked his head curiously as well. "What is it, Captain?"

The new title coming from the Emperor's lips himself felt radiant in Karim's ears. It took him perhaps a moment too long before replying, "This man is a speaker. He has a particular affinity for sea creatures. With your permission, I'd like to conduct his questioning as far away from the coast as possible."

"Very well, I understand. You have my blessing, Captain. I want the location of that Glass as soon as you have it, do you understand?"

"Yes, Your Majesty. If Shati'ala wills it." Karim bowed.

"If Shati'ala wills it," echoed the Emperor.

"Something else you should know about this man, Your Majesty." Karim turned his words from the Emperor to the rest of the council at large. "The man has contracted stoneskin, as I mentioned before."

The topic of stoneskin seemed to pique Empress al-Nasir's interest as she leaned forward, her mouth pursed behind clasped hands. "How much time does he have?"

"Surgeon Abadi assures me he's on the better part of a year, Your Majesty. For the moment, that's not the issue." Karim looked back to the Emperor. "But our... usual methods of questioning will be ineffective against him."

The Emperor steepled his fingers and pressed his chin into his hands in thought. Karim's eyes were drawn to a sudden movement beside the man, as his son sat straighter in his chair once more to say in his small, but mature voice, "Do you require a telepath from our ranks, then?"

Karim bowed his head to the Prince, then turned his eyes back up to the Emperor. "If one is available, Your Majesty. Yes."

CHAPTER 7

ZALA

Though Mantu had agreed to go with Zala and the others on the *Redtide*, he made it clear he was going to keep to his usual dark corners on the crew deck. It was probably for the best. Zala didn't need him drawing attention, and when they got to the Vaaji capital she'd intended to make up some excuse of splitting up to search more ground for their lost crew. Namely Jelani and Sniffs. Captain Nubia too, if they could manage that along the way.

The only issue with that idea was Lishan.

"Things are going to be a bit different under my lead," Lishan —*Captain* Lishan now—said that morning before they set out. "Our goal is simple: we find and rescue the Captain. No more than that. And no more acting alone or splitting routes." She had settled her knowing eyes on Zala. "For each of Zala's crew, they'll be paired with one of our Rovers. I want each of you linked at the hip. If one of you is tasked to swab the deck, so is the other. If one of you is tasked to pull sails, so is the other. If one of you turns in—"

"We gotta sleep together too?" asked one of the few men of the crew. He started rubbing his hands together and eyed Zala and Fon as though deciding the best option at a feast.

"All right, Kwame," Captain Lishan intoned. "You're with the cat."

Kwame stopped the rubbing of his hands at once, his greedy look traded for dismay, but he didn't dare voice his obvious disapproval.

Zala expected to hear some wisecrack from Shomari. One never came. The pakka just leaned casually along the starboard railings—he hadn't even climbed the ratlines like he usually did during meetings. Hells, it didn't seem like he heard anything Lishan said at all.

Zala frowned. Fon had said Shomari wasn't quite himself these past few days, but Zala hadn't seen it firsthand. Whenever she glanced over to him, his usually pointed ears were flopped down, disappearing in the mass of his black fur.

"You feel me, kijana?" Lishan asked Kwame, who took far too long to answer. He quickly nodded and not so subtly drifted back into the thick of the crowd in shame. Then the Captain raised her voice to the rest. "You *all* feel me?"

The crew answered with half-hearted affirmations. Mantu hadn't opened his mouth at all. Zala could only hope whoever he was paired with was a favorable match.

In the end, Zala was assigned to a stern woman named Ouseni, Fon with Iokaja—likely because they were both aziza, and Old Man Ode and Rishaad were grouped with a pair of former Ya-Seti archers, who had apparently been with Nubia since the former Captain abandoned her country.

Zala had hoped to have more than five others on her own crew. When they returned to Kidogo they had found more survivors of the *Titan*, though Zala couldn't convince any of them to come along. Many of them still couldn't believe something like a sky ship existed, and anyone they shared their stories with laughed them off and usually asked if they also came in contact with the ancient merfolk or the like.

She couldn't blame them for not joining her, really. They had no ties to those who were lost, and they were probably happy to be free of their previous Captain's daily raids. So why would they agree to save any of his crew? Were it not for Sniffs, Mantu would never have agreed. In fact, Zala still wasn't sure why Ode and Rishaad had come along. They hadn't lost anyone personally on their end. Granted, Rishaad did say something about "sticking it" to his old country, and the old man mentioned some such about being too young to retire.

Zala's idle thoughts carried her through the rest of the day and she didn't really snap out of it until a few hours later when she found herself on watch duties with her new partner, Ouseni.

Though the sky was free of clouds, they were going against the wind. Lishan said they'd arrive at the foreign capital in a little over a day. Zala and the *Redtide* crew member had been stationed at the crow's nest on watch for any ships they might've passed. Usually, Zala dreaded being stationed at the crow's nest, where every little turn of the ship was exaggerated, but that day the tide was kind. It would've been nice if Fon was with her, though. They often played a game of which ship would crest the horizon. Zala had a sneaking suspicion the grizzly woman next to her wouldn't indulge.

But maybe small talk would earn a bite from her.

"So… you've known Nubia a while, right?"

No answer. Zala had tried several times to spark up conversation with the woman. But Ouseni was just as stiff as the rows of braids lining her head.

"Have you been to al-Anim before?" Zala tried again. "I've only ever been to the port. Never into the city proper. How about you?"

Still nothing. Zala bit at her lip. She didn't mind awkward silences in general, but that was with people she knew. It had been so much easier getting to know Ekko, Marjani, and Iokaja. She figured all of the crew were at least somewhat social.

She was clearly wrong there.

Zala didn't think the silent woman was a mute. Zala reckoned she was just being given the cold-shoulder. Who knows what Captain Lishan had told her? It wasn't lost on Zala that their pairing was more a matter of babysitting than anything else, of course. Ouseni's only task was to make sure Zala behaved, that she wouldn't run off again like on the sky ship. Maybe if Ouseni knew Zala had no intention of lone-wolfing again, at least not right away... maybe then she could bring down this wall between them.

"*I apologized to the crew at large, but not you,*" Zala said in Mero-Set. Her switching from the Mother Tongue got the first stir from Ouseni's eyebrow, though the woman still didn't turn. "*I'm not sure how long you've been on with Captain Nubia. I know she must've been close to you.*" She eyed the archer tab wrapped around the woman's fingers. The insignia sewn in it was faded, though there were still hints of a hawk imprint. "*From that glove of yours, I'm guessing you've been with her a while. I just wanted you to know, I won't let what happened on the sky ship happen again. We're going to save all the crew.*"

It was a long moment, perhaps longer than it felt, but Ouseni gave the slightest turn of her head and tilted over in a light nod. It wasn't exactly the acknowledgement Zala had been looking for. Still, she was happy for at least a *crack* in the woman's stoicism.

Later, at their midday meal, however, Ouseni kept giving Zala slanted sidelong glances. Zala couldn't determine why until she realized how loud she was chewing, too hungry from a night and morning's watch that lasted hours in the midday sun.

A library's silence hung over the galley—except a library had more activity from huddled scholars than those tables of pirates. It was as though there were some new, unspoken rule that no one could speak—maybe there was, and Zala hadn't realized.

It had been a little under a week ago since the galley had been filled with raucous chatter befitting a fighting pit—an excitement stirred from a sparring match between Shomari and Lishan that some of the crew deemed the best they had ever seen. That had been a good day, a real good day. But now the galley was nothing more than a tomb. And a tomb is where they would be headed to with energy like that.

Zala's gaze found the distinct red cloak of Shomari in the corner. She had expected to see that signature leer of his as he, like Zala had tried to do, attempted to break the wall between himself and his partner. But the pakka seemed satisfied in his silence and, had she not known he and Kwame were paired together, she'd never have guessed them sharing in their meal at all.

Mantu, of course, was tucked away next to his own dimly lit table at the far end of the room. He didn't care to sit anywhere near Marjani, his own "partner." The long-haired woman, who wore yellow beads in her locs today, didn't seem to care though, as she was huddled up with her husband Ekko at their own table a little ways away.

Fon, who had just come down from the weather deck along with Iokaja, seemed to be the only one with *some* pep in her step, sharing in some joke with her fellow aziza. The pair's light giggling died the moment they settled into the galley though. Quietly, they got their serving of fish, injera, and soup, then found a seat next to Marjani and Ekko.

This was no way to go into a rescue mission. Zala could appreciate keeping focus and respecting the seriousness of it all, but all this walking around like lumbering *eloko* and conversational mutes wouldn't do either. Someone needed to shake things up.

Pushing back one end of the bench—not caring for Ouseni's sudden glare—Zala marched to Fon.

"We're not to leave each other's side," Ouseni said.

"Ah! Glad to see you actually speak." Zala rolled her eyes away from the woman. "You're not to leave *my* side. And I'm just going to speak with my friends. I'm not gonna break eye line with you or anything, don't worry yourself."

She didn't wait for a response as she shuffled over to her friends' table. Fon's large-set eyes went bright when she saw Zala approaching.

"Gods, did someone die in here?" Fon murmured as Zala took her seat.

Iokaja chewed through a mouthful of injera-wrapped meat as she said, "We've never been without the Captain before. Not even for a little while."

Zala watched as Iokaja did her best to be gentle with her spoon. The stone covering her hand and arm crunched every time she strained to flex them.

Zala swallowed before asking, "How did the potion taste? My husband always tells me my brews smell like turned meat."

"It wasn't... terrible." Iokaja shrugged meekly, her freckles bunching in a bemused expression.

"It's crazy you can brew it at all," Marjani said at Zala's side. "You were one of those academy scholars or some such in Jultia, weren't you?"

Despite their previous conversations, Marjani still couldn't let go of the fact that she had uncovered where Zala had come from before her stint with pirates. Zala still didn't care to admit she was right though. "I've no idea what you're talking about."

"See! Shit like that, just right there. 'I've no idea'... If you're gonna be a pirate you gotta talk the part, chana. Throw in some ain'ts and cusses from time to time if you're tryin' to cover up that noble tongue of yours. Yem, help you, child."

"She'll need more than Yem." Ekko elbowed his wife. "I'd throw Ula in there for her. Can't go wrong with the Ocean *and* Star Gods."

Zala laughed. "My husband would love you both. Can't wait for you all to hit me with all your talk of the Gods."

"Oh?" Marjani perked up. "He's Jo'baran?'

As though saving Zala from another interrogation, Iokaja cut in, "I've had worse potions. Though, I admit, I've had very few." She shrugged as she finally found a good grip for her hand around her spoon. "What matters is that the stone stops growing. I can't thank you enough for that."

"It's the least I could do. Once we get to the bazaars in al-Anim, I'll restock. You'll have at least two days more until it grows again."

Iokaja nodded gently. If anyone had reason to be pissed at Zala, the aziza was right at the top of the list. Zala might've lost Mantu's lover, or the crew's Captain, but those had the potential to be reversed. The stoneskin spidering up Iokaja's arms, on the other hand... not so much. Yet the pirate had never given Zala the cold-shoulder or fixed her with a glare like some of the others. That was almost worse.

It filled Zala with a sickening guilt.

"Seriously, you could hear a quill drop in here," Ekko said through a slurp of his soup, his pale skin reddening from the heat. "How're you all holdin' up, anyhow?"

"I'd be better if I didn't have that Ouseni woman hangin' over my shoulder." Zala braved a glance behind. At the edge of her sight, Ouseni gazed at her with slitted eyes over a goblet. "I know I've known your crew, what, not even a week? But I didn't think it could get this…"

Fon found the words before Zala could. "Bleak? Grim? Hollowed out?"

"Yeah, any of that." Zala turned to the other downcast heads of the room. "We just need to get them back on their feet… I just can't think of how. We gotta do something to build some trust. And I know it's my fault that this is all messed up to start with."

She tapped her boot against the table leg in thought. Pacing was her typical way of working out her thoughts, but that would just put everyone more on edge than they already were.

"What about *The Tokoloshe, The Eloko, and The Kongamato*?" Fon said brightly. Everyone else looked at her like she was crazy. "C'mon, don't look at me like that. You know what I'm talking about."

Zala pinched the edge of her brow until she recalled what those three creatures referred to. "A child's game? Really, Fon?"

The aziza gave a bashful shrug. "It might be for children, but it's still a fun game. It's better than everyone drinking themselves stupid."

"I'm with Zala on this one," Ekko said. "Can you imagine some of these scoundrels waddling around and acting like bubbling tokoloshe?"

"I've a better idea!" Zala sat up quickly. "Something better than sitting in here and sulking. C'mon, let's go up above deck."

"What about Shomari?" Fon asked.

"Already on it," Zala answered with a wave over her shoulder as she made her way to Shomari's table.

When she dipped into the shadowy space, she squinted her eyes. Were it not for Shomari's bright cloak she'd never have seen him there leaning his head lazily against his arm.

"C'mon, cat," she said. "Time to get up."

He lifted a languid ear and kept his head stuffed into his shaggy arm. His voice came muffled against it. "There is no way there's another set of sails that needs stitching."

"No," Zala said, inhaling and wondering if she'd regret her next words. "I'm challenging you to a fight."

CHAPTER 8

ZALA

The setting sun painted the ocean's horizon a pink-orange hue as Zala shook her arms out one after the other. She hopped up and down atop the creaking deck in one place to loosen the tension in her cramped calves. The grip around her blunted training sword tightened.

"This is a very bad idea, Zala," Shomari said flatly with hunched shoulders. He hadn't even withdrawn his rapier yet.

"It'd be a fair fight with just Ekko and Marjani at my side," Zala retorted as she rolled her shoulders and cracked her neck. "And Kwame here looks ready to rip your head off."

A deep and throaty rasp of a chuckle came at Zala's side. It took Ekko and Marjani some convincing, but Shomari's forced partner was more than willing to take a swing or two at the pakka. Shomari stood seven strides away from them along the main deck of the *Redtide*. Fon and Iokaja watched from the stern-castle along with Zala and Ekko's mandated companions. Shomari would never agree to fight Fon, considering his fondness of her, and as Iokaja said, "*I fought that cat once. I learned my lesson the first time.*"

Ouseni nodded in agreement. Zala was surprised she had come along, but she probably just wanted to see Zala get pummeled. "The cat's right," she said. "This is a shit idea."

"Hey, hey." Zala swung her sword ahead of her, measuring its weight. "We know the rules now. First blood, and then we're done."

"And what about magic?" Shomari asked as he eyed Ekko in particular, but it was Marjani who spoke up.

"How does me reading objects help in a fight?" she asked coyly.

"I am not speaking to you, chana." He nodded his chin to her husband. "I am knowing what this one can do with an illusion at play."

Ekko bowed his head with a smirk. "Don't worry, friend. Four on one is enough of an advantage. No need to add my Blessing in the mix as well."

Shomari looked unconvinced.

Ekko held his hand to his heart and said, "I swear it on the tide law and the Mother's Oceans."

A twitch came at Shomari's ear, and he licked at his nose. "Very well." He still didn't draw his rapier. "Let us be getting on with it then, yes?"

Zala gestured to her co-fighters to huddle up. Kwame didn't move at all, save for his tapping foot.

"Kwame, you too," she said.

The pirate grunted, and gave her a rude gesture. "Bah!"

"Fine, suit yourself." She leaned in close to Marjani and Ekko to murmur, "Okay. So I didn't tell you before, but we're gonna lose no matter what."

Ekko drew back. "You mean throw the fight?"

"No," Zala replied. "I mean, no matter what our best effort is ain't gonna cut it."

"So why are we fighting him?" Marjani asked with a scowl.

"To get him out of his rut. The point is to ring his bell, and shock him into himself again, not win—as impossible as that is on its own. Al-Anim will be hard enough with a full-on Shomari. With the one we have now..."

Ekko lifted his hands in a light wave. "I think we get it. What do you need us to do."

"Well, I was hoping there'd be four of us but..." Zala peered over to Kwame who looked ready to pounce already. "Maybe we'll just *use* Kwame…"

Zala explained to them the rest of her altered plan. Shomari wasn't going to like it, but it was their only play.

Marjani's nostrils flared, taking in what sounded like all the air in the world. "Okay…"

"Good." Zala nodded quickly, ignoring the questioning looks of the husband and wife.

Swords raised, they approached the pakka, Zala with cautious steps along with Marjani and Ekko. Kwame, as Zala expected, led with a charge. Shomari took a lazy step back, his free hand behind his back and his weapon hand limp and casual. Zala had been wrong about one thing: Shomari didn't need three strokes to put Kwame down. It only took one.

As though jumping onto some invisible ledge and vaulting off its side, Shomari sprang up and twisted in the air over Kwame's mad dash. Then, the pakka unsheathed his rapier and swung in one motion. His hilt flicked into his target's neck with a *thwack*. And Kwame took a nap between a bundle of ropes.

Zala knew Kwame must've been taken aback by Shomari's move. The pirate might've seen him fight before—hells, Zala had been witness to the cat's exploits for several moons, but Shomari always seemed to have a new trick beneath his fur even when he was only going at it half tilt.

This, however, was no time to ogle.

"Ekko, now!" Zala commanded.

Giving Zala a short nod, Ekko placed a hand to his temple, and she knew he was concentrating. Zala opened her mouth to shout her next order to Marjani, but the woman was already making her move at Shomari's right flank.

It's nice when they actually listen to my plans, Zala mused. *Now, my turn.*

With her hilt lifted to her chest and blade pointed straight ahead, she rushed for Shomari's left flank in a show of faux menace. Zala knew better than to fully commit against an opponent like the pakka. She just needed to draw his attention. Instead of driving through her forward assault, she came up short just as Shomari made ready to parry.

A glint shined at the edge of Zala's eye line. Had she not expected it, she would've never seen Marjani materialize from thin air at her side. Shomari saw it though, his feline instincts in step with Zala's expectation. He redirected his angled blade from Zala to Marjani in an upward block with extraordinary speed. And though his rapier bit into the true edge of Marjani's saber, he was still a finger's length too short. The woman's overhand cleave drove through the high guard, and caught Shomari at the tip of his pointed ear.

For all their effort, the strike only seemed to bring a twitch to the pakka's ear, not the bell ring Zala had been hoping for. Shomari rolled with the blow and twisted low in a sweep kick that caught Marjani at her ankle. The woman went tumbling onto the deck back-first alongside Kwame who still lay unmoving.

Zala cut at Shomari's leg, but found nothing but air. A shockwave sparked through her body. That was as sure a cut as any, and Shomari was entirely open. She looked down at her feet to see her foot had caught on a loose and moldy piece of deck wood.

Zala barely brought her head up in time to see Shomari's pawed foot ready to put her to sleep as well. But Ekko planted his heels into the cat's chest in a drop kick. The pakka cried out and flew back into the mainmast.

"Well, that didn't go as planned," Zala huffed as she drew back from the loose board's grip.

Ekko chuckled. "Nah, that was great. You set me up for that one. That cat is crazy good."

Zala was supposed to be the one to drop Shomari, but she wasn't going to complain about the results.

Shomari kipped up from his fall. "How did I know an illusion like that was coming?"

"Hey! It was Zala's idea." Ekko flourished his saber in front of him. "Still got you anyway, pakka."

"'On the tide law and the Mother of Oceans', ya?" the cat scoffed. "The tides must be fickle at the moment, then. That's what you get for writing laws on waves, I guess."

"What can I say." Ekko shrugged. "I had my fingers crossed."

Well, Zala got exactly what she wanted, and fear sliced through her at the heat in Shomari's slitted yellow eyes.

What was that saying about Pula the Prince who poked a pakka that was pissed?

Zala was feeling a lot like Pula right now.

Shomari went on the offensive, his rapier whizzing like a wasp looking for nectar on honeydew. And that sweet sugar ran red within Zala and Ekko. It was all Zala and her fighting partner could do to play keep away. But she couldn't keep the smile from curling her cheeks. *This* was the Shomari she was looking for.

It was also the Shomari who had never challenged her to a fight because, as she discovered on her third and fourth dodge, they weren't anywhere close to being in the same league. Hells, they weren't even swimming in the same ocean. Shomari was like a tsunami in a storm, and Zala, the coastline drowning beneath him. At least she had Ekko to help her out.

Ekko went down with a thud, his loose curls seeming to flex like springs as he fell.

Shomari had put him on his ass with a drop kick of his own. In fact, Zala reckoned Shomari took so long to disable him — a whole twenty seconds — solely to return the same blow Ekko had tagged him with. Were he not aiming for that specific kick, something told Zala that Ekko wouldn't have made it past a handful of strokes.

Now she was alone, and it was just a matter of losing with at least *some* of her dignity intact.

"Just you and me, chana," Shomari purred. "I will allow your concession if you will give it."

Why couldn't I have been born a mystic, she mused as she and Shomari paced each other in a semicircle. She would have even settled for just a basic talent for swordplay at this point. Anything that might give her a sliver's chance against the pakka. Still, she couldn't help the butterflies flapping against her stomach. Not from nerves. Well, not entirely from nerves. They came by way of the smirk at the edge of the pakka's lips. *That* was the Shomari she knew.

Biting her lip and waiting for Shomari to make his first move, she reminded herself she still had one thing going for her. She knew Shomari and the way he fought. He may always have a new trick ready to surprise her with, but at least she knew enough by now to expect most of them.

As though on cue, Shomari's eyes flitted subtly to the ropes above him. Zala knew what that meant. The cat wanted to finish her off with a little of his old swashbuckling showmanship.

She wasn't going to let that happen. Just as Shomari vaulted up, Zala scanned over to where the rope started, and, taking a step back and up to the crates beside her, she gave the right line a swift cut.

Shomari was at the height of his jump when his rope went slack. He came hurtling down onto the deck where he fell back-first. Zala pushed off the crate she was on and brought her sword overhead. But Shomari, in yet another impossible display of reflexes, blocked her blade with his own. The sidelong parry drove Zala's sword deep into the deck, where it stuck in the wood. Shomari's countering blow came up from where he still lay on the floor.

A sharp pain bit into Zala's exposed shoulder, but it didn't feel like the pakka had pierced skin. Yet.

Before Shomari could commit a second strike, Zala withdrew her dagger and drove it into the hem of the cat's cloak. The action halted Shomari's cut as he choked on his cape's collar. Zala drew back, abandoning her sword and dagger to the deck, where they were lodged for good.

She had no idea how she got out of that one, but instead of letting Shomari know that, she gathered a steady and confident breath to jab cheekily, "I always did think cloaks were pretty silly to wear in a fight."

"And I thought we agreed on blunted weapons only." Shomari pulled the dagger from his cloak. Stitching came away with it, adding to the already frayed edges of the bright red cloth.

"My mistake," Zala said, then added innocently, "It was just a reaction."

Shomari lifted to his feet and pulled Zala's sword from the

deck. He flourished both his rapier and the sword in a dual-wielded stance.

"Well, then." Shomari bowed. "Let us be ending this, yes?"

Zala might have yielded were it not for one thing. Just below and ahead of Shomari's right paw was the rotting piece of deck board she had tripped on before.

"What?" Zala egged. "Think I'm going to give up because I don't have a sword?"

Shomari looked at her like she was a madwoman. The other pirates that watched at the sterncastle shared in his bewilderment. Even Ekko, Marjani, and Kwame, who were stirring on the deck, peeked over their own injuries with raised eyebrows.

"Yes, chana." Shomari deadpanned. "That is exactly what I expect you should be doing."

Zala scoffed. "I think you're just scared I can beat you right now. I've almost had you three times already. You're not yourself right now, and you know it, kijana. Or... maybe you're just getting old."

Her last words brought a near scowl from the pakka and he dipped low, ready to pounce. One was never meant to make light of a pakka's age. Everyone knew that.

There you go, Shomari. Come at me.

Zala gestured to the welt at her shoulder. "I mean look at this. Can't even break skin in your current state. Hells, a Jultian fencer could have done a better job of it."

She knew that would do it. Shomari was always going on about how shit the fencers from her homeland were. *"Anyone can be fighting in that silly sport. As if landing a light strike is the same thing as driving a true thrust deep,"* he would say.

Dashing at full tilt, Shomari got three steps before his paw dipped into the rotted floorboard and he went tumbling into a head-first roll.

"Zala, catch!" Ekko said as he flung his saber Zala's way. Her hand met its hilt at the height of her jump and she brought it down around Shomari's exposed back. The threading in his cloak ripped and Zala's heart fluttered as she thought she saw skin breaking beneath... but it was only the outline of the light armor he always wore around his torso. Before Zala could remount a second attack, Shomari swept her at the leg where, finally, she was put on her back like all the rest.

"All right, you win," Zala gritted, knot swelling on the back of her head. "I yield."

Shomari didn't listen, whacking Zala along the welt on her arm to make her bleed. Then he flourished his rapier and stuffed it in his scabbard to say, with a smile, "*Now*, I am winning."

"Ugara's spear!" Zala hissed. "That hurt, cat." Zala rolled her head to the others nursing their wounds as she caressed the bottom of her open welt. "Maybe it's best if we *did* play that children's game."

SHOMARI HANDED ZALA A PIECE OF DAWA ROOT A FEW moments later down in the sickbay. "Here you will be needing this for there," he pointed to a cut on her head, "there," another on her arm, "there," her cheek, "and there." He poked at Zala's raw ribs.

"How did you know I was injured here? You can't even see it."

"Decades of doing this, chana." He grinned, then did his best to hide a wince of his own.

Between the hanging cots and potions lining the walls atop shelves, shadow dominated the little chamber they shared. Even so, Zala could still see the swipe she got along the back of Shomari's cloak. "So, besides those Vaaji who nearly did you in… was I the first one to get a proper hit on you?"

Shomari glanced up at the creaking wooden ceiling above in thought. "In a straight fight like that… skies, you might be. I have had plenty of near misses, of course, been kicked and punched a few times. But I reckon, yeah, you are the first one to be landing a proper blow."

"Some of the crew and myself were wondering if that tale about cats and their nine lives were true."

"That is what we would be liking you to think, at least."

"Hurry up in there, you two!" shouted Ouseni outside the

door. She had been waiting for them to come out, taking her duties of watching them far too seriously. Kwame didn't even come down with Shomari.

A brief silence hung between Zala and Shomari as they continued to dab their wounds. Zala wanted to ask Shomari how he was feeling directly. There were glimpses of the old Shomari when they fought, but somehow then, even as they spoke, she didn't quite feel he was back to normal. She was foolish to think one sparring match would wash away that sort of trauma. If she had gone through something like that, she wouldn't have wanted to speak on it. So she stayed her tongue and kept rubbing dawa root into her wounds.

The little green roots numbed her pain, but her cuts weren't sealing like they were supposed to. Scanning the sickbay shelves for something stronger, she landed on a fair-sized jar of sea water the surgeon used for certain potions. Then she opened the jar, dunked the dawa root into the water and passed it over her arms.

"Neat trick," Shomari said as Zala watched her wounds finally seal. "Was not knowing salt water mixed with dawa root could do that."

"It's something I did as a child," she explained. "It doesn't work for everyone, though."

Shomari stuck out his hand to try it out. He lifted the root over his shoulder and started to rub. Another silence was threatening to fall between them when Shomari said, "Thanks, chana. You're a shit fighter, but a clever one. Maybe I *should* have challenged you back on our old ship."

"Anytime," Zala replied with a weak and awkward smile.

"I mean that, Zala." Shomari gripped her tight around her forearm. "Do not be giving me that look. I forgive you for what you did that day. I understand why you did it."

Zala didn't think she deserved his forgiveness. At least not yet. She'd make good on all that once they found Jelani and took that sky ship back. Then, and only then, could she accept Shomari's word. But until that point...

"Come, let's get back up there and play Fon's game."

Shomari snorted. "You would not be catching me dead playing

a children's game around this sort. Fon leading us or not. The crew respects me, especially after my near-death heroics. I am not trying to tarnish that."

Zala shrugged and stepped away toward the room's tattered door. "Fine, I won't put in a good word to Fon about you. And to think I told her you were a free-spirit who didn't care what others think. That's her favorite quality in a partner."

"I told you already, chana. I'm a cat, not an ass."

Zala rolled her eyes and walked into the corridor, but not before Shomari halted her with a last few words. "But… do you think Fon would appreciate someone who'd be into her little game?"

"Yes. Yes she would. Not if you're going to be all downtrodden, though. Give her that cocky smile of yours."

Shomari struck his best smirk, though it was entirely exaggerated and borderline monstrous.

"Yeah," Zala giggled. "That'll do just fine."

<hr>

Zala felt her cheeks flush while Fon explained the rules of the game. They were simple. Each pirate was to be grouped at three separate ends of the top deck and assigned a creature. Each of them had to close their eyes and make a sound, whether it was the mumbling grunts of a tokoloshe, the eerie ring of an eloko, and—in Zala's case—the loud squawk of a kongamato. The object was to find your clan of like-sounding creatures until everyone was in their appropriate groupings. First group to find their clan was the winner.

Kwame grunted, "To hells if you think I'll run around clucking like some long-dead bird."

Old Man Ode, who had come hobbling down from the sterncastle agreed as he dodged Fon, who was trying to put a blindfold around his eyes. "You get away from me with that blindfold, damnit! I'll clip that wing of yours clean off and feed it to the kubahari."

"Oh, come on, Ode," Fon said with a pout, putting her large

eyes to work as she guilted the old man with a downright innocent look that the strongest willed man couldn't hope to defend against.

It only took a single moment for Ode to snatch the scarf and tie it around his eyes, but not before grumbling, "Damn aziza and their bloody charm."

"Move it, Ode." The young Rishaad gave him a pat on shoulder, then handed him a bottle of rum. "Take some of your silly juice, that'll get you right for it."

To Zala's surprise the game was a lot more fun than it had any business being. But it went without saying, the silly creature play involved a lot of bumping into one another. At first, it was awkward and uncomfortable, yet those first brush-ins with one pirate or another led to genuine laughter that quickly broke down the walls that had been there before. Even Ouseni had let loose an uncharacteristic giggle when she and Zala found each other, both women screeching and yapping all the while.

The fun and games were infectious, and more and more pirates poked their heads out from belowdecks to join in. For a moment, Zala watched as grown women and men—the tough kind with old scars and hard faces—waddled around like children. Under the snapping of the sails, chuckles of mirth mixed in with the cacophony of beastly creature calls, and not a single face was left without a smile.

Even Mantu had peered around the corner of stacked crates as the sun started to dip below the horizon. He didn't join in on the game, but at least, Zala caught the slight arc of his mustache betraying a smile.

A slamming of a door came from behind just then. Everyone shot up and turned their heads to the thundering sound.

"What's going on here?" came a booming voice from the double doors leading into the Captain's quarters.

Zala almost thought that Captain Nubia was back among them, like she had never left at all. The voice was uncanny. But when she turned her gaze to the stern, it wasn't Nubia who stood there with hands on her hips.

It was Lishan.

CHAPTER 9
ZALA

"What's with all this racket?" Lishan seethed. Her tight braids looked like two large snakes crawling over her head and down her shoulders. "You all look like a bunch of damn fools."

Fon, perhaps still caught up in the previous zeal of the games, said, "You should join us, Captain. You'd make a wonderful tokoloshe."

Kwame sniggered at Fon's side, but quickly reigned in his chuckling beneath the weight of Lishan's hot glare.

"We're a mere night from al-Anim, and you all thought it was a good idea to play games and leave the deck in this mess?" Lishan said as she lifted the cut rope in her hand.

Zala swallowed long and hard. It had been her cut that did that. She forgot it had been left there. In fact, as her eyes traveled along the deck she noticed how disorderly the deck had become: barrels overturned from people bumping into each other, rum crates left open from those who wanted to top off, not to mention the spots of blood from the earlier fight.

Lishan scowled at each one of her crew who dared to meet her eye, doing her best imitation of their previous Captain. If her face hadn't been oblong instead of heart-shaped, and her skin more a russet hue than a midnight one, Zala would have thought Lishan and Nubia were related.

Lishan cleared her throat before saying, "I need you all sharp for what we're about to do. Those of you not with us on that sky ship didn't face their soldiers. The Vaaji aren't what they used to be. They've made adjustments and are a serious threat. Playing these juvenile games ain't gonna do it. It'll only make us soft."

Zala considered saying they started with a fight, but she knew that wasn't the response Lishan was looking for.

"Who's idea was this?" Lishan asked the crowd.

A few heads made their slow turn to Fon. One of her pointed ears was covered by her long hair, but the other—exposed against half a head of braided hair—flared red. Lishan was halfway to figuring out where most of her crew's eyes had landed when Zala stepped forward.

"It was me, Captain."

Lishan drew in a long and deep breath as her cheek pulsed with the grinding of her teeth. Zala's throat felt as dry as sand. At least two dozen bodies stood between her and Lishan, but the captain made a straight line towards her. And the crew parted like a wake before a ship's bow.

In only a few strides, Lishan was on top of Zala, flinging out her hand and gripping hard around Zala's neck. The woman didn't let go even as Zala stumbled back into the port railing and bent back along its edge.

A few gasps came from the crowd as Zala fought for air in staccato rasps. She shifted her eyes to Shomari, who she knew was already reaching for his rapier. Though she struggled in her frightening restraint, her wide eyes told the cat to stand down.

"Captain Nubia might have allowed you to keep your title and your hold on your little crew," Lishan spat. "But I ain't havin' it while I'm at the *Redtide's* helm." She tossed Zala along the deck to fall between folded sails. The wound at Zala's arm opened wider and smeared blood along the off-white cloth.

Lishan raised her voice to the rest of the crew. "We don't have *guests* on the *Redtide* anymore. If you are on this ship, you are on this crew. If you reject this, then you will become our prisoner, or," the Captain turned to Zala, "our enemy. Captain Zala of the former *Titan* here will pledge herself and her crew to us, or she will be thrown from the ship." She crossed her arms. "Anyone have a problem with that?" No one said a word; no one even seemed to move. "Good." Lishan peered down to Zala. "Official proclamation, please. I'm tired of you having free rein. I won't have the sky ship happen all over again when we make our landing in al-Anim."

Zala felt hollowed out and shamed. Everyone was looking at her now, waiting for her acceptance or their Captain's challenge. She could almost hear Mantu in her head telling her it was a bad idea to come along with these "crazy Rovers." But whenever Mantu made his hushed complaints on the *Redtide,* she always imagined it would be the large man sprawled out on the deck before Lishan's wicked stare. Him, the begrudging crewmate, not her, who was actually trying to *help* with crew morale.

The captain was already thumbing at the dagger at her waist as she waited impatiently. Zala had no desire to give the woman what she wanted, but it wasn't just her who'd suffer. She needed to think about the rest of her group. They were outnumbered six to one. Maybe less than that if she tried to test how loyal some of the *Redtide* crew were to Lishan personally.

Maybe if Zala could convince—

"Well, what will it be," Lishan grunted with a tap at her waist. "The ship... or the sea?"

A pair of ideas struck Zala then: One, she didn't give a damn about the lawtide or the Gods it was built on. So she could promise whatever and go back on it. Two, lawtide made it clear that anyone pledged under the same flag couldn't strike one another—save for training or capital punishment. And even then, an altercation between pirates of the same crew could only be officially resolved under the judgement of one of the Tide Lords. If Lishan's true desire was to harm Zala, she messed up. The Captain was essentially giving her immunity.

Lishan scowled. "I'll take your silence to mean the sea..."

Zala remembered one of her conversations with Nubia, that she claimed the Meroé Rovers and the *Redtide* were "true rogues of the sea." Hadn't Shomari told her they operated outside of the scope of the Golden Lord and his tide law?

"How can I pledge to you," Zala finally said, her voice hoarse and weak, as Lishan approached, "when this ship is not recognized by the Golden Lord?"

A second silence deepened within the already hushed crowd. Zala smiled inwardly at her quick-wit, but Lishan's expression didn't falter. In fact, Zala would have sworn she saw the woman's lip upturn at her cheek as she said, "Before leaving Port Kidogo, I paid my homage to Tide Lord Ganaji. The *Redtide* is now a ship under the protection of Golden Lord Zuberi and his Gold Fleet. The Tide Lord signed us onto the list herself."

Lishan lifted her chin upward, and Zala followed the path of her gaze to the flag that snapped above. Sure enough, the *Redtide* banner was altered with a signature trim of gold around its red-and-black cloth. How could she have missed it? She was only stationed up there for hours...

Zala's mouth twisted in a frown. The deeper it went, the more Lishan's little smirk seemed to grow. Zala rolled her head to the rest of the crew, and she caught sight of Marjani with her yellow hair beads in her locs. Even one of the few allies she had on the *Redtide* wasn't willing to give her any support.

Well, like Zala had said... she didn't give a damn about the Gods. At least she'd be making her half-hearted pledge on everyone else's behalf.

Inhaling deeply through her nose, she said, "By the right of Yem, I, Zala of the fallen *Titan*, pledge myself and my remaining crew to Captain Lishan and the *Redtide*."

Lishan narrowed her eyes again. "Go on..."

Really? Zala thought. *She wants the* whole *spiel? Fine.*

"In dire sickness, and perfect health," Zala gritted. "I, and my crew, will be at your services and always remain true."

Lishan, finally, let her thumb fall from the handle of her dagger. Then she shifted her shoulders to her crew, who said in unison, "And we bear witness. May Her waves be merciful."

"May Her waves be merciful," Lishan finished. "Now, get all this cleaned up. I want all of you belowdecks and resting in an hour. And you." The Captain directed her chin down to Zala. "Make sure to get that blood out of the sails. We keep a clean ship here."

Get the blood out of the sails?

She couldn't be serious. That would take forever, and was damn near impossible to boot. But Lishan stood there like a specter of the night, and she tilted her head to one side as though she were waiting for a retort, any excuse to slap Zala across the mouth.

"On this ship," she said, "crew members are to answer their captain in the affirmative."

"Yes, Captain," Zala said softly and bitterly. But the look on Lishan's face told her that wouldn't do. "Yes, Captain," she said louder but flatly.

"Captain," came another voice from somewhere to the side. "How are we supposed to clean all this in an hour with the light almost out."

Zala had barely noticed that twilight was upon them.

Lishan stomped toward her quarters and, with the slightest of turns over her shoulder answered, "Maybe you find a tokoloshe to help you."

CHAPTER 10

KARIM

KARIM ADMIRED THE MEDALLION SET IN HIS HAND BY HIS newly appointed military steward, Jamal Bitar—now the boy could *actually* serve him without breaking official protocol. Back then, Karim was merely an acting captain. Now, he was the real thing.

Karim traced the outline of the metalwork: a carving of an ancient roc with its sharp beak and hooked talons glistening with the palace corridor's lanterns. No man or woman in the entire world could claim this piece of metal: the new insignia of a Vaaji Sky Captain. Perhaps one day the airships would be just as large as the ancient rocs they were modeled after.

And Karim would be at the helm.

"Captain, is everything okay?" his steward asked.

Karim shook the stupor from his face. "Everything is perfect, Bitar."

"Oh, I almost forgot. This letter came in for you through Nabila." The steward handed Karim a folded piece of parchment.

"Thank you." Karim opened it and it read:

Karim,

Collector Vaziri says we didn't give him enough last time. Says

"When did this come for me?" Karim asked sharply.

Nabila had been locked away in the palace, just like everyone else was. Surely his father would know better than to send a direct message to him through her.

"Yesterday, Captain. But I was told not to give it to you until after the debriefing."

Karim closed the letter in a huff. One success always seemed to be met with another problem yet to be solved. Perhaps he could speak with this tax collector directly. Now that he was a captain, he would have more pull in any confrontation with the man. Or so he hoped.

"Thank you, Bitar," Karim said as he curled away his anger under the thin line of his lips. "Go ahead and get yourself some rest. You deserve it."

"And what about you, sir?" Bitar asked with wide eyes.

Karim gave the steward a half smile. "I'll rest when I'm dead."

With a deep inhale, Karim turned and made his way out of Jasmiin Towers. Each time he passed one of the guards, they acknowledged him with a salute and a quick "Evening, Captain" whenever they made note of the medallion at his breast.

It was almost half an hour before Karim had finally descended the many hundreds of stairs from the Royal Family's keep, through the Admiralty offices, and, finally, to the soldier's barracks. It took another five minutes before he was outside the main gate and walking down into the port city, where the night air trailed cooly across his face.

It had been moons since his first *real* return. Ever since he transferred to the Navy, most of his years were spent out at sea and—more recently—in the sky.

Every time Karim returned to al-Anim, no matter how briefly, there seemed to be a new addition to the city. When he had left for *The Flying Viper Project*, the builders were still constructing a large pair of statues in Emperor and Empress al-Nasir's likenesses. Now it seemed completed, save for the final paint job. It stood as the last of a long line of statues trailing to the top of the capital hill. Rulers of the past told the story of their city on plaque bases behind him. A young history that started with Moharam the Uniter and ended with the al-Nasir family, the Shepherds of New Vaaj.

Al-Anim itself was cut from a flat bay to a large hill. At its top were the buildings set for the nobility: the palace, the homes of the governors, the great temples—and even greater libraries. It had once served as the "Chief's Hill" before the Vaaji Empire officially formed, bringing the old tribes together under one banner, and one God: Shati'ala. Now it was much more grandiose, turning sand-swept roads into polished streets with fancy lantern lights and elaborate fountains—though the name "Chief's Hill" stuck around as the district's unofficial name.

Karim had thrilling memories from here when he and his ruffian friends sneaked into the bathhouses. The "hillers," as they used to call them, always seemed to have carefree faces, strolling the stoned pavements or getting driven around in carts as if they owned them both—in many ways most of them did.

As Karim walked down the central street known as the Spine, which was a long, straight shot from the palace all the way down to the harbor, essences of fragrant perfumes wafted through the air. Noble couples spoke in airy tones, meandering their way through the streets. Soon Karim passed from the elite district to the rustic smell of metalwork and the whoosh of mechanical weavers: the welcoming notes of the central borough.

Though it was evenfall, the merchants who resided here still worked under the blue light of moonstone lanterns. Here, in the district called Merchant's Row, one could find a blacksmith to forge a scimitar, a miller who could toil one's harvest into grain, or a tailor to fashion a stylish agal for a kaffiyeh. Of the latter, fashion was a huge draw for those who visited Vaaj. Where people in most other regions wore nothing but the same rags until they fell off their shoulders, what one wore in al-Anim was seasonal and ever-changing.

Karim peered down to his own outfit. The moment he was dismissed from the war council, he had torn off his formal clothing in favor of a loose tunic that bore a military cut—sharp edges at the shoulder and cuffs. It was a simple thing, no ornate blood lilies or embroidered flowers. He was never very good at keeping up with fashion trends, though he and his old friends had always wanted a nice agal wrapped in gold, or a robe layered with expensive silks just so they could show off back in the slums. He could even remember how one of his friends tried to dye his hair blue once—to a not-so-appealing effect. As Karim chuckled internally at the thought, the worker scent turned into a downright stench as his feet met flat ground at the hill's bottom, the residence of the laborers, a ward one would never find on a respectable map: Lowtown.

There was no time for animated conversation or a fashionable collection of clothing down here. In this borough of literal rock bottom, the only fashion was plain clothes and hard faces. Street faces. The kind Karim often wore when he found himself away from "good, noble" company—hell, even in "good noble" company sometimes.

Karim navigated his old ward by memory, the sharp corners and tight alleyways etched in his mind. He had covered his silver medallion at his chest and hid it from the eyes of thieves beneath dimly lit corridors. It was a good instinct, but unnecessary. No slummer would be stupid enough to attack a naval officer, even during the night, especially here where most of the ward's people were followers of that old "pious" religion.

After cutting through an alley, several lines of drying clothes, an abandoned shanty, and a dead field where children played, Karim arrived at what looked like an abandoned, fallen temple. The Great Temple of Jo'bara.

The district known as the Scars.

Relations between the old and new religion were not always a simple divide of taxes and their collection. At one point there had been vicious fighting, with the end resulting in dilapidated temples like that one, the very thing Karim's father had always wanted to avoid.

At its height, the temple had several statues and pillars carved into the images of the Old Gods. Karim brushed his hand over one of the sand-dusted towers as he tried to recall which of the hundreds of Jo'baran Gods it had represented. He stopped himself when he realized remembering was a futile effort.

The time for the Old Gods had long passed.

But this fallen temple had more meaning for him than just a religious site. It was once his home. Many devotees of Jo'bara clung to their fallen temples, making homes of the cracked and neglected rooms that were slowly being built over by the new city.

Karim ducked his head under a pair of crossed and fallen pillars that served as the district's unofficial entrance. As he passed through, a thick musk filled his nostrils: the stench of too many people clustered together in one place. Karim held his breath as he made his way to his father's home, through the disordered collection of shanties that were sheltered by a pockmarked high ceiling. Eventually, he found his father's dwelling among the tattered shelters built between the once holy and unsoiled rooms.

How long had it been since Karim was there? Two years? Three? He couldn't recall. Images flashed before his eyes. Just down the row of shanties behind his father's was where he used to meet with his friends before they went out for their near nightly bouts of thievery. And just a few paces from there was where Issa's family used to live before they moved farther south, away from the city, away from the tithe imposed by Qibasi tax collectors. Issa had still visited, of course. But it was never quite the same without her in the years she was gone.

Karim smiled despite himself. Times were rough here, that was for certain. There were good memories too, though. But the district didn't seem to have done any better for itself in the time since he had left. He could understand why Issa would want to come back and clean up the place. It's not that the people were intentionally dirty or negligent. Between their overlong work hours and the excessive taxes that seemed *designed* to displace them, they simply didn't have the time.

Karim shook his head back to the now. As he passed the threshold into his father's home, he kissed his hand and touched the wall—an old custom he thought lost until a few days ago when he met that pirate Jelani plagued with stoneskin.

His father's space was small, but bigger than most other shanties. As the district's shaman—a role that saw the old man performing ancestral rituals that he believed brought his patients back to health—the slummers offered him better accommodation. At first, when Karim was young, he thought his father really did accomplish it all with magic. But since his time at the academy, he knew his father's true magic lay in the tried and tested methods of medicine, even if the old man refused to see it.

Just ahead of Karim, under a bushel of sage working his "magic", stood his father. This time his form of "mysticism" came by way of ginger root for a sickly old woman whose paling skin didn't need magic as much as it wanted for sunlight and fresh air.

"Just keep taking this ginger root," his father said, "and make sure to pray to Ọfun three times a day, or else the properties of the root won't work and your throat will lock up like the palace dungeons. Do you remember at which times?"

"At daybreak, at sun's peak, and at nightfall," the woman croaked harshly in answer.

"That's right." Karim's father nodded, his white teeth stark against his green-painted ceremonial skin. "Now, you be on your way."

The woman turned to exit, and gave Karim a brief smile. It was then that his father took proper notice of his son.

Unlike most old men, whose hair fell from their heads only to sprout more thickly on their cheeks, his father's white beard was patchy, failing to compensate for his harsh widow's peak. Still, the old man gave Karim a wide smile, his scraggly whiskers lifting high on his discolored cheeks. "Thank Deh'ala, your travels have been safe. How've you been, son?"

Karim bent a knee, tapping the ground in front of his father—another old show of respect. "I'm doing well, Baba. I hope you are the same."

Karim raised his head to take in his father's appearance again. Through the earthy paint his father's skin was darker than he remembered. Karim wasn't particularly light himself, but his skin looked almost fair by comparison. The old man must've been taking more labor jobs out in the sun again. Large bags sagged deep below his graying eyes, and as he moved he seemed to teeter on the edge of imbalance.

Karim watched as his father attempted to "clean up" his home, tossing supplies onto different heaps of piles, which were seemingly organized in a way that made sense to him. Though his old man's shanty smelled of a flowery scent of jasmine mixed with a thick incense, the place was an utter mess with pots, pans, old rugs, and rotting plants scattered along the ground. As the only medicine man in the district, he must've been overburdened. Karim had made his fusses about the home his father kept but he knew nothing could be done for it, just as with the district at large. Not without help.

But what good would military education do to help this place? Karim wondered, his thoughts back on Issa.

Karim's father slumped off as he put away a basket full of herbs and spices. The man simply didn't have the time to keep tidy. It didn't matter to him if his home was clean when someone in the slums needed a broken wrist mended or a fever broken.

"I am glad to see you've not lost respect for tradition." His father nodded to a still kneeling Karim. With a slanted grin, he gestured for his son to rise. "And what's this pinned to your chest?" He pointed to the medallion, which Karim noticed must've exposed itself as he knelt, then the man moved to a large pot of water to begin washing the green paint from his sunbaked face.

"I've been promoted to Captain."

"You have your own ship? The seas will be open to you now!"

"Yes, my own... ship. But it comes with a new assignment, one that I fear may be near impossible to complete."

"Nothing's impossible for my son." He coughed. "Nothing too great for an el-Sayyed. What's this mission you got?"

Karim couldn't help but smirk. Despite the differences he held against his father, the old man had always been supportive. "You know I can't tell you that, Baba. Do you want Their Majesties' carpet vipers after you?"

"Bah!" His father threw up a wrinkled hand as he dug a second splash of water on his face. "No one comes to visit us unless they want our hard-earned coin."

"Which reminds me." Karim withdrew a sack from his tunic. "Will this help for that extra payment?"

The old man grabbed and lifted the sack, weighing it in his hand as the coins clinked together. "That should do for tomorrow, at least."

Karim's brow grew tight. "I don't understand, I sent you two moon's wages over a week ago. How much can that collector possibly be taking?"

"It's not just me that needs it, son. There's your cousins, there's Old Fatima with her bad hip, the little ones with the sniffles I was telling you about in my letter last moon, and the Ali family just had twins. They'll need a bit of coin to—"

"The coin I send is for *you*, Baba." Karim's voice was more stern than he intended, but he wasn't going to apologize for it. He couldn't maintain his father's charity. The regular tithe was already hard enough to keep up with with just *one* head to manage. With his father constantly doling out money as he saw fit, they'd both be broke by year's end.

"So now that you're *Captain* el-Sayyed," Karim's father ignored him, "does that mean you will have more time to visit your family?"

Karim took a seat atop a stained pillow. "No. The opposite, I expect. Especially with this new assignment."

"Don't work too hard, Karim. You're old enough now to start a family. Even your cousin, Ketifa, is finally marrying that boy." His father took a cloth and wiped the last of the paint from his face.

Karim gave an animated gasp. "No! Not... not *Hamid*? The boy's fancied her since we were five."

His father smacked his knee, a cough interlaced within his laughter. "And a wise move it was. Ketifa has grown into a beautiful young woman. Your aunt is happy to see her starting a family too." The old man's smile curled down into a frown. "She saw you at the palace today, though. She was sad when you didn't say hello after all these years."

Karim racked his mind, but he could not recall seeing her. "I don't know what you mean."

"She said she served you and another young woman food. You were angry about something so she didn't fuss about it, though."

Even with his best efforts, Karim could not recall the young woman who might've served him and Issa that day. If it had been his cousin, he wouldn't know. The last time he had seen her, she was losing the last of her baby teeth.

"Can't believe Aunt Kamila agreed to it." Karim changed the subject.

His father sighed, then sat himself down on his own dusty pillow. "Like I said. He's a good boy, good heart. If he can get even Ketifa to marry, then there's hope for you yet, my boy."

The brightness on his father's face only made Karim's shoulders fall as he looked down at his hands uncomfortably. Any of his honest answers would only serve to disappoint his father. "You know I'm too busy for all of that, Baba."

"I've heard them nobles and priests in the market. The Empire encourages its military to marry. A man your age… I'm sure there is *someone* you like, at least." His father gave him a rough, soil-caked pat on the pack.

"I haven't given it a thought," Karim said slowly, though he couldn't help being reminded of Nabila's perfumes. "I'm too busy trying to figure out how to get Their Majesties what they want."

A rapping came at the pocketed straw door. Without waiting for an answer, a member of the palace guard — Karim couldn't tell if they were a man or woman through the thick armor — stomped into the small shanty.

"I have a few wants of my own." A light, almost effeminate voice came from behind the guard, then Mahir Vaziri, the tax collector of the slum district sauntered into view.

He hadn't changed a bit since the last time Karim saw him in passing years ago in the academies. Like Grand Admiral Awad, he had a particular taste for fashion, sporting a checkered yellow and black turban, with a sleek, ankle-length tunic the shade of midnight. If Karim's eyes hadn't betrayed him, gold was sewn into the hems of the cloth, *real* gold, which seemed to reflect in the man's hazel eyes.

Karim took another glance at the guard, who held a hand over the hilt of their saber. Between their full head wrap, which only exposed their eyes, Karim could see they shared the greenish-brown eye color with Mahir.

When his father had said a "Vaziri" was coming to the slums in his letters, Karim had never thought he had meant in person. He had assumed the Collector would've sent one of his underlings. Why was a district official doing his own collection, and why so late at night?

It *stank* of corruption.

"Good evening, erm, el-Sayyed," Vaziri said to Karim in his smooth use of High Vaaji. "And good evening to you, Elder Ismail. Do you have the Emperor's coin?"

"We wasn't expecting you 'til morning," Karim's father said cheerfully, replying in Common Vaaji. Karim tried his best not to scowl. It was the kind of tone his father used when he was appeasing the noblemen. It was too meek, too docile for his own taste. Karim got none of his passion from his father—everyone had always said Karim took after his late mother.

The old man lifted the sack given to him by Karim. He laid his head low as he offered it to Vaziri. "Right here, Your Majesty."

A seemingly honest moment of sheer disbelief overtook Vaziri's expression before he spat, "I'm not your *Emperor*, slum rat. You may address me as 'sir.'"

"Apologies, *sir*." He bowed his head even lower.

Karim gritted his teeth. This was exactly the type of noble he had always loathed, even more so than Malouf. The district official reeked of "hiller" narcissism.

"Take it easy, Mahir," Karim gritted.

Vaziri's guard took the sack of coin from his father's hand, measuring the weight of it in their hands. "Seems a bit light," she said, as Karim identified the woman's voice. It sounded strangely like Vaziri's.

He's nepotic too? No surprises there.

The district official pinched the bridge of his nose. "Elder Ismail, you do know you were to provide the tax for *all* those in this neighborhood, correct?"

"Of course, sir. Is that not enough, sir?" Karim's father stretched out his hands as though to check the amount, but the guard withdrew the sack out of reach, leaving him to grab awkwardly at the air.

Karim stepped forward, his voice sharp, his eyes sharper. "You've given *plenty*, Father." He turned to Vaziri. "I haven't heard word of Their Majesties' tithe going up."

"There are a lot of things you military grunts have not heard of." Vaziri angled his bronze glare on Karim. "That tends to happen when you spend so much time away from the capital. I see that you're fitted with a new medallion..."

"They're not giving you any more coin, Vaziri." Karim's voice was final, challenging. "The Emperor and Empress demand only a single gold piece per head for each of Àyá's moons. What you have there is more than enough."

"Ah, but there are two more heads this week, are there not?" Mahir turned to Karim's father, who couldn't maintain eye contact. "Correct me if I'm wrong, but A'isha Ali had twins a few days ago. You left that out of your report when we last came."

The elder sunk his head down low.

"Doesn't matter," Karim said darkly. "Every parent of al-Anim is given at least one of Yem's moons to pledge their children to al-Qiba. If the parent or parents choose not to after said period, then and only then, must they submit the appropriate tax for the child —or children in this case."

Mahir frowned as Karim's father's eyes darted between the two men.

The pregnant pause in the room hung heavy.

Karim had hoped he got the wording of the law right. It had been a while since he had had to defend anyone with it, though he had always done it almost automatically when he ran into noblemen like Vaziri as a youth. Sometimes his smart mouth had gotten him out of troubled situations, other times —most times —it had led to punishments like the scar running down his chin.

"If you say so, *Captain.*" Vaziri eyed Karim's medallion. How did he know it was a captain's insignia? "But you can't keep giving these rats money. Eventually they'll run you dry, especially those you call kin." The man twisted to his guard. "Let's go. We still have a few spots to hit before the night is through."

Vaziri and his bodyguard left the shanty—Vaziri in a hurried and flamboyant huff, his guard in a clanking stomp. Through the makeshift door, Karim saw six more bodyguards fall in line behind Mahir, each of similar height and build.

Why so many guards? Karim scowled.

It was a good thing Mahir didn't try to force the coin out of him or his father. If it came to a scrap, it was one Karim couldn't win.

"Don't pay him any mind," his father said dismissively.

Karim felt himself get red in the face. "He can't keep doing that. I'll report him to the Admiralty."

"Don't do that, son. It's not worth it. You're doing so well, don't risk your position, especially not now. With this," he tapped the medallion at Karim's chest, "you'll be able to build up this place for our people again, maybe even get Their Majesties to ease up on us, yes?"

His father placed a hand on Karim's cheek, then gave him a gentle slap.

Karim didn't have the heart to tell his father he'd converted to al-Qiba. Even if he had the funds to rebuild the district on his own—and at this rate, that was more than doubtful—his coin could never go into refurbishing a Jo'baran temple. The military council and his colleagues, save for Issa, would never accept it. He'd be committing himself to professional and social ostracization.

"You know it'll be easier if you all—*we all*—just converted to al-Qiba," Karim said. "The tax would go away, just like that. I've been looking into it myself. It's not all that bad. It's the same religion, really."

"It dismisses all other Gods but one, son," his father said with the commanding tone of a patriarch. If only he could muster such ardor with Collector Vaziri.

"I know, but if you gave it a chance, a *real* chance, you might be able to find something useful out of it. Come by the temple and listen to one of the priests."

His father spun on him with shock. "And forsake centuries of tradition? I'd rather have the hillers' tax."

"Shaman el-Sayyed!"

"Oni'baro Ismail!"

A group of children barged into the small home, shouting at the top of their lungs.

"We need your help! The little one got hurt in the mines!"

Karim's father gave the children a kind smile, though his eyes looked beyond exhaustion. "I have my son here and it's been a long day. Is it truly an emergency this time?"

"She can't move her leg," one of the children said. "There's a bump coming out of her skin."

Karim's father's sigh came deep, and the old man aged a decade before Karim's eyes. But then, as though the moment had never happened, he lifted his shoulders with a duty-bound and youthful vigor that did not match his wrinkled skin and weary bones.

"Was it Katya again?" he asked. "I told her not to mess with those bigger rocks, even if she's an elemental."

"It's okay, you can help them," Karim said, placing a tender hand to his father's back. "I should go, anyway. I'll talk to Collector Vaziri, see if I can get him to ease up on you and the rest. But I'm serious about going to the temple. The Faith teaches us—the other soldiers—about being self-sufficient. The sermon at sundown tomorrow will be very enlightening if you take the time to come by."

"The Gods provide us with everything we need," his father said as he gathered supplies. "They left us a perfect world. And we are ruining it. I've heard rumors about what the nobles are doing. No one has been able to visit the Holy City for several moons now. And now they use children for their labor. Slavers might be gone, but there's nothing good being done there, I say."

If only Karim could believe such a thing, perhaps his life

would have been simpler. As his father was dragged at the arm by the children, Karim nodded his goodbye.

The day's events seemed to hit him all at once as his mental energy drained. How long had it been since he slept? A full day? Perhaps more. There was so much on Karim's mind, so much he had to do. But none of it could be done with his wit at its end. He would need to be fresh if he was going to think up a way to stop, or at least slow, Collector Vaziri. More importantly, he'd need to be alert for the coming day.

In the morning, he had a critical session with a telepath… and a certain sea-speaking pirate.

CHAPTER 11

KARIM

Karim got exactly what he asked for and more when next morning came.

Not only did the military council move the pirate Jelani to a new location, but on the new Sky Captain's orders, the prisoner's latest accommodations were immaculate.

For one, the builders stripped the holding room of its typical drab wood paneling, and replaced them with lavender rugs. Azure silks strung up from the wall. Though there was no window to let in fresh air, a light incense perfumed the room, a single stick lying atop the only table present. There wasn't much in the way of furnishings decorating the space, save for a small set of bedding and simple chairs, which surrounded the beige table, each spread out enough as not to feel jammed or crowded.

With all these delicate accommodations, one might expect they were hosting some esteemed guest. Perhaps a dignified king, a noteworthy scholar, or a noble priest. But it was a farce as fraudulent as a trickster's promise.

Karim would certainly never call himself a nobleman, and the women who sat at his side—an instructor and her telepathic student—while invaluable, were no queen or princess themselves. The room's delicate design was for the benefit of their prisoner, and not because they were aiming to dote on the infected man.

They had deliberately chosen every aspect of the room to soothe him into comfort and complacency so that he might be more receptive to what was to come.

The weary, weakened man sat slumped in his chair, eyes unfocused and head gently listing to one side.

Before him, Khadija of the family Ganim sat with her clenched hands atop the smooth table, her forehead lined in concentration. Beside her sat her mentor and instructor, Proctor Halabi.

"Do not force your will on his own," she told her student through tight lips. "He should guide you to the truth without realizing it."

Karim watched as Jelani the pirate shook in his chair, his bald head shining against the gentle light of the room. For the past half hour, the pirate and the telepath both had been through short episodes of spasming jolts as each fought the other across the table in their minds.

Karim had seen nothing like it before. He had heard of the telepaths and the ways of their inner voices from stories—and his time in the academy—but nothing quite prepared him for the sheer absence of the action before reaction as both parties twitched in their seats.

It had discouraged him, however, to see that Khadija had convulsed almost three times as much as the pirate Jelani had. He couldn't begin to understand the process of telepathy, yet he couldn't help but see it as a bad sign.

Several times, Karim had wanted to ask for a report, some sort of communication of progress or lack thereof. But each time he opened his mouth, Proctor Halabi's fierce expression shut down his commentary.

"He's..." Khadija finally strained out. "He's... not resisting me. His active thoughts are clear but... all of his words make little sense. It's... a language I do not know."

"Can you repeat to us what he's saying?" Halabi asked calmly, placing a considerate hand over Khadija's clamped one.

After another bout of spasms, the young telepath did her best to recite what she heard. Halabi's face scrunched in confusion at the gibberish, but Karim let out a low sigh. Though he couldn't make out all of what she was saying, he got the gist.

"He's praying." Karim pinched the edge of his brow.

Halabi turned her withered, graying eyes to Karim. "You understand that babble?"

"It's the Old Tongue, the Origin Tongue."

"And how is it you can identify that dead language?"

"Many prayers in the Old Faith use the tongue," Karim explained, though he didn't want to go into how he knew it. "It's a bunch of mumbo jumbo to most of those Jo'barans as well. Very few *actually* know the meaning of the words."

Khadija's muttering came suddenly to a stop. Her thin brows did little to prevent the sweat streaming from her forehead and into her eyes as she opened them.

"I'm… sorry, Maji Halabi," she said through labored breaths. "I thought I was ready."

Karim tilted his head to the side slightly. "*Thought* you were ready?"

"I can go again," Khadija said quickly to her mentor, ignoring Karim's interjection. "I just need some time to settle myself."

Halabi gave her a nod. "Very well, take some time to—"

"Can your pupil not pull more than words?" Karim cut in, lifting in his seat with agitation. He glanced at the pirate whose spasms had stopped as well, though his eyes remained half closed and his head hung to one side.

As the telepath closed her eyes again, breathing rhythmically in a strange, staccato pattern, Halabi shot slitted eyes to Karim.

"Captain el-Sayyed," she started, lifting the incense in her hand and wafting it below Khadija's nose. "What do you know of the mystical art of telepathy?"

Karim knew that tone all too well, the one that came before a lecture. He had suspected that this woman was not one to be crossed, and he had the odd feeling he was about to find out why.

Taking a small swallow, he said carefully, "I don't claim to be an expert. But I've studied up on the craft before our session. Telepaths have a kind of… second voice. One in your head. I was under the impression they could do more than pull out phrases, though. I had heard they could pull images .. locations."

"That is true of very few," Halabi said, never moving as she spoke. "Only Zaakiyah Najjar and a few of her personal acolytes have shown such power this past generation. And it has been many generations before we found her. Not to mention the decades of *grueling* training she went through."

"Yes, I've heard of the woman." Karim watched as Khadija continued to struggle. "Why was she not invited today?"

"She has more important matters than this to tend to."

"Does the location of a new Skyglass deposit not constitute importance?"

Proctor Halabi sat forward in her seat, her face one of irritation. Clearly, Karim had asked one too many nagging questions for her liking. But he was here for results, not an extended training session for a mystic student.

"Certainly you know of the deposit which rests within Mount Junga?" Halabi asked.

"Of course."

"Then you should know that Najjar is needed there. Her power is key to leading the troops and hindering the Junga defenses. Securing the mountain is paramount to the Master General." Halabi's words were final.

Karim knew he'd get nowhere trying to dig deeper, so he changed tack—and his tone. "And why is it your pupil can't go any deeper?"

"Because. She. Keeps. Being. Interrupted," Khadija said out the side of her mouth. It was the first time Karim had heard her voice so sharp and direct, all too similar to her mentor.

Halabi put a wrinkled hand on Khadija's shoulder. "Though it is true the Captain here should hold his tongue, in the battlefield you shall face far worse. Hold your focus. Nothing we say or do should distract you while you're within your subject's mind."

Khadija gave her mentor a short nod before centering her posture once more and breathing through her mouth in that odd cadence.

"It's a delicate art." Halabi turned her attention from her

student to Karim. "If she's not careful, she can ruin the man's mind or, worse, lose her own." There was a brief pause before Halabi's gaze shifted back to Khadija. "Haste would have helped us little in that event, don't you think, Captain? Besides, I am quite fond of my student."

There was a steely edge to her trailing tone that Karim did not feel wise to ignore. He settled back into his seat, leaving the young telepath to continue with her work. But after a long fifteen minutes, where he tried to occupy the time with idle thoughts, he couldn't help moving in his seat again. They were so close. All they needed was the location to that damned pirate cove with all the Skyglass. Couldn't Khadija just focus on the pirate's past and figure out what he and whatever shamans were with him did to lock it away? What was so difficult about that?

Karim lifted in his seat as a thought came to mind. "What if we wait until he sleeps?"

"Dreams *are* easier to read..." Halabi said. "But they result in faulty information. And it would seem we are working with a strong mind here." Her gaze landed on Jelani's shakes and quivers. "I don't believe we'll manage to pry anything useful. Not a distinct location or how to reach it."

Halabi gave the back of Khadija's hand another tap. Throughout the session, she had done this to make sure her student was still lucid. Karim waited for the standard response —a tap on the table from the young telepath—but it never came.

Khadija managed to lift her fingers above the table, but they seemed still, like the stiffening of joints when one had passed. For the first time, a shadow of worry passed over Halabi's face as she gave her student a second set of taps. Khadija did not respond, her fingers as fixed as stone, just like the very real stone hand of the pirate a few inches from her.

"Listen to my voice, apprentice." Though Halabi's voice came out as cool as usual, Karim caught hints of concern nearly boiling over. "It is the twenty-seventh day of the eleventh moon. Your name is Khadija of the family Ganim. I am Proctor Halabi of the Military Academy of Sciences and Magicks. You are sat across from a pirate named Jelani. Sky Captain el-Sayyed is just to your right. Remember where you are."

Karim's eyes flitted between telepath and pirate as each of their convulsions grew more violent. Then, Proctor Halabi began to sing. At least, singing was the best way Karim could describe it. Despite her raspy voice, her voice intoned a subtle and sweet melody. The small room filled with the words of her hymn as Karim realized there was more to the old woman's song.

He had wondered why Halabi was linked with the young Khadija. The woman herself didn't seem to share any mystical abilities with her apprentice. Karim had pondered if she was a mystic at all. But as her voice seemed to fill more than the room, driving straight through and around Karim, bringing bumps to his skin —

A soother? Karim thought as he recognized the flow of her a'bara.

With each raised pitch and harmony, he could feel his spirits lift. But he knew the calming effect was not for his benefit as he gazed upon the young telepath and her subject. Their bodies subsided to minor shakes as Halabi repeated a pair of couplets.

> *Remember, remember the emerald bay of home.*
> *Remember, remember or you'll remain alone.*
> *Remember, remember your home of silks and sands.*
> *Remember, remember your state, your fertile lands.*

When the repetition of the lines droned on, almost too redundant to bear, the young woman stirred. "I... can... do... this..." Khadija stammered, though her hands were still locked up tight. "Images... stonebeasts... oni'baro... a cave!"

"I command you to break your connection!" Halabi ordered harshly. "You've done more than enough today!"

"Just... one... more..." Khadija grated, but then her head hit the desk hard. Jelani gasped for breath as though he had come up for air after a long time underwater. His eyes were bloodshot and his skin looked to be turning purple beneath the patches of infected stone skin along his brow and cheek.

Halabi sprang from her seat, rubbing Khadija's back as she spoke softly in her ear. Karim couldn't make out her words, but he assumed the Proctor was trying to bring her back to consciousness.

Guilt seared through Karim's veins as he watched helplessly. Had it been he who had pushed the young mystic too far? Perhaps there was something he could do to help. He lifted a hand to Khadija's headscarf, but Halabi slapped him away firmly.

"Do not touch her head," Halabi barked. "You could force her mind into an endless dream state."

"I'm sorry, I was only trying to—"

"Just… check on your prisoner."

Karim flipped his head to Jelani, who had finally caught his breath. Karim was surprised to find worry in the man's dark eyes.

"She all right?" he gasped. "I ain't mean her no harm, but—"

Proctor Halabi silenced him with a curse, her calm demeanor stripping away more and more as her student remained unresponsive.

Then suddenly, Khadija lifted up in her seat like a springboard, her eyes milky-white. Her mouth moved faster than an auctioneer in the al-Anim market wards as she spoke. The words she said, however, were unintelligible and there were no breaks between each utterance.

"More of the Old Tongue," Karim said half to himself.

He gave Jelani a sidelong glance. What had the man done?

"Good, good, get it out, young one," Halabi said as she hefted Khadija onto her shoulder. "Captain, get the door." Karim didn't move, too shocked to do anything. "Captain!"

"Right!" Karim stirred. "Right away, right away." He moved to the door and opened it.

Halabi ignored his agape mouth as she led a ranting Khajida out of the room. In the hall, Karim could hear the Proctor saying, "Let it all out. We'll get you a nice cleansing…"

For a moment the room was left in an odd silence. The quiet sinking deep after the chaos that had just filled the room. Now there were only the soft breaths left by Karim and Jelani.

"On Ogó'ala, I ain't meant to do none of that…" Jelani held his head low.

A set of pounding footsteps filled the hall outside the room. They grew louder and louder until Issa materialized at the door's threshold, thumbing a hand over her shoulder. "What in the world happened to her?"

<hr>

AFTER LOCKING JELANI AWAY IN HIS NEW AND FAR LESS decorated holding room, Karim explained everything he could to Issa as they rode back to al-Anim proper on a pair of camels. The secret base, which had been cut into a cliffside once known as The Great Rise, grew smaller and smaller as they rode, spotted against the blue-orange morning horizon above scattered streaks of cloud. Ahead lay nothing but rolling dunes, with the small hint of the Jasmiin Towers only a league away.

"That pirate's persistent," Karim seethed, clutching hard at the leather reins in his hands. "And the telepath they sent was just a student."

"Did they get anything out of him?"

"Just some Old Tongue gibberish."

Issa tilted her head to the side, her red head wrap wafting against the morning winds. "He was speaking in the Old Tongue?"

"Not verbally. But he knew to cloak his thoughts with it."

"But he *is* Jo'baran? A *true* one." Issa asked too eagerly for Karim's taste. "I've not heard anyone truly speak the Origin Tongue since we were children."

Karim replied through gritted teeth. "Yes…"

"The Old Tongue…" Issa trailed off, almost to herself. Then she started to turn her camel around. "Maybe if I speak to him —"

"He's resting right now."

There was a brief silence as Issa set her camel to trot again. As they passed over hills of sand, Karim noticed her stealing glances his way. She must've been looking for the right moment to speak up. But Karim wore nothing but a scowl, his mind absorbed on everything *but* Issa's want for further conversation.

"Look," she said so low her voice was almost taken by even the gentle desert winds, "we didn't really talk about what happened in the war room."

"There's nothing to discuss. You denied my request, which is your military right."

Issa brought her camel ahead of Karim to slow him down once more. "No, I should've explained myself better. It's not you or the position itself I was denying. It… it…" She frowned and bit at her lip.

"It's the Empire," Karim finished for her, his mouth dry. This revelation wasn't entirely a surprising one.

Issa had been hinting she wanted to leave the Navy for more than a few moons now. Karim just didn't think it would happen so soon, especially on the heels of them being accepted as the pioneers of a new sky fleet.

Karim sighed before saying, "Why didn't you ask for relief from the Vice Admiral? You've served your mandated term."

"Because we were supposed to do it together, Karim. *We* agreed to that when we joined."

It was hard for her to say, Karim knew. The way her skin flushed red and her shifty eye contact told him as much. She wanted him to leave with her, to go back to… to what exactly? Back to the slums where they'd go hungry for endless nights?

Karim didn't give her a response. What could he say to her that wouldn't hurt her? Another long silence seemed like the best solution to the hanging weight between them.

Like most times, it was Issa who snapped that weight. "I visited your father yesterday." Her tone was light. At least for now she, like him, wasn't ready to poke at the differences between them. "Why'd you ignore your cousin at the debrief?"

Karim scoffed, rolling his eyes. "I didn't recognize her. She was barely walking when your family left. And when I went to the academy, she hadn't even lost all her baby teeth."

"They're all struggling. Worse than I thought."

"It's something to do with this new tax collector." A heat rose in Karim's belly. "Goes by the name of Mahir."

"I've heard that name. He's not a Vaziri, is he? The same one as—"

"No, he must be his son or something."

"That's why Ismail asked for more coin, wasn't it?"

Karim nodded. "I don't know what can be done for my father or the others." He scrunched his face in thought. "What would Admiral Shamoun have me do? All *I* can think of doing is giving Vaziri a good beating."

Issa raised an eyebrow as she looked over her shoulder. They were at least a league from the base and perhaps half a league more to the city gates. "You don't need to go saying that so loud. Look, I'm sure if we talk to him we can figure something out."

"Not with this man, not with his family. The greed in them runs too deep. Besides, I don't have the time right now, anyway. We still need to figure out what's to be done with this pirate."

Issa thought it over for a moment. "Let *me* do something about it, then."

"So you can give him a beating and not me?" Karim asked bemusedly.

"No, nothing like that." Issa waved a hand. "But I can figure out what he needs all that coin for. Rub the right shoulders, as Admiral Shamoun would say, yeah?"

"I don't know…" Karim turned his head out and forward, squinting against the brightening sands. "Sounds like too much of a risk. What if he catches on to you?"

"You don't trust me?" she asked, slapping his shoulder with the back of her hand. "You did see me working ol' al-Zoubi during the debrief, didn't you?"

Karim chuckled through his nose. "All right, fine. But be careful about it, that's all."

"I'll pray to Uqapele and make sure I'm blessed with His discretion."

Karim gave out an audible groan.

"What?" Issa asked with a look. "I'm telling you… you

would've made the Admiralty by now if you had prayed to the Gods more. How do you think I do the things I can?"

"Because *you* are trained, *you* are astute, because *you* put in the time and work to become so. "

"You and I are only a vessel for the Gods —"

"Not right now, Issa." Now it was Karim that turned his head to the empty dunes. But just as before, there was no one there to hear them.

Karim let his usual retorts rest, and the two rode in silence until they arrived at the city gates. When the guards identified them and let them in, Issa asked, "What were you planning for today?"

"I'm not sure, yet." Karim stared off into the morning crowds. The districts had already started to bustle. "I think I'll go some-where and clear my head." Without a second thought, he hitched his camel to a post attended by the al-Anim citywatch, then walked toward one particularly infamous street.

"Oh yeah, I hear the courtesans clear plenty of heads down in the Silks," Issa quipped. "Fine then. Tell Ishtar and Majd I say hello. While you go and get yourself off, I'll go pay our mutual friend a visit."

CHAPTER 12
ISSA

S HE COULDN'T REMEMBER WHO SAID IT, PERHAPS IT WAS written in some book back in the academy, or a scroll she found during research, or maybe it was just an old maiden on the street, but she would never forget the line: *If the Sycamore Square is the great vein of the capital, then the Harbor's Flask is its heart.*

Located just north of al-Anim's center, the tavern saw patrons from all walks of life: from bootstrapped laborers who could still afford the Flask's cheaper offerings, to shifty merchants who frequented the tavern instead of the overtly seedy ones as a "respectable" alternative.

And, sometimes, serving host to military officials like Gunner Chief Issa Akif.

Whenever she introduced someone to her favorite hole-in-the-wall, she always described the place as "not-quite-a-shithole", but not somewhere you'd bring a noble prince to either.

Between sips of sweet wine, she surveyed the stonework along the walls that were perhaps a moon or two past the point of needing maintenance—which she knew Innkeeper Akbar would say "didn't need changin' 'til a draft keeps off the payin' customers."

Traffic was light at this early hour, however. Only the miners coming from their night shifts and those going out for the day seemed to fill the oak tables with faces of fatigue, tiredness from a restless night prior or a long day ahead.

Issa could tell the difference between the two by the drinks they held in hand: The morning crews held hot brews of coffee, while the graveyard-shift workers drank down cups of wine. That left Issa alone at the bar as she waited, nursing her own goblet—more out of anxiousness than thirst.

Her eyes flitted to the loft that overwatched the rest of the tavern where Hajjar sat cloaked as he rolled a steamy cup of coffee between his hands. He must've been nervous too. Issa thought it'd be a good idea to have another of the crew to watch her back. And who better than one of the most talented elementals she knew?

"You know, you don't look the type to come in here at an hour like this," came a sultry voice at Issa's shoulder. She turned to find a dark-skinned man—no, a young man, a *very* young man—with perhaps the most flawless complexion she'd ever seen. His eyes were bright and golden, outshone only by the glitz of his canted smile.

Issa didn't often find herself at a loss for words when it came to suitors at a bar, but somehow her usual retort of telling the man off or calling Innkeeper Akbar over to shoo him away didn't come to her. Instead she sat there transfixed, as though she didn't quite understand what the man had said to her.

"Let me guess." He sidled next to her on a stool. "You're a noble's daughter taking a day off classes at the academy of…" He tapped his lip with his finger. "Language Arts. No… what do you Vaaji call it… erm… Geometry?"

Issa hummed under her lips. "Why not the daughter of a priest?"

"With that long hair of yours exposed?" He shook his head with an alluring rhythm. "Not a chance."

"Who said anything about an al-Qiba priest?"

The man drew back a little, perhaps surprised by Issa's quick comeback. Under the light of a hung lantern she could see now that the man wore his hair long in locs. And when he leaned closer to her, licking his lips in what she assumed was the start of some smooth line, his eyes appeared to rotate into themselves.

Issa went for her goblet to whet her tongue, but as her fingertips brushed it, it felt to her as though it was a gentle stream of water falling against her fingertips. That was odd. It was just a regular cup, and nothing was spilling over.

The man's lips were moving then. Clearly he was speaking, yet she couldn't make out his words...

"I told ya to leave the girls at the bar alone, you scoundrel." The thick-necked and broad-shouldered innkeeper, Akbar, waved the man away. "That boss of yours said you was 'posed to be across town already, didn't he?"

Without turning his hazel gaze from Issa's, the man curled another smile her way and sauntered backward. He avoided every table and chair like he had eyes in the back of his head.

"Well," he said to Issa, "if you ever show up here again, ask for N'Kota. I'll be around. Next time we'll work on that name of yours."

The man pushed his back into the tavern door casually and the smell of the city's herbs and spices seeped into the tavern. Then he turned on his heel and disappeared into the morning sea of turbans and headscarves.

And just like that, it was like some veil was lifted from over Issa's eyes. The once vivid colors of the Harbor Flask's lanterns seemed to dim, the cool touch of the goblet went back to feeling as mundane as it should, and the air tasted stale to her lips.

Issa sighed inwardly and turned to the innkeeper. "Let me guess… an empath?"

"I thought so too," Akbar said as he took up the man's glass and put it away to wash. "But I had one of them Seekers come in to sniff him out. He ain't no mystic as far as they could tell."

Issa eyed the door. "He could be using Draft of Dulagi to cloak himself against them. I've been hearing it's been making its rounds the past few weeks throughout the capital." She turned to Akbar. "Keep an eye on him for me, will you? I might want to speak with him again."

"Sure thing, *saabi.*" Akbar lifted a flask of wine to refill her cup. "Top you off?"

"No, I think I've had enough." If any more empaths were going to pay her a visit, she didn't need to help them along.

Akbar gave her a smile and put the flask away. She had always liked the way he grinned, even if it was hidden under the mass of a mustache and beard, which had compensated for the man's balding head. "Whatcha doin' here so early anyway, Mistress?"

"Oh, you know, just catching up. Waiting for an old friend to show." She flitted another glance up at Hajjar, whose eyes were narrowed over a goblet. He needed to make his overwatch duties a lot more subtle than that.

"Ah," Akbar said, "I see, I see."

"You said something about that man's boss?" Issa sipped the last of her wine. "Who were you referring to?"

"Oh, I've never met the saabi, but I pass his messages for a bit of extra coin." He raised his hand with a serious look and a tilt of his head. "If you want me to stop that, you just let me know."

"No," Issa said swiftly. "No… see if you can get a face to face, then come back to me. Plus, I wouldn't want to unduly cut between you and some extra coin. I know it's hard to come by these days."

Issa's eyes traveled behind Akbar's bar, where the All-Seeing Eye of Shati'ala hung from a hook near a shelved jug, the premier symbol of the New Religion. When she was a kid, Akbar was a devoted Jo'baran. But he had since converted to evade the nation's tithe. Despite the switch, she still caught him exercising the old customs by habit—kissing his hand to door frames before passing through, or placing his chickens in final rest before killing them.

Thoughts of the old al-Anim drew her back to Karim. She used to love sneaking into the bar with him on the nights the Flask hosted traveling aziza singers. That went on for, Gods, she didn't know how long, until Old Akbar caught them and put them to work in the kitchens. At first they thought it was just a punishment, then they realized the old man was giving them a legitimate way to see those performances without getting in trouble with the citywatch.

A gentle crease came to Issa's cheek. It took a moment for her to realize she had been smiling. But then her ponderings turned to yesterday's meeting, the grave look in Karim's eye when she declined him, the dower mask he wore when they rode in from the desert.

In truth, sticking with the military past their mandate had its merits. She could admit to herself that she never would have had the access to information that she did now without it. But she could hardly think she'd make a career of it. If she did, when would it end? When would she have the time to give back? Karim should've seen that too. If it came down to their people, or their country, the decision wasn't very difficult at all.

"Shati's tit! You know, if you frown so hard you'll get wrinkles, right?" came a familiar voice at Issa's side.

Issa laughed as she turned to her old friend Nadya Utbah. "And who told you that bull?"

"My first husband."

"Oh yeah?"

"Why do you think he was my first?"

The pair chuckled as they embraced each other in a huge hug, then kissed each other on the cheeks. "Ogó'ala is Good, Sister."

"Oh, you're still on that shit?" Nadya pulled away with a bemused frown. Issa gave the plump woman a look of her own. "Ah, what can you say? Shati'ala made none of us perfect. Not even you, big-shot-military-whatever rank you are now." Her friend measured Issa up and down. "And by the skies and stars, I like what you've got on. Who made it for you?"

Issa did a little turn in her outfit, and gave her friend a coy giggle when she made a round. She never got to wear frilly dresses or loose tops she could breathe in. Plus, it would do no good to wear her military garb in a place like this.

When Hajjar saw her that morning, he barely recognized her, for one.

"Why would I tell you?" she asked coyly. "So you can bite off my style?"

"Yeah, yeah, yeah, come on, let's talk up in the loft, saabi."

Issa followed behind the flap of Nadya's simple cloak and sandaled feet as they passed by the tables leading up to the tavern's single loft. Though the main space of the room was relatively well lit, designed for the more respectable customers, the overhanging loft fell naturally into shadow where it attracted the less *particular* sort. It wasn't like the lower level was some grand thing, but Akbar kept it swept and relatively clean, with flowers set in vases at each table's centerpiece—though many of them were wilted—and imperial banners of black-and-red strung up on the stone walls. Up above, however, flower centerpieces were traded for ashtrays, imperial banners for wanted posters.

As Issa climbed the last stair, she could understand why certain clientele would appreciate the spot. There was a perfect vantage point to the entrance. Any thug or other less savory miscreant could easily tell who was going in and out. And if necessary, they had a route out through the arched windows at either side of the loft.

Issa did her best not to look at Hajjar, who only sat a table away.

"How long has it been, Issa?" Nadya gestured for her to sit first.

Issa took her seat, nearly tipping over to one side from one of its legs being not quite level. "Oh, I don't know. Can't be more than a decade, right? Gods, maybe more?"

Though Nadya was several years older, she and Issa had been good friends before Issa and her family left the capital. At that time, Nadya was a mousy little thing, all skin and bones, who wore rags for clothes—well, they all looked like that back then. Now though, the woman was working on a second chin, and her head wrap was lined with sapphires.

"I'll admit," Nadya said as she waived over a barmaid, "when I got a message from the palace, I didn't think it would be from little ol' One Tooth. Glad to see your smile filled out nicely." She gestured for two drinks of the "usual" as the serving girl passed by. "So, what did you want to meet up for so goddamned early in the day?"

Issa shrugged and leaned back in her chair. "It's been a while since I've been posted to al-Anim proper. Just wanted to know what's been goin' on. So much has changed here. Did you know the springs are covered over by a fountain of Moharam?"

"Yeah," Nadya said. "That happened a few years after you left. Let's cut the small talk though. This isn't the palace. I know you've not been in the *real* city for a while—and not very long—but time is money around these parts."

"Fine," Issa huffed lightly. She wasn't the biggest fan of small talk herself, but it did help cut at the awkward edges of things sometimes, and she *had* missed her old friend.

She interlocked her fingers and set them to the table. "You work for one of the merchant guilds, yes?"

"I do."

"Under the leadership of a man named... el-Yasin."

"That's the one."

"I've just been wondering." Issa flitted her eyes to the entrance. "Has there been a lot of coin moving around the city where it shouldn't have been lately?"

Nadya scratched at her brow. "There's always coin movin' that shouldn't. You'll need to be more specific."

"Imperial coin," Issa intoned. "In the form of tithes."

Nadya took in a deep breath through her wide-set nose, and Issa knew there was a hint of a smirk threatening to creep behind her pursed lips. "Okay... so we're talkin' 'bout some serious shit here."

Issa lifted a brow. "I don't know. You tell me."

"Do me a favor, and I'll do you one. What you got for me?"

"Nu uh, I asked first."

Nadya settled back into her seat as the barmaid brought her and Issa their drinks. The merchant took a sip, gritted her teeth with a grunt, then said, "I can't get into specifics of course, but I *can* tell you Lord el-Yasin is pretty pissed about one of our rivals, a man named Hamza al-Turabi."

"Why's that?" Issa asked, ignoring her drink. She knew al-Turabi fairly well.

"Just last week there was a council meeting—conversation

about your military gearing up for expansion. Great for you lot I'm sure, bad for us and our trade routes if shit gets out of hand. We've got plenty of vested interests outside of Vaaj, you know. Well, al-Turabi kept sayin' stuff like 'taking matters into our own hands.' So I suppose this little conversation of ours overlaps. Now, you tell me... what's the military got brewing?"

And so the game begins, Issa thought.

It was an enterprise she had become more proficient in during her time with the military, especially in the academies. There wasn't anything in this world, she had learned, that couldn't be bartered, coerced, or uncovered through a little bit of verbal sparring. One's currency, and the value it held, was grounded in one's ability to manufacture stories that could be sold at a profit—even if the truth in those tales were not altogether authentic.

Issa knew she needed to play it safe with Nadya though. She might've trained up rubbing shoulders with military officials and nobles, but that was nothing in comparison to the kinds of circles this woman likely ran in. She knew she wouldn't get anything worthwhile from the woman if she didn't think she was getting something good back from Issa herself.

It was a good thing Issa brought Hajjar along. Had she invited any other crewmember, they were liable to rat her out to the Admiralty. Hajjar, however, had come from the slums just like her. Anything Issa traded in favor of making the plight of their old boroughs better would be worth it in his eyes.

"The military is mustering," she murmured to Nadya, "though still slowly. But I can tell you it's for something big."

Nadya chuckled through her next sip of drink. "Oh, Little One Tooth. You gotta do better than that. We're going for fair trade here. We hear plenty enough rumors floatin' around. A simple *confirmation* isn't going to count for much of anything."

Issa bit her lip, playing the part of a novice in information trade. It was one of her preferred moves. It was true enough that she hadn't been to al-Anim in any formal capacity in some time, but she knew plenty about its changes and what had been going on.

Where strong, play weak. Where weak, play strong — just as her old academy instructors always taught.

Obviously, Issa couldn't say anything about the airship. She just needed something juicy enough for Nadya to sink her teeth into, something that would whet the merchant's appetite but not satiate it.

Nadya chuckled again. "Stop it, stop it." She laid a hand on Issa's wrist. "If your eyes dart around too much they'll fall out of your head."

Issa snorted, "And who told you that?"

"My second husband." She smiled. "Look, I'll make it easy for you. This secret of yours... it has something to do with that General, doesn't it? That Najjar woman? The one headed eastward? I heard the troops out there are having trouble taking down even the little villages. But them higher-ups aren't sweatin' it cause they got some sort of asset in the works, right?"

Issa fabricated the way her throat gulped, waited for the line of Nadya's eyes to brighten slightly at the "misstep." Then, when she was satisfied with the awkward silence Issa replied, "Yeah, the military does have a new asset, though the whole thing is still under consideration."

"I knew it." Nadya slammed down her empty cup on the table. "By Shati'ala and Her Will, I knew it."

Issa stammered, "K-knew what?"

"They've found a True Blessed, haven't they?"

Mouth falling agape, Issa's shock this time wasn't entirely theatre. Nadya had just fucked up. Royally. In this game, one never wanted to lead information out of their second party. And true, there had been rumors of the Prince being a True Blessed, a mystic that only sprouted up once every three or four generations, but only the small council in Jasmiin Tower knew its falsehood, a falsehood Issa had believed in too if she hadn't had a certain conversation with a certain senior officer named Abaza the day before. Perhaps it was Their Majesties' spies throwing out the false rumors about their son's not-so-mystical abilities, she wasn't sure. Whatever it was, it was the best way for her to win this little bout with her old friend.

Lifting her cup to her mouth for the first time, Issa said, "You didn't hear it from me."

Nadya zipped her lips and threw away an invisible key as Issa sipped her first bit of drink. She half choked at the fire in her mouth. Whatever it was Nadya had ordered, it didn't taste like anything Issa had tried before. She had sampled hard liquor in her youth, but whatever this was, it tasted closer to acid. It ran through her chest and down her gut like burning oil.

Nadya let out her loudest guffaw yet as she got up to pat Issa on the back. Even Hajjar lifted his head to see what the commotion was about.

"Get it out, get it out." Nadya laughed. "Oh yeah, it's gonna be a little while yet until al-Anim suits you again, Little One Tooth." After Issa's coughs tamed down to intermittent heaves, Nadya took her seat again and continued in a low voice. "It's the Prince, isn't it? Anyone who's met him has said he's kinda... different. I expect you'd have to be with all that a'bara in you mixing up like a bad blend of stew, right?"

Issa cleared her throat, indicating she'd given enough and that it was Nadya's turn to come forth with her end of the trade. "Tell me more about al-Turabi. He's an old friend of mine. Do you think he's serious about this 'take matters into our own hands' business?"

Nadya lifted her sandals onto the table. Issa would have smirked if she had been alone. The woman thought she had already won. Whatever information she was going to give, she felt was *way* under the value of what Issa gave.

"Well, I don't really know what he's capable of," the merchant said. "He's a whole lot of talk most of the time, always goin' on about this conspiracy or that, but... he's been meetin' with this saabi who never goes anywhere without at least a handful of guards posted around him. I've never spoken to him directly, but his guards keep trying to set up a meeting with my lord and al-Turabi. When I ask them for a name though, they never give, they just spit out the usual 'someone you'd like to know.' And then I have to smack them down and explain that *that's* not how this game works."

Issa rubbed at her throat, the last of its throbbing going away. At the corner of her eye, she could've sworn Hajjar was chuckling at her through his cup of coffee. He'd hear from her later.

"That reminds me," Nadya said. "I need to see what's going on with my guy. He's supposed to tail this mysterious saabi, but he loses him every time. I hear he's a pretty man, keeps his eyebrows threaded and all that, you know, that sort. Thinks himself Shati'ala's gift to mankind or some such. But he's been getting bolder these past few weeks—so far I've uncovered he's part of some old family who used to run with the nobles. But there's about a million players in this damned city... it takes time, you know? Anyway, is that enough for you?" Nadya finished, folding her arms.

"I think that'll get me started, thanks." Issa pushed her cup away.

Nadya gave her another laugh and took the cup. Then she downed it in one gulp. She hissed out the side of her mouth and belched.

"Well." Issa cleared her phlegmy throat. "It was nice doing business with you, old friend."

"Same, Little One Tooth. Same." She was positively beaming. "Please don't be a stranger to the Flask. I'm here at least three times a week to score with one of them aziza singers. And I wanna hear more of what goes on up in that palace of yours."

CHAPTER 13
ZALA

"Land ho! Land ho! Al-Anim on the horizon!"

Zala forced her heavy lids to open, and she was met with the image of Shomari's hanging paw a finger's length from her face. He had slept just overhead in a hammock above her own, where Zala had quickly discovered the pakka never slept in one spot for more than a pair of minutes.

Rubbing her eyes and yawning, she dodged the cat's arm. The faint and cool orange-blue of morning streamed through the sleeping quarters to reveal the rest of the crew, who, like her, were slow to rise. They all smelled of morning breath and sweat. Blowing in her hand to smell her own mouth, she knew fixing it was in order. So, Zala reached for a loose twig she kept in her traveling bag, then rubbed some salt and chalk along its end for brushing. As she thrust the twig into her mouth, she poked at Shomari.

"Get up, cat," she slurred through her brushing.

Shomari grumbled. "Give me another hour."

She kept to her prodding. "Ain't no hour to give. We'll be in al-Anim soon. I know you heard the watcher."

"What can I say." He turned away from her. "You tired me out good yesterday, chana."

"He's not your problem," Ouseni intoned at Zala's shoulder.

The woman already had on the black garb with red trim all the Rovers wore. Zala wondered when she'd get her own uniform now that she was "one of the crew."

"Come on, girl. We gotta get up there and make ready for landing. Kwame will take care of the pakka." Ouseni marched off and started her climb up to the weather deck.

"I'll see you up there soon, ya?" Zala asked Shomari as she put her twig away.

The pakka didn't answer. She knew it was impossible for him to have fallen back to sleep that quickly, but she got the message and walked off.

"Zala," he groaned.

She turned back to find Shomari slumped over his hammock, looking at her straight on.

"What?" she asked.

"I am not there yet," he pointed to his head, "but thanks all the same. For yesterday."

"You already said it… a few times if I recall correctly."

He flashed a smile. "Right. Such is the curse of the sarcastic types. We have got to make a point of things if we want them to stick. I will say this though… *you* have never acknowledged my gratitude."

Zala tilted her head. "What do you mean?"

"Maybe you humans do it differently from us pakka, but usually when someone says thank you, it is followed by a 'you are welcome.' Mutual recognition of good will or some such nonsense, yes?"

Zala looked back on the times Shomari had thanked her—there weren't all that many to picture. He was probably right. She was never very good when it came to appreciation or acts of words, save for when she was with Jelani, but that was an outlier. A *gargantuan* outlier. With anyone else, she always favored acts of action above anything.

"It was Fon's idea to play the game." She shrugged.

"Zala…"

"I only wanted to fight you because you looked so—"

"Come on now, chana. Just say the words."

Zala threw her gaze to the ceiling. "You're welcome, Shomari."

"Can I be getting a little eye contact this time?"

Zala shot a finger out at him. "Don't push it. Now come on and get off your ass. I don't need you getting into any trouble with the Captain."

"One hour more," he purred as he disappeared into his cot again.

Zala let out a sigh that turned into a laugh before moving away and up to the weather deck.

She was met with the cool ocean breeze of crisp morning air. Though the foot traffic above was still light, with stragglers still appearing from below deck with lethargic shuffles, the crew that *was* awake was busy at work.

Above them all snapped a new flag in the coastal breeze: a simple thing, a patterned field of green, red, and white, with an emblem of a blood lily stitched overtop. It was the banner and symbol of the merchant ships of Vaaj. Sometime in the night, one of the crew must've swapped it out for the *Redtide's* personal flag. It wouldn't be wise for one of the most notorious pirate companies to ever sail the seas to boldly wave their flags when approaching what had once been one of the greatest navies in the world.

Zala snorted. Being a part of Lishan's crew wasn't her favorite plan, nor her primary one, but after a good night's sleep she didn't think it was so bad. At least now she didn't have to lead. Plus, the Rovers wanted exactly the same thing she did—and now Zala didn't have to shoulder half its weight alone.

Let *Captain* Lishan take the blame if something went to shit.

A pair of seagulls squawked overhead as they flew past the ship and toward the desert coast of Vaaj. Just beyond the kuba-hari horns of the *Redtide's* bowsprit, the visage of al-Anim grew larger. From their distance, all Zala could see was the bespeckle of a reflected window off what looked like a lighthouse posted on an island offshoot.

"I think that's al-Abaar," Fon said at Zala's waist. The aziza stretched her arms wide and yawned. "One of the greatest light-houses of the Esterlands."

"Tell that to the Aktarians in Pyrus."

"Hey, I did say 'one of', didn't I?"

"That you did." Zala smiled.

"And, hey… thanks for what you did with Shomari…"

"Oh, no. I'm not going through that again. Here, help me get these ropes ready for mooring."

"Aye, aye, Ca—" Zala shot Fon a look of warning. "All right, sorry, sorry."

"You too, Rishaad," Zala called over to the boy, who looked like he was in need of some direction as he watched everyone else work. "It's rude to let a pair of ladies do all this labor alone."

"Right, right." The young man hustled over. "I just haven't been back home in so long. Got caught starin', was all."

As al-Anim grew closer, the three of them worked together to coil, wrangle, and coil the rope again in preparation for their arrival. Zala had thought Rishaad a great bore when she had first met him. And sure, his voice could be rather monotone and sleep-inducing at times, but ever since saving him from the sky ship he seemed to be opening up somewhat. He had a way of making the funniest—if a bit random—little one-liners when no one expected it, like—

"Do you ever wonder if Lishan's butt cheeks are sewn together?" he said out of the blue as Zala tied a knot in a rope.

She gave him a questioning eyebrow, then he nodded to the passing Captain. Zala looked up to see the woman surveying the deck with that hawk's glare she always had. She couldn't say she had ever taken any extended looks at the Captain's rear-end, but she reminded herself that with most men, butts were a prime source of conversation. Now that she took a look… yeah, she guessed it was above average. But sewn together? Not so much.

"No, I've never wondered," she answered. "Why? D'you like what you see, Rishaad?"

"What?" he shot back. "Oh, no! Well, I mean… yes. But that's not what I meant." He cleared his throat and pulled up his trousers nervously, then. "I just wonder how she'd keep that stick so far up her ass, without the sewing, is all."

Fon, surprisingly—or perhaps not so surprisingly—was the

first to laugh. The giggle drew the attention of some of the other crew, who, up to that point, had been conducting their work in silence. Even Lishan had dark eyes for the aziza from across the far end of the deck.

Fon quieted her laughter, then murmured. "I get it. That's a good one, Rishaad!" She held in her gut to quell what Zala assumed was a second bout of giggles. "Oh, oh, I got one. I bet one says to the other, 'between you and me, some shit's about to go down.' Or no, wait, this is even better. They'd say... 'I can't keep this shit together.'"

It couldn't be helped. Fon and Rishaad both burst out laughing in fullness. Even Zala couldn't hold back the smirk escaping across her lips as she smacked the pair to quiet them down. Even if a joke wasn't funny, sometimes it was the reactions that got you. "You two have been spending too much time trying to cheer up Shomari with children's jokes."

"Not true." Rishaad choked through his chuckles. "I heard it from a boy turning sixteen. So technically, not a child's joke, ya?"

"And might I ask *what* is so funny?" Somehow, Lishan was able to reach them from the sterncastle to amidship in the space of a few heartbeats. A sickle of ice sliced through Zala as she tried to come up with some sort of excuse.

"What's the matter, pirate? Pakka got your tongue?" Lishan spat.

"It's nothing, Captain, really," Rishaad said as he lifted to his feet. "I'm from this city, and I was tellin' them a joke. Have you ever heard the one about why the pirate turned red on the desert coast?"

"No, and I don't think I—"

"Cause they were marooned..." Rishaad trailed off, catching on a beat too late that the Captain was not in a joking mood. Ever.

"I told you yesterday to cut the childish shit." She lifted the rope they were working on. "If the crew isn't sharp we can't—" She tried to pull the knot Zala had made apart, but it was locked in place good, a tie befitting any decent sailor.

Zala watched as Lishan struggled, how the woman's face

turned an uncomfortable shade of red—not unlike Rishaad's pirate who was left on a desert coast. She knew the Captain was looking for a reason to reprimand them, but she clearly couldn't find one good enough this time. If Zala had been in better standing, and hadn't felt the strong grip of Lishan's hand the day before, she might've tried her luck with a "is it too tight for you, Captain?" But Zala wasn't exactly filled with the audacity to say something so bold that morning.

Despite it all, Lishan always found *something* she could come back with.

"Who organized these here?" Lishan demanded, nudging the crates behind them. "They shouldn't be stacked upright like that. They should have a stronger base, lest we hit rough waves and they topple over. And they need netting and a counterweight."

Zala gulped, then looked to Fon and Rishaad. *She* hadn't been scheduled to the crates, but one of *them* might've been. Unlikely though, neither of them would have had the muscles to move them. If anyone would have been charged with stacking crates it would have been—

"It was that big one, Captain." Ouseni said near the hatch leading belowdecks.

Lishan whipped to her. "Which big one?"

"The one from Asiya Bay. The quiet one."

"With the scraggly beard?"

Ouseni nodded. "That's the one, ma'am."

"Ah, yes." Lishan uncurled the fist she had been making. Zala wondered if the Captain was irritated she couldn't choke Zala again. "Bring him to me."

"Right away, Captain."

Lishan handed the rope back to Zala. Her next words seemed to be pulled from the depths of her throat, but at least, she said them, "You think you can prepare us for mooring… pirate?"

Zala nodded proudly.

"Show me." The Captain's voice was close to something resembling respect. Maybe that stick up her ass wasn't lodged too far up.

As Zala got back to her work, she looked ahead. They were

already close to the city. The ship was just approaching al-Abaar, whose lighthouse stood much, much taller up close. Beyond it, the bronze mountain range and the haze of desert about it, started to clear to the impressions of a proper port city. Now, even more windows reflected the morning sun along what Zala assumed was the harbor. When she was back with Kobi on the *Titan,* they had never made port at the city, favoring the more deserted and less risky piers of the southern towns and villages, who were more likely to turn a blind eye to pirates cleaning barnacles from the bottom of their hull.

As she stared at the indistinct images of buildings lining the coast, she wondered where Jelani could've been, where the Vaaji would hide that sky ship of theirs. It was possible the thing wasn't even stationed in al-Anim. Then she considered if they would've even kept her husband on the ship. It was more likely he was in some palace dungeon as they interrogated him about Kidogo and its protected cove. What had he told her before they parted?

"The Vaaji can't get the Glass, Zala. They can't. They won't make me talk."

Anytime she thought back to his voice, no matter the context, she gave a squeeze to the songstone hanging from her necklace. The only reason she went on was because she knew he was still with her. She hadn't told the others, but every so often Jelani sung her their song through the stone. It happened almost every night, she assumed, right before he slept.

As Mantu ascended above decks, a confused expression on his face, Zala thought back to the lover that he'd fought for, and she turned to Lishan with a soft voice. "Go easy on him, Captain. He's been a wreck ever since… you know. He lost someone on that ship. Just like we all did in one way or another."

Lishan didn't turn fully to Zala, but she said, "I'll go *somewhat* easy on him."

Zala smiled a little. Lishan wasn't a total monster, it seemed.

Her mouth, however, thinned to a line when she saw that Mantu's face was a touch more than just curious. His eyes kept shooting between the crew around the deck, up in the crow's nest, at the sterncastle, port, and starboard. There wasn't anyone at the bow though.

A wave of shock pressed down through Zala's chest. The pirate must've thought he was in more trouble than he was. He must've reckoned that—

"Do you know what an orderly ship looks like, pirate?" Lishan asked as Mantu stopped several paces ahead of her.

Zala could tell the man was suppressing his gulp. She wanted to shout at him, to tell him to get a grip on himself.

Lishan put a finger to the crates and gave them a little shove. Whatever was in them must have weighed several stones, but she was going to make her point. The top-most crate teetered ever-so-slightly and if, like she said, they hit a rough patch of water, it would've likely toppled over.

"This," Lishan went on, "is unacceptable on this ship, you hear me?"

Mantu still wasn't quite meeting her gaze, still eyeing around him and watching for every little movement. Zala knew the look. It was the same one she had likely had when she met with Captain Nubia a week ago. The look that said: *where are my exits*.

"Mantu," Zala said, "it's okay, just—"

Lishan snapped her fingers. "Nope. Nothing from you. This is between me and *my* crew." She took a step to Mantu and the man flinched. "Not only did you stack these poorly, but you've left them dusty and dirty. You know, our former Captain used to say that a clean ship is an orderly one." She took another step forward. "And I agree."

"What you want from me?" Mantu drew back again, his eyes bloodshot. "I ain't polished the thing, but I dusted it."

"Then you did a poor job of it. Your previous Captain may not have held to very high standards, but on this ship we—"

"Don't you go talkin' 'bout Captain Kobi like that," Mantu seethed. "You ain't know him."

Zala rocked on her feet, on the edge of pushing forward. This was not good, not good at all. She leaned forward, but Fon stopped her with her small hand and a shake of her head.

"You're right," Lishan said. "I didn't know him. And I don't have to. I've seen his crew. But you know what I do know? Looking at you… No wonder your work is so half-assed when you keep yourself in rags. I'll make it known right now, I won't have my ship grow as unruly as your beard. Honestly, I should have you cut the thing off. That would be a step in the right direction to set you rig—"

This time Mantu took several steps back, like some fish retreating to a reef from a shark. "You come anywhere near me, and I'll have more than words for you."

This was too much. Mantu had the wrong end of the stick here. The Rovers didn't know anything about his past or the tattoos he hid on his cheeks—a set of tattoos that were the mark of the Meroé Rovers' sworn enemies.

Zala stepped forward to say, "Relax, Mantu, the Captain's only giving you a hard—"

"Enough!" Lishan spat in Zala's direction. "You will shut your mouth, or I will shut it for you."

But she couldn't shut her mouth. If she did, Mantu was going to go mad and blow the whole thing. Then a flash of recognition seemed to pass over the Captain's face as she made a slow turn of her face from Zala, whose chest was heaving, to Mantu, who was near to hyperventilation, his fists curled tight and his stance crouched.

"Mantu…" Lishan deadpanned. "An odd name for someone of Asiya Bay."

She doesn't know, Mantu. Keep your head, kijana. Keep. Your. Head.

"Tell me, Mantu. What are you hiding under that beard?"

Zala could have screamed at Mantu's next words if she wasn't in such shock. But he clearly thought himself a deadman. Mantu just wanted to go out with his pride standing tall as he grunted, in the Aktarian Tongue, "*Mudwa, Umtet. Heseti em netek.*"

Zala felt her heart coming up in her throat. Most of the crew would have heard gibberish, but she, and a few dozen or so Ya-Seti on the deck knew the phrase in all its dirty history: the war cry of the Aktarian Navy. The Ya-Seti's—and Rovers'—centuries' long enemy.

Mantu had just killed them all.

CHAPTER 14
ZALA

"Grab him!" Lishan shouted.

Before the Rovers could so much as draw their bows or march toward the pirate, Mantu threw down the set of crates he was supposed to stack at his side. Wood cracked against the deck and he went running for the bow of the ship in a sprint Zala never thought him capable of.

But he had nowhere to go.

Al-Anim was growing larger ahead of them—the sails of docked ships and national flags flapping against the morning winds—but it was still too far away for a swim.

Mantu slowed at an archer's perch where a station of oiled arrows were lodged. He took up a bow and set an arrow to flame with a quickness Zala had only ever seen from Shomari.

Where's this *Mantu coming from?*

Then, in the space of a single breath, Mantu loosed his flaming arrow at the crates he had pushed over and they went up in an inferno. Zala glanced at the rough script that lined the boxes: rum.

"Stay back, you filthy savages," Mantu shouted as he backed to the kubahari-horned bowsprit. His head kept spinning wildly between the flames and the bow behind him. The fire had bought him time... but not much.

The Rovers lifted their swords, inching closer and closer to the fires as Lishan shouted, "Someone get Arus and Iokaja and have them get this fire out now!"

Zala heard but didn't see marching feet heading off below deck. Some of the archers, the Ya-Seti crew in particular, took shots where they could, but Mantu dipped behind the foremast for cover.

Idiot, Zala thought.

She turned to Fon and said, "We'll need to make the switch now, Fon."

"B-but," the aziza stammered.

"We don't have a choice. Just like we said… 'when all the hells break loose.'"

"What are you two going on about?" Rishaad asked.

Zala gave him a quick look, then turned to Fon again. "And take Rishaad with you."

Though worry dominated the lines through Fon's forehead tattoo, and utter confusion prevailed in Rishaad's brow, the aziza grabbed the young man's wrist and they both took off across the deck and up to the crow's nest. No one seemed to pay attention to either of them. Not yet, at least. In fact, no one seemed to pay Zala any mind either.

Every bloodlusted gaze was for Mantu.

Once the pair got up top, Fon and Rishaad started working their fingers as fast as they would go along the lines. And soon they reigned in the faux merchant flag and hoisted the ship's true colors instead: red, black, and now gold.

Zala had planned this as a last resort—one she had *desperately* wanted to avoid—but with Mantu's little stunt, all she could do now was roll the dice. Once the citywatch caught sight of the flag, they'd alert the local navy of a pirate ship inbound. True, having the Vaaji Welcoming Fleet barreling down on them wasn't the best outcome she could've asked for, but if they managed to slip past them, while they focused their attention on Lishan and her crew, they might have a chance.

As soon as Fon and Rishaad had the pirate's true flag up, they turned their heads back down to Zala. Fon pointed below deck.

Zala gave her a questioning stare, then remembered that Shomari and Old Man Ode must've still been down there.

With all the attention still on Mantu, who had now started hiking up the kubahari horn, Zala backpedaled below deck. The inferno along the deck had started to climb to the first level of masts when she lost sight of the insanity. And it wasn't long before she found Shomari, who had genuinely fallen back to sleep in his hammock.

"Wake up." Zala poked at Shomari's side. "Wake up! We've got to go."

"What is going on? I have told you I need my beauty rest.." Shomari turned his back to Zala, his tufted ears twitching.

"No time. Mantu is trying to escape the ship."

"So let 'im."

Zala scoffed. "I said *trying*. Lishan and her crew have him pinned."

"Ugh… that dikala." Shomari sighed, sitting up in his hammock and dropping lithely onto the wooden floor. Zala hadn't realized he was "naked" under his blankets. "Just give me a moment to freshen up."

"What!? We don't have time!"

"Just a *moment*." Shomari brushed a comb casually across his chest.

Zala clenched her fists in front of her face. This was *not* the time to have the old Shomari back. "Shomari! We can't waste a single—"

"Okay, okay, do not get fussy," he groaned. "I do not work well under these conditions, is all. Tangled fur can get in the way. You know this."

Zala shook her head, annoyed at his rolling purr, and hoping her eyes would convey her earnest. "Where's Ode?"

"Over there, at the far end." Shomari pointed with his leg as he pulled on his trousers.

A blast outside sounded and the ship rocked to one side.

That would be the Welcoming Fleet, Zala thought.

"All right, I'll meet you top-side," Zala said over her shoulder as she shuffled through the sleeping quarters. When she found Ode's lumpy cot she started jabbing at him.

"What's with the poking and prodding?" he grunted.

"Sorry, but we've got to go. We've arrived at al-Anim and we need to make a hasty exit."

"Godsdamnit, who was it?" Ode heaved himself from his cot with a groan as he rubbed the sleep from his eyes. "Did the pakka blow it?"

"No, it was the twitchy one, of course," Shomari said, pulling on his gold bracers. "But thanks for thinking of me, kijana."

"Well, damn…" Ode said as a second blast followed by another jolt shook the ship. "How much time we got?"

"*None*," Zala said. "Mantu's pushed to the bow. I wouldn't be surprised if he's already leapt overboard. Can you move with your leg?"

"I'm a bit wobbly, but I'll manage." Ode stood up on both his legs at a slant. The wooden stake the Rovers had given him was a fair bit too short, but it was all they had. "I've been through worse."

"All right then," Zala said. "Let's get above deck before—"

"There they are!" A pair of pirates ducked their heads below deck, both brandishing swords. When they walked into the lantern light, Zala could see it was Kwame and Ouseni.

"Shomari!" Zala shouted.

"I got them, I got them," Shomari replied casually as he withdrew his rapier and sauntered over to the duo. With such a confined space he wasn't able to somersault or vault about as he usually did, but he could still side-step the pirates, forcing them to collide into one another as he darted about.

"Try not to kill them if you can, please!" Zala shouted down the room.

"Noted," Shomari said as he set off a riposte.

Boom! Another shake rocked the ship.

Zala turned to Ode. "Listen, we don't have time to get to their armory, and they probably have it guarded, anyway. So we'll need to make a… a run for it."

Ode looked down to his wooden leg. A silence hung in the air for a moment too long.

"I guess I'll say it then," Ode grunted in resignation. "We both know I'm only going to slow us down."

Zala shook her head firmly. "Just stick to my ass and I'll get us out of here." She took Ode's arm, slung it over her shoulder, and made her way toward Shomari. "Cat! What's taking you so long?"

"I told you," he grunted as he parried a blow and gestured to his unruly fur. "It is hard for me to work," he blocked another strike, "under these," another dodge, *"conditions."* He kicked Kwame's front legs out from under him before lunging at Ouseni. "Besides, it is the first duel of the day, I have not done my warm-ups." Shomari ducked under another sidelong swipe. "And thanks for remembering, but I just went through a traumatic experience not long ago." He threw the flap of a hammock into Kwame's face. "And *you* try winning a fight quickly when told killing's off the table—"

"Okay, okay," Zala interrupted as she approached the fight with Ode in tow. "Just finish it."

"Three more moves." Shomari flourished his blade and disarmed Kwame. "One." Ouseni came in for a stab, which Shomari knocked down and away with a low block. Then the pakka used his hilt to hit the pirate across her face. "Two." And with a short leap, gripping at the roping on the ceiling above, Shomari kicked down at the pirates' heads with the soles of his paws. They flew back into the deck—and stayed there. "And three!"

"Good. Now run," Zala shouted, already dragging Ode halfway up the deck.

"No 'thank you'?" Shomari scoffed.

Zala was about to swear aloud at the damned cat when she reached the top of the stairs. A cold spiked up her spine at the sight before her: A Vaaji battle squadron was already moving to crane the *Redtide,* half their ship line already stretching out past the portside bow.

Mantu was nowhere to be seen. Some Rovers were running to

man their cannons, while others still were diving overboard to try and escape the threat.

They had put out the deck fire, but that didn't really matter with cannon blasts and fireballs impacting the ship's hull. Warning bells blared from the harbor, drowning the shouts and screams of the pirate crew. The Vaaji fleet was so great and vast, they nearly blocked out the rising eastern sun.

Fon dropped from the ratlines with Rishaad ambling down behind her. Her half wing was still badly wounded, but she had enough movement in her span to glide at the least, though her flight path was far from balanced.

"It worked just like you said!" Fon beamed. "Mantu made off into the ocean as soon as the Vaaji came in. The Rovers don't know what to do!"

"I didn't think the Vaaji would take too kindly to one of the most ruthless pirate companies sailing into their port," Zala admitted. "I didn't expect such a massive fleet, though. I hope we can all get away."

"I saw Marjani and Ekko getting overboard safely, they're good. Hopefully."

"They're probably pissed at us."

Fon fiddled with her lip. "Oh, right…"

Another cannon impact sent splinters rushing in their direction. They all ducked, covering themselves from the worst of it.

Maybe they do *have the sky ship somewhere close,* Zala mused as Ode slumped against her side.

"How are we gonna get *ourselves* out of this?" the old man asked.

Shomari nodded an agreement. "The Rovers are busy, but the Vaaji will be having eyes on us, same as them."

"We'll figure it out along the way. Just stay close to me." Zala's feet pounded on the deck as she dashed away, and the others followed suit.

Shomari jumped from rope to rope above them. He moved with awkward balance, his injuries—or his wounded spirit—still plaguing him. Even still, he dodged the Rovers that tried to clutch at his legs or snatch his tail. Though they were coming shockingly close to grabbing him.

With Shomari's acrobatics distracting most of the crew, Zala, Fon, Rishaad, and Ode cut a swift path to the bow of the ship. Fon floated just behind Zala, keeping pace, but only just. Zala couldn't see where Mantu swam off to, but there was nothing she could do for him now—if he hadn't been caught by an arrow from the Rovers already. Zala just had to trust that he was crafty enough to slip away. Ode didn't seem like he was going to make it though—his shoddy wooden leg was already giving out from under his run. Zala needed to get them off the ship and to the port, but she couldn't just leave Ode behind.

"Hold my hand tighter, kijana!" Zala shouted. "And stay close. We'll get out of here."

Beyond the ship's figurehead, Zala could make out the grand palace of al-Anim, the sheen of domed temples, and the crowd gathering to watch the spectacle. The bells continued to boom— the continuing warning call of pirates Zala had become all too familiar with. She just needed to make it to the port where she could hide in the thicket of bazaar patrons. That's all that mattered at that moment.

"There they are! Grab them!" bellowed a voice from the side.

Zala didn't turn to look. The bow of the ship was approaching fast.

"Get ready to jump," she called out to the others over her shoulder. Zala knew Fon would make the jump fine. The port was not so far, and Fon could glide the rest of the way, even with her wings working at half capacity, but the same could not be said for Ode. "Can you do it, Ode?"

"Uh… I can make the jump, but I ain't knowin' about the swim," Ode said, hesitation and doubt lacing his tone.

"The port isn't far, the tide will take us in," Zala assured him.

"I don't know…"

"Don't worry, I've got you." Zala slowed, grabbing Ode by the shoulders and hefting him overboard before he could react. The motion cost Zala precious seconds and the first of the Rovers caught her at the last moment before she could get overboard herself.

Fortunately for her, the pirate was one of the faster ones, not a stronger one. Zala would have still lost a fistfight with the man, she knew that well, but she didn't need to fight him. She dodged the first two jabs directed at her head and moved to jump overboard. Before she could leap, a final blow caught her just under the chin. It was a vicious uppercut. It took everything she had not to black out, dots spotting the edges of her vision even as she fell awkwardly into the water below.

Most times, the rush of water at her ears felt liberating, cleansing, but her dizzy head had her completely off-kilter. It didn't help that her deafened ear made the muted sounds of underwater tones unnerving. She fought the odd sensations as best she could, thrusting her hands through the sea, making sure to stay below the surface line and—she hoped—enemy arrows and bolts.

Distantly, she could hear the impact of arrowheads against the breaking waves, could feel them rush past her ears. But there was no time for fear, no time to ponder any of the arrows catching her shoulder or back. All she could think about was her hands, one in front of the other, as they tugged against the current.

Usually she could hold her breath much longer, but the stress, or perhaps the panicked pace she swam with, made her lungs tiny things. She shot herself up for a second breath, straight to the surface until her head broke through to open air. She gasped in great lungfuls, as much as she could. Vaaji spice laced the ocean breeze and wafted into her nostrils as she inhaled. The bazaar couldn't be far, probably just over the closest rocks near the port's beach.

Where had Ode gone? He couldn't have swum far with his leg. Did the Rovers get him? Was he shot? Perhaps the Vaaji picked him up?

"Ode! Fon!" Zala shouted hoarsely, turning herself in the water. "Shomari! Rishaad!" she tried again, with no answer.

The Rovers seemed all but subdued by the Vaaji fleet. The *Redtide's* sails were shot through and burning. Zala had swam at least a hundred strokes from the sinking ship. If Captain Nubia was still alive to see her ship in ruin, Zala would certainly face her wrath.

But only if she could manage to survive this.

It wouldn't be long before someone on one of the imperial ships noticed her in the water. She turned and made her way to the large rocks jutting from what she hoped was the port's edge.

A moment later, Zala grabbed at a lodged stone, then another, climbing as fast as her tired arms would allow, but the damn rocks were so slippery. As she reached the top of her climb, an arrow tip shattered just two paces to her right. Zala jerked her head over her shoulder to see an archer aiming her way from the *Redtide's* sinking bow—a certain archer with braids running down her head like snakes.

There was nothing she could do but continue her climb and hope Lishan continued to miss. The Captain was a mystic with the Blessing of short-sight, not eagle's eye after all, right?

As soon as Zala reached the summit of uneven rocks, she pushed to her feet and ran. She didn't take the time to look back, though her gut told her something *was* behind her. Had one of the Rovers jumped after her? If she was lucky, they were still in the water.

But when am I ever lucky?

Zala turned down to her right, where the large rocks cut deep into the beach and on to Port al-Anim. Far to her left, she saw Fon's tiny figure. The aziza was running straight into the port's bazaar, right where the crowd was at its thickest.

Atta girl, Zala thought.

Oh, what she would've given to be Fon's size right then.

Zala bounded through the market, past the stalls selling potions, where a man haggled prices, past a stall trading maps, where a woman asked if the scrolls were outdated, past a snake charmer, where a toothless elder performed for men smoking from elaborate pipes. Zala couldn't take it all in properly. The market quickly became a blur of colors, the many voices around her merging into simple noise, several languages colliding in a babble. If only she had two good ears to pick out potential pursuers.

Heads turned as she rushed past, likely wondering why a

soaking wet woman was making a mad dash through the market, but she couldn't afford to pay them any mind. After ducking around a stall selling flutes and riqqs, Zala threw a glance over her shoulder for anyone stalking her. When she found no one, she turned back and pulled a set of robes from one of the merchant displays and wrapped them around her head in the style of a Qibasi devotee—and to cover her wet clothes.

She backed against a stone wall and looked back on the crowd. She caught her first sign of pursuit as a set of Vaaji city watchmen wearing green kaffiyehs and black agals came running into the market yard. Quickly, Zala moved to the nearest stall and picked up the first item she saw, then asked the small wind flute's price from its seller.

Before the merchant could even finish answering, the guards had vanished back into the crowd, and Zala dropped the flute back on the wooden surface, apologizing and moving on through the market square. She was only a few steps on her way when she caught the wide eyes of Mantu, who was hiding behind a slimy bundle of fish netted at the side of another stall.

His gaze was fixed on the Vaaji guards that had just passed. Zala observed as the citywatch faltered, doubling back toward the crouched pirate beside the stall. Mantu stepped back, staying low, but Zala saw he was backing straight into a pair of Rovers making their way out from a separate avenue. Their wet dark clothing and red trim stuck out among the vivid colors of the market.

Zala waved her hands at Mantu, trying to warn him of the trouble he was about to find himself in. When she got his attention, she pointed to the crew behind him. He turned his head, ducking behind the fish again when the Vaaji soldiers made eye contact with the Rovers.

"Hey, you! Stop right there!" they shouted in Common Vaaji.

The Rover crew stopped cold before turning to sprint in the opposite direction.

When she was sure the coast was clear, Zala shouldered her way over to Mantu through the crowd.

"How'd you make them?" he asked, water coming around his brow.

"I have eyes," Zala seethed. "You have a few things to answer for, kijana. But there's no time. Follow me, we need to go deeper into the market."

Mantu shook his head, his beard casting sea water. "No way. We'll be cornered."

"Trust me. This is our best play. Unlike you, I'm *not* fixing to die today."

Zala led Mantu toward the end of the bazaar, making sure to walk and not run—though she knew she was looking over her shoulder more times than she should've been.

"Once we get safe, we need to talk about how to keep our cool." After her fifth look, she turned on her heel only to slam into another figure. At first, she thought it was the garment merchant chasing her down for stealing, but then she peered into the figure's robes.

"Shomari? Is that you?" she whispered as she looked him up and down. If she hadn't bumped into him, knocking down the hood of the dark—likely stolen—cloak, she wouldn't have known he was even a pakka. Shomari had hidden himself well, his robes hiding his fur and his turban covering his pointed ears.

"Yes," he answered, voice muffled through the cloth. "Would you like to be announcing it a little louder for everyone? Some of the merchants over there did not quite hear you."

That left Mantu the only one undisguised, though Zala figured they all should be fine, his deep olive-toned skin matched most of the other patrons in the market. But just for good measure—and to sell the lie—Zala grabbed Mantu's arm.

"What you *playing* at?" Mantu flinched at her touch.

"I'm *playing* your wife. I can't walk around without a husband in this getup."

"*Again?*" Mantu rolled his eyes. "Is there somethin' you need to tell me, chana? Because I think I'll end up breakin' your heart."

"Give me your arm already," Zala said irritably. "We got Rovers and citywatch on us, fool."

"All right, all right." Reluctantly, Mantu snatched up Zala's arm again, placing it around his waist. Zala had to take his arm and roughly place her own through the gap of his elbow.

"*This* is how a woman holds you," she explained, bemused, as they walked on. She did her best to suppress her vexation. Mantu groaned before they turned a corner into the food markets, a new rush of cumin, za'atar, and cinnamon filling their noses.

It didn't take them long to find the end of the bazaar through the labyrinth of stalls. But a quartet of Vaaji soldiers blocked off the entrance into the city, all of them brandishing long spears and glinting sabers. Quickly, Zala pivoted her group away from the guards' eye line, but there was nowhere else to go. She tried her best to think. The nervous pounding in her ears was no help. Going back into the market was the wrong play, but talking to the guards directly was too risky.

There has to be something…

A new thought slipped into Zala's mind.

Tugging on Mantu's arm, she led them back along the market's edge, between al-Anim's outer wall and the food stalls.

"Why are we going back *into* the market?" Mantu said nervously.

"I'm looking for another way out."

"By going back *in*?"

Zala grunted. "You can't talk. '*Mudwa, Umtet. Heseti em netek*'? Honestly!? If you're going to kill yourself, do it on your own time, please and thank you."

"They was talkin' 'bout shaving my beard! I wasn't gonna die without slingin' an insult or two."

Zala ignored his bullshit of a retort as they continued through the hustle and bustle of the crowd. At one point she thought she saw the red trim of Rover tunics, but it had only been a caged hummingbird's feathers. The few Vaaji they passed paid them no mind, however. With Zala and Shomari wrapped in robes, there was no reason for the guards to stop them. And though Mantu was more than a little wet, anyone might expect his level of damp clothing near the port's market, where so many fishmongers sold their stock.

When the paved walkway turned to the soft sands of the beach, Zala finally found what she was looking for.

Mantu pinched his fingers around his nose. "Please don't tell me your idea is to hide away in there."

"My idea is to hide away in there," Zala echoed flatly as she eyed a small opening off-shooting a grimy sludge of brown. She and Shomari could fit through easily enough, but she wasn't so sure about Mantu.

"Come now, Zala," Shomari purred. "These robes are too fresh to soil. I have already compromised my fur for you today."

"This isn't up for discussion," Zala insisted. "Either we go in there and stay alive, or we keep wandering the market and run into the Rovers."

Mantu chewed on the thought, looking between the sewer and the bazaar several times before deciding, with a begrudging sigh, "Into the waste we go, I guess."

CHAPTER 15
ZALA

Several minutes passed as Zala peeked through the tiny hole of the sewer's off-shoot. Fortunately for her and the crew, the sewer drain spread wide once they had squeezed through the initial opening.

As expected, there was no problem for her or Shomari, though Mantu had trouble getting his large mass through the cramped gap. The moment he fell through, though, almost too unceremoniously, he had spat a curse, none too pleased with the thick grime or the rancid stench. Zala couldn't quite blame him. The whole space permeated with the smell of shit, and the heat from outside cooked the putrid dark stones. Even standing away from the worst of the waste felt like simmering in a cauldron of muck.

"As much as I love the decor..." Mantu nodded to a mysterious green-black spot along the stone wall, "I think it's time for us to go."

A pair of voices stilled Zala.

"Wait," she whispered, grabbing Mantu by the wrist.

The pirate pulled away from her out of reflex. "What? Ain't no one followed us—can't guess why—you want to stew in here longer?"

"No, listen." Zala pointed a finger at the grating leading out to the beach.

The timbre of a male and female voice grew louder. Zala stuck her head into the hole to see two figures dressed in black lurking away from the bazaar and onto the sands. Like Zala, they had both wrapped their heads in disguise, but their garb was unmistakable.

"It looks like some Rovers got away after all," Zala murmured. "Shit, they're coming this way."

Zala pushed away from her vantage point in haste, and she slipped in something wet and mushy. She fell back, her heart thumping against her chest, knowing full well the following splash would give them away. But before her back landed in the waste, furred hands caught her by her shoulders. A pair of yellow eyes pierced the darkness above her. She had almost forgotten Shomari was there with his black cloak hiding him so well in the shadows.

Zala mouthed a silent "thank you," and Shomari gave her a short nod before hoisting her upright again.

"Do you see them?" came the voice of the female pirate, echoing through the tiny hole. It was Ouseni.

The man's voice, Kwame's, came next. "Nothing. We should head back. The Captain wants us all at that plaza in the city. She knows some people who'll hide us."

How in the hells did they get away from the Vaaji fleet? Zala thought, though she had to remind herself that if she could pull it off, others could too, least of all the most notorious pirate crew. Lishan had learned from one of the longest standing pirate captains in the Sapphire Seas, a position that usually shifted hands within two or three moons, and it had been years since Nubia took to the seas.

"Do you know if Arus made it?" Ouseni asked.

"Yeah, I saw her near the coast. She had that old one and the aziza dead to rights."

"Flutter..." Shomari stepped away from the sewer wall to get a closer look. Mantu held him back with a single hand while Zala turned to the pakka with a finger held to her lips. But she couldn't help suppressing her own slice of worry going through her chest. The pirates hadn't mentioned Rishaad. If luck was on the young man's side, perhaps he escaped—or at least survived. This was the boy's home, after all. He should know it well.

"They gave chase," Kwame continued. "Hopefully, by the time we get out of the city, they'll have them."

"What about that Captain of theirs?" Ouseni asked.

"No time to stick around. We'll need to lie low."

"Should we try in here?"

Kwame laughed. "Ain't no way I'm fixin' to crawl in there. You can if you like."

Shomari drew his rapier, and Zala knew he was ready to stick whoever's head came through first. Zala couldn't bring herself to tell him to keep them alive, not this time. She bit at her lip nervously as she waited for Ouseni's response.

"It is only being two of them," Shomari purred quietly.

Though confident in the pakka's skill, Zala preferred avoiding any further confrontation. A loud sniff brought Zala's attention back to the hole as the woman seemed to judge the smell of the sewer drain.

Kwame let out another chuckle. "Don't worry, I won't go tellin' the Captain you didn't want to go lookin' for them through that. I ain't blamin' you none myself."

"Shut up," came Ouseni's disgruntled response. "Fine, let's go then."

"Aye."

Zala, Mantu, and Shomari held their heads low as the pirate's feet shifted away in the sands. Zala's heart thrummed in her stomach. The Rovers were serious when they held a grudge. Her one meal with Captain Nubia, and Lishan's thick grip around her neck, had shown her what that could look and feel like. Their persistence only solidified the notion.

She shot a glance at Mantu. Not for the first time, she understood his paranoia. Zala could only hope that the Vaaji were far less cruel with Jelani, whatever they might be doing to him.

The silence between the small group persisted, as though none of them wanted to be the first one to breathe for fear of being caught out. Zala expected most of them were thinking the same as she.

After a long moment, Mantu spoke first. "How... in the hells—"

"I know, I know," Zala huffed. "I thought most of them would get captured."

A tiny pang of guilt punched her in the gut. Most of the crew would've been killed if anything else. She couldn't say she cared for most of them, but she at least hoped Marjani and Ekko were okay. Even if she knew them barely a week, they were kinder to her than the rest. It was a shame she couldn't speak to the couple before she set their plan in action. They might've come with her and the others. Now... they were probably just as pissed as the rest of their crew.

"Most of them probably were captured," Shomari surmised, already tiptoeing down the sewer farther into the dark. "We can only hope the Vaaji got Lishan or we will have her to be dealing with while we are here."

Mantu shook his head with a sigh. "Told you them pirates were crazy."

Zala gave Mantu an annoyed scowl, but it was unlikely he could see her expression through the dark. She really had thought they'd be able to broker some sort of genuine alliance with them. They were just on the cusp. It was Mantu who ruined it all in the end.

"You can't talk, kijana," she said as she followed Shomari—and his cat's eyes—down the darkened path. "Were it not for you, we wouldn't be in this situation."

And if it wasn't for me, his lover wouldn't be in Vaaji hands, Zala thought sadly.

"They was gonna shave me!" Mantu exclaimed.

"Lishan was just lookin' to chew you out for that mess you left. That's all, you fool."

"Yeah, yeah." Zala could hear the eye roll in his tone. "Water under the bridge. I fucked up. I get that. Let's move forward now."

The group padded through the drain in silence, their walk punctuated by intermittent tip-toes into the shallow black waste. Whenever Shomari took a large step to one side, Zala followed suit, knowing the pakka's feline eyes would avoid any questionable piles.

"I barely knew Ode," Zala said after a time. "But I feel like I've let him down, you know?"

She could still see Ode's eyes, still see how he struggled with getting off the ship. She didn't know if she had done the right thing in throwing him overboard, but what other choice did she have? She could only hope it had been quick for him if the Rovers had caught up to him. She had a dark feeling the pirates weren't in the mood for prisoners at that moment. Her mind wandered back to the Aktarian prisoner the Rovers had strung up by his thumbs only a week prior—and that was the Rover's mode of operation when they were in *good* moods.

"We've got to find them before the Rovers do," Shomari said, a hint of uncharacteristic unease in his voice. "They said they are having Fon."

"As much as I'd like to go lookin' for the others, it ain't the smart thing to do here." Mantu sighed, doing his best to navigate the small tunnel with his large size. "We need to make sure them Rovers are gone first."

Zala put a hand to Shomari's shoulder as a light from overhead gratings shone through. "Don't worry, Fon is a hard one to find when she wants to get herself lost. They might've seen her, but she'll get away. I saw her make it into the market before any of us. She's probably hiding and worrying herself, waiting for us to turn up somewhere in the city."

"Same with Ode," Mantu added. "I can't tell you how many times that old kijana has survived impossible odds. A cockroach would envy him. Duma too… I know he's still out there."

Shomari's next words could have been better chosen. "Someone like Sniffs… folks like the Vaaji don't keep a big guy like that alive for too lo—"

Mantu pushed around Zala to get to the pakka, nearly tripping her in the process. But she managed to step between them awkwardly. "Will the both of you calm down? I'm sure they're both fine. They're *all* going to be fine. They survived as long as they did under Kobi, and they made it out of that first battle with the Vaaji too. A little chase with the Rovers should be nothing. This is Rishaad's home, Fon can hide anywhere, Ode's hard to kill, and Duma isn't dumb."—Well, not entirely dim—"He'd've known when to lay down his axes on that sky ship." She nudged her chin up as they passed more sealed grates. "Look at this place, there are so many holes to hide in." The passing feet above looked as though the people they belonged to were shoulder to shoulder.

"We should keep to the sewers for now," she went on. "Those other two will come back when they realize we must be in here. We'll have a lead on them though, even if they do manage to get into the city, but still..." She paused, sighing. "We can't afford to be fighting amongst ourselves."

Then it occurred to her... how would she ever be able to tell Mantu the truth about Sniffs and her hand in getting him captured.

Putting the thought aside, Zala turned to the spot-lighted abyss that was the onward stretch of sewer. She gave another great sigh, pinched her nose, and continued farther into the stench. Shomari followed next. Then Mantu brought up the rear.

"I can't believe this is really al-Anim," Mantu said as they peered through the holes of the sewer. "My great nan used to tell me not so long ago this place was just a fishing port with maybe one temple to its name. Now it beats out some of the cities in Aktah."

"I suspect it has something to do with that sky ship," Zala said.

"That's a good guess," Mantu agreed. "We shoulda been raidin' al-Anim instead of attackin' ships at open sea. This where the real money at."

Shomari threw up a furry finger. "Let us not forget it was Zala who was suggesting we raid al-Anim in the first place during her speech for Captain."

"Yeah, yeah, but she ain't *really* know what al-Anim was."

Zala ignored them both, pushing her way through the rising sludge. The deeper they went, the more it seemed to build up, and with it, a foul cloud hung in the stale air, which slipped past even their covered noses.

After a while, they came across a group of children huddled in a corner of the sewer. At first, Zala thought they had been hiding as well but when they approached closer, she could see the children picking off mold from bread, then shoving it into their mouths like it was a fine steak.

Zala shuffled toward them, avoiding what looked to be more human waste on the ground. "Don't do that! Do you want to get sick?"

She slapped the bread out of the nearest girl's hand. The child went for the bread again even though it had landed directly into the sewer water. Zala was about to follow, but Mantu's meaty hand wrapped around her wrist.

"It's all they have," he said as he shook his head.

"There has to be something better than trash for them." Zala swatted the bread out of the little girl's hand again when she put it to her mouth.

"Come with me," she said to the girl and her friends. They gave her blank stares, so Zala repeated herself in Common Vaaji. Now there was recognition in their eyes, yet still the children refused to follow her.

"They don't know who you are," Mantu said. "What makes you think they'd come with you?"

The children ran off deeper into the sewer, molding fruit and old meat covered in waste stuffed in their hands. Zala frowned, a lump in her throat. She could almost remember when she was their age, rummaging through Jultia's own trash. That was all before...

She shook the thought from her head. Now wasn't the time. They needed a way out and fast. Another grate sat overhead. She set her hands against it but it wouldn't budge.

"We should probably get out of here too," Shomari said as he crept around the edge of the green water. "Children means there is likely a way out."

"We should," Mantu agreed. "But where we gonna go?"

"I think I know a place," Zala said as she made her way to the next sewer opening down the tunnel. "Follow me."

"Aye, aye, Cap'n." Shomari saluted.

Zala pushed against a second grating. This one was looser than the first, a stone missing near its edge which must've once held it together. The children likely came through this way.

The day's light hit Zala across her face warmly, the welcome smell of Vaaji spice filling her nostrils once more. She found herself somewhere in the middle of al-Anim, where women towed laundry above their heads, and children hung from windows along tattered building sides. A man dressed in a high-top head-dress stood at a wooden balcony down the street. His voice echoed and boomed against buildings packed into each other. The sing-song nature of his words sounded like some prayer, his booming tone boosted by what Zala assumed was the mystical touch of a sonamancer. The words of religion, however, were of the Old Way, not al-Qiba.

Good, we're still in the lower boroughs, Zala thought.

"My lie to Nubia about knowing someone in al-Anim wasn't entirely a lie." Zala pulled Mantu up from the sewer hole.

"The best lies always have truth in them." Mantu smiled. "Wonder where you got that from?"

Zala did her best not to break face. She didn't need to feed Mantu's ego anymore than necessary.

"There's a woman here I know," she said. "She works out of a place called the Whispers. Her name's Majida. Madam Majida. She doesn't have shipping routes for us, but she does know every-thing else that goes on in this city."

"A working woman, you say?" Shomari lifted his shaggy brow, needing no help as he slinked out of the sewer. "How did you come to know someone like that?"

"She's Jelani's cousin," Zala said as they walked between a set of women with a bucket of wet clothing. A man in noble robes brushed her shoulder roughly without as much as looking at her. He must've thought her a slummer like the rest in this district. Playing the role, she made sure to relieve him of his coin as he did. "I forget how close of a cousin she is to Jelani though, at least third or fourth."

In truth, Zala didn't expect the woman to know much about the rest of the crew. But Jelani was likely brought to the city soon after Zala's last meeting with the Vaaji nearly a week ago. The madam had plenty of time to know at least *something*.

Mantu kept looking over his shoulder nervously. It helped that he smelled like literal shit so everyone stayed clear.

"What good would a madam be for us?" he asked.

"Her business is known for peddling more than just pleasure," Zala answered. "She, or one of her workers, deal in information prized from their clientele."

Zala walked through the crowd like she owned it. She much preferred big cities to small island towns. It had been a while since she'd been in her urban element like this.

"There's one issue, though," she said. "Something I've never understood about her profession in this place. How in the hells am I supposed to find a brothel here? Aren't they supposed to be forbidden in Vaaji cities?"

"I'm sure they are, those spineless dikala," Mantu huffed. It looked as though he was walking backward with how much he turned to watch his back. "But that won't stop them from existin'. Finding one should be easy enough… just follow the men."

Mantu set off ahead of Zala.

The trio continued on as the city started to slope upward, the ruined buildings left behind for more well-kept edifices. The crowd changed from the bootless masses, where naked children roamed the street and hunched-backed elders were plentiful, to the hardened faces of working folk. Far more nobles were found here, many of them procuring their expensive satins. Zala made sure to make their purses a bit lighter as she went along behind Mantu.

At one point, a pakka blacksmith seemed to sniff something in the air when Shomari passed, but dismissed it in almost the same moment. Zala caught sight of Shomari, who was still covered in his dark turban and robes. He took up the far side of the cramped street, as far away as he could get from the suspicious blacksmith.

"A cousin of yours?" Mantu joked.

Shomari scoffed. "That is prejudice, Mantu. That one isn't even having the same coat."

Zala laughed a little, but couldn't help clenching her fist as she worried about how pakka were treated in this city. If there was a pakka craftsman, maybe Shomari wouldn't stick out so much. Whatever the case, it was likely best they both remained hidden until they figured out the social dynamics of Vaaj.

After a short while of following Mantu, and a few short conversations with men he had seemingly chosen at random, they found a district called the Silks, where a small building was pressed between a barber salon and bootsmith. Anyone could have easily missed it. Above its simple wooden door, with chipped paint of crimson, read, *The Whispers,* in a beautiful yet faint script.

"Good job, Mantu," Zala complimented.

"Kobi didn't name me Captain for nothin'."

"Perhaps as a Sea Captain. How much coin did you get on the way here?"

"Huh?" He raised an eyebrow. "What you mean?"

Zala lifted three tiny sacks of coin in her hand. Shomari walked up to her and handed her five more.

"You've spent too much time at sea." Zala smirked. "You need to keep your hands busy, especially in a place like this." Zala nodded toward Shomari, who was filching a kabob from a grill. "Make yourself useful. You can learn a thing or two from a pakka; they've got light fingers."

"Yeah, yeah, whatever you say." Mantu tried for a tone of dismissal, but the reddening around his ears betrayed otherwise.

With another smirk, Zala started into the brothel, but Mantu's giant hand stopped her. "Where do you think you're going, *Captain*?"

"To find out about this sky ship..." she trailed off matter-of-factly. "To see how we can get our people back."

And to figure out where Jelani is, she thought.

"Not with *that* you ain't." Mantu pointed to her covered head. "Men and women of al-Qiba devotion ain't allowed in a place like this. You'll get snatched up before you get anywhere close to that cousin of yours."

"Oh, right." Zala pulled off her headscarf and robes, revealing her tattered pirate clothing. "Better?"

"Much, but you still stink of shit." Mantu waved a hand over his nose. "At least now you won't be stoned on sight. Still, not sure about this Majida woman, though. We don't know where her loyalties lie."

Zala shrugged. "She's family. What could go wrong?"

"I ain't never cared none for given families. It's the one we choose that matters. But suit yourself, and holler if you need anything. That way me and Shomari can make a break for it."

"Not so that you can rescue me?"

Mantu smiled. "What kind of pirate would I be if I did something like that?"

CHAPTER 16
ZALA

ZALA FOUND HERSELF INSIDE A TIGHT AND DUSTY ANTEROOM. Like outside, the space shared in the chipped paint aesthetic of the front doors, except that instead of faded acrylic, the chamber was littered with cracked marble and cobwebbed corners.

It was all a front for the Whispers.

A faint scent of mildew entered Zala's nostrils, and she wondered if this place had once served as a bathhouse. At either side of the room sat two arched thresholds, which led to ascending stairs. Between the archways, a large hanging banner fell from the ceiling to the floor, and an armored man whose size challenged even Sniffs' stood ahead of it. Two short swords swayed at his hips as he rocked from heel to toe.

"You one of them new girls?" the man asked her.

His voice was deep and gravely, yet somehow homely. He looked her up and down. Though the gesture read initially as a cautious one, the man's eyes were oddly kind and bright.

"Yes…" Zala lied very slowly. "I'm here to see Madam Majida."

The guard thumbed behind him. "Mother's right inside, at the end of the red pool. Can't miss her."

Zala nodded and made to walk past him but he stopped her with a single hand, a spiral tattoo marked at his wrist.

"But you can't go in there smellin' like you do," he said.

Zala's face flushed with heat. "Sorry I—" she started to say, her ears reddening.

The guard held out his hand and waved it casually. "Don't worry yourself none." He tilted his head to one of the stairs near the arches. "There's some baths up that way. They ain't the cleanest, but *some* washin' is better than none."

"Thank you." Zala nodded.

"It's two silvers for entry..." the man trailed off. "But just go on up and I won't say nothin'."

Zala stuffed her hand into her loose wrappings and pulled out the fee. "No problem."

The guard lifted his brows in surprise, then bit each coin. When he was satisfied with their authenticity, he nodded his approval. And, lifting his large arm to one side, he beckoned Zala forward.

Zala followed the direction of the man's outstretched hand and made her way to the second level. There she found a set of four small pools, each of them a different shade of brown. Choosing the lightest hue of amber slush, she disrobed and set her clothing just under her bottom so she could sit with her feet hung over the lip of the pool instead of dipping all the way in. To her surprise, the water was warm, and beneath her wiggling toes she could just make out hot stones at the base of the dingy pool.

The water's warmth nearly made her forget what she was doing there in the first place.

Shaking the stupor she was entering into, Zala rushed the fetid water over her shoulders, atop her torso, and against her legs. She didn't want to waste time lounging in some sauna. She and the others may have made it into the city first, but Lishan and her Rovers could bump into them at any time—that and she was eager to finally glean some new information about Jelani.

After drying off, she put her clothes back on, then walked back out to the antechamber to find the guard speaking with a smaller man—a boy, really. There was only the slightest of stubble about the young man's cheeks.

"Is Ishtar working today?" he asked eagerly.

The guard hoisted his eyebrows up, where they disappeared under his head wrap. "You know she's top coin, right? I got in trouble last week for lettin' your slow-ass in without countin' the right funds."

"I got it, I got it, I got it," the boy said rapidly, then dug into his purse to reveal a small well of gold. "See?"

Like with Zala, the guard put a few of the coins to his bite. "All right then, get your silly-ass in there and try not to hurt yourself."

The guard drew back the banner behind him to reveal a patchy stone wall, and, after whispering some words into it, a simple wooden door materialized before them. He gave the chipped oak a few knocks, a rhythm too specific not to be some sort of code. There was a moment's pause before another set of knocks came back at him in answer. The guard replied with a last set of knuckled hammerings and—finally—the door swung inward.

"In you go." The guard gestured.

The boy didn't need to be asked twice, he practically skipped inside. Zala noticed now that the hanging banner was in the image of a mother with seven children surrounding her. Each toddler clung to their mother around her arms, legs, and torso—wherever they could lay a hand. She knew it had something to do with the Jo'baran religion, something Jelani must've told her about time and time again, but she couldn't remember what.

Presuming she was free to proceed, Zala followed behind the boy, but the guard stopped her with his weighty hand. "Wait, wait. Give me your hand," he said.

"You know you ain't supposed to leave the door open," came another guard's voice from a second dark room within.

"I know you didn't just use that tone with me," the first guard shot back. "This'll only take a second, don't get yourself in a twist." He turned his eyes to Zala.

She gave him her hand without protest. No need to have him shooting her with one of those glares. The man dabbed a liquid on her wrists and then on her neck. It smelled sweet, the aroma maybe cinnamon, the same mixture Zala had smelled when she entered the port markets.

"That should be good enough for your meetin' with Mother. Not much can be done about those rags on your shoulders. Don't take too long though, this stuff won't cling long. I hope you get the job; you got an interestin' face."

Not the most refined compliment she'd ever received, but she could tell he meant it earnestly, and without the typical lust of a man who worked at a place like this. Zala gave the man an honest smile and walked through the dark curtains and door frame to the second room.

"About time..." murmured the young man waiting on the other side as the guard closed the door behind her.

With the entrance room closed, they were left in darkness as they waited for another exchange of knocks from the opposite side. Then, after a short moment, another door opened, and the subtle glow of coral and lilac washed over them.

Dashes of the hues blanketed the main chamber. From the ceiling above hung a tent of red cloth that curved at least twelve-paces high, surrounded by streaks of purple material wrapped around the wall's floral pillars. The sun's light peeked through cuts of the silk, through thinner cloth filters that shone coral patches around the room.

Zala almost didn't catch the drop her mouth was lazing into.

"I love coming here," a woman in imperial tunics who was snuggled up with an aziza spoke from the side. "The architecture alone is worth the trip."

In the middle of the chamber sat a steaming pool with a stone walkway flanking its sides, all lined with scented candles of lavender. The room's vapor clung to the back of Zala's neck. She reached up to rub her skin dry and her eye caught a trio of naked women within the bath ahead. The pool was certainly red as the guard had said, stretched narrow and long with lily pads floating atop its surface. The women turned to Zala to show themselves fully to her, teasing her with a nipple and then ducking back under water. At first, Zala paid them no mind—until her eyes settled on the one in the middle. She wasn't exactly a human woman, at least not in full.

For a moment, it might have looked as though Zala's attention *was* intrigued. But the half-aziza who flaunted her assets to Zala hadn't piqued her curiosities because of her glowing and flawless skin, but because the brothel worker looked far too much like Fon, even down to her forehead tattoo. Zala halted in her tracks as she shook the blank expression from her face. She had already convinced herself that her friend was okay. The little one made it into the city before any of them.

Her expression must've revealed her attention, because the aziza swam closer to her in the pool. When Zala made it clear that there was no sexual interest on her part, the aziza and the human women who joined her turned to the other patrons within the room. Their focuses instead alighted on the young man Zala had followed in, who was staring, transfixed.

Guards lined the walls, each of them wearing a necklace with a spiral charm at its end—not unlike the front guard's tattoo. Zala only then recognized it as the same symbol Jelani had on his wrists. But he was an oni'baro, a pious man. What were flesh-peddlers doing with the symbol?

At the end of the room sat a severe-looking woman, her sharp features in stark contrast to the rest of the tranquil room. She settled casually on a large cushioned chair between a canopy of lavender silks, and she wore a long bandana of teal laced with silver. Sterling earrings hung from each of her ears, almost down to her shoulders, catching the light that peeked through from above. Though clothed, the silks about her curvaceous body hid very little—at least for Zala's taste—just enough to give the subtlest impression of what lay beneath.

Next to her stood two shirtless men wearing simple white loin-cloths, equally evocative. Each of them had hair dyed the shade of bright indigo, wavy crowns and thin mustaches alike.

Before the three of them stood a man and woman of noble garb. They spoke with the madam just ahead of Zala. The brothel owner looked as though she was repressing some choice words for the nobles, her eyes still and mouth thin.

Not wanting to seem an eavesdropper, Zala turned her head to the dancing girls who stood before each pillar. They shook their bellies to the beat of light drums and lighter flutes performed at the edges of the room. Uncomfortable with the sensual gyration, Zala relented, deciding that this was a place she simply had nowhere safe to look. Instead she turned her eyes upward to admire the drapes and light piercing between them.

Her good ear trained in on the nobles despite herself. The man seemed to be doing all the talking, though at first Zala thought his voice belonged to the woman—it was so light and airy. She darted a glance back down to steal a look at the noble. He sported a sharp beard with an intricate design. His checkered head wrap and long black tunic looked as though they were cut and sewn that very same day, clean and free of any tatters or loose seams. The woman at his side didn't quite have the same flare, wearing a green tarha and dark under-wrapping to cover her face. Zala suspected the woman was some bodyguard by the way she kept looking out the corners of her eyes and the insignia on her sash.

"This is the last time we'll take your tributes late," the bearded man said. "You know, if you just took up the teachings of al-Qiba, these taxes would go away."

"All I know is this brothel," Majida said, her tone flat. The deadpan in her eyes betrayed a wave of anger deep within. Zala knew the look too well. "If I took up that religion, what would I do for a living?"

"You're not too old." The man flashed a sleazy smile. "I could make an honest woman out of you. I've not taken a first wife yet."

"I'll decline, thank you, as *beautiful* as you are," Majida said the word "beautiful" as though it was the most wretched thing that could've crossed her lips. "Perhaps it is *I* who should offer *you* a job."

The man didn't look at all pleased with her response. Eventually, Majida nodded to one of the men next to her. The servant, or whomever he was, shuffled into a back room before returning with a small purse.

"You'll find everything is there," the servant said, his scowl matching Majida's.

"Oh, I'm sure it is," the fashionable man replied, "or else I'll have my friend here return and shut this godforsaken place down." The man tilted his head to his bodyguard, who made no change in her expression. "See you on Yem's next, *Mother*. Don't be late next time."

The man turned and "accidentally" tripped over a candle, setting one of the curtains alight. Majida's men rushed to stomp it out. The nobleman gave a half-hearted apology before passing Zala, who lowered her head. It was unlikely any of the Vaaji knew she was a pirate, but better safe than sorry. As he passed, the man gave a few curt nods to the other imperial officials lounging around the red pool.

"Madam Majida." Zala stepped forward, her voice deferential. She wasn't sure if she should bow, kneel, or if she could even look the woman in the eye. So she just stood as still as possible as the blue-haired men stomped out the last of the flames dancing around the curtains.

"Yes, that's me. Are you the new girl?"

"I…" Zala wasn't sure if she should maintain the lie, but remembered she was here for a reason. "I'm not, no. I'm here about…" Zala turned her eyes to the men.

"What you wish to say to me may be said to all before you."

"I need information about the military here in al-Anim… the Navy, specifically." Zala kept her voice low. Majida might have trusted the men that stood at her side, but Zala didn't trust the others in the room, most of them Vaaji nobles. Besides, Majida probably thought Zala would ask something about brothel work, not Vaaji secrets.

Majida laughed and said, "You came to this place to ask me something like that? Why do you think I would know anything about Vaaji military, of all things? Don't you see where we are, child?"

"Your reputation precedes you, *Mother*."

Majida canted her head a little, and the hints of a smirk started at her wrinkled dimple. "Who are you, exactly? Who are you working for?" She scanned the sides of the chamber as though searching for someone lurking in the shadows.

Zala waved her hands frantically in front of her. "Oh, no, no. It's nothing like that. I'm not working for anyone. Someone close to me was captured by the Vaaji military recently. I just want to know where he's been taken to."

"I see..." Majida turned to the men, and her expression softened slightly. But still, there was an air of restraint in her voice as she spoke to the one to her right. "Altair."

"She's speaking the truth, Mother," he said. Zala flitted a look to him and realized he must've been an empath.

"Very well," Majida said with a sigh. "Latif, if you'd be so kind. Altair, you can join him."

"Yes, Mother," they said in unison. The pair of them gave short bows, then moved to the outside of the canopy. The taller of the two, Latif—Zala presumed—drew the curtain closed around Zala and Majida. Though Zala could see outside the thin silks, chit-chat running across the patrons lips and musicians playing their instruments, a familiar vacuum of air sapped away as the flutes, harps, and giggles of the room extinguished.

She's got an empath and a sonamancer. This Majida doesn't play any games.

"So, what is it you would like to know?" Majida asked once she was satisfied that they wouldn't be overheard.

Zala bent her head close to the woman, whispering. "What do you know about ships that can fly?"

"Oh, I don't know much..." Majida stuck her hand out. Zala understood this to mean she wanted coin—the universal language of transaction.

"You don't understand... *Jelani* was taken by some sort of... sky ship."

Majida withdrew her arm in a fist. "How do you know that name?"

"I knew you wouldn't remember me." Zala sighed, trying her best not to sound offended.

"Oh, yes." A new light shone in the woman's eyes, one of objection and dissatisfaction. "You're that girl he ran off with. What's happened to my cousin?"

"We were attacked at sea. The Vaaji came. Jelani's alive, don't worry, that much I know. We've a songstone between us. The Vaaji Navy has him, and I also know if anyone knows anything about where they are keeping him or the location of that ship, it's *you*..."

Majida went silent for a moment as she touched her necklace. Zala's eyes widened when she realized what kind of beads hung from the woman's neck. How hadn't she noticed it before? "Wait, your neck... that can't be —"

"Yes, they're darkstones," Majida confirmed casually.

"It can't be," Zala gasped. "You'd be covered in the stoneskin if it were."

"Not all of us are infected by its touch, and it's a good repellent for those who might want to cross me." Majida glanced down to Zala's retreating feet. Zala stopped herself when she noticed. It couldn't be helped. She had no interest in becoming infected herself. "You may have noticed that that imperial guard didn't come very close to me. Her kind are especially threatened by the darkstones."

"Her kind?"

"Magic users. Mystics. The Blessed. Those with a'bara. Whatever you know them as."

"Like Jelani."

Majida's eyes went far off, as though a long-suppressed thought had resurfaced. "Yes. Just like him."

"So you'll help me find him?" Zala said, perhaps too eagerly.

"I said no such thing. I haven't seen him in years, not since he went off with those islanders—and then you. Never understood why his side of the family didn't join the rest of us here. And to leave us for that old *religion* of all things."

"Aren't you religious, too?" Zala asked, thinking back to the entrance's tapestry. "Isn't that why that man took your taxes?"

"He took his taxes because of the profession I've chosen, not because of the gods I may or may not pray to. The nobles and those Qibasi are opposed to my business. I'm sure at some point they'll shut me down, but they'll be hard-pressed to with my clientele. I'm sure you noticed some of them when you came in. Most of them are on Their Majesties' payroll. Still… they are doing quite well with these extortionate tithes in the meantime."

Zala dropped her head and pursed her lips before saying, "I'm sorry to hear it."

"I'm sure you're not," Majida shot flatly, her deadpan returning. The stark honesty in her words threw Zala off for a moment. "Tell me, what happened to my cousin?"

Zala told Majida all that she could remember from the past moons and that fateful day. How Jelani contracted his disease. How they decided to take up pirating, and, of course, the circumstances that split them apart. "Will you help me? Help *him*, at least?"

Majida turned her head, sticking out her hand again. Zala deflated, but she dug into her shirt and pulled out what she had stolen all the same. When she placed the sack of coin in Majida's hand, however, the woman did not move. So, reluctantly, she withdrew the sack of coin Shomari had given her as well. But still, Majida did not move or speak.

Zala's mouth fell open. "How much do you want? There isn't a… family discount or something?"

"Well, let's just say that I hope that was not the last of your coin."

Zala's silence and hanging jaw were answer enough. Majida rolled her eyes and slipped the sacks between her silk robes. "The information you seek will cost a fair bit more than what you've given me."

"How much?"

"Well, there are more ways to pay me than with coin. I can always," Majida ran her finger down Zala's arm, making her flinch, "use your services. I have a client coming in a few days who has a soft spot for the boy-ish types. He pays handsomely and you're flat enough for that job." Majida's eyes fell over Zala's figure. It was all Zala could do not to cover her body with her hands. "We'll have to get that ear fixed up, though. I have a healer who can get that done. And you've an odor about you. We'd need to do something about that straight away."

Zala would've liked a proper healer for her ear—the one on

the *Redtide* only reduced the flare-up, and even the brewmaster on Kidogo said nothing could be done...

But she knew the life of a brothel worker well enough; her time on the isles had shown her the toll it took many times over. She and Jelani had discussed it as an option before delving into pirating, and both agreed it wasn't something they ever wanted to do.

"I'll pass," Zala said as, out of the corner of her eye, a dancer enticed a patron with a contortion she didn't think was possible for humans to make, "as appealing as that sounds."

"Well then, that concludes our business." Majida lifted her hands, her jewelry clinking like music.

"But what about the coin I gave you?"

"What about it?"

Zala suppressed a groan as an angry static rose through her head. She should've known better than to give out her coin so quickly. Frustrated, Zala clutched at the curtains surrounding them. But before she withdrew them to exit, she turned, an idea springing to mind. "Even with the coin you took, I don't think that'll be enough for what that man who came here earlier wanted."

"Who? Vaziri? That nothing of a man is all talk."

"Perhaps he is. But that woman that was with him seemed like she meant business. She's a Vaaji elite, no? A mystguard... or, is it *sindisin* they call them here? That's what that insignia on her sash meant, right?"

"*Sindisi.* You've a sharp eye, love. But remember my lucky charm." Majida lifted her necklace. "I think I'll be fine."

"That might keep most people away, but it won't help you indefinitely. If a noble like him wants you, he'll have you."

Majida ran her fingers over the stones on her necklace, considering Zala's words. "And what exactly are you offering in assistance?"

"If I handled your tax collector problem..." Zala trailed off, her tone leading. "Would that give me the information I want?"

"It would." Majida nodded. "But that's an impossible task.

Vaziri surrounds himself with dozens of guards. And even if you did get rid of him, another would simply take his place."

Zala gestured with casual hands. "I'll work out the details."

"So… what? You're going to undo decades of imperial policy? That seems a lofty goal."

"Either way, what do you have to lose? I'm the only one taking any risks here."

Majida pressed her fingers into her chin, her forehead creased in thought.

Zala continued in haste. "Look, I'm not going to do anything with the information, not like you're thinking. I couldn't give a damn about what your Navy is up to, or what taxes they want from their people. I just want my husband back…"

Zala didn't understand why Majida was so resistant. It seemed as though she didn't care for her cousin at all, as though she had written him off as just some religious zealot long ago. The woman couldn't hide her displeasure for this Vaziri person, yet still, she sat stewing in her thoughts.

Abruptly, Zala saw a change in her expression, like the woman had been going through the same thought process as she, and drew to the same conclusion. In the end, all the risk fell on Zala's shoulders.

"We have a deal…" Majida searched for a name.

"Zala. My name is Zala."

"Zala," Majida repeated sweetly. "A beautiful name. Are you originally from the Isles? I don't remember. Your accent is a bit off."

"It's not where I was born," Zala confessed. "But it's where I went when I was old enough to know what was better."

Majida drew her fingers over her lips inquisitively. "You've the grit of the Isles with none of the stupidity. You may well be able to deliver as you say, then. But don't take too much time. I'll give you this much for free: our great and glorious military doesn't make a habit of keeping prisoners for long."

"Thank you." Zala bowed her head. "Trust me, I'll get it done."

Excitement charging her limbs, she pulled the curtain away

quickly and dashed straight into a tall, robed figure. The low grunt of a man sounded off in shock, and the figure stumbled for a moment, his hood falling back from his head.

"A-apologies, sir," Zala said, her voice stuttering as she helped to steady him. "I-I didn't see you there."

"No, forgive me," the man strained, turning to her with an odd expression.

A shockwave cut through Zala's chest at the sight of the man. He had a distinct scar down his chin which cut through a short beard over olive-toned skin.

No…

It couldn't be him…

She was seeing things. It's just what she wanted to see, not what actually was. But before she could get another look at the man's chin, he was already pulling on his hood again to hide it.

"I've already had my fill today. I don't need another," he said. Zala hadn't noticed she was still holding him up tightly as she stared at his shadowed face. "And you're not my type, girl. Latif, Altair, have her unhand me."

"Let him go, won't you, love?" Majida intoned politely before either of her men could move forward.

Zala let go of the man, though everything in her being screamed for her not to. Instead she stood there shell shocked as he walked away.

"I thought you said you didn't wish to work for me," Majida chuckled.

"I… I don't," Zala answered almost to herself, still eyeing the man as he exited.

"What's wrong?"

"I think… I think I may know him."

CHAPTER 17
ZALA

THE MOMENT ZALA ESCAPED THE BROTHEL, WITH ITS PUNGENT smell of flowers and perfumes, and back out to the stink of the city, Mantu bombarded her with a wave of questions. When she told him how she had given up all their money for very little information, he almost burst a vein.

"You was 'posed to get information on that sky ship and Duma, not take on some job against a damned tax collector!"

Zala wasn't looking at him though, staring at a certain dark cloak through the crowd. "She wouldn't give me the info without somethin' in exchange."

"Eight sacks of coin ain't enough?" Mantu shook his head. "You got played, chana."

Zala bit back her retort. There wasn't much she could say in rebuttal. She knew she had got the short end of the stick, and Mantu's words didn't help her confidence.

"If you two could stay your bickering for one moment." Shomari pointed a finger into the crowd. "I think I might be knowing that man."

Zala followed the path of Shomari's finger, and her heart leapt as she realized he was pointing to the same man she had bumped into.

"It's him, isn't it? That dikala from the sky ship, right?" Zala watched him press between two commoners. "How would you know though? You can't even see his face."

Shomari continued with a purr. "The dikala gave me a good fight. I do not forget someone with moves like that. He's got the walk of a real swordsman." Zala couldn't see it. She shrugged. Shomari waved a paw with his signature grin. "Novices like you would not be understanding."

"Then what are we waiting for?" Zala asked. "Damn that tax collector. This one can lead us straight to Jelani."

"And Captain Nubia, possibly," Shomari reminded her.

"And Duma," Mantu added. "And I ain't forgot about that sky ship you promised us either, *Captain*."

Right…

Zala nodded. She would need Mantu and Shomari if she was to subdue the man when they caught up. No need to ruffle feathers. "Just stick with me and we'll find them all. We need to be careful though, we'll easily lose him in this mess if we're not." She gestured to the masses clustered shoulder to shoulder. "And if we all follow him together, he'll make us. So we need to split. I'll be his shadow."

"All right then, Cap'n," Shomari said as he split off into a side alley. "I will be taking the high ground."

Mantu cracked his knuckles. "And I got your backs."

The trio followed the man on their three tracks. Shomari took to the rooftops, hiding behind raised towers and low overhangs. Mantu shifted between the entrances of bathhouses, food vendors, and blacksmiths, feigning interest in each before moving on. Zala was the most straightforward, keeping as close to the man as she could, letting the crowd guide her small frame.

She saw more young children as she went, most wearing rags for clothing that hung from boney shoulders—if they wore anything at all. After crossing a district filled with crumbling temples, they passed into an area with large, newer structures with golden doors only a few strides from the starving children.

The stark difference nearly stunned Zala to a halt, but she forced herself to focus on the retreating back of the robed man ahead of her. For all its faults, her home city would never be so negligent of their poor and needy. How could there be such a difference between two capital nations? How could the noblemen here simply step over those who were suffering?

The contrast became less and less severe as they pushed higher into the center of the city and up the hill. Zala caught sight of Shomari, who stood atop a roof, blending against a statue set atop a temple's high dome. She turned to look for Mantu, who wasn't hard to find—he was almost a head taller than everyone else in the throng. He gave her a small salute, then pretended to ask the price of a vender's wooden figurines.

After turning down their twelfth corner, they crossed into a wide street and the sky filled with the sight of dozens of marbled statues, which Zala assumed were the likenesses of kings and rulers from ages past. Each of them sat poised along a stair landing of their own, and they all led up to a mountain of a palace. Before the massive structure stood a wall the height of six or seven men stood tall. Where the rest of the city held buildings of two, maybe three stories, the structures within the wall stacked high into the sky, growing larger and larger atop the hill they stood upon, where a multi-towered fortress rose above the rest: The palace of al-Anim.

Jasmiin Towers.

If Jelani was going to be anywhere, it had to be there.

But Zala needed a plan. How could she stop the man they followed and question him? There were too many eyes on the wide road. Zala looked over her shoulder to find Mantu—perhaps he could think of something. But as she scanned the bustling sea of commoners and nobles she could no longer find his towering figure.

Stopping in her tracks, she darted her eyes to every corner, every vendor and storefront she could. Her breath quickened and her skin warmed with nervous heat. She saw nothing but chins and shoulders, too damned short to see anything else.

Shoving through a trio of noblemen, she found a set of crates alongside a storefront and climbed onto them for a better vantage point. She ignored those who complained about her pushing as she shielded her eyes from the high-noon sun.

C'mon, ðikala. Where'd you go?

Zala did her best not to think the worst as the seconds raced by. But there was no sign of the pirate at all. She turned her gaze up to Shomari, who was continuing his movement from rooftop to rooftop. Zala followed the pakka's gaze to the hooded target, who had thankfully stopped to inquire about something near a hash vendor.

Taking another scan of the streets, Zala saw a flash of light glint between a dark alley. A darkened *empty* alley. Her eyes traveled farther down the road as a second glimmer caught her attention. Zala whipped her head back to the alley with raised eyebrows. There was nothing there that would glisten, no metal, just a collection of tattered crates. She squinted, doing her best to make sense of the dark shadows. There was no mistaking the perpetual shine that seemed to flutter from nowhere. It could have just been a child playing with some glass somewhere…

Just as she was about to discount the flashing as a trick of the light, a disembodied head and arm broke through an invisible plane of the alley—Mantu's head!

Zala blinked twice as the pirate strained against the unseen, his brow cut through with a deep gash, blood trailing into his beard. His mouth opened in the shape of a scream, but nothing came out. Instead, his face contorted in an eerie silence. Before he could shout again, the unseen force pulled his floating head and arm back into the empty alley.

Zala's heart dropped. *Ekko…*

The Rovers had found them.

Zala looked to the Vaaji officer they had been trailing. He was already exchanging his coin with the vendor. Zala couldn't go back for Mantu *and* keep her eyes on their target. But the image of Mantu's twisted face kept flashing in her mind.

Maybe if she got Shomari's attention she could have the pakka go back to check it out. But as she waved her hands up to the roof, Shomari didn't as much as twitch his ear, his focus too keen on his target.

Her turmoil held her feet to the crates she stood on in indecision, but one voice within her rang out louder than the other. It told her she needed to turn back. There was only one thing she could do, she *should* do.

She could almost see Jelani's smile as she made the decision. The smile she so desperately needed to save.

Damn you and your morals, Jelani.

Zala hustled into the crowd, squeezing her way toward the dark alley. As she approached, the glint of light continued to flash like a firefly. And like before, she saw nothing but an empty back street, no different from any other. Zala stomped forward across the alley's threshold.

The sight before her made her heart stop.

Entangled between two women robed in Qibasi fashion, Mantu twisted on his heel as he dodged a wicked dagger strike that caught the sunlight at its tip. The air tasted oddly sterile on Zala's tongue, and the sounds of the fight seemed to be trapped within the tight corridor.

Zala caught sight of a third figure at the far end of the alley. He might've been wearing full Qibasi robes too, but she knew it was Ekko. He sat with crossed legs, his back to Zala in what looked like a meditative state. Without the use of Gods' Glass, even maintaining the image of a back street was too much for him. And to think he cloaked an entire ship a week ago.

Zala shot forward, pulling at the closest woman's arm before the pirate could sink her dagger into Mantu's shoulder.

The woman responded with an elbow to Zala's gut. Zala hunched over, her breath stuck in her throat. She lifted her gaze with a hardened expression, and she hardened her mind.

For once, Zala had a size advantage on her opponent. And it seemed the other woman knew it too, crouching in a low stance as she circled Zala. Then, with a slow movement, the woman attacked again.

Zala dodged the first of the woman's intermittent and sluggish stabs. Had the Rover not been clearly tired, Zala suspected her opponent could've won with speed alone. But her strikes came slow, drained of any bite. Zala could thank Mantu for that later if they survived.

After two more missed strikes, Zala became comfortable with

the distance and timing of the blows, and on the next move from the Rover, Zala intercepted the dagger and twisted it out of the woman's hand. Before the other pirate realized she was disarmed, Zala stabbed her between shoulder and breast in pure reaction.

The woman slumped over with a thud, letting out a pained shriek. Zala could only see the Rover's bloodshot eyes through the veil she wore—a pair of eyes she recognized. In the woman's fall, the head wrap that had covered her head had pulled slightly loose to reveal a single loc beaded in yellow and black.

Marjani? Zala thought in horror as the woman's body folded down, still as stone.

Zala's gaze shot instantly to Ekko at the far end of the alley, Ekko who had turned at the sound of his wife's shriek. He and Zala locked eyes with one other, and despite Ekko being covered save for his eyes, Zala knew his mouth must've been slack. Sweat dripped down his eyes. There was only an instant, but Zala tried her best to convey her sincere apology.

"Concentrate, kijana," grunted the woman who tussled with Mantu, and Zala recognized with a stab of fresh fear that the voice belonged to Lishan. "Don't break the wall. I'll handle these two."

Lishan clutched Mantu's wrists then kicked off his chest. Her Qibasi robes flared at her sides as she twisted in the air. At the top of her spin, she uncurled and landed a few paces from Zala, the dagger in the pirate's hand like the pointed tail of a scorpion.

And Zala knew too well how lethal that tip could be.

CHAPTER 18
ZALA

SHIT, SHIT, SHIT, WAS ALL ZALA COULD THINK AS SHE PARRIED Lishan's slashes with her own dagger.

She never liked knife fighting. It was too damned precise and too damned hard to deflect and defend in such short distances. Lishan seemed to know that too. That must've been the reason she lunged for Zala in the first place.

The easier target.

Get up, Mantu! Zala shouted to herself. But that kick he took was nasty.

Within seconds, Zala had already taken three cuts to her blade hand at the knuckle, wrist, and forearm. Lishan was like a panther, relentless and exact with her attacks, her eyes cold and unforgiving, a shadow with a knife. And it seemed like she knew what Zala would do before Zala did it. Which, of course, she did.

Damn mystic seers and their short-sight.

A pair of weighty, blistered hands spread out and over Lishan's chest. Mantu pressed her in a bear hug and lifted her from her feet. Surprised by his heroics, Zala almost missed the opportunity to stab at her very vulnerable opponent. And when she did lunge, she was too late. Before Zala reached even halfway close, Lishan threw out a kick with the heel of her boot, catching

Zala's blade at its flat—an impossibly precise move for any normal fighter.

Zala's momentum twisted backward as she slipped and fell over a loose rock, and her head slammed hard against the ground. Mantu hefted the would-be assassin into the side of the stone building, where she too thudded against the dirt-ridden alley.

"Gimme that," Mantu grunted, snatching the dagger from Zala's hand. "The woman's a bloody seer."

I know, Zala thought through a ringing head as she rubbed at the knot welling beneath her short hair. She would've said it out loud but she was in too much pain to speak.

Mantu rushed for Lishan as Zala thought back on what Jelani had told her about seers with short-sight. There was only really one defense against them: false reads—mind feints, as he called them. That had always been difficult for Zala. She was always so blunt with her words, her thoughts, and intentions. No wonder Mantu was able to surprise her too. Zala, and most everyone else who fought the seers tended to forget they didn't actually have a sixth sense of danger—unless they were particularly powerful— they just could see images of the near-future.

Lifting to her feet, Zala watched as Mantu pushed forward. She had seen him fight many times. He was usually more brutal, more forward with his height and weight advantage. Yet as he struck at the Rover, his feints seemed twice as many as she had usually seen from him. It almost looked like he was fighting as Shomari would. And it was working. Lishan's steps stuttered, her feet unsure whether to dance her forward in offense or backward in retreat.

Zala raised her eyes to the rooftops. Shomari must've noticed she and Mantu were gone by now. Where *was* the damned cat? With Lishan working through fatigue like she was now, Zala knew the pakka would be more than a match for the woman. He proved as much only a week ago. But even if he backtracked to find them, he'd see nothing but an empty alley as Zala had.

So, she narrowed her gaze onto Ekko, who still sat with pinched eyes at the alley's end. She might be no help to Mantu, but she could do something about the mystic.

Rushing around Mantu and Lishan, Zala ran toward the illusionist. When she was mere paces away from the man, he opened his eyes, the illusion of his wall flickering at his back. He was crying.

I'm sorry, Ekko.

In rhythm with her run, Zala kicked out with the heel of her foot, forcing the pirate on his back. The mirage broke, revealing the city dwellers behind it. Zala tried to shout for help, but no sound escaped her mouth. She glanced down to Ekko, who had a hand held out in her direction, silencing her.

A flash of the sky ship came to Zala's mind again. Like then, she wanted so badly to call out to Ekko, to let him know this was all a misunderstanding, and that they could work this out. Maybe that would've been possible if they hadn't switched *Redtide's* flag, or if Zala hadn't just stabbed Marjani.

They were past explanations now—Ekko's snarl and tear-streaked face made that plain enough, and he lifted his second hand, oscillating it toward the open alley where his illusionary barrier materialized once more.

Zala was trapped, and she knew there was only one way out of this: *through* Ekko.

But she didn't have to hurt him, she just needed to break his concentration. Zala flung forward another kick, but this time Ekko caught it and held her leg in place. He buckled his own legs around Zala's right calf, pulling hard, and Zala fell to her side with a gasp—straight onto her wounded ear. Pain seared through her head as she felt the warmth of blood pouring from the reopened wound.

Hurt stacked upon hurt.

The mystic pounced on Zala, giving her no time to reorient her dizzying head as she gasped another silent shriek. His hands wrapped around her neck and squeezed hard. Was Ekko really about to kill her? How did he not know she'd never want to intentionally do him or Marjani harm? Just a week ago he was saving her ass. Now his eyes filled with the red heat of anger.

Zala tried to kick at Ekko's back, his knees, anything her feet could find. But her legs were just too short. The longer she struggled, however, the less focused the man became. At the corner of her eye, she saw the illusionary wall dwindle again. Through each flash, a new image materialized—a group of merchants walking by, a mother and father chasing after their children, and then... a dirty urchin who canted his head at the alley.

The child rubbed at his eyes twice. As Zala continued to twist and turn under the pirate's grip the fake wall broke for longer periods, and with it, intermittent spurts of sound leaked through. During one of these stretches, Zala grunted and waved her hand at the child, whose mouth had dropped down in shock. When he finally decided he wasn't crazy, he ran off screaming and calling for help, though his voice cut off every other moment.

"Damnit, we have to go," came a strained voice from the side. Zala couldn't turn her head but she assumed it was Lishan. "We're no good to the Captain caught or killed."

Ekko, still squeezing at her throat, didn't listen. His glare was laced with unadulterated murder.

"Citywatch, there's a man attacking a woman!" the little urchin screamed. A few gasps followed as other city dwellers made sense of what was going on within the alley.

"Get away from her!" purred a voice from above. Shomari's voice.

"Did you hear me, kijana?" Lishan seethed again. "Let's go."

"She killed her, Lishan," Ekko cried into Zala's face. "She deserves—"

But Zala couldn't hear the rest of what she deserved. Lishan rushed over her, tackling Ekko away and pulling his hands from Zala's throat. Zala coughed and rubbed at her neck as she watched the Captain practically carry Ekko away into the crowd. The illusion finally broke and people started their double-takes down the alley. One would-be hero even tried to grab at Lishan but she swiped at him with her dagger and continued on her way, shifting like the shadow she was.

Shomari—still disguised in his turban and dark robes—jumped down from the rooftops just behind Mantu. He was already brandishing his rapier.

Mantu turned on his heel. "Where in the hells have you been?"

"He couldn't see us," Zala explained through a rasp as she heaved herself to her feet, thumbing behind her. "It was Ekko. He had an illusion up."

"Besides," Shomari said, "I cannot be saving you hairless *all* the time. I am glad to see you can handle yourself, though." He nodded to Marjani who lay still. Fresh guilt festered through Zala's stomach. Clearly, the pakka hadn't recognized who she was. "Were you not saying to me 'no killing' this morning?"

"As much as I love a compliment," Mantu said, eyeing over Zala's shoulder. "We've gathered a bit of a crowd."

Shomari pulled at Zala's arm, pushing his way through the back street, away from the commoners who had started filling the narrow path. The nobles watched from a safer distance away. Mantu brought up the rear, pushing Zala forward and hiding his bloodied face from the citywatch who approached.

"Make way!" one shouted, holding up his curved sword above his head. "Make way, you gutter rats!"

"Over there," Mantu nodded toward another dark alley cramped between a bookbinding shop and a dye maker. It was out of the way yet still in view of the palace gates, the other alley, and the wide road.

Once they had settled into the shadows, Mantu pressed his fingers around his face, wincing at every sting. It looked like his nose may have been broken too—Zala could never tell with him; he'd broken it so many times. After a few more tender touches and some flinches, he caught Zala staring at him.

"Thanks, chana," he said.

"Don't mention it," Zala frowned, pressing her hand into her throbbing head. Blood came down her arm and onto her cheek.

It was bad enough they broke what Zala assumed was the start of an *actual* alliance. It was worse that it seemed Ekko and Marjani were pissed enough to want to see them all dead. If only she had a minute to explain to them... none of this would have happened. At least not as bad as it went. But it was impossible to clue them in, and they would've refused helping Mantu with the lie about his past revealed to them.

Shomari dabbed some essence of dawa root on Mantu's wounds as they observed the citywatch carry Marjani's body from the alleyway. In her haste, Zala hadn't even realized she was stabbing at the woman's heart. It was just all out of pure reaction. Judging from the woman's bloodied torso, her aim had been true. Zala turned her gaze away from Marjani's body, away from the beaded loc that rocked to and fro under the lifted hands of the citywatch.

It seemed like the whole borough had come to see what all the fuss was about. Zala scanned the crowd, hoping no one had followed them out the back alley. They seemed safe for now, but anyone could start asking questions. She didn't think she had the energy to talk her way out of another bad situation. She was injured and her spirits were beyond drained.

"Here. Take this." Shomari handed her some dawa for her wounds.

"It was Marjani," she choked near to tears. "I killed… Marjani… we shouldn't stay here."

"It was going to be you or her, chana."

"I know, I know, but—"

A dark robe caught her eye at the back of the growing crowd. She couldn't be sure, but it looked like their man. What did Shomari say about the way he moved? She watched and waited a moment, and her breath caught in her throat as she held a hand out to Shomari, who had started dabbing dawa root at her brow.

Come on, turn. Let me see your face.

But the figure was too keen to get a good look at what was going on, his head bobbing left and right for a crack in the crowd.

"Hang on a moment," Zala said offhandedly, pointing to the man. "Tell me, is that our kijana?"

Shomari's ear twitched, and he stuck his nose out in the air. When his eyes became slits, Zala knew she was right. And in the next moment, the hidden officer peeled away from the crowd and headed back to the palace gates. As he turned, Zala caught sight of the distinct scar across his beard.

There was still hope, or at least some semblance of it. That's what Zala told herself to forget about Marjani, at any rate. There was still a mission at play, and it still needed getting done.

"Stay here," she said, handing the root back to Shomari. "I'll need a distraction."

"What are you going to do?" Mantu asked. "I ain't tryin' to get attacked by them Rovers again."

"I don't have time to explain. Can you do it?"

Mantu furrowed his brow in thought as he looked to the guards at the palace gates. "I think I know what you got in mind. Go for it, chana."

Zala grinned, and slipped along the edge of the crowd, using the grand statues leading up to the gate for cover.

"Someone, help me! This wretched pakka tried to pickpocket me!" Mantu pointed to Shomari, whose cat-eyes went wide as though to say: *what in the Gods' names are you doing?*

"A pakka?"

"Yeah, yeah, he attacked that woman!"

"He's over there!"

"That's what I said, saabi. He's beating on that man now. Look at his nose!"

The guards at the palace gate caught sight of Mantu and Shomari. The taller one waved the black-robed man inside the fortress, while the shorter went to check the commotion. Zala pressed her back against the fortress' outer wall, sliding closer to the gate. A smear of blood stretched across the sandstones, so she ripped a piece of her shirt to stay the bleeding. Though only one guard left his post, Mantu and Shomari's antics distracted the other. She just needed him to stay that way while the gate closed slowly behind her target.

"I thought the cats weren't allowed this far up in the city!" Mantu raised a fist.

Shomari slipped out of his disguise and raced up the side of the adjacent building. He climbed atop a statue in full view, wagging his tail with mirth.

"What are you playing at, cat," the guard spat. "You think we won't chase you?"

The rest of the crowd raised their voices and pointed to the rooftops as Zala inched her way forward on the gates. Two more paces and she'd be at the threshold. She held her breath tight, and hoped the guard would not see her out the corner of his eye. The helmet he wore should've obstructed his view, right?

She grabbed the edge of the gate for balance and peered into the fortress' courtyard. There were a dozen soldiers training with sabers, and a dozen more with crossbows. Even if she slipped inside, there was no way she'd get past them all. But the black-robed man would be lost into the palace if she didn't move.

"Rabi, hurry and get that damned thing down," the guard called out with agitation.

Zala almost jumped out of her skin; his voice was so close. It was now or never. She bit down on her lip, trying to find her courage, then pushed forward.

But a tiny grip around her ankle stopped her.

"They said to look for the woman getting herself into trouble." Zala turned to see a small child with two missing teeth and rags strewn over his shoulders—the same kid who had called for help earlier. "You the one they is calling Zala?"

"Who's 'they?'" she whispered.

"Don't go. They'll kill you good in there. Or worse, capture you."

Zala kept looking between the child and the distracted guard. She didn't have much time. "You haven't answered me."

"That tiny woman sent us."

"Us?" Zala asked. The boy pointed to other children tucked away in the crowd. One of them tugged at Mantu's tunic pointing to an empty market stall to hide in. "Tiny woman? What do you mean?"

"The one with the wings."

Zala's heart leapt. "Fon? Where is she?"

"Back home. But we must go," the child said, still tugging.

Zala turned her head back to the entrance. She couldn't be sure she would find this mysterious man again. And who knew if she could trust the child? Maybe he was sent by Lishan as a trap. No, that made little sense. The kid had saved her from getting choked out. If he was one of Lishan's, he'd have let it happen.

"Come, come." The boy kept to his pulling. "Before the guard comes back."

"All right, all right." Zala grabbed at his wrist to stop his tugging. At the very least, she knew where the man was headed. Maybe that would be enough. At least now she knew where to start her search. But first…

"Take me to Fon."

CHAPTER 19

LISHAN

"We have to go back," Ekko grunted loudly in Lishan's ear. It still rung from one too many blows to the head from that damn giant of a pirate, sending her head into a spin. "Did you hear me, chana? We have to go back!"

Lishan grabbed Ekko by his collar, shoved him into an alley between two weaver's shops, and threw him against a wall. "What did you just call me?"

"Sorry, Captain, sorry… I ain't thinkin' straight." Ekko twisted uncomfortably under the weight of her grip. Unlike most women, Lishan had weight, reach, and height against the man. And that didn't even account for her short-sight Blessing.

Ekko's next words came much lighter and strained. "But we can't just leave her behind."

Fear laced the man's eyes like a dog scolded by its master. Lishan loosened her grip and drew back from his round face blotched with red. She hadn't even realized how close in she was on his neck—much more and she'd have crushed his windpipe like some wolf to its prey. Had it really come to this? How did Captain Nubia manage it? How had she always kept the crew going? She would hardly ever put hands to them, yet they listened to *her* without question. What was Lishan doing wrong? It had only been a day under her command and she had already lost almost everything they had worked for all these years.

Lishan always trusted her gut for good reason. And ever since they hooked up with Zala's crew on that deserted isle, she knew something ill would come of it.

"The citywatch will have Marjani," she finally said, freeing Ekko from her clutch. "She had those Qibasi robes on. They'll treat her kindly if she's still..." She trailed off at the sight of Ekko's haunted look. "Let's just regroup at the Harbor's Flask first. We need to see who's still with us. Whatever's going on with Marjani, good or bad, she'll be taken to one of the healers in the city. These Vaaji are supposed to have fairly good... what do they call them? Hospitals? Going after her now wouldn't help none."

Lishan looked Ekko over. His robes were caked in blood on one side. She stared down at her own garb which had been torn through and tattered with a few streaks of blood lining the hems.

"Take those off," she ordered. "They'll do more harm than good now in our state. Take off the Rover uniforms too."

Slowly, Ekko stripped himself of his robes as Lishan did the same. Peering out of the alley, she saw they were just on the border of a new district. Opulent villas had dwindled the farther down the hill they had come from. Lishan hadn't wanted to stop so soon. They were still too close to the palace and the watchful eye of the city guards for her liking, and Sycamore Square was still a few districts away. If it hadn't been for Ekko's chatter in her ear, she'd still have them moving.

"C'mon, let's go," she said harshly as she discarded her robes near a bucket of old wash rags. "And be quick about it."

Back straight with a gait befitting a local on a normal midday stroll, Lishan pushed them forward through the market stalls until they came upon an open plaza. There was an ornate fountain set between a collection of shops and flats; the statue that sat within the fountain depicted some large man bedecked in animal skins and a necklace made of what looked like manticore quills. His hand stretched out overhead and the fountain's offshoot sprayed out and arched like a waterfall.

"I don't recognize that statue," Lishan murmured to Ekko at her side.

"That's Moharam the Uniter," Ekko answered. "He was supposed to be Vaaj's last True Blessed. That was over five-hundred years ago. And then—"

"Okay, okay, didn't need the whole spiel on the man," Lishan told him as she scanned the district. She knew how Ekko could get when he started reciting facts, a defense mechanism against the sorrow that was surely threatening to swallow him whole.

The air smelled of forest shavings mixed in with a fragrance of grilled meat. A few youngsters lounged near the fountain, while others ate and chatted. Lishan thought there was some festival taking place, until she realized it must've been a midday break for these carpenters. A sonamancer walked along one of the balconies to start chanting an al-Qiba prayer.

It was all too crowded for Lishan's liking. She glanced over her shoulder, making it look like she was interested in a wood carving of a weaver bird. A quartet of city guards brought up their rear near the steps they had just climbed down.

"Keep your wits, but do you think we've been made?" Lishan asked Ekko as she moved to his side to look at another vendor's offerings.

Ekko faked a cough into his arm and flitted a glance upward. Then he turned back to the fountain to say, "Maybe. Can't be sure. Does your sight need more time to make a read? I know that fight took its toll."

"I've been trying," Lishan admitted, but right now she could only muster half a heartbeat of the future, which was less than useless to them.

She glanced to their exits. Two other avenues cut into the plaza, each of which were watched by a pair of guards.

"What's the play?" Ekko asked. "More disguises?"

"No, they got a vantage point on us," Lishan said as neutrally as possible. "Us trying to get into another disguise will just give us away. Just act like we're on break like everyone else. We'll make our way *very slowly* to that western avenue. The play is not to be seen if you can manage it... how are you feeling? Sorry I didn't ask before."

"I've settled down a bit. I'll be all right," Ekko said as he followed behind Lishan through the bustling crowd.

The plaza was packed tight with domed structures and arched entrances into shops and homes. But this particular area was free of the usual back streets, even tight ones.

As they approached the center near the fountain, Lishan braved another look over her shoulder. Two of the guards who had come down from the stairs stood waiting. The other two... she couldn't see.

She made an effort not to turn her head quickly as she scanned the square. As her eyes passed over one of the storefronts with brightly-colored dresses hung from lines, she saw one of the cloaked guards. Most in that situation would've turned away and avoided the eye-contact—a mistake Lishan had learned not to do years ago. The welts she earned on her back from her father's guards all those years ago served as a constant reminder. Instead, she held the guard's gaze, even gave him a little grin. And just like she thought he would, he looked away, his searching stare more interested in a suspicious pair near a rug shop nearby.

Ekko, however, was not as subtle.

"Shit, I think I've been made," he whispered in her ear. "The guard just by that stall sellin' riqqs. I know I shouldn't have looked away, but it's habit, ya know."

Lishan held Ekko close and laughed like he had told her some funny joke. Though her eyes were squinted in a fit of giggles her gaze was intent. Sure enough, the guard Ekko spoke of was shouldering his way through the crowd toward them.

"Yeah, he marked you," she said through a faux chuckle. "We're gonna make a move, but don't be too quick about it. Just behind you there's a chicken coup near the group of elders playing King's Way. I need you to walk by it and accidentally trip over the latch."

"Understood," Ekko answered a bit too nervously for Lishan's taste.

"Good," Lishan said. "All right... be slow about it. Go in three, two, one."

She and Ekko split.

At the very least Lishan knew her side was free of any suspicious eyes. Ekko just needed to lose his tail. After a few strides and a few "excuse mes" through the crowd, Lishan found herself under the shadow of the sonamancer's balcony. The man above began singing a hymn.

Again, Lishan eyed the western exit where the guards stood tall. She didn't think they'd have enough time to be informed about what had happened near the palace, but she didn't know the city well enough yet to know how fast word could travel. There were already a few checkpoints she would've liked to have avoided when she was tracking Zala and her wretched crew. Right now, she didn't have the time to hit another roadblock.

The high-pitch of a series of *"bwok-awks"* drew her attention to where Ekko had made off to. Almost all the heads in the plaza turned to see a mess of feathers drifting through the air. One of the chickens even knocked over the King's Way board the elders were playing with, which earned a tirade from the old women as they chased the browned-feathered birds. With all the commotion, Lishan expected to see Ekko making his hike away with no issue, but she caught sight of his pale face heading *back* to the fountain.

What in Yem's name is he doing?

Then she saw that the guard hadn't fallen for the ruse at all, and was just behind Ekko. Lishan flitted her gaze to the second guard who marched from between the flowing hung dresses and straight for Ekko. The fool was gonna get pinched.

Lishan let out a long sigh. Ekko wasn't the best at this whole losing his tail thing.

No wonder Marjani tracked him at Pyrus so easily, she thought, knowing it was entirely the wrong thing to tell him when she saved his ass.

Digging into her belt, she pulled a sack of coin and threw it into the air while shouting, "Praise Genizebi!"

Shimmers of silver and bronze rained down across the square to the raucous fervor of the laborers taking their breaks. Where before the air was filled with the sonamancer's sung hymns and the workers who sung back to him, now the plaza was filled with shouts and screams. The crowd converged where the coins fell, not caring who they shoved or trampled. Lishan pushed forward, dipping in and out the crowd like a leaf through a cyclone of elbows and knees.

On instinct, she steeped herself into the flow of her a'bara, using her mystical eye to pre-judge each movement within the mass of bodies. Ghostly images sprang before her just before their movements became reality. It didn't take long for her to snatch up Ekko's arm and pull him away. His dark curls were disheveled and falling over his crazed-looking eyes.

"Quick," she shouted over the crowd's hollers. "We don't have time to talk our way through a potential check-point. How long can you hold an illusion right now?"

"Five seconds, maybe."

Lishan grunted. It was possible… but the timing of it needed to be perfect.

"Ugh, fine. Follow me," she said as she set her short-sight to work again.

Factoring in Ekko's trailing body and awkward sway was more than difficult though. Despite her mystical abilities, this time she took a few elbows to the gut as she passed through. Twice when she recovered from the blows she looked back to find that all four guards had been giving chase now, but they were doing far worse than she was through the sea of people.

Lishan's heart raced as she and Ekko were free of the densest portions of the crowd. The guards at the western exit were thankfully preoccupied by the pandemonium. But at any moment they could cast their eyes on Lishan and Ekko.

"Right now," Lishan ordered. "It's gotta be right now."

Over her shoulder she saw as Ekko furrowed his brow in concentration. Just beyond him, one of the pursuing guards was still stuck between shoves and jabs as he shouted, "Stop them!" But his voice was lost in the cacophony.

Then, with bloodshot eyes, Ekko said, "We're cloaked. Let's go, let's go, let's go."

Lishan dashed forward between the guards, not caring if they felt a strange wind brush past their ears. The path behind them led to a dark avenue shadowed by two tall buildings on either side. Lishan counted the third second of Ekko's mystical time limit in her head as she saw a nook she and Ekko could slip into. She counted the fourth second as she pulled Ekko in with her. Then, on the fifth, when they were exposed again, she hunkered down and waited. Old rugs had been thrown against the sand-swept walls, barely covering them. If anyone made a proper look, they'd be caught, but Lishan was hoping any pursuers would just pass in haste.

"Where did they go?" came the voice of what Lishan assumed was one of the pursuing guards.

"Where did who go?"

"The two fugitives that were headed this way."

"Fugitives? What are you —"

The guard didn't get his answer as marching footsteps came echoing against the cobblestones. Lishan gripped her dagger tightly as one, two, three, and four of the guards passed by. None of them turned to look to where she was. It was a moment later when she finally allowed herself to let go of the breath she held trapped in her chest.

"Fucking hate palace guards," she heard a voice from the square say. "Come on, let's break this up. Whoever threw that coin must've tossed a fortune."

The pounding of boots receded into the plaza, then Ekko let out a long breath against Lishan's shoulder. He must've been holding his in even longer. "That was close…"

"Let's go," Lishan grunted. "Once they realize they've lost the trail they'll double back."

Returning to a casual walk, Lishan led the way through a series of corners and descending slopes she only vaguely remembered from her last visit to al-Anim, despite Captain Nubia telling the crew to remember all port towns backwards and forwards. When she entered a plaza with a large white-barked sycamore at its center, she knew they had made it. The descending afternoon sun shone through the red-orange leaves of the tree, and just beyond the tips of the low-hanging foliage, she could make out the arched entrance to the Harbor's Flask.

"Let's hope the others made it," Ekko said with a sigh.

"If Her waves were merciful, yes," Lishan answered as she made her way to the tavern. This plaza was far less busy than the other one, she assumed because the midday breaks for prayer and food were dying down now. Besides her and Ekko, there were only a few town dwellers that sat outside storefronts, some smoking from hash pipes, others just taking a breather.

"I sure could go for one of Akbar's Andalan Reds right now," she murmured as she pushed against the Flask's door.

"That was quite the little chase." A voice came from behind them before she could push fully into the tavern. "You might be just what I'm looking for... *Captain* Lishan."

There was no point trying to turn and fight. But the fact that they weren't already knocked across the head meant whoever was behind them wanted to talk. Lishan made a slow turn around, Ekko following her lead. They were met with the image of a slender man wearing a lilac tunic that stretched to the ground. His beard was sharp, and his hair was long and pulled back, no strand out of place. The posture he held, and his arms folded within his cuffs, spoke loudly of his utter confidence.

Lishan gave him the start of a scowl before saying, "How do you know who we are?"

"Unlike the Sapphire Isles, you pirate lot will quickly come to realize that information carries more weight than gold in this city." The man waited for a reaction. Lishan and Ekko didn't give him one. "That stunt you pulled at the harbor wasn't the smartest thing, bold as it was. If you want to survive here, you'll need to be sharper—"

"It was a traitor that gave us up."

The man pursed his lips. "Hmmm. Then perhaps you need to know your crew a bit better. Captain Nubia never had such troubles when she was at the helm, did she?"

Without thinking, Lishan shot forward with a sneer, but she was held back at each shoulder by a pair of hands. She turned to see two guards concealed in head wraps that covered their faces.

Next to her, Ekko was trapped in a similar hold with two more guards at his sides. Where had the guards come from? It was like they had materialized from thin air. She twisted hot eyes back to the man in lilac.

"Ah, I see..." he trailed off. "You've never had a ship or crew of your own, have you? Not as easy as it seems, is it?"

The man brushed past her and put a hand to the door leading into the Harbor Flask. He turned and said, "They call me the Collector, by the way. But you may refer to me as Vaziri." Clearly the man aimed for his name drop to be some great revelation, but Lishan didn't so much as twitch. "Come. Join me for a drink, pirates. The rest of your surviving crew awaits. I've a job for you lot."

CHAPTER 20
ZALA

T HE JOURNEY BACK DOWN TO THE HARBOR WAS MUCH EASIER than the one headed up toward the hills and the palace.

"We call this big street the Spine," the young urchin that led Zala and her crew said. "Fastest way to get through the city."

Zala and her crew followed the young boy—and several other youngsters who joined them along the way. At first, Zala thought they were headed back to Majida's brothel, but just before they turned the corner toward the Silks, they shifted onto an older, dilapidated road. The children slipped down paths that Zala wouldn't even think to take. Occasionally they'd come across a low-hanging gap that Mantu couldn't fit under.

"This is Old al-Anim," the boy said. "'A home for the forgotten and lost.'"

"Or at least that's what the shaman says," another small girl said as she limped at their side, a child-sized crutch under one of her armpits.

Zala ducked beneath a low-hanging stone that looked like it had once been a statue's arm before asking, "You're all kin?"

"Orphans," Mantu whispered into her ear. "They always come in spades in big cities like this."

"I'm not *that* green Mantu, even here."

That "always" wasn't strictly true. You wouldn't find many

orphans back in Jultia, Zala thought. But she didn't voice that aloud—she wasn't about to spill her humble origins to Mantu of all people, much less these children. Mentions of Jultia always led to obvious questions, and she had no time for them.

Zala watched as the children skipped ahead, each of their "outfits" more dirty than the last. Zala pondered if some of them were the same ones she had run into among the sewers.

The boy leading them kept staring at Zala, and eventually she couldn't help but ask, "What? Something on my face?"

"You have a death wish or something?" the boy asked. "You don't take on the masters and their fortress. No one survives in there."

"Well, I didn't have much of a choice," Zala said, then turned a frown to the boy. "And did you say 'masters'? I thought slavery was abolished here?"

The boy's face turned red. "Baba says we still is slaves. Even if we don't work for free no more."

Zala thought the other run-down buildings and mud huts outside the main city were bad, but they were nothing compared to the cracks that ran through the district they walked through now. The foul odor that stuck to its crushed pillars smelt like that kind that couldn't be scrubbed away without a whole lot of elbow grease. Many of the people had sick faces of green and mouths filled with yellowed teeth. Yet, surprisingly, few wore the dower faces that would normally match such ailing appearances.

In one corner, a quartet of children sang hymns from the Old Way. In another, a man dunked dirty clothes into a bucket for washing as naked children awaited their rags. Older women told children stories, using figures and dolls Zala recognized from when Jelani did the same years ago. The stories reminded her of the villages in Kidogo. Her husband had always been the children's favorite storyteller.

Zala continued to follow her tiny escorts into a small dwelling tucked between a collection of shanties. The children said they weren't allowed inside, but they let Zala go forward between the threshold hung with beads. Inside, shamans painted in greens of sage, emerald, and fern spoke in tongues, waving burned roots that billowed smoke above a dirt mound. When Zala got close enough, she could see the edges of a translucent wing—Fon's wing.

Despite her deafened ear, Zala almost fully heard the storm that thundered at her side, the storm that was Shomari rushing to Fon's side. Despite the very disgruntled looks of the shamans, Shomari lifted Fon's limp head, brushing her hair out of her bruised face.

"What happened?" Shomari asked in a panicked voice Zala thought she'd never hear from the pakka's maw.

"The Rovers happened," Fon replied, through a delicate rasp. "I... tried to disguise myself as... a child, but it's hard to hide... these things." She pointed to her wings, one of which was missing altogether. "One... of the Rovers... cut it clean."

Zala put a hand to her mouth to cover her gasp, coming to Fon's other side. "C-can you still—"

"Fly? No..."

"But you can still glide," Zala bit back the hitch in her throat, "like you were doing before when it was damaged, yes?"

The aziza shook her head sadly. "The shamans... don't think so."

"And what about Old Man Ode? Or that boy Rishaad?" Mantu stepped up behind Zala, making the very tiny room feel entirely too cramped. "Was they with you? Did you see 'em?"

"I didn't... see Ode, no," Fon said as Zala struck a frown. "But Rishaad was in the markets. He's—" She coughed up phlegm, which stuck to the bottom of her chin.

"Don't speak," Shomari cried and cleaned Fon up with his paw, not caring about the spit webbing between it.

Fon put a hand to Shomari's cheek and stroked his whiskers. "It's... okay, Shomari. The only reason I got away was because of... Rishaad. He distracted the ones who did this to me. There were so many of them though... I don't know how he got away."

"This is the kid's home," Shomari assured her. "I bet he knows a fair few holes he could hide in. I mean, look at us. We found a way."

Zala felt her eyes water as they traveled along the edge of

Fon's ruined wing, now laid out along the dirt mound she was lain against—completely unconnected. Her wings were not unlike that of a butterfly, four appendages that grew from her back. Most times, they seemed to shimmer with a perpetual glow. And that was still true of the two right wings that were still attached. But the other disconnected ones were almost as dull as the dirt they laid against.

Was this *Zala's* fault? Had she done this? Try as she might, Zala couldn't think of anything any of them could have done differently to get off that damned boat, but surely there had to have been something. She just couldn't see it.

This was the life of pirates.

Mantu was protecting himself, and seeing how serious the Rover threat was, Zala understood his caution. Fon knew that too. They all knew that when they agreed to do business with the "aggressive entrepreneurs" of the Sapphire Seas.

Zala turned to one of the shamans. "Thank you for taking her in. Do you think you can help her?"

"There aren't many aziza around these parts," the oldest of the shaman said through his patchy white beard. "Don't reckon there is much we even know *how* to do. We just been easin' the pain."

"There's no one here who can help her?" Zala asked anxiously.

"We pass our knowledge down from elder to elder," another shaman with loose and wavy hair down her shoulders said. "Over these past few years we've lost too many. And aziza are barely allowed in the city, except for those wretched whorehouses."

Zala looked the group over. They were younger than most shamans she had known. And when she walked into the slums, she had only seen one or two people she could truly call old.

"You all can stop looking at me like that, I'm fine." Fon pouted. "I have my life, at least, and nothing else is broken. What about you?" She nodded to Mantu, whose cut above his brow looked larger than Zala remembered. "Or you, friend." The aziza eyed Zala. Zala could only imagine what state she was in, but she felt fine. "Did the Rovers get to you too?"

Mantu nodded. "I had a little run in with a certain captain, illusionist, and—"

"Pather." Zala pinched the side of her temple. "That's how they found us so quickly when we made it out of the sewers. Marjani… she was sniffing us out."

Fon's eyebrows hiked up her forehead. "Marjani and Ekko did that to you all? I thought they would've understood why we had to do it…"

"It was mostly Lishan who did the actual hurtin'," Mantu snorted testily. "No surprises there."

"Well, at least Marjani and Ekko made it out okay…" Fon trailed off at Zala's look. "They are okay, ya?"

Zala swallowed hard, thinking back on that single beaded loc… She couldn't bring herself to say she killed one of their closest allies on the *Redtide*.

"Zala didn't have a choice," Mantu said for her. "It was her or me."

Guilt ate away at Zala's insides. It wasn't so cut and dry as all that, if she were honest with herself. If she had known Marjani was hidden away under those dark robes, she wasn't so sure she would've taken such swift action. Maybe there was a situation where she could stop Marjani and Ekko. Then it could have been four on one against Lishan.

"We gotta know how many of them Rovers there still are out there." Mantu knelt down to Fon. The shamans still stood in shock, a few of them seeming to want to cast the pirates out, but Mantu stood taller and wider than three of them combined.

"Did you get a good look on who had you?" Mantu asked Fon. "Did you see any others chasin' Rishaad?"

Fon arched her back and lifted herself on her elbows to speak. Her eyes pinched with pain. "It was Iokaja who had me pinned. She knew just where to cut to make it hurt. Rishaad tackled her off, then he told me to run, and I did." Fresh tears welled in her eyes. Shomari held her close, purring and nuzzling her to settle her weeping. "The citywatch came. I saw you all going into the brothel, but before I could get to you, the Captain…"

"Lishan," Mantu finished for her darkly.

"She had me when I wasn't looking. But then these little ones helped me." She pointed to the children who stole glances into the shanty.

"May Yem's waves bless you, little hairless," Shomari intoned his thanks in earnest, bowing his head deeply.

The boy who saved Zala smiled through the beads at the threshold. "We was thinkin' she was one of us at first. We ain't never seen a tiny woman with wings before."

"Nuh uh, I saw one walkin' down Shroud Street," the little girl argued from outside the beaded entrance.

"Yeah, yeah, but you always lie, Katya."

"My kind are usually much smaller. But I'm only half-aziza," Fon told the boy, gesturing for him to come closer. He shuffled his way into the room and sat next to Fon's dirt bedding, fiddling with his hands all the while. The shaman with the wavy hair gritted her teeth but stayed her tongue.

"Ah... zee... za," the boy sounded it out. Had he never heard the term before? Did the Vaaji really suppress wageni to that extent?

"That's right." Fon touched the boy lightly on his cheek, and he grinned warmly.

The wavy-haired shaman cleared her throat loudly.

"So. What brings you all here?" the shaman with the patchy white beard said. Perhaps he was the leader. He had great big eyes, and, under his paint, his skin showed a deep olive skin tone —the type of complexion brought on by hard labor. "The children tell me you were sneaking into the palace."

"One of the nobles has something I want," Zala confessed.

"I thought you were following that kijana because of Fon and Duma?" Mantu shot, stepping forward with a canted head.

"I... I was," Zala started. "But I also hoped he'd lead me to—"

The shaman cut in. "Whoever told you walking into Jasmiin Towers was a good idea, did not have your best interest in mind."

Mantu clinched his hands into fists. "We don't have time for this. We should just take Majida and force her to tell us what she knows."

"No, we shouldn't," Zala shot back. "I'd rather not go making more enemies than we already have. Or are the Vaaji and the Rovers not enough for you?"

"So, it was Majida who introduced you to the man?" the shaman asked as he dunked his hands in a barrel of water.

"Not exactly. We…" Zala turned her eyes away from Mantu. "I sort of ran into him. It was Shomari who recognized him properly."

Mantu stepped closer to Zala, whispering. "So why did you have us tail him all through the city? You could've led us straight into one of their dungeons. Did you even know that man could lead us to our people?"

"No…" Zala confessed. "I was hoping he'd lead me to Jelani specifically." Mantu's face screamed disbelief. "Don't give me that look. I didn't know what else to tell you! It was in the moment, and I knew that officer had to know *something* about him."

"Jelani's dead, Zala!" Mantu bellowed. "When will you get that through your head? He was my friend too, you know. One of the best men I knew. But he's gone, along with all the others."

"You don't know that!" Zala said, her voice demanding he take it back. "And I've got my songstone. He sings to me every night."

"Fine, so he's not dead *now*, but once they find out he's infected, they'll cast him aside, same as all the rest."

"They were keeping him with a bag over his head. They want something from him. But I can't wait around for them to get it. I don't have the time. You know that."

"What *I* know is that we tend to get into trouble whenever you put your husband first, chana." Mantu drew forward, his breath hot on her nose. "What about Ode… or Ajola… or Siya… or Duma. They all had their own shit too."

"Damnit, Mantu, I *know*. I didn't have to choose you back on the *Redtide*. I care about all of us, but he's my *husband*. I wouldn't hold you back from chasing Sniffs!"

He fixed her with a look. "Yes, you would."

Zala thought about it for a moment. *Shit.*

"What? You think I ain't know you were the reason Duma got captured?"

"Okay," she conceded with a sigh.

"You think I'm as dumb as a tokoloshe? That's all the Rovers talked about was how stupid that 'Captain Zala' was."

"Okay, I get it."

"You're lucky they didn't hang you from your thumbs. Were it not for Ekko and Marjani—"

"Stop it, Mantu. You win." She hated it, but it was true.

"All right, this is over now." Shomari stepped between them. "We have our friend back. This is a good moment and you two are souring it." Mantu tried to get past Shomari to put a finger in Zala's face, but Shomari was too fast, clutching Mantu in an arm lock. "It is time for you to be taking a walk, I think. Shake it off, big boy. Little Flutter needs her rest."

The wavy-haired shaman nodded in agreement with an exaggerated pout.

Mantu gritted his teeth, from anger at Zala, or Shomari's hold he couldn't get out of, or both, Zala couldn't tell. The large man glared down at Zala longer than he needed to before stomping out of the shanty and into the thick of the slums.

Once he was gone, Shomari turned to Zala. "Is it true? Did you have us chasing down that man just for your own?"

"Yes…" Zala held her head low.

Shomari laughed through his nose. "I would say I am disappointed, but I understand. Give Mantu some time. If Sniffs was here, he would not be so miffed. Hells, if he thought following that hairless would have led us to his man, he'd be asking why we are here and not in that palace as we speak."

Silence hung in the room as the shamans looked toward Zala and Shomari. None of them seemed to know where to place their eye lines. Most decided to cast them into the dirt. Even the little boy's gaze next to Fon went no farther than a side eye as he caressed the aziza's arm nervously.

"Tell me," the bearded shaman said again. "What business did you have with Majida?"

"I'm sorry, I didn't catch your name…" Zala said softly, regret curling through her chest as her shoulders slumped. Maybe she should've taken a walk too.

"Ismail, my lady." He lifted his hand to his heart and bowed in greeting. "Ismail el-Sayyed."

"I'm no lady," Zala said. "And I told the Madam I'd deal with that tax collector… Vaziri, I think his name was."

A few mumbles sounded between the shamans. The wavy-haired one, whose previous scowl turned to a curious one said, "Brother Ismail. It is a Blessing from Ula. The oni'baro left us, and now they bring us these people."

Ismail pressed his finger to his chin and stroked the whiskers beneath his lip. "That may be so, Sister. Her Stars still favor us." He turned to Zala. "And yes, we all have trouble with Collector Vaziri. But trying to get into that palace by force is suicide. Well, unless you have an army and the Grace of the Gods, I reckon. After hearing your stories, maybe you have their Grace, if not the army."

"Tax collector?" Fon asked as she nursed her cut wing. "Is that why your people are in the state they're in now?" Her little companion continued to rub at her arm as well, placing his head on her shoulder.

"Yes," Ismail said gravely as he dunked a ladle into a boiling cauldron. "And Mahir Vaziri tends to take extra off the top. He's been forcing us to work ragged. I'm not sure how long we'll last if we stay in the capital."

"Which is exactly where they want you," Shomari added. "Not a bad plan, really. They do not have to be forcing you out through persecution or war, they can just be driving you out with coin."

Ismail emptied his ladle into a wooden cup and drank, his wispy eyebrows dancing at his brow in what looked like thought. "It's good to talk to someone who understands." He looked to Zala as the painted spirals on his skin glowed against the dim fire light. "You all seem like you can handle yourselves. I might be able to help you, where Vaziri is concerned. But first, let's get your little friend looked at. We're not done with our ritual."

"And it seemed rude to…" the wavy-haired shaman trailed off. "Well you know… you and the big guy had Ọkụ's fire in you. And you know what they say about sticking your hand in Ọkụ's fire…"

Zala inclined her head, feeling herself blush. "Sorry about that…"

Without another word, the shamans slipped masks on their faces. Iron slats like metallic shells bedecked the mask and, as they all bent over Fon's fallen wing again, it looked like a collection of some ancient creatures Zala had never seen before were going to work. Two of the healers flanked the table as they waved their hands in unison. A hymn in the Old Tongue rolled from their throats.

Zala bit at her lip as she watched Fon's face turn pale. Misty wisps swirled around the aziza's head, dancing about like smoke from a hash pipe.

"Come on," Shomari said to Zala and the boy who still held one of Fon's arms. "We should be giving the healers their space."

Zala let herself be turned away as she looked back to Fon. The room was already filling heavy with the scent of incense as she pressed her hands into her lips. She didn't pray as a rule.

But for Fon, she was willing to try.

CHAPTER 21
LISHAN

"THE ADMIRALTY CAN'T STOP TALKING ABOUT HOW THEY'VE captured the Great Captain Nubia," Collector Vaziri was saying, kicking back in his great big chair in the Harbor's Flask. "I'll give it another moon before the information is public knowledge. And when that happens, every Great Nation who was wronged by that woman, namely Aktah, will want a seat with Their Majesties."

The Collector wasn't lying about there being others of Lishan's crew. At their large, round table of chipped oak, Ekko the illusionist, Iokaja the aziza, Ouseni the famed archer, Kwame the blademaster, and Arus the elemental, flanked Lishan.

Just one day, one brief morning, and her crew went from nearly a count of one-hundred, to six. And at that moment they were fenced in by no less than a dozen guards, nine looking like the typical Vaaji sort, and three others who looked foreign to the land, each with dark skin and long-flowing locs down their backs.

If Lishan did choose to fight, as ill-advised as that'd be, at least the Harbor's Flask had been cleared out. The moment they entered, Vaziri had thrown the barkeep named Akbar a hefty sack of coin. He didn't even have to say a word before the balding bartender made a call to the other patrons that he was closing shop for an hour.

As the Collector chatted away in his cavalier way, she couldn't help being reminded of her father. Vaziri was just as arrogant, just as "all-knowing." He even crossed his legs and smirked the damn same. If she and the others weren't surrounded, she would've already smacked that smile off his face, just like she did with her father.

"Of course," he blabbered on. "If what I'm about to propose to you works out, the Admiralty will have a… what do you pirate sort call it? Ah, yes… a shit show. They'd have a shit show on their hands." Vaziri set his goblet onto the table with a bit more heft than he needed to, breaking up Lishan's reverie as he said, "You are listening to me, aren't you, Captain? I would think this meeting would serve us both."

Lishan straightened. "Yes, of course."

"Good." He leaned back as he took another sip from his goblet. Then he rambled on again about taxes and what have you. Men like him always took forever to get to their point.

How had it come to this, Lishan wondered.

She had spent a lifetime waiting for her moment. For much of her adolescence she had tried grasping for anything that would set her apart from the twenty other brothers she grew up with. As the only mystic child, she'd been taught to strive for Yem's Moon, to never settle for second best. No, she wasn't taught by a mentor or a parent; it was the cruel harbors of the Sapphire Isles that served as her teacher. And the lessons they imparted, those written in blood and bruises, were never forgotten.

Yet her father, Tide Lord of Zanziwala, never cared for any of it. The man only cared for what her brothers were doing out in the Sapphires, only cared when Lishan could give him mystic children.

"*You are meant to be a good wife, not a warrior,*" her father would say. "*You're a daughter of the Golden Court. Let your siblings go out and play the pirates, you need to protect your womb, Ayanna.*" That had been her name then. "*Our family needs more mystics, and you're our best shot.*"

All of her siblings—and the children they sired—were plain and ordinary like their father. No magic. Nothing special. For a time, Lishan almost believed birthing mystic children was all she could ever be worth.

It wasn't until she met Captain Nubia when that all changed.

The woman was unlike anyone Lishan had ever met, a surrogate mother who embodied integrity, resilience, and vision. Lishan had known many people in power. Hells, that's all she knew existed until she set off on her own. Yet Captain Nubia wasn't just power, not the kind that could be bought. She was, to put it plain, an enigma of authority.

"... and I'll never understand why the harbor masters won't allow me to spruce up their docks..." Vaziri went on.

Lishan was barely listening.

Were Captain Nubia in this situation, she would have talked their way out of it back out on the streets. Or else, she would have found a way to escape Collector Vaziri's incessant drivel.

Maybe Lishan could never live up to that, perhaps that wasn't the role she was supposed to play in all this. Not everyone was cut out for the leading role, not everyone was meant to be the fancy golden dome atop a temple. Lishan resolved that perhaps she was something else. Besides, what was a beautiful edifice without its foundation?

If she couldn't lead a crew, at least she could save the one who could. And as she listened to this Collector Vaziri, and his self-involved plans, she realized she really had a chance to save her Captain. But first...

"I know you must mistrust me, as you rightly should." Vaziri seemed to be reading her thoughts, though anyone could've guessed that. "But your flitting eyes won't find an escape from my guards. At the very least, hear me out before you start letting your mind wander to murder and escape, yes?"

Like always, he ended with that crooked grin of his. It was made worse by the fact that it was genuinely a beautiful one.

Lishan crossed her arms. "And what is it you are proposing? We already know Captain Nubia is captured, and that you Vaaji are holding her. So far you've talked about your favorite kind of drink, asked all of us what our's were, rattled off about the failings of your Admiralty and the poor state of the harbor districts—and every time you bring up our captain's name you expect us to grovel for whatever reports you have on her." Oddly, the Vaaji guards didn't seem to react at all, but the foreign ones shared side-long glances with one another. "So, what is it, Vaziri? How do we play into whatever scheme you got cooked up?"

The silence then could've been cut by a blunted janbiya. At the corner of her eye, Lishan could see her crew didn't budge an inch. There was a reason they had survived. They were true Rovers. Hardened. And who knows, perhaps there were more of her crew still out there. But she was glad of the ones she had at her side now. She could've smiled if she wasn't already fixing the Collector with a pointed glare.

Vaziri sighed. "Oh, what is this city coming to… a confluence of ruin and silk. There was a time when even thugs such as your-selves would humor conversation at least for a time. It's always straight to the point without any of the fondling these days. How are we ever to know we're a match for one another without a bit of light repartee, hm?"

"If you're hiring thugs," Lishan said. "Then I don't see how pleasantries and quips would do you any good."

Vaziri rolled his goblet between his manicured fingers. "I suppose you're right." He turned his chin and rested it on his shoulder. "A shame isn't it, N'Kota? Me, you, and your brothers have such great exchanges. Why, just last week we were talking about the merits of…" he trailed off as he snapped his fingers for the thought. "Oh, what was it…"

"The virtue of open-ended questions," answered the tallest of the foreign men standing behind Vaziri, his smile so bright it nearly made Lishan squint.

"Oh yes! Not just that, but one's ability to include the whole table in a conversation, not just one individual. It's a lost art these days."

The tall man named N'Kota nodded. "Yes, sir. That's right."

"You see," Vaziri turned back to Lishan and the pirates, "I've yet to learn anything about you, Lishan. Sure, I know your name already, and of course I've heard rumors about your exploits. But who hasn't? The *Redtide* has been a thorn in every Great Nation's side for years now."

"I'm a Daughter of Ugara who graduated the Zanziwala Mystic Academies top of the class at the age of fourteen," Lishan started. "Then I went on to win the Golden Arena in Zanziwala not once, not twice, but three consecutive years before I decided the shit was boring and wanted something more real. So I applied for Golden Lord Zuberi's court guard until that got boring too. Then I met up with Captain Nubia and—" Lishan stopped herself short. The truth behind her initially joining the Captain wasn't something she was willing to divulge. "Well, you seem to know all about my time on the *Redtide*."

Vaziri let the moment hang for a beat before he started tapping on his chin to say, "That was a fabulous outline of your experiences. I especially like the touch of 'Daughter of Ugara'. I wasn't aware the Old God of War had one. But what I really want to know is what makes you tick. I want to know how you dwell under pressure. I assumed I was mistaken when I heard you foolishly threw up your flag in the middle of our bay, but as you say, that was a traitor in your ranks. Tell me, do you trust the others at this table?"

Lishan didn't have to look at them. "This lot, for sure."

"None of them would be sympathizers to the ones who broke off from you, would they?"

It took Lishan a moment longer to answer this question. Were this a day ago, she would have thought perhaps Ekko, Marjani, and Iokaja would have been on that pirate Zala's side. But after today, after seeing Iokaja slice that other aziza up real good, after seeing how murderous Ekko's eyes were after Marjani got stabbed... she knew where their loyalties lied without even the shadow of a doubt.

"None of them," she answered.

"And what about you, Captain Lishan?" Vaziri asked. "Do you think you're fit to lead them?"

Lishan was on the edge of saying a quick "yes" when she realized that wasn't what Captain Nubia would have done. Instead she answered, "You can ask them."

Another smile stretched across Vaziri's face. But this one was different. This one was free of any of his usual conceit. It was more... honest. Like an older brother's grin. Something she never got from her own.

"All right, then." He eyed the others. "Would you follow this woman?"

For the first time since they sat, Lishan surveyed the rest of her crew. She couldn't honestly say how they'd answer. Sure, they wanted to have Captain Nubia back, and they wanted to see Zala and her crew dead, but that didn't mean they wanted Lishan as their head.

Ekko was first to respond. "Aye. I'll honor my pledge."

"Same here," came Iokaja's reply next.

"Aye, aye," said Ouseni and Kwame in unison.

Arus placed folded thick-set hands on the table. "Ain't no one at this table got more spirit than Lishan. If any of us got the grit to get our Captain back, it's her. I'll be with her and the *Tide*, no matter if it's at the bottom of the bay or not."

"Very well." Vaziri sat up straight. "Here is my proposal. As I've been saying, the Admiralty can't shut their mouth about Captain Nubia, but they have had tighter lips about certain other things... certain vessels that you and I both know exist that by all reason shouldn't." Lishan didn't make a show of confusion, so Vaziri went on. "This job I have for you will kill two rocs with one catapult, as it were. You see, I want this vessel badly, very badly. But that's not all. There are whispers in the palace about a very important target having a particularly unique form of lodging. Whereas a vast majority of the most important of our detainees are kept in the dungeons of Jasmiin Towers, this specific prisoner has been left on this... floating craft. Are you following?"

Lishan nodded, realizing then that she had been leaning forward onto the table a bit too deeply.

"Good," Vaziri went on. "I want what you want. If you can save this target, you can also have the vessel. And in return... you will answer to me much in the same way you would to your Golden Lord."

"What stops us from just making off with the thing ourselves?" Lishan asked.

"Well, this will be a joint effort, of course." Vaziri thumbed to his guards. "I'll be leaving N'Kota and his brothers, Ikeji and Keta, with you all." The shorter two foreigners inclined their heads, their locs falling over their noses. "You will find they are quite *influential* in their own ways. They'll be vital for the final stages of this plot. And some of my guards will oversee some of your work from time to time."

"You seem to have your fingers on the pulse of this city." Ekko spoke up to Lishan's surprise. "Tell me, where's the nearest healers by the palace?"

"Ah, I see." Vaziri tilted his head to the man. "That business with the religious folks dressed in Qibasi robes being attacked was you then? Rumors are already stirring about the slummers and a band of oni'baro getting heated about the rising taxes here. Anyhow, why do you ask?"

Ekko's shoulders were slumped inward and down, but his voice was steady. "I just gotta know where my wife is being tended to."

Vaziri pursed his lips and tapped his fingers along the table. "Very well. Give me until the end of the day and I'll have that information for you. One of the brothers here will take you over."

"How long do we have to hide out here?" Lishan asked. "I already have a relationship with one of the frequent visitors at this tavern. Should we keep our distance?"

"Oh no, you can do as you please within the city. Just know that I'll have eyes on you, of course." Vaziri sat up straight and snapped his fingers. "Oh! And any of you who are mystics... careful in the city. Mystic-kind are heavily regulated by a league called Seekers. So if you do go out, one of the brothers will be with you... for your protection." He surveyed the pirates, seemingly looking for a measure of them all. "And if all goes to plan, we'll make our final move at the start of the new year."

"A whole moon?" Ouseni blurted with crossed arms.

"Why yes," Vaziri said with a lifted brow. "It takes some time to arrange a banquet... especially one serving as distraction."

Lishan looked to her crew, trying her best to give them even looks of confidence. "Whatever it takes to get the Captain. So... what's our first assignment, Collector?"

CHAPTER 22
ZALA

Moments.

Moments were a cruel thing, Zala decided. They didn't allow for forethought, or caution. They laughed at deep planning and poked fun at calculated deliberation.

It was a moment that plagued Jelani with stoneskin. It was a moment that had Zala choosing to switch flags or compromise. It was a moment that got Fon's wing cut. And it was a moment... a moment too late that saw Zala stab and kill Marjani.

There were a number of reasons she had forsaken the Gods, a reason she didn't play their games of fate and fortune. This was just one more argument she could add against them on her already long list. How could they be so callous? How could they force that kind of life-altering decision on their creations and give them only seconds to make it?

It was heartless, and it was unfair.

Nearly an hour passed before Zala found shelter from the sweltering sun. There was little to be found in the slums — where houses were made of patchwork and broken clay. The slummers had taken shelter near an old Jo'baran temple, its fallen statues and pillars repurposed as walls and roofs. Locally, the whole district was apparently known as the Scars.

After an aimless shuffle, Zala found an unoccupied shanty that

had at least a sliver of consistent shading. To keep her mind off of
how Fon was doing, or whether Jelani was even in al-Anim at all,
she found herself watching a group of children dancing in a circle
hand in hand. In unison, they sang a disturbing song:

> *Boy better have the emperor's gold*
> *Or he'll lose his hands, we've been told.*
> *Girl better have her bronze and silver*
> *Or she'll be drowned in the river.*

The kids fell down and mimicked drowning in a river with fits
of giggles and laughter. It was a terrible sound to Zala's ears.
Memories of past suffering willed themselves to the surface after
so long. She felt her stomach churn at both the sight and sound.
The bread in her hand looked far less appetizing, its stale and
brick-like texture notwithstanding.

"Dulagi got you in a bunch, dear?" An old woman with a
toothless smile and rancid breath asked, making Zala jump a little.
"Don't mind the lil' 'uns. It's all just fun and games."

She chuckled and waddled off, a too-short stump lodged into
her right leg. The sight reminded Zala of Ode and his lopsided
gait. She wanted to think the old man was all right, but after
hearing what happened to Fon... The aziza's story didn't include
any sightings of the seasoned pirate and her own chances had
been much higher to begin with. But regardless, Zala knew hope
would do no good. It would only serve to disappoint her.

Zala wouldn't have minded the children's dark song on most
days. She'd heard plenty of them at sea. But when it came from
children at play—*that* hit closer to home. It was no better than her
academy days, of children cut from a better cloth, perhaps, but
with the same casual regard for suffering.

Shaking the thoughts from her head, she returned to the hard
bread block in her hand. The man who had heated it called it pita.
Zala called it disgusting. At least it was better than something
from the sewers.

She didn't look back up at the singing children. She turned
her eyes farther down the street where more youngsters were

chasing rats in their own game — or maybe their own survival. One girl, who seemed to be the group's leader, controlled the leading rat as the others gave chase.

A sewer speaker, Zala thought as she watched.

She had heard the term before but never had a visual of the mystic type. She'd only ever seen the courts and academies of Jultia, and Kidogo lacked the infrastructure for sewers. The mystic child reminded her of Jelani and the way he used to play games with the fish along the shoreline of their home isle. Granted, his games of flips and spins were much more innocent than this one.

Eventually, the girl allowed one of her friends to catch the lead rat, and the boy who caught it skipped and celebrated all the way to his waiting mother. The disheveled woman stuffed the rat into a basket full of other rodents.

"Jaali, what did I say about using your a'bara like that!" another old man came scolding the one who had controlled the rat in her game. "You know what Maji Arba told us about keepin' you a secret. You want the Seekers to come and take you away? And you playin' with rats of all things!"

Zala stared down at the egg stuffed between her pita which was spotted with gray blotches. Suddenly her day-long hunger had vanished as though it hadn't been there at all.

A gilded light shone bright from the shamans' shanty. Zala followed the glint to where it shimmered along what looked like Fon's repaired wing. Shomari and Shaman Ismail stood at her side with expectant looks, each of their hands at the aziza's shoulder. Zala could see Shomari mouthing something down at the aziza but Fon didn't seem to listen. There was a frown that stretched deep across her face. Shomari mouthed something again, and Fon heaved her shoulders in anger. She sprang into a half-jump in the air, hovered a foot from the ground, the afternoon light twinkling through her translucent wings, then came crashing down in almost the same moment.

The aziza's plummet matched the drop that came to Zala's stomach. Flying was Fon's thing, her *literal* identity.

Shomari and the shaman lifted helpful hands to heave her up.

Fon did as best she could but the tears leaking from her eyes couldn't be helped. Zala strained to beat down the lump welling up in her throat as her own eyes watered.

"We can't eat them straight away," came a voice at Zala's side. It was a young woman with bushy hair, bushier eyebrows, and a long, freckled nose. Zala sucked in her tears, pinching her eyes as the girl gestured down to the pita filled with egg and the mysterious blotches in Zala's hand. "Rodents have diseases and a poor diet. We have to feed them right for a few weeks before we cook them. I prefer them fried, personally." Zala turned her nose up at the meal. "Don't look so disgusted. You'll get used to it. Badu must like you. He gave you the good bread, at least." The young woman pointed down to Zala's pita. It was true the cook had been particularly nice to her. "If you don't want it—" Zala handed the pita over before the young woman finished speaking. The young woman snatched it and bit down on it as if it were a juicy cut of beef. "Name's Ketifa."

"Zala," she replied with a sigh.

The girl named Ketifa sat herself next to Zala. "You're new here, I take it? First time in al-Anim?"

"Yes, first time."

"And what brings you to this side of the capital? It's much nicer down by the markets, or up by Sycamore, you know."

Zala decided that, in this district, the truth would play just fine. "I'm here on a job for someone about some tax collector."

"Oh, Mahir?" Ketifa's eyes lit up. "Did he take their coin too or something? Do you know him?"

"I only saw him in passing. Can't say I've had a conversation with the man."

Ketifa nodded her head beyond the collapsed entrance where two of the citywatch passed by. They glanced into the fallen temple with dark eyes but kept moving along.

Ketifa cleared her throat, then said, "Then you don't know that the *man*," she snorted derisively, "has *at least* half a dozen guarding him at all times. And he's been adding more to his ranks every day since them soldiers came back."

"You know about the soldiers?"

"Yeah, my cousin is one of them. He just got back from one of his tours."

"Who's your cousin?" Zala wondered if that return tour had involved a certain sky ship.

"His name's Karim." Ketifa dusted a stray piece of egg from her entangled hair. "What, you a sailor too?"

"In a way…" Zala hedged and turned back to watch the children chasing their second rat. "What do you know of Mahir?"

"Only that he's a pain in my side."

Zala raised her eyebrow.

Ketifa canted her head and sighed in answer. "A few of us do some work for him now and then—well, slave under him is more like it."

Zala shifted her shoulders back to Ketifa. She didn't ask what *work* meant for someone like Vaziri. She knew his type and could imagine well enough what he'd have young girls doing for him.

"Oh, you do?" Zala asked with a tone of guarded interest. This might be her way to get close to the tax collector without his guards hovering around. If he had more than just that woman Zala saw, he must've meant business.

"Well, I don't work with him directly, I suppose," Ketifa went on. "A few of us work the kitchens at Jasmiin Tower. The western keep. I usually just serve the soldiers, but sometimes Mahir uses the palace staff for private dinners and the like. Pays pretty well, and all my coin goes right back here." She gestured to the ruins around them. "They even offered me a house up the hill a year ago. I took it but sold it off. That was a good season for us."

"And they let you sell it?"

"No, but I got someone payin' me for my *privilege* in my stead. I try to come out of the place every few days to make it look like I still live there, but the rest of the time…" She gestured to the streets again. "And don't look at me like that. I'm not stupid. The saabi livin' there wouldn't sell me out. He's got his own thing goin' on on the side."

Zala flattened her expression. In truth, she had thought the girl a bit daft. Already in the space of a few moments she had entrusted a complete stranger with information that would land her in serious trouble with her Empire.

And she worked in the palace? There had to be something else at play here.

"They just let you into their palace freely?" Zala asked, doing her best to curtail her skepticism.

Ketifa shrugged. "Freely wouldn't be the word I'd use. We're only allowed into the kitchen areas, sometimes the courtyards. Everything else is strictly off-limits. If you're caught outside of it." She ran her thumb across her throat. "No one's that stupid though. And if the nobles like you enough, you can even sign on for proper work in the military. That's how my cousin got his start. Well, his start was in the shipping yards, but same difference. Nobles like hard workers."

Zala's forehead scrunched together in confusion. "Why would anyone want to sign up to serve an empire that leaves its poorest poorer?"

"'Cause we don't want to be poor no more," Ketifa said matter-of-factly. "Or we want educatin'. It's free to those who join, you know."

"And you're okay with your cousin doing all that?"

"'*The Hustler King reigns Supreme in these parts*'. That's what everyone says, right?" Ketifa spread her hands out wide in a casual wave. "Life's been a lot easier for Karim from what I've heard. He even has enough to send us money, way more than I ever can. I can only ever cover the tax for maybe a dozen of us at best. Whenever Cousin comes through, though, the whole district eats for a week. Not well, but we eat. Just yesterday morning he came with a whole sack full of coin. And he'll have another set for us in a week, no doubt. He always comes through when we need it most. But even he can't keep it up."

Ketifa ended somberly. Her eyes rose back up to Zala and she asked, "So what's this job you got goin'? I'll help anyone take Mahir down a peg. We need the help ever since those oni'baro started workin' the whorehouses. Can't blame 'em. They're paid better over there."

"Can't tell you the specifics," Zala said, "but let's just say my certain someone wants the problem of Collector Vaziri dealt with as much as you."

"Oh," Ketifa said, elongating the end of her exclamation like she had made some great revelation. Then she lowered her voice even further. "You an assassin or something like that?"

Zala barked a laugh, trying to cover the outburst with a cough. "Me? Definitely not."

"Oh right, right… that big guy and that pakka you came in with must be. You're just the middleman—or what do they call it—a contractor or somethin'."

"No, no. We're just… well, it doesn't matter." She sighed. "And no, I don't plan on killing the man. That wouldn't help with what I'm trying to do. I just said I'd fix it so he doesn't take any more taxes—more than he should be anyway. Which we can make happen, I just need him alone is all."

"Ah." Ketifa nodded. "Well, his guards come through here all the time. He only shows up himself once a moon, though, so he won't be here again for a while. But like I said, he doesn't go anywhere without his guards. Not outside the palace anyway."

"Great," Zala groaned as she slumped her head into her hands. "So we only have to break into the most secure place in the whole damned Empire to get him to ourselves."

"Maybe not…" Ketifa lifted a dirt-caked finger. "Mahir's got another one of his banquets happening soon. Some big ol' thing for the nobles to *bring in the new year with some showmanship*," he said." She brushed her thumb and forefinger together. "If you got the coin, I sure could do with a few days off…"

Zala smiled. Now they were getting to the brass tax. The girl wasn't all sunshine and rainbows and loose lips for nothing. She knew what she was doing well enough.

"How much?" Zala asked.

"Whatever the palace pays you, plus a finder's fee of let's say… a bronze for every hour you're in there."

Zala chewed on the inside of her cheek as she considered the offer. She and Shomari could make a few runs pocket diving in the markets and pick up enough for that. But with the Rovers out there hounding them it was probably best to lay low as much as they could. After all, Mantu practically told the whole of the city-watch that it was Shomari who caused all the raucous in that alley.

"We can just swap with you just like that?" Zala asked skeptically. "There's no catch?"

"Well, what I'm *really* selling you is this." Ketifa reached into her threadbare tunic and pulled out a parchment with a blood lily sigil along its crease. "Just show this to them, and they'll let you through. But it's up to you not to muck it up. If you don't cook to their standards, they'll chuck you out. And you'll need to do better than even that if you want Head Chef Hadi to pick you for the banquet. A week should be enough to make a good impression, though you have more time than that. The banquet isn't for another moon. I know a few nobles got a bit of a sweet tooth so maybe you can get in that way. There aren't very many good bakers."

Zala began to understand then. Ketifa didn't really think Zala would be able to do anything about Mahir. The slummer just cared about capitalizing on whatever madness—or paycheck—had Zala making the attempt. Her attitude was clear enough from her story of the house on the hill, and Zala couldn't blame her for it. Besides, from what she could tell, the money would be going right back to the girl's home and people. That was more than Zala could have said of herself had she been in the same situation.

"I've got a wedding coming up," Ketifa said. "And well, you know, my family's having a hard time coming up with the funds. And I can't contribute to the district *and* make my way—"

"I understand," Zala said quietly as something caught her eye.

Zala peered back up to Fon and Shomari, the latter of which held the former in his arms as they sat. The aziza wasn't crying anymore, and Shomari kept nuzzling her cheek. The sight brought new tears to Zala's eyes and she had half a mind to go over and see how Fon was doing but thought better of it. Fon and Shomari were having a moment that couldn't be interrupted.

Brushing her lids free of the wet welling at their base, Zala sniffed, turned to Ketifa and knew there was only one choice. The longer Zala sat idle, the sooner Jelani would be in the position Fon was in. Only he wouldn't just have something broken. If the Vaaji had their way, he'd never be made whole again.

Cursed moments.

There might be no stopping them, but that didn't mean Zala would just heave anchor and let them sail. She'd do what she had always done and keep crafting her schemes.

What other option did she have?

There weren't any shortcuts to these things, and a moon's cycle slaving in some kitchens would hardly be so bad. But she couldn't do it alone. Even if she did curry favor with this head chef, even if Collector Vaziri picked her to serve at his banquet, what could she do by herself? She turned her gaze to Mantu who had positioned himself at the broken temple's entrance. His back was hunched and rigid, his own gaze searching for, Zala assumed, more Rovers.

"Could you get me a second slip?" Zala finally asked. "I've another man who I'll need to go with—"

"My betrothed will be the second, on the added condition we throw in an extra bronze an hour." Ketifa stuck out her hand. "He'll give you an additional slip. Just don't go losin' it."

Zala grabbed the girl's hand and gave it a firm shake. "Then it's a deal."

<hr>

"You want to what?" a red-faced Mantu asked a few minutes later.

Zala rubbed at the back of her head nervously, taking second glances at Fon and Shomari who had accompanied her. Fon thought she was there for emotional support; Shomari, for protection.

"Listen," Zala hurried. "If we can keep our heads down for a fortnight—"

"A *fortnight?*—"

"We might be able to find out what happened to Jelani—"

"I already told you what's happening to Jelani—"

"And, if you let me finish, we might find out more about that sky ship."

Mantu kept his mouth shut at that. Zala could feel Fon behind her rocking from left to right in nervousness, and at the corner of her eye she could see Shomari's tail flicking with alertness.

After a short moment, Mantu said, "I thought you only told me that shit back on the *Tide* as a way to convince me."

Zala tilted her head from left to right. "Yes and no. Look, if you're right, and my husband doesn't have long, the next thing I want to do is take that ship of theirs."

"I don't get it." Mantu shook his head. "How does becoming cooks get us a sky ship?"

"The kitchens that some of these people work at are within that palace," Zala said, "which has a keep specific for their military branch."

Fon nodded. "And military compounds tend to have military stuff in them."

"Secret stuff, if you get their meaning," Shomari added.

Mantu thought it over with a scowl on his lips. "I don't know the first thing about cookin'."

"It's easy," Fon said, her single wing flipping up a touch. "It's just choosing good ingredients, prep, and cutting."

Mantu looked unconvinced.

"Just give it a moon, at least," Zala urged. "Just so we can be sure we can't see where they keep that thing. Who knows... if we do good, Majida might end up finding information on the ship itself. She seemed to know something about it."

"Hold up, you just went and said *fortnight* a second ago."

"A fortnight, a moon, whatever gets the job done."

Mantu shook his head, turning away from Zala, Fon, and Shomari to peer out of the temple entrance with a very heavy sigh. "I don't know. I still think we should take that Majida woman and force her to tell us what we want to know."

"That'd be impossible," Zala said. "She's surrounded by guards at all times. Not everyone in that brothel were regular workers. Ketifa was saying some faction of oni'baro are protecting her. My husband was part of the Kidogo faction. They're peaceful and all that but most of them are very powerful mystics. That's probably why Majida hasn't been shut down already."

"And there were more of those sort posted outside her brothel," Shomari added. "Attempting to take her would be ill-advised."

That was saying a lot coming from the renowned pakka. And that usually would've settled it for someone like Mantu, who had known the cat longer than Zala or Fon did, but still the man spat the question, "And sneakin' into an imperial fortress is better?"

Shomari shrugged. "At least they won't know we're coming."

"I don't like it." Mantu frowned. "I should leave y'all to your own deaths. I could be spendin' my time in this city lookin' for a new crew. Duma is out there somewhere."

"Just like Jelani is out there somewhere." Zala stepped forward and touched him lightly on his wrist. "I know you care for Duma as I do for Jelani, we've been through that... And I'm not about to throw his potential death in your face to motivate you." *Like you're doing to me.* "If Duma is gone like Jelani is gone, wouldn't you want to get the Empire back for that?"

Mantu turned to the others and replied with sad eyes, "I would..."

"It also doesn't help that the Rovers might still be out there, and it's possible the Vaaji have your face marked. So right now, your best option is to stay with us."

"Well." Mantu crossed his arms. "It ain't seem like I have much of a choice, does it?"

Zala smiled. "Let's get to work. Fon, we'll need you to teach us everything you know about cooking."

CHAPTER 23
ISSA

IF ISSA HADN'T JUST WALKED UP FOUR STEEP HILLS THROUGH desert trails, thorny brush, and narrow canyons, she would've thought she were in some tropical oasis, not al-Anim.

Though the Suhul Steppes were not technically classified as a desert, sitting between the truly barren south and the lush thickets of the north, it still couldn't be called anything more than an arid wasteland. Despite that, Merchant Lord Hamza al-Turabi had managed to carve himself nothing short of a retreat befitting royalty.

"It's the only way to get away from al-Anim's stink," he had told Issa during her first visit to his revered villa.

Issa wiped her damp brow, thankful she had plaited her hair in two braids down her shoulders as she gazed upon al-Turabi's estate.

"Rumor has it," Hajjar said at her side, "that the Merchant Lord purchased this lot of land—and the crumbling structure that sits within it—despite the stories that the fields are, well, haunted."

Even now, Issa could see the architecture of what looked to be some temple or sanctuary shrouded beneath. What was unique about the edifice was that it seemed to be a blend of Old Vaaj, with its simple blocky sandstone, and New, with domed roofs and arched pillars. It didn't even look like it was built all at the same time, with splashes of the old at the foundation of its three tiers, and the new seeming to rise above it. The one feature that seemed to bring both styles as one were the vines that grew along its side and the palms that lined its perimeter.

The trailing plants were the source of the rumored haunting… that nefarious spirits had called forth the weeds to swallow the structure whole. But al-Turabi had been living here for decades now without so much as whispers on the cool wind. Though he always had a complaint or three concerning red palm mites, the only pests he ever encountered on the land.

"You know, you didn't have to shadow me today," Issa told Hajjar as they waited to be greeted.

Hajjar shook his head, his thick eyebrows furrowed. "No way I'd let you come to the haunted Suhul Steppes without an elemental at your side, Chief. But let's be quick about it. Get more info on Vaziri, and get out. This place gives me the creeps."

"Ah, Lady Akif," came a voice from the estate entrance. "And guest of Lady Akif. Welcome to the al-Turabi estate."

Issa turned to the short man who stood waiting for her, and he inclined his head almost immediately. He was the caretaker of the estate. Issa had often mused if his crooked height had been brought on by perpetual bowing.

"Afternoon, Caretaker." Issa gestured above her. "My partner and I were taken by the design."

"Very beautiful." Hajjar bowed.

"Please, please," the caretaker blurted with the speed of a woodpecker's beak. "Get yourself out of that sun. Have a sit by the pool… Master al-Turabi has guests at the moment, he'll be with you shortly. I'll bring you both a drink. You still like your carob juice with mint, yes, Lady Akif?"

"Sharp." Issa nodded.

"Always, my lady." The caretaker rubbed the back of his hands and headed off, disappearing into a veritable forest of shrubbery. Issa had long since stopped trying to correct him whenever he called her "lady." In truth, it was nice being doted on with the phrasing. It almost made her think she was meant for a court.

With an inward chuckle, she and Hajjar made their way out onto the grounds. It did not take long for them to find the thin pool set along the stone path, not because Issa had been there before, but because of the stream of giggles that were echoing from the garden-draped pool. Within its long stretch lay the most beautiful men, women, and aziza one could find. They chatted with each other—whether hanging from the lip of the pool or lounging along its side—like they had known each other for years; more likely, Issa mused, they had only recently met. Al-Turabi never had the same crowd hanging around his villa for more than a week or two... everyone knew that. It was a bit of a game to see who could hang on the longest, and the winning formula for those who did remain was, like anywhere else in al-Anim, a subtle rubbing of the right shoulders.

As Issa found an empty chair under the shade of palms, she caught a glimpse of herself in the lapping water's reflections. Though she preferred her flowing dresses and looser tops, today her uniform was a bit more traditional, with just an added dash of flare: an ankle length dress of simple blue, set with studded bronze to line its edges. It was well-known that al-Turabi's guests were invited for their allure by way of exposed shoulders, thighs, or what have you. Issa wanted to make it clear she wasn't here to become one of his courtesans—she was here to conduct business.

Hajjar, however, couldn't stop taking glances at the guests among the pool.

"Stop your gawking," Issa told him in a playful murmur. "Keep your eyes on the hedges."

"What—I wasn't... I mean... yes, ma'am."

Issa laughed as a familiar timbre, al-Turabi's baritone voice, came over the hedge. "I've already told you, saabi, either you allow my caravan priority passage through Moharam's Pass, or you can forget about the extra tariffs I pay you. I've other routes I can use, you know."

"I can't have it, Lord Merchant," came a second voice, female. "Your cargo will have to wait like everyone else—"

"Then we have nothing more to discuss. Good day. May Shati'ala guide you to a lord with deeper purses than my own."

The woman continued with another set of excuses, but they fell on deaf ears. Al-Turabi came stomping around a corner, his cloak billowing around him like emerald wings. The bird-like image was made more stark by the magenta feather protruding from his turban. He didn't even seem to slow as his guests turned their chins to him in wait of his attention. Even as he approached Issa, his gait did not abate.

"I hope you've got better news for me," he grunted, brushing past.

"Stay here," Issa told Hajjar.

Issa, taking al-Turabi's meaning without a word, followed behind and did her best to keep up with his long strides. Avoiding the series of head turns from the others, she commented in a light voice, "I was hoping to catch up before all of that."

Al-Turabi either didn't hear or chose to ignore her. He kept to his steady march down the stone path bordered by topiaries in the likeness of animals and ancient creatures. He seemed to carry his shoulders in a tight hunch as he grumbled to himself about tariffs and good-for-nothing help. But as he descended farther into thick greenery dotted with lavenders, his walk eased from its previous rigidity to the more loose saunter that Issa was used to seeing from him. At first she thought the change was brought on simply because the Merchant Lord had put more steps between him and whoever it was he was consulting with, but then she realized it might've been because of where they were headed.

Issa had never come to this part of the estate before. Where the main compound was certainly dense in its cluster of palms, cacti, and vines, the grove they were heading into now grew so thick, it was as though they weren't in the middle of the Suhul Steppes, but some bonafide tropical rainforest. Soon, cages and pits lined the clearings through which they walked, each of them bringing a smile to al-Turabi's lips, though the smell of dung and other animal waste brought a twitch to Issa's nose.

"Oh, aren't you precious, Little Flopper," the man said in a cutesy tone as a caged desert lynx of an orange hue tumbled onto its back in greeting. The cat even nuzzled its nose against al-Turabi's finger, which the man had stuck between the bars with a tiny flutter.

"You're actually doing it, then?" Issa asked. "You've actually started your sanctuary?"

Al-Turabi was making kissing noises at the lynx before he turned to answer. "Yes, yes. I only found this lovely little lady a moon ago out in al-Haru." He started to pet around her half-torn ear. "Poachers were having their way with her when I got to them."

Issa surveyed the other cages with curiosity as the various animals stirred at their arrival. One of them—a baboon by the looks of it—hollered excitedly and climbed atop its bars. It shook them harshly; whether in anger, or to seek his master's attention like the guests at the pool, Issa couldn't tell.

When last she had visited, some of the creatures had been held within the main villa in cramped rooms barely fit for storage, let alone live animals. She was happy to see that they had been moved outdoors and given much more space. The sight of the animals, common and rare both, reminded her of the gift she had acquired for the Merchant Lord.

"Oh, before I forget," she said, pulling a tiny envelope from her tunic. "I came across some tickets… but I don't have much interest in them. I realized you'd be the *perfect* candidate."

Al-Turabi eyed the envelope as he moved toward the first of the pits, which held a mountain lion within. "This is the seal of Arba al-Zilu. You better not be playing me for a fool."

"It's not exactly a seal that's easily forged." She nudged her chin forward. "Go on, open it. I want to see your eyes alight."

For the first time, al-Turabi gave Issa his full attention, a smirk sneaking across his goatee-outlined lips. Slowly, he broke the seal and withdrew the note within. Then he read, *"A War of Storms: The Last Tale of the Rocs and Kongamatos."* He snapped the parchment around so it faced Issa. "How did you come by something like this? This isn't one of al-Zilu's public performances. This… this is one of her private productions. No one can get an invite just like that, not even me."

"I'm offended, Lord Merchant." Issa feigned her indignation. "All these years you've known me... an invite to a private party is nothing."

"That may be so, but—"

"I'm sorry, my lady, my lord," the caretaker's voice came at them from the sanctuary's entrance. His feet were *pat-pattering* along the path, and the pair of glasses on his tray *click-clattered* as he walked. "I looked for you all through the pool. I did not realize Master would be showing you to the sanctuary."

"Don't worry yourself." Issa tilted forward to help steady the tray under the man's grip. It looked like he had spilled some of the carob juice and hastily cleaned it up, save for a few droplets on the edge of the tray. "Thank you for bringing it."

He bowed. "Of course, my lady. And, Master, I brought your usual. Two pinches of sugar, and a hint of cinnamon as you like it."

"Thank you, Khadim." Al-Turabi took up the glass, downed it in three chugs, and set it back down. "Go back up to the guests and make sure they're entertained. I won't be long."

"Right away, Master."

Issa watched as the caretaker scurried away. She took her first sip of the juice and felt almost immediately refreshed by the cold chocolate-like flavor. When she turned back to al-Turabi he was still ogling the parchment in his hand.

Issa asked, "Can I take that to mean I did well?"

"You did *very* well, child." The Merchant Lord folded the slip as carefully as a mother tucking her child to bed before slipping it back into its envelope and placing it into his sash belt. "Come, I want to show you something. Or perhaps I shouldn't... seeing as an allusive production of *A War of Storms* is not of interest to you."

Issa smiled through a second sip of carob juice. "Oh, you know I'm always open to being enlightened."

"You know... every time we part I forget how much I like you, child," he said through a smirk. "Do you do this intentionally? Leave me with just enough of an impression but not enough to remember why I'm fond of you."

Issa followed at his side as he took her down a curved path

deeper into the jungle he built. "I must be doing a poor job," Issa said. "I'm always looking for your favor. Perhaps you are just too busy to remember who you even speak to these days. I bet you know the names of all these animals you keep, but you'd be hard-pressed to name the guests you have here today. In fact, can you even name one?"

Al-Turabi ducked between a low-hanging branch before answering, "Of course I know those who visit my home. That one saabi in the pool, the one with the thick curls... his name's Alim... or Alem... or Amir... maybe it could have been Amiri, actually. One of the four of those is correct. Mark my words."

Issa didn't bother jabbing at his poor recollection; the bemused look they shared between one another was enough.

"It's my fault, in part," Issa explained, "the Navy keeps me busy. My visits to you have become less and less frequent."

"Well, regardless, I hope it is I who can leave the impression on you this time around." Al-Turabi stood before an iron gate inlaid with the images of ancient creatures in a collage of spread wings, fixed roars, and strike-ready, saber-length claws. "Once I'm ready with this, I won't need to meet with other merchant lords or bureaucrats or nobles. If all goes to plan, I'll have an attraction to al-Anim that'll rival even the 'bathhouses' of the Silks." He withdrew a set of keys and slotted one of them into a keyhole the shape of a manticore's maw. "May I present to you a sanctorium like no other, a refuge for the lost and exotic, an exhibit that'll send you back to a time when magic and Her creatures ruled all the lands. Welcome to al-Turabi's Zoological Garden of the Ancients!"

He pushed the door inward to reveal a space Issa would have likened to its own village. Though still cloaked under a thick canopy that blotted out the sun, the greenery was almost like an enormous dome that rose several hundred paces in the air. Through the brush came the pounding hooves of unicorns, at the edge of a great central lake, the head of a grootslang exposed its monstrous trunk to the temperate breeze, and from between the high rising trees flew the rainbow-colored wingspans of kongamatos.

"It's like you carved out a piece of the Kunda Jungles and transported them to al-Anim."

"That's the idea. I'm trying to give people the Kunda Jungle experience without the risk of being maimed, poisoned, or… you know… otherwise killed."

"Is it safe?" Issa asked, never letting her gaze stray too far from what she didn't want to believe was a sphinx peering through a thick set of ferned tree trunks.

Al-Turabi walked right into the middle of the path to stroke the beak of a curious impundulu. "Entirely safe. I've got the top alchemists on my payroll. Once a week they refill the lake with a sedative potion to make the creatures docile." He pointed to the central watering hole where another pair of lightening birds cupped water into their beaks. "And I've elementals and harvesters who keep this manifested jungle from drying out. I'm told in time, I won't have to do that anymore, that the land will stick, much like Kunda does today. I want to make sure visitors can never see the outside world, total immersion."

Issa could say confidently this was not what she was expecting. She knew of the Merchant Lord's fascination with creatures and animals of all kinds, it's what fueled his desire to earn the coin he had in the first place, but she never would have thought he'd go so far as this. Many of these creatures were thought extinct. Others were surely endangered.

Al-Turabi must've caught her look because he said, "And before you get to thinking about the legality of this all, don't worry. My lawmen and advisors tell me I'm well within my rights."

"How?" Issa asked, trying her best not to offend with her question. They were still in the small talk phase of conversation. Unlike with Nadya, she'd need to play into the typical shams of feigned interest Karim so often scoffed at. Though it wasn't a fabricated intrigue Issa was battling with at that moment. Rather, she tried to hold back the smatterings of revulsion crawling up her stomach at the sight of majestic beasts being pacified for the pleasure of a merchant lord. A man probably more wealthy than half the court in Jasmiin Towers, a man who could likely wipe out the plight across the slums with one of his smallest purses. Instead, he spent his hard-fought earnings on… a zoo full of half-beasts.

"I'm sorry." She corrected the scowl starting on her face into a half smile, though she kept her distance at the entrance of the sanctuary. "What I mean to say is, well, the impundulu you're petting now… it's deemed as endangered by those Jultians, no?"

"No, even better. They're deemed extinct by those Jultian humanitarians."

"Oh, right…" Issa's voice hitched a little, her tone clear that her true question of legality hadn't been answered.

"You see, once a creature is deemed extinct, all previous laws of being endangered are cast aside. So in my case I'm technically not operating outside the law unless a new one is drawn up. Even if they are deemed endangered again, my people say my papers will absolve me because I came in ownership of these few after the proclamation of extinction."

"I see." Issa turned her eyes to the lake's edge where a ghoulish gray creature seemed to materialize from thin air. "What about that one?"

Al-Turabi halted the stroking of the lightning bird's feathers under his hand to follow Issa's gaze. "Oh! Grunt, there you are. Don't be shy. We have a guest today." Al-Turabi turned back to Issa with the eager eyes of a child with a new toy. "Did you know tokoloshe can turn invisible from time to time?"

"I might have heard that in passing. I've also heard that some of them are considered thinking beings."

"Key word there is *some,* and even then that's generous. I can count on one hand how many thinking tokoloshe I'm aware of."

"One of them works out of the markets near Sycamore Square."

"And he's one of how many?"

Issa didn't have a good enough rebuttal to utter.

"I know you're worried about me. But trust me… a vast majority of tokoloshe are just as dim as my lynx. No, that'd be too cruel of the lynx. These gremlins have no more wit than a tree stump. *And* they aren't anywhere near extinct—the pests they are to their native lands. So I'm clear on both counts there."

Issa was about to question the legality of the sphinx who was still staring at her between mossy tree trunks, but she knew al-Turabi would have an excuse for that one too. She wasn't here for a debate about ethics, she was here to learn more about Vaziri and his collections. The time for catching up was over.

"It seems you have everything covered, as ever." Issa inclined her head. "The expense must be a heavy burden though. I mean, it sounds like you have a mystic academy and a unit of advisors to keep paid."

"That's why I have you, right?" He flashed a smile Issa only half returned. "I admit, I could be doing better. And I don't like these rumors about war on the horizon. That'd be bad for both of my current endeavors. My sanctuary, in particular, will only truly flourish under the current peace. It wouldn't be so bad if my mystic crew still had their steady supply of Gods' Glass. I can't risk them using half-expended material. That's a dangerous sport, that is."

"I've heard through the grapevine you've had qualms with the new head of the refinery sites..." Issa canted her head, "that you claim it's some collector who's making ruin of your situation. But there's something I don't understand about that—I was under the impression it was Overseer Fahir who was managing the sites."

"That's what it looks like at the surface." Al-Turabi frowned. "But it's Vaziri pulling his strings, I know it. It wasn't like this a few moons ago... but the Overseer has changed. Daveed Fahir was a true gentleman of Old Vaaj, and he was liberal with the Gods' Glass he gave out under the table. Vaziri on the other hand... he's just keeping it all for himself, it seems."

"You don't think he's just going legit? Maybe he's done playing into the black market." Issa knew this wasn't true, not with Vaziri going around siphoning extra taxes off the slummers.

"Not a chance," al-Turabi said, echoing Issa's true thoughts. "Vaziri is as crooked as they come, I'll tell you. The whole lot of that family... They'll do anything to earn back even a sliver of their previous wealth."

"What makes you think Vaziri has anything to do with the refinery sites to begin with? His station's in collections, not mining."

"It's like the Overseer changed over night." The Merchant Lord snapped his fingers. "Just like that. Have you ever had the chance to speak with him in recent moons? He's as dull as they come, doesn't even seem like there's a soul in him at all, you know? And he used to be the life of any party. Something strange is going on. I may not be able to prove it, but I know it. And my gut never sets me wrong."

Al-Turabi rubbed at his goatee as though to recall an old story. "At first I thought Vaziri had the man under some potion or something, I would've bet my estate on it. These days though I've been working on a new theory…" He looked down at Issa earnestly. "Vaziri is an empath, sure as sand is dry. You ever see those golden eyes of his? Most empaths got eyes like those. Well… at least that's what me and some of the other lords think anyway, but the cowards don't want to confront Vaziri about it. Some of them are actually friends with Vaziri. He's always having his little parties and whatnot. And I'll admit, he knows how to entertain… but someone's gonna need to stop him at one point or another."

"So," Issa said, "Hypothetically speaking, what would you say one would have to do to bring someone like Vaziri down?"

"I'd go asking around at the mystic academies. Vaziri's been spending a lot of time with—" Al-Turabi stopped himself. "You know, I'm saying a whole lot without hearing much from you. What do you have for me, Officer Akif?"

"I thought my gift showed enough good faith."

"It got your foot in the door, and perhaps a bit of a rant from me about Vaziri, but I don't see any reason to say anything more unless you've got something for me to chew on."

"I don't think I have much that would be of interest to a merchant lord."

"Sure you do. You're a clever girl. And I know you know more than you should despite your lowly position in the Navy. What do you know of the rumors about impending conflict? I'm sure you know some time tables at least. I already know Zaakiyah

Najjar and her little band set out a few weeks back... Let's start with there, what's that one all about?"

"I don't know," Issa lied. That was something she couldn't give up. Najjar's conquest was in pursuit of more Skyglass. If Issa tipped someone like al-Turabi off, it wouldn't take long for him to figure out why an army was heading off to Junga Mountain, which housed nothing but pacifist monks. Were that information to get out, it would bite her in the rear real quick.

She couldn't let silence be her only answer, though, not when al-Turabi's eyes were darkening. She was certain a dismissal was imminent, not unlike his previous meeting with the tariff officer. So, before the Merchant Lord could open his mouth she said, "But I can give you some *general* estimates of a potential push westward."

Al-Turabi's eyes lit up. "I'm listening. And don't feel compelled to muck up the information by cloaking the truth either. I don't need specifics, I just need to know a date so I can get a head start on getting my assets in order, in case trade lines start backing up. I have my alternatives, of course, but they do need time to set up."

"The Admiralty is planning for westward expansion through Aktah by the end of next year, maybe as soon as the end of summer."

If a certain airship was in order, she added in her head.

"And let's just say, signs of this push will be clear, if a certain telepathic general comes back home with good news. And, let's just say if *I* were this General, I'd probably not make a play until I secured a certain mountain in the East. Then, and only then, would I push back to the West where Vaaj has a few former enemies… ones tied to a certain Inquisition."

Al-Turabi rose from his squat and came within a finger's length of Issa, his face deadpan. Issa could smell the perfume lacing his goatee, the carob juice that still lingered on his breath. Then, gently, he kissed her on each of her cheeks. "Very good, child. Very good. This will serve me very well. Very well indeed."

"Good. So, you were saying something about Vaziri and mystic academies?"

CHAPTER 24
KARIM

Damnit, I don't have time for this, Karim spat in his mind as he replaced another book into the giant stacks of Jasmiin Towers's central library.

He had scoured through the substantial archive of ancient texts and newfound theories for anything pertaining to the Old Way and how he might use their information in his efforts against the pirate Jelani.

His early book selections turned up nothing useful on the old religion itself, but as he had searched he came across a number of alternative interrogation techniques—ones that did not involve torture. The findings had sent him down a winding rabbit hole of research. He hadn't studied like this in... he didn't know how long. It had been years at least, probably for his final exams in the academies. Day and night, rows of shelves became his friends, and old scrolls and dusty tomes became his closest confidants. After his first week, Administrator Ahmadi, an elderly woman with the neck of a bull had gotten into the habit of issuing him the keys to the classified section by default. That wasn't strictly allowed, the section set aside for military officials and certain highly-ranked nobility, but after so many days of the same spiel, tedium prevailed.

He didn't have the luxury of time. Their Majesties wouldn't

wait for him forever. They'd just replace him with someone faster, and the new Vaaji Air Fleet would sail forth without him. He had to get this right, and he had to do it now.

Things might've gone faster if Karim had consulted Issa or his father with regards to the Old Way instead, but Issa was busy tracking Collector Vaziri—plus, she had made it clear she didn't want to use the Jo'baran faith against the pirate back on the *Viper*. And when it came to his father… he just didn't want to get his old man's hopes up in thinking his son was getting serious about the Old Way. So Karim settled with the more comfortable wisdom of parchment and ink.

It was during one of his especially long sessions of looking up more interrogation techniques, where stacks of books bordered him haphazardly, that a small hand drew across his private reading table to light the moonstone sconce at his side.

Is it night again already?

"Congratulations, *Captain*," the Prince murmured.

Karim straightened and squinted as the surrounding space filled with gentle blue light. As the moonstones' light expanded, he could see the thinnest line of a smile on the boy's face. It didn't quite suit him, Karim decided. The half smirk seemed almost strained in its precision.

"My Prince," Karim stood in a rush and bent over a pointed salute at his chest. "I am honored, Your Highness."

Karim could see now that Prince al-Nasir held a trio of books beneath his small arms, each tome thicker than any one that Karim had on his own desk.

"I hear you had some trouble with your assignment a few days ago. Proctor Halabi told us it took two nights to bring her telepathic student back to her own mind."

Karim didn't answer, his immediate response struggling somewhere between royal decorum and answering to a child.

"Speak candidly, Captain," the Prince acquiesced.

Karim nodded. "I didn't think it would be so dangerous. I didn't think the pirate would manage such resistance to telepathy."

The Prince tilted his head back a fraction in thought. "These things do happen. Mystic Khadija knew what she was volunteering for."

"Of course, Your Highness." Karim bowed into another pointed salute.

Something that looked like a dark lasso twisted over the Prince's shoulder, and it took all of Karim's resolve not to shudder when a forked, slithering tongue licked the Prince's jeweled turban. He had almost forgotten that Their Majesties and their only son never went far without their personal guard by their sides—or rather, shoulders, in this case. Karim eyed the Prince's protector warily. Serpent-shifters were a rare and dangerous breed, and the carpet viper seemed to incline its head to Karim's table with an odd look of curiosity.

"Ah, *The Tempting Rope*." The Prince ran a finger across the page Karim had been trying to read. "Al-Dimashqi didn't have half the clue she thought she did. Colorful writer though..." He leaned back and held the withdrawn finger to his chin in thought. "Give me a moment. I have something I think you'll find more suitable."

Karim watched as the boy set his tomes gently on the desk, then shuffled through the rows of books and scroll-stuffed shelves. At the end of one aisle, he caught the attention of Administrator Ahmadi, who nodded and pulled a set of keys from her wrist. Keys in hand, the Prince disappeared around a corner and did not return for several minutes.

A nervous beat ran through Karim's chest. The Prince himself was giving him aid. It was one thing to consider how much the Royal Family depended on him in thought, yet it was entirely another matter when one of them was there in the flesh.

Karim jabbed a finger to his temple as he considered all the scrolls and books he had gone through. How could he get information out of a man he couldn't hurt or delve telepathically into? Perhaps the Prince would have his answer, but Karim doubted it; he'd been in the library several days already.

He gazed through the open chamber he sat within, up to the arched windows above that led to a golden dome. Each window sill held a statue of one of the great minds of al-Anim, each backdropped by the night sky. Issa often reminded Karim that the statues once belonged to the images of the Gods before they were torn down and replaced. He sighed at the thought. One day she'd understand that this was the age of men. The Gods, like their statues, were no longer the true power in the world. The same went for the mystics, and with Jelani. Eventually, the pirate too would fall like those statues. Karim just needed the right tool to see it done.

Karim's reflection broke sharply as a large tome dropped onto his desk with a thud, dust billowing from its cover.

"This should do you well for your... *stony* situation," Prince al-Nasir said through another peculiar and uncharacteristic thin smirk.

Karim's lips parted and he was about to ask how he knew of Jelani when the Prince moved his eyes downward as though to say "take a look." In an eerie mirror of the child, the carpet viper at the Prince's shoulder made the same gesture. Karim followed the boy's and snake's gaze to the volume that had been set down for him. A silver title along a leather cover of deep blue read: *House of Stone, by Ghulam Bahjat.*

Karim lifted his head to the Prince, a knowing glint in the young boy's old eyes and a stray hair curling out of his lavender keffiyeh. Karim had no idea how a boy his age came to know the things he did, even if he *was* the Prince. But he recalled how well the markedly young man controlled the debrief in the war room... like he was some seasoned admiral. Karim decided it didn't really matter how he came to know the things he did, or how he wore the authority of his station so capably so young. The boy was helping, and with the task at hand, Karim could use all the help he could get.

Flipping through the first pages, Karim scanned a few of the opening passages. Though some of his crew thought it best to just beat the information out of their prisoners, this "Ghulam Bahjat" did not seem to agree. The first section of his book mentioned something about the likes of... being the prisoner's friend. Karim shot an eyebrow up at that. He tried that before on the airship and that didn't work out too well for him.

"The key to extracting information is a casual approach," said a new voice at his shoulder. Karim turned to see Vice Admiral Shamoun there with his usual crooked grin. "Well, at least, not one of fear and aggression to start. Don't worry, Bahjat gets into the details in a few more pages."

The Prince gave Shamoun a slight nod. "To what do we owe this honor, Vice Admiral?"

"The honor is all mine, Prince al-Nasir," Shamoun returned with a bow of his own. "And it's good to see you as well, Harith." The viper at the Prince's shoulder nodded.

"You also doing some research, Vice Admiral?"

"Oh no. I'm up to nothing special, Your Highness." He slouched into a seat next to Karim. "I just like coming here for some peace and quiet, especially with the new workload. Not to mention I fancy the view in the main chamber. Yem's moon is bright tonight, yes? I'm sure the mystics of our city are having a nice viewing of Aya's turn from yellow to orange. The bright pair together means the foretellings of a warm week ahead, if I'm remembering that correctly."

"You are," the Prince answered. "At least, as far as the layman sayings go."

Shamoun nodded. "How about you, Your Highness? You're not giving el-Sayyed a hard time here, are you?"

"Just pointing him in the right direction," the Prince replied, and Karim could hear the first hints of a boy-ish tone—one of a youthful buzz. "So much of our future rests on his shoulders, does it not?"

"Ah…" The Vice Admiral leaned back in his chair casually. "You must be procrastinating for your exams tomorrow, aren't you?"

The Prince tapped at the books he left on Karim's desk. "I'm offended, Vice Admiral. I was ready for the exams weeks ago. These are so I can win a debate with Lady Awad about how Moharam came to bring the old tribes together."

"Oh, is the young Zariya Awad with you tonight?" Shamoun leaned his head around a corner. "I can't remember the last time

I've conversed with her. She's a particularly sharp one. You'll have your work cut out for you there, Prince. Watch yourself."

"This is… a lot," Karim confessed, flipping through the pages of the book the Prince gave him. "I'll need at least another week just to wrap my head around the concepts."

The Prince and Vice Admiral turned to him with frowns, even the boy's carpet viper seemed to fix Karim with a stern look. Each twisted to the other as though deciding who should speak first.

"Listen," the Prince started, "it seems a lot to start. But as with anything, you should first focus on the smaller parts—not the whole."

"Take it one step at a time," Shamoun added. "These sorts of things have to be done in sessions. It's a long game. Think of it as a contest of King's Way. You're not going to win in one gambit."

Karim never cared for the game. He didn't see how it helped —despite the love his superiors had all heaped upon the near-sport. Many lectures back at the academy had been made trying to convince him of the game's relevance to real life battle strategy. Karim just never saw the purpose of it all. Like any board game, it was regulated, clean, and predictable. No plan, no matter how intricate or how many times it's been poured over, ever survives the first moments of a battle. When soldiers are staring down a vanguard of giant elephants or a squad of elementals conjuring storms of fire, improvisation was king.

Karim knew that firsthand from his experiences in the sky.

The Prince looked over his shoulder with narrowed eyes and leaned close to Karim. "I'm sure you've heard—the eastern front has found great success. Junga Mountain will be ours soon. If you can secure Kidogo without letting that Golden Lord of theirs know what he's been sitting on all this time, there'll be none who can hope to stop the Empire's expansion."

Karim sighed. It was hard enough extracting the information he needed from the pirate Jelani. Figuring out how they'd swipe the skyglass deposit right out from under the Pirate King's nose was another ordeal entirely.

"Forgive my ignorance…" Karim set the large book down. "Are we not going about this the harder way? Why not request an audience with the Golden Lord? He could be made to *help* us extract the Glass, if he's paid well enough."

The Prince drew back a little, barely a twitch. He seemed to be considering Karim's words deeply... the same look he gave him back at the debrief.

"You want to tell the Emperor that yourself?" Shamoun remarked darkly as he traded a glance with the Prince once more. "He's been very clear on his desire to keep this all under wraps—he and the Grand Admiral both."

Karim stroked his beard in thought. "But that first attack was a fiasco. Surely the Pirate King knows something is going on by now."

"Yes," the Prince spoke up, "my father was most displeased about that. But our spies tell us Lord Zuberi does not yet know *why* the attack was launched. Our diplomats were apparently successful in chalking it up to pirate infighting that just ranged too close to our own seas. In short, an overzealous defense. Still, you're right. The Golden Lord is particularly cautious of the Empire now."

Shamoun snorted a chuckle. "You never fail to surprise me with your knowledge, young Prince."

"Remember what I told you before, Vice Admiral." The Prince gave Shamoun a sharp look before relenting. He brushed his hands free of dust. "I must be off. The longer I keep my lady waiting, the better the rebuttal she'll have in store for me."

Shamoun lifted from his chair and gave Karim a pat on the back. "If you need me for anything, I'm stuck in my quarters for the foreseeable future. Don't be a stranger."

"Right, of course, Vice Admiral," Karim said, then he turned to the Prince. "It has been a true honor, Your Highness."

Karim watched as the two walked away, their voices receding deeper into the library's rows. With another sigh, he turned back to the book.

Well, this isn't going to read itself, Karim thought as he flipped through the first pages once more.

CHAPTER 25

KARIM

AS DAWN BROKE, AND AFTER A FEW MORE HOURS OF READING—
and re-reading—the first chapter of *House of Stone,* Karim finally
set out at the break of dawn to test what he had learned.

The book had been well-crafted for a novice like Karim, and it
turned out he didn't need to spend the week pouring over it as he
had first feared. When he had turned the pages to the second
chapter, he realized the very next section detailed the second stage
of a long-term interrogation. In fact, the end of the first chapter
advised outright that:

> *The interrogator should step away from the subject to let seeds of*
> *doubt grow in the individual's mind, to let the hard work under-*
> *taken thus far bear fruit.*

Karim had noticed a perhaps over appreciation for metaphors
in Bahjat's writings—but he heeded the words all the same.
Instead of distracting himself with what was to come, he closed
the book and decided he was confident enough in the foundations
to proceed with at least the first steps of Bahjat's instruction. He
just needed to mold the scholar's musings around what he knew of
Jelani specifically… his religious fervor.

As he marched out of the temple and back out into the desert's morning, he enjoyed the refreshing, cool wind as it chilled his face. He considered his plan of action. Bahjat hadn't argued that torture was completely out of the question, as Karim had first assumed. There were times when a more assertive approach was necessary, such as in time-sensitive or combative situations, or perhaps against a subject about to perish. But in scenarios such as the one he was in at that time, when a subject's fortitude was so far above the average expected of them, a more delicate approach was necessary. And when the interrogator had such a read on their target—Bahjat also seemed to write very sympathetically regarding his subjects—was when they could play with the more nuanced and labyrinthine depths of emotion.

The Gods, like always, were in the details, the end of the section had said.

Karim took issue with the dated line each time he read it. Not *everything* the talented author had put down was of use to him it seemed. He could almost sense Issa over his shoulder, telling him, "See? A thinker who puts faith in the Gods."

Forcing her voice out of his head, he continued to toil with his strategy as he passed through the palace's main gates, through the polished stones of noble dwellings, and back to al-Anim's outer wall.

He nodded a greeting to the young man who attended the camels by the portcullis and mounted one of the desert creatures. With a pat at its side, Karim adjusted the camel's head to the rolling dunes of the north just beyond the gate.

"All right there, Captain?" the stablehand asked as he gave Karim the reins and raised the gateway.

Karim took the straps and bellowed a short yip at the camel, then he turned to the stablehand and said, "For the Empire's sake, I hope so."

The camel lifted and trotted through the dunes. A half mile from the city where the huge plateau of the base broke the horizon, Karim pulled out his book from the camel's saddlebag and reread the second page.

... Being overly complacent and submissive to a prisoner's sensi-

Karim had no interest in pressing Jelani any further than was warranted. The telepath he had forced on the prisoner went through enough trouble with that on her own. Karim just needed the pirate to see reason—for his own sake as much as Karim's. So how would he soften the man? While Bahjat's words were helpful in theory, they provided no solid examples that matched Karim's own scenario. Perhaps they were hidden further in the text, but Karim didn't have the time to find out.

The Empire was depending on him *at that moment.* He had the eyes of the highest-ranking officers of the Admiralty watching over his shoulder. Skies, the Emperor himself had apparently taken a personal interest in his mission—his princeling son even more so, it seemed.

So, when he arrived back on base, instead of going straight to Jelani's new cell—which had been moved from his previously over-decorated quarters to a more conventional one of low-light and lower heat—he turned to the kitchens. There he prepared the one thing he knew how to make well: a simple carrot and onion soup. Once he'd finished making the soup, he poured it into a wooden bowl, slid the bowl onto a tray, and made his way to the prisoner's room.

When he reached the pirate's new lodgings, he gave a swift nod to Hajjar, who had been posted at the door. The young mystic returned a salute as Karim leaned his head close to the door.

"Step away from the door and against the wall," Karim called out. He listened for movement but heard none. "I said move yourself against the far wall." When no answer came he withdrew his janbiya and traded a look with Hajjar, who snapped a chilled ball of ice into his palm. It looked like a floating snowball with jagged, almost translucent crystalline edges.

Good choice, Karim thought. *A fire would not be smart right now.*

For a moment his mind wondered if Hajjar was truly capable of freezing the pirate in place, then he remembered that not too long ago the young man had thrown a prisoner over the airship railings. It had taken him little to no effort to hold the captive man up, simply through a thin water line connected to a frosted point.

Karim mouthed a silent countdown from three and opened the door quickly, ready for an attack.

What he found was the pirate's back.

Jelani sat cross-legged atop the wooden floor, facing the far wall as though in prayer. At first, Karim couldn't make out the words Jelani was muttering to himself, but then he realized the pirate was singing that song he did every morning.

Karim sighed, tilted his head to Hajjar, and spoke out the side of his mouth. "Don't worry, Hajjar."

"I can come in with you, if you please, Captain," the young man said eagerly, head held high.

"That's all right. If I need anything, I'll let you know."

Hajjar nodded and closed the door behind him.

"Is that onion I smell?" Jelani said, lifting his head and turning.

"Onion *and* carrot," Karim corrected.

He set the tray on the ground in front of Jelani and tapped a finger next to the bowl—an old tradition of the Jo'baran faith. He just hoped the gesture wasn't *too* obvious. This play would only work if the pirate thought Karim was slipping into old habits again.

The clay-like stone clumped around Jelani's cheeks caught Karim's eyes. In the short time he was away, the plague seemed to have worsened far greater than he had anticipated. "I'm still looking for a brewmaster who knows his way with stonesbane," Karim said. "Abadi thinks he can do it, but he says it'll take some time. The condition is quite rare."

"And thank the Gods for that. It's all good though, I 'preciate you givin' it a try." Jelani leaned forward, bending hungrily to pick up the bowl. He blew a quick breath across the soup's surface before tilting the contents to his mouth. After many deep and swift gulps, he rested the bowl back down—half empty already—and looked back up at Karim. "I been lookin' for a brewmaster myself. I get it half right, most of the time, but it never lasts long—only a day or two. My… well, I know others who can do it better than me."

"We don't have all that many mystics in this country that aren't regulated." Karim nodded as he pulled up a chair resting against the room's far wall. "Therefore, any use of Gods' Glass is heavily regulated in Vaaj, especially here in al-Anim. So we have very few infected. It's been years since the last time I saw someone plagued with the disease in person. The rare few permitted use of the glass know to stop before they reach the darkstone."

The pirate waved a hand. "Don't worry none. I ain't dyin' tomorrow."

"How do you like it?" Karim nodded to the soup.

"Better than what we used to get on our ship, your cooks are pretty—" Jelani glanced up at Karim properly for the first time, his eyes trailing over the silver medallion hooked on his chest. "So you been made a captain then? For real this time."

"How did you know this is the medallion of a captain?"

"Me and my crew got to know you and your Navy good and well."

"Regardless, let's not talk of pirates and empires." Karim waved, recalling the first step by Bahjat. It was too soon to begin the true questioning and Karim wanted to get them there on his own terms. He had to make Jelani forget who his true enemy was, as difficult as that would be with him confined and imprisoned. Not to mention the fact that Karim had set a telepath on him not too long ago.

Jelani folded his hands in his lap and Karim saw a slight shift in his expression. It wasn't any less guarded, but perhaps more… inquisitive?

"What you wanna chat 'bout then?" the pirate asked.

"I want to know more about you." Karim maintained his casual tone. "Who were you before life turned you to piracy— besides an oni'baro, of course."

Jelani gave him a wry grin. "How do you know I haven't always been in the life?"

"You don't seem the type." Karim shrugged one shoulder. In

truth, it had only been a guess, but the more knowledge Jelani thought he might know, the more he may be willing to let slip as a given between them.

"Right. Well, it weren't my first choice." Jelani raised his fractured hand, gesturing at Karim. "What about you? How does someone from the slums come to be in such high service of the Vaaji Empire?"

Karim swallowed hard, trying his best not to show his surprise. How could the pirate know? Surely he had to be bluffing too.

"Just a guess." Jelani smiled, his eyes seeming to read the shock through Karim's mask. "You got the look of the streets about you."

"I suppose I'll have to work on that." Karim played along, adjusting himself in his chair uncomfortably. It was important that he not let any hostility rise between them. Especially not from himself. Thinking on it further, he realized that his elevated seated position may have come off wrongly. So he discarded the chair and sat himself on the floor, matching the pirate's eye line.

There was a long silence that came after that though, interrupted only by Jelani's now slower slurping. His initial hunger must've already been sated, but he was clearly savoring the meal as much as he could. Karim tapped at his knee. He had never been good at casual conversation, least of all small talk.

Jelani put the bowl back down and broke the silence for him. "So, you think I'm old, do you?"

"What?" The question caught Karim off guard.

"When you put down the tray you tapped the ground. That's what younger people do to elders as a show of respect." Karim suppressed the smile that tried to loose itself at his lips' edge. He traded it for a look of confusion, raising an eyebrow as Jelani continued. "You sure you're not a child of Jo'bara?"

Karim chewed at the inside of his lip in mock nervousness but he stopped at the third bite. Jelani thought he caught Karim off his wits, that's what needed to be the truth here if this was going to work.

"I'm sure I'm not." Karim let out in a guarded tone.

"My body might be cracked and broken but my eyes work plenty fine. Seems you carry a lot of old habits with you. Why you give it up?"

Jelani's eyes were casual, unassuming. He almost shrugged as he picked up the bowl again to finish the dregs.

Karim played the act of irritation as he pursed his lips tightly. Even as he played his part, he could appreciate how… *arresting* Jelani was. He must've been a good oni'baro—a seasoned orator. His words were far too measured, too soothing. Karim considered if the man was twice blessed, some sort of empath perhaps. But the academies had trained him to sense that sort of influence and none of the elusive signs were there. The words were the man's own. He was just good at speaking them, despite his broken accent.

"The Vaaji frown on the Old Way," Karim sighed, pressing his fingers to his forehead as though in shame.

"No, that ain't it. Or it's more than just that." Jelani set his bowl down for the final time, contents drained to the last drop. He crossed his legs again, his chains scraping against the wooden floor. "You agree with them, don't you?"

"My Empire? The Faith?" Karim wondered what would work better here. The truth or a lie. Should he placate and show remorse for rebuking the Old Way, or should he admit that in reality he truly was converted?

"I do," Karim confessed. The truth felt like the right call. "I do agree with them, that is. And what of it? It makes sense. Are you going to tell me I shouldn't forget the other lowly Gods?"

"Not at all." Jelani shrugged. "I'm just curious is all." There it was again. That casual ease about him. Karim didn't feel the need to put up his guard as he did with Issa or his father. He had half expected a fight from the pirate, some sort of dogmatic rebuttal about the righteousness of Ogó'ala, or some such.

Karim sat forward, considering his next words. "It's really very simple. The Gods were gone long before you or I were even thoughts. Shati'ala gave us the ability to defend ourselves; she gave us humans magic of our own. Not the pakkami, not the azizas, not the scaled, but to men."

"They have a name, you know," Jelani interjected. "They're *kadal*, not 'the scaled.' I ain't never understood why of all the wageni, you Vaaji piss on them the most."

"Shati'ala gave us the supreme power," Karim ignored Jelani, "she gave us our minds. Magic is dying in this world, *you* know that better than anyone right now." He gestured to Jelani's stone-skin. "Great Nations are clamoring for the last of the mystics, but they are only delaying the inevitable. One day our magic will be gone, our gift from the Supreme One will dwindle, and then we'll be on our own. There will be no gods to save us, none of their tools left to use. We need to start preparing for that."

Karim waited for Jelani to rebut, but no counter came. He simply sat and waited like he always seemed to do. Maybe the previous silences weren't silences at all. Perhaps the pirate always took twice the amount of time to ponder his words, regard them against Karim's own, and then respond.

Karim had been so used to the military, where concise speech and swift responses were coveted.

"Most credit the Supreme One for the power she sacrificed to us," Karim went on. "But that's not the best of it. Our greatest power isn't our ability to manipulate fire, or see into the, to be honest, *fickle* future, or even to talk to whales." Still, Jelani did not waver. "Our minds are what created our greatest achievements, it's what will bring Vaaj back into power."

Jelani gave his nose a small scratch. "That's interestin'."

"What's interesting?" Karim asked almost defiantly. What would this man say? Would he dismiss his words altogether? Tell him that Deh'ala will not grant the Vaaji success because they did not pray to him or the others?

"What you said…" Jelani went on. "I'm used to your people repeatin' the words of your holy text. But those words were your own."

Karim paused and raised his eyebrows in genuine curiosity. He had never given any thought to the way he spoke. He was used to conversations on military strategy, not his own philosophical opinions or musings. It made him think. Looking inward, he hadn't realized how deep into the Empire's machinations he was.

Had his own world view aligned so closely to his empire? He had only thought he knew so much about their sensibilities because he wanted to be a good soldier.

"I agree with you, for what it's worth," Jelani said. "My kind ain't gonna last, but our minds will. We do put too much faith in the abilities given to us by Shati. But it ain't mean I'll deny those who came before me, Gods or ancestors. There's beauty in all things."

Karim appreciated that Jelani did not chide him. Instead, he spoke about what the Gods meant to *him*, not what they *should* mean to Karim.

"Who taught you the Old Ways, anyway?" Jelani asked, again, the catalyst for the conversation.

"My father," Karim replied without hesitation.

"Is he well?"

"He's in good health."

Jelani dipped his head low. "Even with all the taxes?"

Karim scratched at his beard to hide the shock his lips would surely betray. "How would you know about that?"

"Your guards get bored easy." Jelani glanced at the door. "Sometimes I think they forget they guardin' me. It ain't their fault though. I'm a very quiet prisoner, 'cept for my singin' every now and then. But them boys have loose lips."

Karim logged the thought in the back of his mind. Hajjar and Damji were slacking.

"Yes, my father has had some trouble with the taxes," Karim conceded.

"And what he think 'bout you puttin' faith in with al-Qiba?"

"I haven't told him. He's a stubborn man…" Karim trailed off, his lips twitching with the realization of what the pirate was doing. He wasn't about to let the tables turn so easily. He took a breath, settled his expression again, and continued, "If you know the time for mystics is ending, why do you protect your Glass so closely?"

"Ah, I was enjoying our conversation. I suppose we should get to business, then." Jelani leaned back on his hands from his seated position.

Well, I'll be... Karim thought. The pirate was far more keen than he let on, or perhaps Karim simply kept underestimating him.

"Where is the Glass, Jelani?" Karim remembered that using the subject's name supposedly made them feel more at ease.

Jelani's following shrug was almost too cavalier. "Honestly, I don't know. They always movin', you know, Ula's Glass tends to do that."

Karim bit back the heat running up his tongue. "When our soldiers breached the caverns on your island, most of them were gone. We *know* your people moved them somewhere."

"You got the wrong kijana if you're lookin' for *that* kind of secret."

Appeasing the pirate with soup and sweet words was clearly not going to work, so Karim switched tack. "Do you know of Shati'ala's Justice?" Karim took Jelani's stilled expression as an affirmation. "Oh yes, I'm sure an oni'baro like you would know of it. There are many like you who have fallen to Her due process—"

"You're wastin' your time with your threats. I can't be hurt while I got this here plague, we been through this."

"Who said anything about hurting *you*?" Karim's last word came as sharp as the janbiya tucked in his belt. He could see from the subtle twitch in Jelani's eye that the man understood it too. "I merely wanted to invite you to one of these... viewings. I assure you, it's not too grotesque. Certainly nowhere near as bad as what you pirates get up to. I've heard about the way that *Redtide* crew treated their prisoners."

"You wouldn't," Jelani cut in. "And we both know the Rovers are outside the Golden Lord's authority." The pirate shifted on the floor with discomfort, from the flat wood or unease at the conversation—Karim couldn't tell. Either would do.

"Nah," Jelani continued after a short silence, his head shaking so slowly Karim could barely tell it had moved. "Nah, you wouldn't do that, Karim. You're a good man. Perhaps your Emperor would have me watch my holy kin being executed before my eyes. But you..." The few muscles left in his shoulders seemed to relax. "I don't see it."

Karim felt his neck stiffen and he brushed a speck of dust from the floor to center himself. "Don't presume to know anything of what I would or wouldn't do, *pirate*." Karim rubbed at his beard once more. He could almost hear the mocking laugh under Jelani's flat expression. "You think yourself a good man: noble, pious, don't you?"

Jelani laughed through his nose. "No, I just know my sins better than most."

"Then there must be something you're not proud of."

A darkness curled over Jelani's eyes, one Karim would have never expected to cross his gentle gaze if he hadn't seen it before. Despite this though, the pirate's tone came light as he said, "I stole fruit from my village once when I was ten. Took some coin from my father's table when I was twelve. Then there was the time—"

"You know what I mean."

Jelani's smile hung for a few moments before a new thought colored his deep, dark eyes. "There's a story behind why this didn't kill me." He lifted his stoney fingers. "But I prefer not to tell it, just like I'm sure you don't want to tell me yours." He indicated the scar through Karim's beard by running a finger down his lips.

Another uneasy silence fell. The first true one, at least. Karim decided that he was terrible at this form of interrogation. Maybe he should have got someone else to do it in his place—maybe asked for Issa's help after all. But she already had her fair share on her plate and was probably faring far better than he was with it. It was time for him to buck himself up and pick up the slack on his end. They had decided to meet later that day. If the rest of this talk went aground, then maybe he could ask her...

That wasn't good enough, he decided, not when senior officers and princes were backing him and practically giving him the answers in a damned manuscript. No, he needed to crack Jelani now or suffer another week of coming up empty in the eyes of the Emperor. His new title could be taken as easily as it was given.

"Listen," Karim said. "You seem like a decent enough man..." *Make him feel like your friend*, Karim thought. "But I can't help you out of this if you don't give me something I can work with."

"Even if I did know," the pirate began, rubbing his hands together with an eerie cracking sound. "I ain't seen shit from the Vaaji to suggest y'all gonna do right by the Glass."

"Why cling to them? They are of no use to you. No mystic can use them. Unless you're telling me the last of the cloud dancers still roam the skies. *We* can actually put them to use. We're reasonable people, once you get to know a few of us."

Jelani waved his hand dismissively. "It's hit or miss with you kijana. I'm sure even *you* don't get along with everyone in your Empire. I saw that Captain before he went down. What was his name... Malouf?"

Karim's mind darted to the groups he had conflicted with, Malouf and Vaziri at the forefront. "It doesn't matter if I get along with them or not. What matters is that we do our Majesties' bidding."

"Ah, you were doing so well." Jelani leaned his chin into his hand. "Every word was your own until just then. No man should submit to another's without question. I know you believe that too."

A knock came at the door though neither Karim nor Jelani stirred, attention fixed on each other's eyes. How dare the pirate assume and pass judgment? He was the one who pillaged and stole. How could he ever presume to hold himself over Karim like some saint?

"Enter," Karim called out without breaking eye contact.

The door creaked open and a pair of feet came pattering in. "Urgent message for you, Captain." It was Nabila.

Karim finally broke the stare down, closing his eyes and breathing heavily through his nose. "Is it paramount?"

"It's about Collector Vaziri, sir," she said. He turned to see her holding her hands tightly as though she were waiting for him to become angry. "He's returned and is making demands about the twins. The one who gave me the message said you'd understand. And he said he found a way to deal with the situation."

"Your fight ain't with me, it seems," Jelani said with a mellow grin. "Seem like your fight's with your own."

CHAPTER 26
KARIM

EXHAUSTED WITH THE WEIGHT OF YET ANOTHER FAILED interrogation, Karim couldn't find the energy to return to al-Anim proper and see his father in the flesh alongside Nabila; besides, he was to meet with Issa soon anyway. Instead, he directed himself toward one of the crimson military tents left mostly for the soldiers protecting the desert's secrets. For a moment, Karim marveled once more at the base carved from the lofty plateau as a gentle wind gave him a short start, waking his heavy eyelids.

"It's really incredible what we've achieved, isn't it?" Nabila said at his side.

"Indeed it is," was Karim's answer.

He recalled his conversations with Engineer al-Kindi. The man had been the one to suggest establishing the airship's base at the top of the uplifted earth once called The Great Rise—the perfect way to keep wandering eyes from her secrets. Karim wondered how many elementals—and how much time—it took to carve out the base. He might've stood there a bit longer ogling at what the Empire achieved, and pining for what it could still do with a united effort, had fatigue not directed him to his tent.

As it were, since coming back to al-Anim he'd made little use of his own lodgings, save for the storage of his coin. He wasn't sure how his sore feet and his drooping eyes carried him through the rows of tents, until he and Nabila reached an off white tent stitched with his new sky captain insignia, a twin to the one on his chest, though the emblem was sewn with a silvery satin where his was pure silver.

After a lazy rummage through his wooden chest, he sent Nabila off with another sack of coin to help supplement whatever had been lost in the old district. For the first time, he had to dig into his own personal funds to cover the amount. Had he been more awake, drawing from his own coin would have left him with renewed anger, but it seemed as though that early morning weariness had other ideas for him. Mere moments after sending Nabila off—not without yet more advances from the woman—he fell backward into his cot, one arm and leg hanging over the side.

Mere moments after falling asleep—he was sure of it—a warm touch against his cheek roused him. He clamped his eyes shut, scowling. "Not now Nabila, I told you to get that coin to my father."

"Ah, so that's who you shared your time with within the Silks, then?"

Karim's eyes shot wide, his vision blinded by a stream of sunlight beaming through a slitted tent flap. Silhouetted against the orange light of—*dawn?*—was a figure he couldn't make out, but the voice was unmistakable.

"Issa?" he asked, rubbing sleep from his eyes.

"Afternoon, Captain." She turned away to set something against his desk. Her blue uniform contrasted vividly against the reds and maroons of the tent's furnishings.

"Wait," Karim said. "Did you just say—"

"Yes, *afternoon*." She spun around, her headscarf whipping with her. "I came by this morning but you looked too precious to disturb."

Karim snorted at her coy remark. "It can't be. I only just knocked out. Nabila was just here. I'd just come down from interrogating—" He stopped himself short. "I need to get on top of my sleep…"

"Here, have some of this." Issa knelt down and stuck out a plate of steaming pita with a side of what smelled like hummus on his bedside stool. Karim reached for it, still reclined on his side, and tore into his first bite of the warm bread. Issa sat up and took her own seat on one of newly stitched red cushions.

After his dozenth ravenous bite, Karim finally asked the obvious question, "So, I'm guessing there is news about the Collector, then?"

"Mahir is up to something," Issa said with crossed arms, jumping straight to business. "He's had several meetings with a handful of nobles and senior officers. Dahlia Fahyad, Umar Jad, Anwar Rashid, Hamza al-Turabi, Nadya Utbah, both the Maloufs, and even the Grand Admiral."

"Is there anyone in the nobility he *hasn't* met with?" Karim remarked dryly.

Issa poured him a cup of coffee which he hadn't realized had been brewing on his low table. She blew on the steaming drink before handing it to him. "His meeting with Admiral Awad was the shortest," she said. "I'm guessing it didn't go well."

A smirk crawled against Karim's lips. It'd been barely a week and Issa had already procured an entire profile on Vaziri's personal dealings.

Issa always surprised Karim with how effective she was at gathering information. Several times during their military training she had been offered spy work in the East but she declined, always wanting to be close to Karim. As Karim watched her list out more peculiar circumstances from Vaziri across all her fingers, a shadow of a frown slipped his lips. There had been so many times when he wondered if each of them was holding the other back.

"What's he planning?" Karim asked as he sipped the first of his brew.

"I don't know. Nothing good. He's been spending a suspicious amount of time at the mystic academies, rubbing shoulders with the instructors. Al-Turabi says there's rumor that Mahir wants a travel pass. He's trying to craft an alliance with the Ya-Seti. But I think he just wants to study abroad."

Karim broke from his reverie. "Study what?"

Issa shrugged and poured herself a cup. "Therein lies the

question. Al-Turabi thinks he's an empath, influencing that over-seer at the old refinery, but so far I don't have any supporting evidence for that. Give me another few days, maybe a week or two. I'll have it figured out."

Karim shook his head in frustration. "I just need him in the same room. Every time I get close, his guards are there to block my path."

"Then we may be in luck," she smiled.

"How so?"

"Mahir wasn't just interested in speaking with the nobles. There are plenty of people interested in a few words with the Gunner Chief who led the *Viper's* first assault." Issa winked, pointing a proud thumb at her chest.

"You didn't...?"

"I did. Awad's right. You've really got to get connected with these types. It's not all that hard. You just have to get them talking about themselves—the nobles at least. Once you start that ball rolling, you just sit back and listen. Not a lot of fun, but you pick up a few things: their connections, what they really want, how long they've been with the Faith. You could learn a thing or two from me, you know?" She smirked her way through the faux boast.

"Your coaching would, as ever, be welcomed," Karim acquiesced gracefully. He'd long since learned to let Issa have her moments of fun. "But how does this get me in a room with Vaziri to catch him in his plot?"

Issa leaned back on her arm, sipping at her coffee. "He's throwing an end-of-year banquet. All the major players will be there—save for Their Majesties and the Admiralty. And guess who got herself invited?" Issa withdrew a folded parchment from her uniform. It bore the three-coined sigil of the Vaaji treasury.

"Better you than me, I suppose. Just make sure Mahir isn't—"

"We're allowed to bring a guest, idiot," Issa said with a playful laugh. "You're coming with me."

"He's allowing guests? But I thought this was some secret meeting?"

"From what I can tell, no. It's just a banquet. I reckon he's just softening up the nobility before his next round of meetings. All perfectly above board. Although..." She shrugged, motioning her cup to the side as she trailed off.

Karim pressed his head into his hand, prompting her to go on.

She peered up from her drink, clearly surprised he hadn't followed her thoughts. "Well, even the decent noble types have back room gatherings at these events. It's just the done thing. Maybe he'll try and take advantage of that, I don't know." She shrugged again.

Karim considered it. *What's Vaziri playing at? What's his endgame?*

He took a sip of his own coffee and his eye caught a lump of fabric stacked atop the desk that Issa must have brought in. "I suppose those have something to do with the banquet."

"Why yes, yes it does." Issa practically skipped her way over to the low table—an inherently unusual movement in the official garb of her uniform—and lifted the first bundle of fabric.

Karim couldn't help smiling at her giddiness. He hadn't seen her skip like that since they were children. Her coy remarks may have remained—adapted to meet the expectations of her rank—but her jubilation, the genuine *joyous* quirks, had all but washed away from years of military institution.

Or so Karim had thought.

"Now, I *know* this is just a way for us to uncover what Mahir is up to, but..." she trailed off yet again, flapping the first piece of fabric in front of her to model. "I see no reason we can't enjoy ourselves while we're at it. Now come on, help me pick a dress!" The silky garb was discarded on the cot, thrown carelessly over Karim's legs. The bright blends of oranges and reds paired well with the darker furnishings of the maroon tent.

Typical that she wouldn't like that one, then. Karim thought with amusement. *She* hates *blending in.*

Issa quickly drew the next garment to her chest—though the chest part seemed to Karim to be somewhat... missing. "It looks even better when I put it on! Look—" Issa walked to close the flap at the tent's threshold, then promptly started to undress.

"Wait! W-what are you doing?" Karim held up his sheet to cover his eyes.

"Showing you my dress," she answered matter-of-factly, her trousers already thrown over his side table chair. "You can't judge it until I've put it on."

"Some warning would be nice next time."

Issa sucked at her teeth. "What's the problem? Our families used to bathe together down by the river all the time." Karim could see her pulling the skirt of her dress up her legs through the silhouette cast against his sheets.

"That was before you were a woman—and before al-Qiba deemed it indecent. Families don't do that anymore, remember?"

"Right…" Her voice was sad. "Okay, I'm *decent* now."

Karim rubbed his eyes and lowered the sheet. When he got a proper look at Issa, he rubbed his eyes again. He couldn't believe what he was seeing, where had his childhood friend gone? Her tan arms were left completely exposed, her shoulders free and neckline low. Her athletic legs, however, had been mercifully covered by the flowing length of luscious greens and sensual blues. The skirt of the dress's trimmed lining was streaked in fine silver. The details of her every aspect were outlined perfectly, the effect—even for him—was… aggressive.

Though taken aback by the woman before him, Karim couldn't help softening at the twinkling of her eyes, the honest smile on her lips.

"So… what do you think?" Issa gave a twirl. It looked like she was dancing through the flow of a majestic forest river—half naked.

Karim didn't approve. "It's a bit immodest…"

"I prefer 'exciting.'" She stopped her twirl and kicked up her skirt with her legs, holding the edges out to the side.

Karim averted his eyes again. "Where did you even find something like this?"

Issa scoffed. "You need to get out more. We're in the capital, Karim. Al-Anim has some of the most diverse markets this side of Esowon. You can find anything if you look hard enough." She dropped the trimmed edges of her skirt and spread out her arms. "So, tell me what you really think."

"It's a nice dress," he admitted. "Really, it is. But maybe for…"

Issa crossed her arms, and Karim could sense an imminent foot tap coming on. "For what? Go on. Spit it out."

"It's something one of the women in the Silks would wear."

She sighed. "Well, I know *you* like the dresses the women in the Silks wear well enough—you spend enough of your shore leave down there."

Karim ignored her barb. "Right… It's just, I don't think it's appropriate for the banquet is all. What kind of attention are you trying to attract?"

"I told you, you have to start making connections. A little flirtation helps grease the wheels."

Karim pointed to the open cut of her breasts. "You're certainly going to be greasing something."

"I thought you would have liked it…" Her voice came low as she fiddled with the strappings of the dress, struggling to take it back off. The sight was strange for Karim. He had grown so used to seeing Issa shouting orders at her deck crew that he had forgotten how sensitive she could sometimes be, or perhaps he was simply being too harsh.

"What about this one?" Karim lifted himself from his cot and picked up another dress. It was a simple blue, straight with a silver trim and a loose fit. Classic and conventional.

Issa's eyes drooped along the dress like it was as interesting as watching paint dry. "It's more traditional… but I'm not so old yet."

"But it's respectable. It's a nice color too. If you pair it with this orange-ish sash, it'll look great. Beautiful and prudent."

"You're no fun anymore." Issa snatched the blue dress from Karim, stomping into a corner to change. "Well go on, turn around." She rolled her eyes, waiting for him to turn.

Karim did as she said, shifting his head to the corner where a single vase lay on a table, a set of incense sticks branching up from its base. "Is there someone you're trying to impress at that banquet?"

"No one you know," she joked.

"What about that elemental in gunnery? What's his given name… Tahir?" Karim feigned forgetfulness. He only just saw the young man a few hours ago.

"Hajjar? He's a child."

"I've seen the way he looks at you. He's always at your heel, and you seem keen to have him around."

"He's got a good head on his shoulders, that's all. I would never… no. Just no." He could hear the shudder in her voice. "I do think he'd be a good fit for the *sindisi bahriin* though. He keeps asking for a recommendation. But, you know, mystics can't really protect other mystics, right?"

Karim peered through the shiny surface of the vase. Through its reflection he caught sight of Issa's bare back. He averted his eyes to the smoking incense tips at first, but his gaze kept returning to the reflection. He might've known Issa since they were children… but he wasn't blind.

"Well, the kid should be a bit more discreet about how… fond he is of you," Karim said—mostly to distract himself.

"The same discretion you have when you visit Majida's?" Issa retorted.

"What I do during my shore leave is my personal business."

"As is mine," Issa returned coldly.

"And what I do is at least sanctioned under al-Qiba."

"By the barest technicality," she snorted. "You can turn around now."

Karim took a look. The dress was more unassuming. And the tarha that covered her head was far more prudent. She did seem a bit more uncomfortable in her stance, stiffer, as though the plain dress didn't sit right on her shoulders. There was no smile or twirl this time.

"That is much better," he said. "I don't understand why you have to be so immodest against the Faith."

"No need to get defensive. Besides, *our* Gods have nothing against harmless fun. Illopa and her seven children teach us the seven ways of love. I'm not doing anything any of them would disapprove of."

Karim let his groan out freely. "Always with the Gods with you."

"Well, you never listen," she retorted.

"I listen fine. I listen too much. If it's not from you, it's from Baba. If it's not from him, it's from that damn—" Karim stopped himself short of saying "pirate." Instead, he let out a great sigh, pinching the bridge of his nose. "The Old Gods don't matter anymore. When's the last time you've spoken to one—and before you say it, I don't mean those echoes manifested by ritual. When's the last time they've *done* anything for what goes on in the world now? *Right* now. Today."

Issa gave him a look of a reproachful mother. "We can't forget where we came from Karim. We can't just cast our traditions aside."

Karim placed his hands on her now covered shoulder. "I'm just looking out for you is all. You can't keep to the Old Way anymore. It's dying—dead, even. It's had its day. I worry about what will happen if the Navy realizes you're not truly converted. You can't go to the banquet and be that open about your... disagreement. There may be a time and place, but this isn't it."

She frowned deeply. "I'm not abandoning my ways just because the Empire demands it."

"What does it matter if you change your clothes a bit if it keeps you alive?" Karim asked.

"It matters a lot to me, Karim." Disappointment was laced in Issa's eyes. "And it should matter to you. What are we fighting for if it's not for *our* people. If we fight for whatever al-Anim is turning to... we're just protecting, what... merchant villas and greedy collectors?"

"What matters to me is bringing that Mahir Vaziri down."

Issa sighed, turning around and dipping to the low table to take a sip of her coffee. She walked to the tent's slit and unfurled it, letting in the afternoon wind. Outside, a few soldiers passed, walking shoulder to shoulder with spears in hand, their forms set against the bright light of the dusty orange and cloudless sky.

Issa stood there for a long moment, looking out into nothing, still as stone. After a while Karim joined her with his own cup, sipping silently. They let the quiet moment rest, as always, easy between them.

Farther along the row of tents, a pair of soldiers stood around what looked like a miniature arena crafted from mud. Karim couldn't see into it, but judging by the sweat beading atop the women's brows and soaking through their head wraps, they were engaged in a battle of speakers—desert speakers, more specifically. It was likely they were fighting a mock battle where they controlled a set of ants, or scorpions, or whatever creature they got their hands on, an effective ground-up training regimen for the more complex desert creatures they brought with them into battles. Their eyes flitted with sharp precision until finally one of them won out and their furrowed brows flattened once more.

"I've been thinking about that." Issa nodded in the direction of the mystic soldiers. "Mahir meeting with the mystics… making power plays. After our first mission, when we retrieved a few of those pieces of Gods' Glass, was all of it turned over to the military like it was supposed to?"

Karim thought it over. He didn't oversee the transport of the deposit. At the time it had been above his pay grade. "I heard rumors that some of it was sold off on the streets. But I thought it was just being distributed among the slummers."

Issa hummed under her pursed lips. "Next time you see Mahir, watch his hands." She finished the last of her coffee then gathered her discarded dresses. "The banquet is still a few weeks off but... wear something besides your uniform, will you?"

CHAPTER 27
ZALA

It took several days for Zala and Mantu to properly familiarize themselves with the kitchens and their mess halls. The workers were only allowed to enter the palace at the start of the morning when it was still dark. After checking them for weapons, soldiers escorted them down several winding corridors until they reached their destination. Zala couldn't determine how big the palace was in its entirety during just their first few days, but she was able to figure out that the western keep was at least one-thousand strides from the main entrance gate.

"Why are you murmuring to yourself like that?" Mantu had asked on their first day as they turned down their twelfth corner —Zala had taken on the continued role of a Qibasi devotee so her entire face was covered.

Lifting a finger to her face covering, she had whispered in reply, "Hush, I'm counting."

"No talking," the soldier ahead of them had said.

By the end of the first week, the most they had learned beyond that was that the head chef, Hadi, liked his onions chopped, not minced, and that he kept mistaking Zala for Mantu's wife—a story they actually didn't go with this time around.

Neither Zala nor Mantu could find any noblemen or officers. Mantu had tried distracting Head Chef Hadi as Zala did her snooping, but there was always too much work to be done and too many guards about the halls.

Zala had even tried to cross reference the steps she took within the palace against her steps outside of its walls when her shifts were over, but every few strides there were always a new set of soldiers standing guard.

Despite the challenges, that didn't stop Zala from gathering as much information as she could. Each day she returned to Lowtown and the Scars, where she added notes to a scroll she kept beneath her sleeping cot.

"Your penmanship is nice. I didn't take you for a scholar," Mantu had told her before their last shift of the week.

"Gods, don't scare me like that." Zala pressed her hand into her chest. "And..." She was going to say thank you but instead, reflexively, replied, "Yeah, I guess it's pretty neat."

Mantu circled around her, leaning his face closer to the scroll. "What are you doing?"

"You can help me, actually. I'm trying to work out how we'll map out the fortress. If we can't do it from within and we can't do it from its borders, how will we do it?"

"Beats me." Mantu shrugged as he hefted his supplies over his shoulders. "I thought it was you who had all them plans."

"Sometimes it helps to have a second pair of eyes. Or at least to have someone to talk it out with. Jelani..." Zala trailed off. Each day that passed without a sign of him was a day Zala lost a bit more hope. The stoneskin would take him if she didn't put her mind to it.

"Well, yesterday I did notice somethin'." Mantu pointed down to Zala's half constructed map. "The soldiers are thickest right before we turn this corner here. And then they thin out the closer we get to the mess hall."

"I thought that at first too. But the positions of the soldiers always change. Sometimes they are concentrated at the front of the fortress and other times closer to the mess hall..." Zala pressed her reed pen between her lips.

"Do you reckon they'd even keep that sky ship there? Where does someone even store somethin' like that?"

"At first I thought at sea. That ship of theirs seemed like it could float if it wanted to. But their bay is too exposed. They wouldn't risk anchoring it there if it's supposed to be secret."

"We gotta find a way out of the kitchens, but it's impossible with all them eyes, and that chef."

"I have a plan for all that."

WITH THE AMOUNT OF FOOD ZALA, MANTU, AND THE OTHER prep cooks had to sort through, one would assume they were baking and grilling for a whole village, maybe two. Between the soldiers in the barracks, the nobles throughout the halls, and the scholars that were served in their studies, the number of mouths to feed tallied near a thousand.

It was as though Jasmiin Towers was a city in and of itself.

She and Mantu had been mostly delegated to the soldiers, who never complained about how dry their falafels were so long as their alcohol was cold. But it was the higher-ups that Zala wanted to impress, the ones that could lead her to Collector Vaziri. The problem was that Head Chef Hadi never allowed it.

"So you was sayin' somethin' 'bout a plan this morning..." Mantu said when they were prepping for the midday meals. He'd been fighting against tears as he cut into his dozenth onion.

"Shhh," Zala hushed him, throwing a sidelong glance to Hadi, who had just entered the chamber.

That day they had actually been allowed to roam the halls to serve this captain or that philosopher, but they couldn't hang around very long—despite Zala's best efforts at striking conversations about tax collections with a particularly social noble's daughter. Still, their mainstay was the tight confines of the smallest kitchen in the keep: A cramped room with sauce splattered walls—three of the newer marks had been made by Zala only a few days prior.

"Girl!" Chef Hadi showered Zala in spittle. "Who taught you to cut a mango?"

Zala surveyed her work and didn't understand what the issue

was. She had got the cut right, just like the display of the fruit platter that lay to her side.

"What you're doing takes twice the effort!"

And all that froth you've just slung from your mouth is going to get someone sick! Zala thought, but out loud she said, "Of course, sir. Apologies, sir."

Chef Hadi grunted, then went along to observe everyone else's work. No one else got a shout down quite like Zala did. Not even the little boy at the end of the line, who couldn't be any more than twelve. Besides her and Mantu, there were four other prep cooks who were usually stationed with them. Two of them from Lowtown's Scar District, where they called their temporary home.

Zala waited until Chef Hadi stepped away from their station before leaning into Mantu to whisper, "So what, I might be no good at fruit cutting, but the other four don't know anything about baking. And I hear General Hashim has a sweet tooth. Fon gave me her rum cake recipe and—"

"It won't do you no good," Mantu sniffed and pointed his knife at her, "'til you actually get your cuttin' clean. Look how much you butcherin' that poor mango you got there. You ain't listen to a word Fon said, did ya?"

"What does it matter? The soldiers don't give a shit how well I cut their fruit so long as they're good and drunk." But Zala's next cuts came more measured, and, more than once, she flitted a glance to Mantu's handiwork. "What do you know about cooking anyway? You didn't even want to come along."

Mantu shrugged. "It's basic stuff, really. For example, if you cut a bit of chicken breast unevenly it's gonna cook unevenly, like Fon told us. And if you go cuttin' a mango like you are now, it takes twice as long." He sighed. "Ain't you an island woman? On Yem's tide, sometimes Zala, I wonder..."

"Okay hush." Zala swallowed, watching him work. "How are you doing it so fast though?"

"What? You're actually askin' me for advice? Has the Great Dulagi come back to gain his coveted and prophesied revenge? Have the Foglands pressed into the southern borders of Wazantsi?"

"Hah. Hah."

Zala went back to her cutting, trying to figure out how she could speed up what she was doing. Chef Hadi needed a lesson in leadership. He only told his inferiors that they were doing something wrong, never how they could do it right or, at the very least, better. Zala figured slicing the mangos down the sides, then peeling the skins made the most sense. That way she could cube them like the display had them piled.

"You know, I could show you how to speed up your cuttin', if you weren't so stubborn," Mantu chuckled under his breath.

Zala gritted. "I'm doing just fine. This is how Jelani taught me to do it when I came to the islands."

Mantu threw up an eyebrow at her. "And your husband came from them southern isles, no? Them savages just go openin' their mangos up with their claws and start diggin' in. No class."

In Zala's opinion, Mantu couldn't talk about class when his beard still looked like an impundulu could lay an egg in it at any moment.

"Here." Mantu took one of Zala's mangos from her station and placed it on another cutting board. He pulled out a clean knife and started to work. "You was right to slice down the side. No problems there. But you don't need to spend the extra time peelin' the skin. Just slice it evenly across and down. See?" He took his tiny knife and sliced under the little cuts of squares he made. "Then slip under and you got yourself some perfect little squares for your platter."

"Hm," Zala hummed. "That's… actually much easier."

"Man, Shomari's right. You're really shit at thank yous."

"Thank you," Zala blurted quickly. "Seriously. Sorry… I'm still working on that."

"Let me do you for another favor." Mantu edged his chin past Zala's shoulder. "How long that been spent over there?"

Zala followed the point of his jaw to the hour glass she had set on the shelf just above her cutting station. It had expired—for how long, she had no clue, but the faint scent of burnt flour pressing into Zala's nose gave her an unpleasant guess.

"Shit!" she exclaimed as she rushed to the other side of the kitchen, where her rum cake was rising as a black puff.

The little twelve year old pinched his nose. "We ain't 'posed to be bakin' right now."

"No one asked you, you little s—" Mantu gave her a look from his station. *"Keeba yuh mout,"* she said in Pakwan instead.

The kid shook his head and went back to his work of separating dates. Zala always resorted to insulting him in a language he didn't understand. She knew it was a bad look to shout down a child who's balls hadn't even drop yet, but how could she help herself? The boy was a little snitch. Chef Hadi would've never known the three stains on the wall were Zala's fault were it not for the little brat.

They were all competing to get the job for the banquet, however. Every cook in the western keep was. It's all any of them could ever talk about, that and all the coin it would bring those who were picked. So anything to show your worth and put someone else down was fair game in the end, Zala supposed.

With slumped shoulders and a pout on her face, Zala returned to her station where she slammed down her pan of blackened waste next to Mantu.

"Okay… we're fucked," she admitted.

That was her last gambit. She tried to impress Chef Hadi with her soup skills, but she was terrible at seasoning. Then she tried her hand at grilling, but somehow she always overcooked her meats. Then Fon suggested the idea of rum cake, especially after hearing about the sweet tooths that some of the nobles had, but that too failed like all the rest of her plans.

"Maybe there's another way we can corner that Vaziri," Zala murmured to Mantu. "Shaman el-Sayyed said he comes to the Scars weekly."

"But he ain't shown up in the last few days…"

Zala groaned. "Yeah… Ketifa said something about her big-shot soldier cousin scaring him off. He might not show his face there for a little while. Ugh! We don't have time…"

"We could always grab Majida and force her to tell us—"

"No. I already told you we're not doing that. Someone like

Majida's connected. We'd have more trouble than all that's worth. I told you she's got a network of oni'baro guards all around her spot."

Zala bit at her lip and peeked over to where two of the other cooks, a young couple, jabbed each other with their elbows playfully. "Heh, I could try flirting with Hadi," she joked. "I used to do it all the time at the taverns in Kidogo. Free drinks were always better than the ones you paid for."

Mantu stopped his cutting and edged his chin to the spotted ceiling.

"What?" Zala asked.

"That might not be a bad idea. We ain't got much time left. At this rate, I *might* get picked for this banquet. But *you?* You're not going anywhere."

Zala gave Mantu's words some serious thought. Chef Hadi wasn't much different from the patrons she used to scam drinks off of, just as rude and repulsive.

"All right then. Come break time, let's see if I can still work my game."

Over the next few days, Zala pulled out every trick she knew: laughing at Hadi's terrible jokes—"Oh, I never heard *that* one before."—light touching of his arm—"Were you born with strong hide, Chef?"—and feigning interest in the man's hobbies—"Oh, you love poetry? Tell me one of your favorites."

Her attempt to woo and seduce him seemed to have the opposite of a desirable effect, however. Each exchange brought her nothing but a scowl or cold-shoulder.

On the fourth morning, when she and Mantu were heading into another shift, Mantu said, "You know, I heard a rumor you was a lady of the night back on Kidogo... I can see why you became a pirate instead."

"I don't understand it." Zala shook her head. "I've tried everything. He just won't bite."

"Hey, not everyone has the gift. We all got to wonderin' why Jelani was with you, honestly—hey!"

Zala had punched him hard across the shoulder. She smiled when she realized she'd got him good—she had banked on her bony knuckles doing the trick. "We do our own thing. Duma saw it. I don't know why you don't."

"I was only pullin' your leg, chana."

"Yeah… well, it's not like you could do any better."

Mantu tapped his lips. "Hmmm… you'd be surprised."

"Go on then. Today, you give it a go. I need a break from shadowing Hadi all day. I can't memorize anymore poems."

"How much time we got anyhow?"

Zala pulled out her scroll and ran her finger along a few dates. "A little under a fortnight."

Mantu cracked his knuckles. "Give me a pair of days, three max. I'll get Hadi to pick us… well, me, at the very least."

Next to their station, one of their cohorts cried into a napkin. Zala gave her a short glance before turning to Mantu to ask, "What happened with her? Didn't get picked for the banquet?"

Mantu pulled Zala aside, lowering his voice before saying, "Nah. It's her son. Them Seekers swept all of Brewmaster's Row, not too far from where we stayin' at. The Vaaji don't play around with unregistered mystics here. Good thing we ain't got a lick of magic, eh?"

"What does a sweep mean? What happens to the mystics here?" Zala wanted to go over and console the woman, but she couldn't bring herself to do it. In fact, everyone in the room was keeping a wide berth from her, as though speaking to her would somehow associate them to her and her crimes against the Empire.

"Ah, nothin' crazy. They don't kill 'em or nothin'…" Mantu gestured down to the plates. "We just end up serving them. You haven't noticed most of their military are mystic types?"

"No…" Zala said softly, watching the crying woman. "I never did."

CHAPTER 28
EKKO

EKKO ROLLED THE YELLOW AND BLACK BEADED HAIR BETWEEN his fingers, their texture rough against his calloused hands. If he recalled correctly, the yellow was meant to represent acceptance in the old religion, and black, the finality of death. Marjani had tasked him to help her switch to the black beads in observance of the final day of mourning she was going through for their lost crew on that damned airship.

'The Six-Nights Celebration,' she had called it.

It occurred to him then that they were on the eve of a new week, which meant the mourning period for all those lost that first day in al-Anim would've been officially observed now. Marjani could've been among them.

Ekko stared down at his partner's body stretched over the ward cot before him. He dropped the single lock of her hair he had been caressing, and his gaze flitted to her torso for the thousandth time that evening. He just couldn't help the fear.

But she was still breathing. Still alive.

"Scholar Judas?" It was Surgeon Abadi. "I didn't think I'd see you so soon. Weren't you just here this afternoon?"

Ekko nearly forgot that "Scholar Judas" was what he called himself when he visited. The handle he had given the hospital workers when he first found out where Marjani was kept.

"I was, yes," he managed through a surprisingly dry mouth.

In truth, Ekko hardly ever left. He wasn't sure how long he had been sat there with Marjani, but it was long enough for his back to slowly set into an ache without him ever realizing it. He stood from his chair, rubbing at his spine and nodding to Abadi as the man came around the hanging modesty sheet—Marjani had come in with Qibasi robes, so she got the Qibasi treatment of chastity, that meant no one but the surgeons and Ekko could see her face.

Ekko didn't know why the surgeon was acting surprised. Where else would he be? Marjani needed him. He'd only left her side twice since she had been admitted to the Hammadi Hospice, and then only because Captain Lishan had ordered it for their latest job for Collector Vaziri.

Ekko glanced down at Marjani's face, checking for breath yet again. The "scholar gambit" had been one of hers, back in their early days. She had been amused—and impressed, Ekko secretly hoped—when he had fully committed to the disguise with fake wisdom beads and a mundane robe to sell the story.

"I was, yes." Ekko nodded sadly, weathering his false Aktarian accent with even falser age. "I try to come as often as I can. Any progress?"

"As much as could be expected with how much blood she lost that first day."

The deep blue of the surgeon's robes nearly swallowed him in the shadow of the room. Were it not for the line of moonstone lanterns at the head of Marjani's cot, Ekko wouldn't have even been able to make him out. The room sounded emptier than it was before—the other cots filled only with the sick or wounded, their shadows flickering along the sandstone walls and Vaaji arches. All of the other visitors must've already left.

Marjani's body spasmed a little under Ekko's touch. The jerky movement always sent a slice of fear through Ekko. The caretakers said it was supposed to be normal, but he never liked it.

"The healers tell me they had a rough session today." Abadi shuffled into the light of the nearest lantern, revealing a wizen faced, gray beard, and tousled white hair that threatened to burst from his turban. "But you've a strong one here, Brother."

That was the second lie Ekko had thrown into his story. The only way he'd be allowed to see Marjani, who had been found with Qibasi robes, was to say that he too followed the Faith. That meant being called either "Scholar Judas" or "Brother Judas" depending on the speaker's preference. With Abadi, it was often both.

"Thank you." Ekko placed a hand to Marjani's cold wrist. "Were you checking up on her, or is this my cue to leave for the night?"

"Oh, no. I was just poking in to check on the elder quarters when I saw you." He seemed to hesitate a moment. "Well, to be completely honest, I did have a question for you, if I could be permitted."

"What is it?"

The surgeon cleared his throat as he lifted the lantern closest to him to angle the light on Marjani. "Your wife, Sister Galia, has an interesting sequence of beads here. Many of the al-Qiba devotees are submitted here, so naturally I have seen their hair, but I've never seen these beads before. What do they represent?"

Anxiety sliced through Ekko for a moment. But he quickly recognized the genuine inquisitiveness in the old man's tone. There was no probing coming from the surgeon. Ekko was halfway to building another lie when he decided a half truth was the safer bet.

"Old habit of hers. She wasn't always a devoted child of Shati'ala. She comes from the islands, where they still pay homage to the Old Way." Ekko brushed his hands along her hair again. "It's something she's still working on."

Surgeon Abadi quirked a pair of bushy eyebrows. "Ah, if her attackers had known that, she may have escaped their targeting."

"Pardon me?"

"Attacks against the devoted have been increasing around here lately. Those radicals, those *oni'baro* sort, normally want to terrorize more... erm... pure devotees—I mean no offense, of course."

"None taken. No one of us is perfect. This was—is—my wife's struggle."

"Of course, of course." The surgeon set the lantern back in place and stood to his full height. "I'll be off. I see no reason to ask that you leave, but fair warning... Mistress Pasha might say otherwise."

Ekko gave him a weak smile. "Very well. Thank you for coming to visit. May Her Will be yours."

"And may Her Will be yours." Abadi bowed, then closed the privacy curtain that Ekko had left slightly open.

He groaned inwardly at his stupidity. The Faith made it clear that any of the devoted were meant to be covered. And since Marjani didn't have her wrappings on at the moment—so that the healers could do their work—that meant that her curtain was to be closed at all times. Abadi was being considerate, or just simply didn't care. But if it had been Mistress Pasha who'd seen it...

Ekko turned back to Marjani and sat down beside her. "Nice old man, don't you think?" He hunched over and dipped his chin over Marjani's cot, his voice low. "Like I was saying. It's been about a week since you were last awake. I got sidetracked looking at your beads. They reminded me of the time that's passed." He sighed, letting the stress of the week leave him, if even for only a moment. "Captain Lishan is still pissed. No sign of Nubia yet, but this Collector Vaziri has us pulling so many jobs that are supposed to lead us to her. I just got back from one, actually. I'll tell you, working the docks for information here is far easier than in Zanzi-wala, especially when these folks think you're religious like them."

A cough echoed off the walls. Ekko stopped speaking for a moment, waiting to listen for a caretaker, but none came.

"Anyhow," he continued to murmur, "I've got this empath fellow shadowing me today. Collector Vaziri still won't let us walk the city alone. I've never met one like him before though—the empath, I mean. I remember you telling me you met a few back home..."

Ekko chuckled at the memory of the story. It was one of Marjani's favorite to tell. She was always telling stories. Hopefully one day she'd tell some more again. But the darkness swelling in

Ekko's heart didn't quite believe it. The surgeon just said that the healers had a rough day, and Marjani was looking paler by the hour. He chewed down on his cheek to stop new tears rolling from his eyes.

"I've been doing my best to find that traitor of a woman," Ekko gritted. "In between my jobs I've listened for anything about her. But the city is too large, and I'm not even sure she's still here. Zala may be—"

Another spasm rocked Marjani's body. Ekko froze up like he always did, his throat tight as he waited for her next episode to pass. But only one shake came across her body.

"Marjani?" He brought his mouth a finger's length from hers. "Can you hear me, love? Was it something I said? Was it Zala that—" Another spasm. Butterflies floated in the pit of his stomach. "Skies above, Marjani!"

Ekko ripped the privacy curtain from them and rushed out into the adjoining courtyard where the healers often took their breaks.

"My wife! My wife!" Ekko bellowed, nearly forgetting the accent he often put on. He cleared his throat and reworked his mouth. "She can hear me. She's moving."

The three healers, all with heavy bags and deep shadows under their eyes responded with muted expressions. Their limp hands held cups of coffee to their lips. None of them jolted or made a move to follow Ekko. They must've heard this sort of thing all the time. Still, eventually, they made slow, shuffling movements from the courtyard into the intensive care wing all the same.

When they approached Marjani's cot, her lips were moving rapidly, as though chewing on something in her sleep.

"Oh, Shati'ala," one of the healers gasped. "She's trying to communicate."

Her companions rushed to Marjani's side and set their hands to her body and forehead with authentic vigor. Ekko's heart raced with an excitement he didn't think he'd feel again. Marjani was going to make it. His wife was coming back to him!

"Hurry, send for Proctor Halabi," one of the healers said. "She was helping in the elder's chambers with one of her students. Go!"

The first healer who had gasped rushed out of the room, her slippers pattering against the marble floor.

"What's going on?" Ekko asked. "Is this good news?"

"Brother Judas, we'll need you to give us some space—"

"But is it good news?"

"It could be if you give us space."

Ekko jerked back with his hands uplifted in surrender. "Right, right."

The few minutes it took for the lone healer to return was torture. The other healers had already worked up a light sweat under the dim light, and Marjani's convulsions never let up. A rush of new footsteps filled the room. Ekko watched as Mistress Pasha led two more females and a single male in her wake: the lone healer, an older woman in Maji robes, and a young boy no more than thirteen or fourteen.

"Come, come," Mistress Pasha beckoned them around Marjani's cot. She gave Ekko a sharp look. "You shouldn't be here, Brother."

"If I wasn't, I wouldn't have been able to notify you," Ekko returned darkly. "What's going on? What does this mean?"

"We might be able to save her," Pasha answered. "Just let us work. Faiza, get him out of here. Now."

The foyer was too damned cramped. How was Ekko supposed to pace back and forth when he could only take a few steps before having to turn around? And why couldn't he just be left to the courtyard? It wasn't like he was going to burst into the chamber while they were working on his wife.

Ekko kicked a bucket of water into the cobbled wall, where it crashed and spilled into the cracks of the marble floor.

That helped. If even a little.

"What's taking so long, saabi?" A sultry voice came from

behind. It was his escort for the night: N'Kota. "Vaziri has us on a schedule. You were supposed to be in and out."

"They think my wife might wake again," Ekko explained. "She's moving now at least. Why do you need me anyway? Can't you and your brothers do the job on your own?"

N'Kota shook his long head, his braided locs ebbing with the movement. "I already told you, you're the most valued asset for this operation. That, and my brothers are working with some of the other crew on something else tonight."

"If I wanted to run off on you all, I would've."

"Oh, we know that. And you'd probably get away. I'm not shadowing you because you might scuttle off; I'm protecting you from Seekers."

"Seeker this and Seeker that, I've not seen one since I've been here."

"Uh… that's the point, saabi."

Since the day they came to work with—or rather, *for*—Collector Vaziri, the man had clearly expressed the dangers of being a mystic in al-Anim, or at least an unregistered mystic, visitor or not. So the magic users of the crew, like Lishan or Arus, needed a special guard at all times, usually the empath brothers. Ouseni and Kwame, who didn't have a drop of mystic blood, could roam freely to complete their daily tasks.

"Look, I don't like babysitting anymore than you," N'Kota slipped next to him with an unnatural smoothness Ekko hadn't quite grown accustomed to, "but the second a Seeker starts asking questions or asking for papers, you'll love having me around. Unless you got a fancy for the embrace of dungeon walls."

A warm wave rolled through Ekko's chest. He hated when N'Kota did that, a reminder of the empathetic influence he could execute. But even Ekko could admit the value N'Kota had in a tight situation where smooth talking wouldn't be enough.

"Brother Judas," Mistress Pasha called from an archway leading back into the hospital wing. "We are ready for you."

Ekko turned to N'Kota with a sigh. "Five minutes. Just give me that."

N'Kota shook his grossly handsome head but smiled. "Fine

then... but that's all, *Brother* Judas. I got a girl or three waiting for me back at the Flask."

<hr>

EKKO WAS NEAR TO SKIPPING AS HE FOLLOWED BEHIND Mistress Pasha. He hadn't expected Marjani to be her full self, but at least he'd get to see her eyes again, get to see that wide smile with the tooth gap he loved so much. She was probably going to be thirsty and famished. He'd get one of the caretakers to fix her one of her favorite meals. The healers had kept her alive, but already her skin had sunken in and she was thin as a needle.

"Mistress Pasha, if you don't mind." Ekko lifted a hand as they passed the kitchens. "I'd like to get my wife some soup. I smelled lentils earlier today. She's very fond of..." Pasha had made a slow turn to him, her long head wrap falling against her shoulder. "What? What is it?"

"Oh, Brother Judas... you didn't think." Ekko didn't like the way she fiddled with the beads at her wrist. "Your wife... the healers did all they could do, but she can't hold on much longer. I told you when you first showed up here. Our healers have never sustained a body more than a fortnight. And in your wife's state, her injuries, I mean... she did much better than any of us expected she could."

Ekko's insides were transformed into a cave, a dark abyss that knew no end. It couldn't be true. She was just moving her lips a few minutes ago. That must've meant she was coming back and getting better, right? She couldn't slip away again, not when she was supposed to wake up and tell him his hair was shaggy, or that he needed to shave. Anything.

"But there is some good news." Mistress Pasha uncurled her fist around her wrist and reached out... almost as though to touch Ekko but thought better of it. "Proctor Halabi and her student have been able to tap into her conscious mind."

"What's that mean?" Ekko's throat was so very dry and his foot started taping on the stone floor.

"It means you'll get to say your goodbyes, Brother." The

woman let the heavy notion settle over Ekko a moment before she went on. "Come. Your wife is waiting for you."

Ekko slapped away the single tear that escaped his eyelid. Marjani was waiting for him, holding on so she could speak to him one last time. It was too much for him to feel at once. He wasn't ready for this.

As he stumbled behind the train of Pasha's simple robes, he battled for steady breaths. He'd had a week to prepare for this moment. Every time he visited, a part of him feared he would get the news of Marjani passing away in the night, or that there were complications and the healers couldn't get her steady.

But thoughts were one thing, reality another.

When they crossed over into the chamber, Ekko couldn't help seeing it for what it really was for the first time: a tomb. The cold stone walls that had often looked so tranquil with the spill of the moonstone's gentle hue, now felt eerie, like some specter was ready to capture each man, woman, and child in their unprotected cots.

The sick weren't getting better. Every cough or sneeze that stirred them from their sleep told a different story, every paling piece of skin and exposed vein just barely holding on. And when Mistress Pasha rolled the privacy curtain away to reveal Marjani, she too looked different...

Ekko had always thought of how she'd look when she'd get better. In his mind she was always going to get better. He never looked at her gaunt face or sickly skin in the inverse, the way her body would look in the next days, weeks, and moons as a corpse. A skeleton.

It wasn't fair. Marjani was a good person. His wife was caring. She put her trust in those who showed her kindness. And it was that altruism that had become her demise.

"So... how does this work?" Ekko croaked, finally realizing everyone was staring up at him.

The healers stood to one side with their hands cupped together and heads held low. The student, Ekko assumed from his plain tunic, cuffed a hand around Marjani's forehead. He whispered something under his lips. His overseer, the woman with the

Maji robes stood at his shoulder, coaching him through whatever mystical art he was applying.

"Mistress Pasha," the Maji said. "Can you give us the room? Your healers have done wonderful work."

Pasha dipped in a low bow, then beckoned her juniors away. When the area cleared out, the Maji cleared her throat. "To answer your question, my student here specializes in *last breaths*."

"Last breaths?"

"A loose translation from our tongue. Put plainly, my student specializes in withdrawing the thoughts of the dying. Their minds, the minds of those soon to pass, use almost a different language, one we among the mystics believe is the true Gods' Tongue. A communication more of feeling than thought. Though for now your wife still speaks in the Mother Tongue, the closer she comes to passing over, the more incoherent she will become. My student will translate for you as this happens. Please, comfort your partner for her final moments."

Telepathy was something Ekko never spent much time studying. The most he knew of it were the Aktahrians who marked themselves to connect with their military captains and generals. He didn't realize there would be divisions of the art. But he couldn't say he really cared for the how of it all right now, so long as he could speak to Marjani.

"Do I just… talk?" Ekko asked as he knelt next to Marjani's body. He placed a light hand atop her own, then slipped it into her palm. She gave him a light squeeze, and Ekko's heart fluttered.

"Yes, Brother Judas," the Maji answered. "Speak as you normally would."

Ekko chewed down on his jaw and rolled the start of a few responses on his tongue. In the end, all he could manage was a, "Hey, it's me."

It killed him that he couldn't give her his real name, or call her by her own. Would she even know it was him speaking to her with the telepath being the bridge between them?

"*Hey yourself,*" the boy said, his voice airy. Though the quality was different from Marjani's, the cadence was the same.

"I... I..." Ekko stammered, sobbing. "I don't even know what to say. I've had all this time and I still don't know what to say." He tried his best not to look at the Maji or her student. But both of them were being respectful, neither making eye contact. "I'm so sorry this happened. I'm so sorry. I —"

The boy cut him off. *"You are my heart, my love, my everything."*

"You know you are my heart. I don't want to lose you... I-I can't."

"You know what you have to do," the boy continued. *"Do it for me... do it for..."*

A silence came then, and Ekko felt his stomach bottom out.

"What happened?" Ekko asked, flustered. "What else is she saying?"

"She's slipping away," the boy said in his own voice. "Hold on I think I have it... something about a woman. Zarra? Does that name mean anything to you?"

Ekko swallowed deeply. Of course he knew what she was saying. "Zala," he droned. "She's saying 'Zala'."

"Oh, yes, that's probably right." The boy furrowed his brow, his eyes moving rapidly beneath his lids.

Ekko glanced between Marjani and the telepath. "What? What is she saying?" Marjani's grip slipped from his own as dead weight brought it down to her side. She was gone. Really gone. Ekko threw wild eyes to the telepath. "What happened!?"

"I'm sorry... she's gone."

"What do you mean? You were just speaking with her a second ago." Ekko wanted to punch something, everything, anyone. He never knew his body could shake and convulse as much as it was then.

"Scholar Judas..." the telepath said meekly. "There was one last message she had for you though." His eyes were wide, his shoulders tensed for another shout down from Ekko. But Ekko settled himself down for a moment, allowing the boy to go on.

"Um..." the boy went on in his small voice. "She said... I think she said... to make sure *she* suffers. To make Zala... suffer."

CHAPTER 29

EKKO

Ekko had left N'Kota in his wake the moment he stormed out of the hospital. "You said we were going to the Suhul Steppes, right?"

"Well, yeah… but I didn't reckon you knew where it was."

"My old captain always had us study any map we could get." Ekko stomped through alleyways and roads like he was possessed.

"What happened back there?" N'Kota pressed between a drunken group spilling from a tavern. "You wanted to see your wife… Is everything all good?"

Ekko increased his pace further.

"Ah," the empath said with muted realization. "Sorry to hear it, saabi."

Ekko bit down on the inside of his cheek. A memory kept invading his mind. His own naive voice trying to convince Captain Nubia that the new pickups were all right. He vouched for them, he *actually* put his own name on the line off the back of one friendly meal over soup. And *this* was Zala's repayment.

His thoughts hadn't even accounted for Mantu. Ekko had always told the old captain that the Aktahrians weren't all bad. Ekko had lived among them for years, but perhaps he had only known the decent ones. Lower Aktah always said Upper Aktah was filled with a bunch of bastards and dullards. Considering Mantu was apparently some sort of soldier, he probably came from Upper Aktah originally. And Ekko's blind trust had taken the love of his life away from him.

But there was one thing that always helped him get through life… a job, any job. And right then, he had one.

Ekko stayed silent the rest of the journey, even as he and N'Kota rented a pair of camels to take them out to the Steppes—though every now and then Ekko could feel N'Kota's a'bara lacing through him. Halfway into the dunes of al-Anim, he got fed up with it.

"Stop trying to press into me. If you got somethin' to ask, ask it."

"Sorry, friend. It's a habit." N'Kota brought his camel up to Ekko's side. "But I gotta question if you're all there right now. You seem like you're kind of tilting on your mount."

Ekko grounded his teeth. "I'm fine."

"Look, I've known many kinds of men in my life. Some who break down with a loss like that, others who do better with… certain motivations. We can reschedule this job, there are others to be done. I only know the guard's itinerary for tonight, but I can get that again no problem. Vaziri will understand with your wife—"

"Kijana, I said I'm *fine*."

"You sure?" N'Kota nodded down to Ekko's wrist. "My eyes are quite good in the dark, but maybe I'm seeing things. Those beads on your wrist, that thread there, that wouldn't be human hair would it?"

Ekko covered his wrist with his tunic sleeve. He'd taken a few of Marjani's beads, and some of her hair with it. It was the only way he could keep a piece of her, something he could still smell of her. He knew it must've looked crazy but he wasn't ready to acknowledge that, least of all with his babysitter of an escort.

Ekko pulled the reins and stopped his camel along the dunes. "You said I can leave whenever I want, ya?"

"That's right, but we all figured you all wanted nothing more than to get your Captain back. This is the way to do that."

"What if I had another request, another reward for this operation we're doing right now?"

N'Kota rubbed the back of his hand over his chiseled jaw. "How much?"

"Not how much… What I want is information. This Collector of yours, can he find anyone in the city?"

"Mostly, yes. Within reason, of course."

"Good. Then I want him to find me a woman named Zala. Her and her pirate crew. I'll *only* do this job if I have his word."

"Well, you got me in a bit of pickle here. You couldn't have made this request back at the city?"

"Only thought of it just now," Ekko admitted. "Sorry, I had a lot on my mind." Without warning, a tear fell down his cheek and he was thankful for how dark it was in the dunes, far away from the lights of al-Anim.

N'Kota swung his camel around to face Ekko's. "Mahir's a case-by-case kind of fellow, but he'll probably agree to it. Considering the nature of our operation, this all should be connected. To the crewmembers who betrayed you, I mean. You lot are all going for the airship, so the best way to cross paths again is doing what we're doing now."

"Good, then let's go." Ekko pushed forward and his camel set off again.

N'Kota sucked at his teeth. "*You* might be satisfied, but you still haven't quelled my concerns. I don't know if you're all there. You probably should be with your crew to mourn your loss or something—"

Still riding ahead, Ekko threw out a single hand. To his side a mini oasis manifested under the moonslight: a trio of tiny trees flanking a little pond with buzzing insects skimming over the water.

"I'm good, kijana." Ekko called out. "Now hurry before we lose the cloak of night."

"All right then…" N'Kota said smoothly. Ekko could hear the surprise in his voice.

They continued trotting through the endless dunes, though on the edge of the north and west border, Ekko could just make out the start of some desert jungle.

"So, what is this job exactly anyway?" he asked. "All you told me was that we're stealin' something from somewhere in the Steppes."

"We're off to this estate run by a saabi named al-Turabi," N'Kota said. "Some madman who got himself his own zoological whatever. Vaziri says he's got a few kongamatos. Shouldn't be too difficult for us."

"Not too difficult?" Ekko halted his camel once more. "No one said anything about flying. And I thought those kongamato things were all dead, just like the rocs and most of the dragons."

"Almost. Were it not for Turabi, they would be, actually. And don't worry about the flying business." N'Kota's golden eyes rotated into themselves and Ekko could feel that empathetic influencing filter through him once more. "That's what I'm here for."

"You can control two beasts at once?" Ekko asked, unconvinced.

"Very, very easily, in fact. The mind of a beast is much easier to influence than a human's. A lot less fuss." Now it was N'Kota that took the lead. "Hey, saabi. I'm putting my trust in you on this one. You gotta have some faith in me too."

Once the Steppes turned into a full-on jungle, Ekko and N'Kota tethered their camels to the first set of trees. Staying quiet and crouch walking, they helped one another to scale a tree where they could survey the estate ahead of them. To Ekko, it looked like some abandoned temple that someone was trying to reclaim from the jungle that tried to swallow it whole.

A pair of voices echoed from below them. Ekko squinted to see two guards marching along one of the walls.

"Hey, what about this..." one of them began.

The other groaned. "Let me guess... another would you rather?"

"This is a good one, I swear." The first guard twirled a golden dagger over his palm and back again. "Would you rather one of them mind fuckers put you in one of those deep sleeps for ten years or spend ten years in them Jasmiin Tower dungeons?"

"Sleep for sure."

"You wouldn't want to live your life? That's ten years wasted, saabi. At least in the dungeons you can make something of it. Skies, you could even make an escape attempt or two."

"Escaping from Jasmiin Tower? I'll have time with Empress al-Nasir before that happens."

"It could happen. You'd just have to…" The first guard's voice trailed off around the corner.

N'Kota tapped Ekko on the shoulder and the two of them vaulted from the tree and onto the edge of the estate wall. Straining against his own weight, Ekko struggled to get his leg over. N'Kota had no such trouble. He was already standing straight; balanced and poised.

"Ah, yes, I forget you're human." He stuck out a hand and lifted Ekko over the wall with surprising ease. He pointed below. "Just over there by the pool. We'll wait until the next set of guards pass through."

Ekko nodded as he walked over to a long pool surrounded by topiaries. Once he and N'Kota found a spot out of sight of the guards posted on the estate's balconies, they waited.

"So, what would *you* choose?" N'Kota murmured to Ekko.

"Huh?"

"What those guards were going on about… sleep for ten years, or the dungeons for ten years?"

Ekko shrugged.

"I'd take the dungeons," N'Kota said. "You see how muscled those saabi get when they leave out of there? Stronger than when they go in, sometimes. Makes sense with all the labor they've got to get on with." Ekko couldn't begin to understand why N'Kota would want bigger muscles. He had plenty enough already. "Not to mention half the dimwits that go in there actually come out literate… even if all they ever want to read is that al-Qiba book.' N'Kota turned to look at Ekko, perhaps realizing he was just talking to himself. "Not a big talker, then?"

"Not when I'm trying to stay quiet," Ekko hissed from a clenched jaw.

N'Kota shrugged. "Fair enough. We only got a few minutes once the next group comes through. The path down to the kongamatos is just past this pool here, but we have to be quick about it. Do you already have an illusion in mind?"

"Yeah, I've got something." Ekko had been taking his measure of the estate since they came in, the look of the stones, the shape of the topiaries, even the shadows they cast.

"Even if you do screw it up, once we get our hands on those kongamatos, we can ride them out."

"I'm not going to screw it up—"

"Shh, they're coming."

The *click-clack* of boots on stone came around the corner. Through the bush Ekko hid in, he could see the furred paw of an orange pakka and the deep brown skin of a human. Neither of them spoke like their cohorts at the wall, but they communicated well enough with hand signals. Just as they passed by where Ekko and N'Kota hid, the pakka stopped and sniffed at the air.

A wave of empathetic influence perfumed the air. Ekko gave N'Kota a sidelong glance to see him concentrating on his a'bara. But it didn't seem like it was working so well.

The pakka was still sniffing.

And his nose poked right between the bushes they were in.

Guess I gotta save N'Kota's ass this time.

Ekko held a hand against N'Kota's chest as the pakka pulled a few branches away. His cat eyes were wide and gaping like the mouth of a cave.

"What you see?" his partner asked.

The pakka gave the air a few more sniffs. "Nothing. Let's keep moving."

The *click-clack* of their boots receded toward the estate and away from the pool area.

"Good job, Ekko. Never doubted you." N'Kota smiled.

"Sure, kijana."

"Now… let's run."

N'Kota was right about the run having a very tight window. Despite Ekko going as fast as he could while suppressing the sound of his footsteps, they still didn't have time to get to the gates that led to Turabi's zoo before another set of guards crossed their path.

The walkway was tight, with shrubbery forcing the path to allow for single file only.

"You see," N'Kota murmured as the guards approached. "We're the dream team here. I've got light feet, you've got the illusion of light feet. It all works."

Ekko threw up another, much larger illusion, but it wasn't going to be enough. Their only option was to double back to the pool.

"No, no, no." N'Kota grabbed Ekko's shoulder. "These ones we don't have to hide from. Give me a few minutes."

Still holding his illusion, Ekko watched as, right before his eyes, the man next to him turned into a half beast.

Bones crunched, limbs contorted, and N'Kota stood on all fours as a hyena manifested from the back of his locs. Before Ekko could make full sense of the grotesque form, N'Kota sprang out from the illusion and attacked the approaching guards.

It must've been a monstrous sight. One moment, you're just walking on patrol, and the next, a demonic shapeshifter springs from the shadows to devour you in a second.

N'Kota was wrong about one thing. The whole ordeal took far less than "a few minutes."

In his wake he left a bloody mess of limbs and hands. The guards didn't even have time to scream.

N'Kota trotted over to Ekko with a set of keys hanging from the jaw of the hyena half of his face. Though the hyena's lips didn't move, a deep and eerie voice came from it. "Aah... that never gets old."

Ekko's heart hammered and thrummed despite the stone face he put on. "What the hell are you? I thought you were an empath, not a shapeshifter. I thought — "

"I *am* an empath." The hyena turned around to show the human side of its face where the voice was coming from. "I'm also a demon. We're called kishi where I'm from." The tone was far too nonchalant for Ekko's liking. "Don't look so frightened. Can you get this gate open for me? Paws aren't great for the job and I'd rather not change back right now."

Ekko hesitated before he took the keys. It took him a moment longer to actually fit them into the gate lock, his eyes still fixed on whatever the thing was that was hunched next to him.

"Don't be so slow about it," N'Kota said with some force, blood dripping down his hyena mouth. "When they find these guards, we'll need to be on the back of a kongamato and in the air."

Finally, Ekko fitted the right key into the slot and they were in.

Most of the animals in their cages were awake, but none of them paid either of them too much mind as Ekko continued holding up illusions and N'Kota kept influencing the various animals to look the other way. It wasn't long before they came to an area in the zoo that was blocked by another gate, which was carved with images of great beasts of the old times.

N'Kota nudged Ekko's hand with his maw, egging for him to try more of the keys. Ekko tried them all, but none of them worked.

"I was afraid of that," N'Kota said, then looked to the top of the gate. It was at least twenty men tall. "You think I can make that jump?"

Even with N'Kota being some sort of half-demon-whatever-he-called-it, Ekko doubted his odds. But each inlaid design looked like they could be a foothold for his paws. Paws weren't made for climbing, though.

"Don't freak out," N'Kota said as he leaped five feet in the air. His paws transformed into human hands that grabbed at the jutted designs and he crawled and rushed up the gate until he cleared the top. There was a brief silence before N'Kota's voice called out. "Ahah!"

A click sounded and the gate shot inward to reveal N'Kota,

who stood upright like a human but still with a hyena hanging from his back. The smirk across his face looked like one of a jester's as he beckoned Ekko. "Nothin' to it. Welcome to Turabi's Little Jungle."

N'Kota outstretched a hand to the space around him, a huge expanse of jungle trees, a big lake, and a host of creatures Ekko thought were lost to the pages of fables and legends: funkwes, n'kalas, lukwatas, a sphinx, and most of all a cluster of kongamatos. Only problem: the flying beasts were lounging in trees too tall even for N'Kota to climb.

"Here's the thing," Ekko said, chest thrumming violently. "I expected there to be a cage or something, some sort of enclosure. How exactly are we supposed to get at those beasts all the way up there?"

"By getting them to come down to us," N'Kota explained. "I've been working on their mating calls all week."

Setting his fingers to his mouth N'Kota made a strange whistle that shrilled and pierced Ekko's ears. A few of the kongamatos—the males, Ekko assumed—jolted and jerked their heads below. N'Kota gave them a second call and they dived straight for them.

"All right, now's the part where you slow them down with your demon magic." Ekko backpedalled and looked for cover. The closest thing was a bamboo forest to his side but it was several paces too far.

"I'm working on it." N'Kota lifted his hands in apparent strain. The kongamatos snapped large beaks and flapped their giant vivid rainbow feathered wings. They weren't slowing down at all. "Oh, shit."

"Oh, shit?"

"Take cover!"

Ekko was already sprinting to the bamboo forest, but he was still nowhere close enough to be safe. N'Kota sprang out toward him and wrapped him in a hug. The kongamato slammed into the man's hyena half. And they both went crashing into the bamboo, tumbling head over heel for what felt like forever. Even as they slowed they kept rolling farther and farther down a sloped hill until finally their tumbling halted against a boulder with a large *thud*.

Ekko shook his head, trying to free himself from the buzzing in his ears. When his vision cleared he looked up to a forest full of yellow and green eyes looking down at him in the night. He wasn't sure what kinds of creatures the fierce gazes belonged to, but he knew they weren't friendly.

"All right, I'll admit it," N'Kota grunted at Ekko's side. Despite taking more of the punishment in that fall, his hyena side looked unwounded, though his human side took a few scrapes. "This... is going to be a bit more complicated."

That was the understatement of the century. The sun was already rising, and they were stuck deep in a mad man's experiment of a jungle.

CHAPTER 30
KARIM

It had been a week and Karim still hadn't made any major headway with regards to the pirate Jelani and the secrets of Kidogo's cove. He'd made it all the way to chapter five of his book on interrogations before he realized that the slow-burn methods he was using weren't likely to see results for another moon.

Karim quickly returned the book to the library after realizing that small facet—and also after seriously considering burning the book first.

But it wasn't all bad. At least now he and the pirate had been talking openly without resulting in any animosity. These days their conversations ranged to anything from the mundane chit-chat of "how-do-you-does", to the deeper introspection of politics, religion, and the greater world. These talks were enlightening, but they weren't exactly getting Karim the results he needed. And it was only a matter of time before Their Majesties or the Grand Admiral sent someone to ask for a progress report.

It didn't help that Mahir Vaziri was still hounding Karim's father and his old home district, even if the man himself hadn't yet returned in person.

A light shined at the edge of his vision. He flitted a glance out of his office window to see the morning sun edging over the eastern dunes and spilling onto the mess that was his desk. There was so little room atop his workspace for the scrolls and tomes he had checked out that some of them were forced to find homes on the floor. If anyone came into the space to check up on him, they might've guessed he had emptied out a whole wing of the palace library.

A knock came at his door.

"Yes?" he called out. "You may enter."

Nabila shuffled into the chamber and closed the door behind her. She bowed lightly. "Sir, your father is here to see you."

"Here?" Karim shot up, displacing another wave of scrolls to the floor. "You mean here as in in the palace… right now?"

"Yes, sir. He said you weren't returning his messages and—"

"Never mind that, how did he get inside?"

"Um… he told the guards he was your father. He has an escort with him. They need to get the okay from you before they let him pass into the western keep, sir."

Karim inhaled so deeply, the whole of the Sapphire Seas could have been sucked up through his nose. "Let… him in."

"Right away, Captain." Nabila bowed again, retreating from the room.

It had barely been a few days. Or was it a week? He couldn't keep track of time anymore. His father was likely there about more taxes. Vaziri must've returned with some other loophole in the tax code, or kicked more of his old neighbors out into the desert lands.

Can I not just get a week to focus on one thing at a time?

The sides of Karim's temples drummed a painful beat against his skin. He rubbed them, but that didn't do him any good. Stomping over to his sitting desk, he pulled out a jug of water and drank from it straight, cups be damned. When that didn't work he cupped the water and threw it onto his face.

Thankfully, it was only a few minutes more before his father arrived.

He quickly dismissed Nabila. This conversation would be best held in private. After a half-hearted apology about the mess his office was in, Karim said, "I told you I'd deal with Vaziri. I was just working on something today. I've just got this military affair to address —"

"Oh, no, no, no." His father lifted pacifying hands, his skin looking, Karim had to admit, a bit more healthy. "I just came to tell you that it's okay. I know you've been busy and got a lot goin' on. But everything with Vaziri is being taken care of."

"Oh." Karim settled slightly in his chair next to his jug. "Oh, that's very well then. I'm glad to see Vaziri is being rational now."

"Well, nothin' changed with Vaziri. But I found some help that will stop his whole tax crusade against our district."

"What? How?" Karim thought back to his father's early letters. "Not those radicals again?"

"Oh no, no… Those oni'baro haven't been around for a little while — apparently some brothel pays them better. Nah, there are other people doing me a favor. Real nice types. They've even got a pakka with them."

"And this help that they are giving… it's staying away from the hill districts, right? You know pakka aren't allowed up that far."

"Of course, of course. They stay down with us. You should come visit. They're nice people."

"Maybe some other time."

Karim's father circled back. "Yeah… it's a good thing they came when they did. A lot of the bandits we deal with don't come around as much. But… one of Vaziri's guards came through saying the twins needed to leave the city for unpaid taxes. But if everything works out, it won't come to any of that."

Karim flared up. "Mahir is still going on about the twins? I already settled all that."

"So much work you got here, son." His father cleared his throat and started gathering the fallen scrolls and organizing them on Karim's desk.

"I told you not to mind the mess." Karim stayed seated but stretched out a hand. "And don't you go trying to change the subject, Baba."

Slowly his father set down the scrolls and lifted his hands in surrender. "It's nothing, really. I just came here to tell you it's all gonna work out fine. No need to worry about our end anymore."

"You're digging your own grave if you go off working with radicals and mercenaries or whoever you're in league with now."

"I told you they are nice—"

"I don't care how nice they are. You risk sparking a flame I can't put out if you involve more people we don't know. None of this would be happening if you and the rest would just—" Karim decided to think instead of say, *If you just converted to al-Qiba.*

Karim clenched a fist and pounded it on his end table. He didn't think his headache could've gotten any worse, but it was overwhelming him now. He couldn't even look at his father. The floor and his tapping boots against it was a better sight. At least he could tunnel vision straight on them and imagine when he looked back up he'd be in a different room on a different day.

To think just three moons ago he was in this very office when former Captain Malouf was informing him he was to be made Chief Officer of the Empire's very first airship. Perhaps he should've said no. He could've saved himself a lot of stress.

"I'm sorry, Baba," he finally said, his voice dry, exhausted. "I didn't mean to raise my voice. I've just got a lot going on."

When Karim looked back up he was met with the image of his father with head down and shoulders slumped. He wasn't even making eye contact, and when he did speak his voice was barely above a whisper. "Well, I'll get out of your hair, son. I was just heading over to the mines for an early morning shift. Just… don't go worrying about Vaziri, you hear me?"

Karim nodded an affirmative, but the moment his father left his office, he made his way straight for Collector Vaziri.

"Good morning, Captain el-Sayyed." Chef Hadi bowed to Karim as he stomped down the high arched corridors. "I'll make sure your breakfast is in your office in another hour. I didn't realize you were up so early."

"Don't worry, I'll eat in the mess hall later," Karim said as he brushed by and marched up the stairs leading to the financial section of the western keep. Just like the officials that filled the offices, each door leading into their workspaces were more opulent than the last, with rubies set along the edges of one, or sapphires around another, even pure gold on a few.

This is where the Empire's coin is going to? Not the old districts?

Stomping up to Vaziri's door, which was perhaps the most opulent of all the others with the Vaziri family crest of a platinum rose embedded in wood, Karim rapped on the door twice. On his third knuckled knock, the door swung open to reveal a tall dark man with golden eyes and long matted hair. His beautiful smile shined bright as he said, "Mornin' um…" He glanced down at Karim's medallion, perhaps unsure how to address him.

"Captain," Vaziri finished for the man from within his office. "Captain el-Sayyed."

"Apologies, Captain el-Sayyed." The man committed a perfect imperial salute. "I've not seen that insignia before. Can't keep up with all the new titles the Empire has. Doesn't help I'm new here. Anyway… the Collector is all yours."

"Oh, Ikeji!" Vaziri called out. "Before you make your morning run, check in with N'Kota and Ekko if you can. They were supposed to report back after their night shift."

"Sure thing." The man named Ikeji gave his superior another salute, and, as smooth as a cat, made his way down the grand hall.

Karim watched him the whole way until he rounded the corner. Were these some of the new recruits Vaziri had doing his bidding, the reason he hadn't been seen in any of the old districts like his usual? Hell, was that man going off to his father's district to scrape even more coin right now? He was certainly big enough for the job. Despite how loose fitting his tunic was, Karim had seen the muscle bulging underneath clear as day.

He threw his theories aside for Vaziri, however. It didn't matter who the man was or what his "morning task" entailed. If Karim could cut the head of the operation then and there, it'd all go away.

"I do prefer my doors closed, Captain," Vaziri called out again. "Were you coming in for a chat, or did you mistake my office for someone else's? Vice Admiral Shamoun, perhaps?"

The utter smugness in the man's voice brought a clench to Karim's fist. Issa's voice needled at the back of his mind. She had specifically asked him not to interact with Vaziri until his little banquet. She said it "hadn't been time yet," but he didn't have time for backdoor meetings and planning when his father was being swindled *now*.

It was time to confront Collector Vaziri right then and there, not later.

Karim stepped into the office and closed the door behind him. The chamber was large, but surprisingly sparse: huge windows, high ceiling, backed by a stretch of bookshelves, which backdropped another line of half-painted canvases on easels. A single, simple desk rested in the center, where the Collector sat.

"I never took you for an artist." Karim said as he walked the long distance to Vaziri's desk. Many of the paintings he passed were near life-like in their portraiture of nude men and women. "Perhaps you are in the wrong line of work."

"Oh, these?" Vaziri waved the compliment away with a limp hand. "They are still works-in-progress. But I've a fortnight before I need them to be properly done. They still lack a certain... realism."

Karim lifted a curious brow. Most of what he saw looked like completed works, but he couldn't call himself a critic of fine art. "A fortnight, you say?" He finally took a seat across from Vaziri. "That'd be around the new year, yes? Any plans? I've heard rumors of a certain banquet. One that you may or may not be hosting."

"Banquet?" Vaziri folded his hands atop his table, leaning forward slightly. "I host so many little get-togethers; I'm not sure which one you could be referring to. Besides, a dedicated servant of the Empire like yourself wouldn't be bothered, especially with how much work you've got on your plate."

So, the man was going to play coy. Karim knew Issa or

Shamoun would've told him to play along, to allow the conversation to flow casually into its true meaning.

Karim was never very good at that.

"I think you know which one I speak of. It's the same one you've invited a number of nobles to, namely Dahlia Fahyad, Umar Jad, Anwar Rashid, Hamza al-Turabi, Nadya Utbah, and both the Maloufs."

Vaziri pursed his lips and gave a light shrug. "I invite many nobles to many events."

"Oh yes? Even the Grand Admiral? I heard he turned you down rather soundly, or did I hear that wrong?"

For the first time since Karim came to the office, that conceited little grin of Vaziri's slipped, even if it was only marginally.

"You ever hear of the Origin Tribes district?"

"Of course, what does that have to do with anything?"

Everyone knew about that district. It was the talk of the city for several weeks, two or three moons ago, especially when the Origin Tribes had been one of the safer and orderly Lowtown areas. Yet the whole district had been cleared out and treated like radicals in one night. One day, it was full of slummers not unlike the ones that roamed Karim's home district, and then the next week they were all gone.

Most assumed there was some sort of midnight massacre, but there was no blood. It took several messanger birds to bring back the news that the whole district was being ushered into the red dune seas by military escort. The rumor was that the whole of the district had unpaid debt. Moons and moons worth of unpaid debts.

"That was me," Vaziri explained. "Their district leader didn't take kindly to my collections. So, to make an example, I got the treasury to back me and kick them out. It didn't even take all that much effort. In fact, if I wanted to do something similar to that again, all it would take would be a single messenger bird. I think Nabila would be a good one to use. She knows exactly where a certain problematic district is, doesn't she?"

Karim had to assume Vaziri knew pretty much everything

about him at that point… about the airship, about his giving money to his father, and now that Karim used Nabila to send that aid and those messages.

And then he brought up the notion of the Origin Tribes district.

Direct threats, Karim thought. *Or as direct as it got within the palace walls.*

So the swords were unsheathing now. That was a game Karim could play, a game much easier to navigate than false words and false smiles. "All right then," he gritted. "Let's cut the farce. What could you possibly gain from suffocating the slums? Don't you have powerful hiller friends you could exploit? Wouldn't they garner you more coin?"

Karim wanted him to respond with a cheeky "Well, I want those powerful friends to remain friends" or a "You don't know what you're talking about, slummer," but instead Vaziri's answer was: "I'm just doing what the Monarchy has asked of me. As a newly appointed captain to our Empire's prestigious Navy, you should know intimately the charge of heeding her call better than even myself. I've read your dossier. The better question here is why *you* are defending heretics."

"Don't try turning this on me. You're the one who's stepping outside of your role."

"Am I? Is it not our Empire's tax that I am imposing and upholding? If we're on the subject of 'stepping outside of our roles'—between the two of us, there's only one who seems to be doing that, unless prestigious new captains also have jurisdiction over policing imperial officials."

Karim dug his nails deep into Vaziri's desk in anger. "You and I both know you couldn't care less about what our Empire wants. So I'll ask again: what could you possibly gain?"

Vaziri took a deep sigh and tucked a loose curl of his hair over his ear. It was sickeningly casual. "I'm not sure what it is you want me to say, Captain. My gain is the Empire's gain. The penalty for unpaid taxes are quite clear. Perhaps you need to get some fresh air or some coffee in you. One of Chef Hadi's morning crew just bought me a fresh brew. I can call for another. You do look rather... unhinged." Karim dug his finger so deep into the desk, it felt like his nail would jam straight into skin. "Even if I was doing this for some undisclosed personal reason... what ever could you do about it?"

Karim had a few words for what he wanted to do and say. Lashing out and strangling Vaziri felt like a pretty good first option. But the man was right. At that moment, there was nothing Karim could do, at least not anything that wouldn't strip him of his title and land him in a dungeon. The whole conversation was a benefit to Vaziri, not him. He had laid out all his cards. He played the game he wasn't suited for. And he had no other hands to play.

Vaziri's next words were like twisting a knife in Karim's gut. "You're wasting your time and efforts with me. Wouldn't your attention be better utilized with that sea speaker you're charged to break?"

"How did you—"

Vaziri lifted a casual finger. "If your true desire is upholding the will of the Empire, that order of business should be paramount, no?" It took Karim all he had not to break eye contact with the man. The scowl that desperately wanted to contour his lips was even harder to hold.

Hearing no response, Vaziri sighed, seemingly disappointed that the game was over. "Was there anything else you wanted to discuss?"

Karim pushed back in his chair, making it scrape against the ground; it was furnished with a soft rug, so the desired screech he was looking for didn't come at all. It seemed that even Vaziri's furniture wouldn't give him the satisfaction he craved. Disgruntled, he shot up, marched the long length of the office only to be halted by Vaziri's last words. "And tell that lady friend of yours I cannot wait to see her at the banquet." The bastard, he knew exactly what banquet Karim was talking about. "You can learn a thing or two from Mistress Issa Akif, I think."

Karim didn't turn around to give Vaziri the satisfaction. Instead, he slammed the grand doors as hard as he could behind him.

CHAPTER 31
EKKO

"Don't move," N'Kota murmured to Ekko. "And stay silent. Very silent."

That was more than easy. For Ekko, everything ached. Moving right now was not his first order of business. He could only hope that the dozens and dozens of eyes staring down at them through the canopy belonged to benevolent creatures and not aggressive ones. He couldn't even tell if they were even all the same creature. Hardly any of them shared in their hues ranging from amethyst, crimson, and sapphire.

"What are they?" Ekko asked in his own murmur.

N'Kota gave him a little shrug, his eyes never moving. "No clue."

They lay there planted for what felt like several minutes as the morning sun peeked through the tall trees and bamboo stalks to reveal the amorphous shape of creatures Ekko had never seen before, even in the books back in Aktah's great libraries. He couldn't distinguish between arms or overly large earlobes—or maybe those were tails? Whatever they were, they clearly knew a human and a half-demon had intruded their space, but none of them moved to attack.

N'Kota started to chuckle, holding his bruised stomach.

Ekko shot him a sharp look. "That's not being quiet."

N'Kota started to stand up, dusting himself.

"And *that's* not staying still." Ekko stared up at the creatures, who still didn't move. They just kept to their curious blinking.

N'Kota stretched out a hand down to Ekko. "Apologies for the scare, friend. I forgot that good ol' al-Turabi has all these creatures docile." Ekko grabbed his paw-hand and stood up. "Vaziri told me that that lake of Turabi's is laced with some potion that cost him a fortune. It makes it so the creatures don't attack on sight, as most of them would do in their natural habitats." He pointed upward. "Those hanging from the trees are called *anjunjun* where I come from—tongue demons." Ekko gazed back up to see the long hanging shadows were indeed tongues and not tails. "Have you been to the Kunda Jungles before?"

Ekko shook his head as he brushed caked mud from his chest.

"Good. Never go. Even for someone like me, it's only good if you have a death wish."

A bell rang out between the bamboo thicket that they had tumbled through. "Looks like al-Turabi's guard found the bodies," Ekko said. "Time to find those flying creatures of yours again. This time, try not to get us killed."

Ekko took a step forward but was stopped by a low growl. The hyena on N'Kota's back went stiff and flipped him over into that unnatural stance on all fours, instantly changing his human hands into paws.

"Wait," N'Kota said in that demonic tone. "Those aren't human bells."

"Not human bells? What's that supposed to mean?"

Through the bamboo, Ekko could make out a figure that looked something like a moving tree, no, a moving bush, like a man had covered himself in fern with a nose made of bark and joints plastered with stone.

Gods, it can't be...

The bell kept chiming, and the morning light caught the edge of the grimy bell that was in the creature's hand. The other beasts who were sat observing in the trees scurried away quickly. Ekko wouldn't call himself a man of nature or an expert of the jungle, but he knew enough that when animals made a mad dash away, you were supposed to follow.

"N'Kota," he muttered out the side of his mouth. "That's... that's an eloko, isn't it?"

"Indeed it is." His hyena arched its back and growled. "Don't worry, it'll just pass us."

"Your little head boil seems to think otherwise."

"He's just shook, is all. Eloko don't take too much of a fancy to my kind."

The eloko broke the bamboo line and looked in their direction, lifting its peculiar nose to sniff the air. It couldn't have been more than two feet tall.

"Why's that?" Ekko asked, not sure his aching body was ready to make a run for it.

"We compete for female flesh. I use my face to lure women in; it uses that bell."

A chill ran down Ekko. He hadn't signed up for all this. It was supposed to be a simple job—well, as simple as any job that entailed commandeering ancient kongamatos could be. He wasn't supposed to find himself in the middle of some deep-rooted rivalry between a beast and a half-demon.

But he needed to make it out of there alive. He could die after he saw Zala hung from a rope or drowned in the ocean.

"Well," Ekko said. "We don't have anything to worry about since that potion you mentioned—"

The eloko screeched, showing all its fanged teeth and purple, sickly-looking tongue dotted with boils.

"Climb!" N'Kota shouted as he bounded for the eloko.

The two creatures met in a clash of fangs. The eloko used its thick bell as a weapon, smacking N'Kota's hyena maw. Ekko turned to find a bamboo stalk with the most ridges for him to easily climb. The battle at his side raged with growls and wails that made Ekko's searching frazzled and hurried. When he decided on one that looked half decent, he realized quickly that the climb wouldn't be easy at all. Despite the stalk having fairly large ridges, his meaty hands and large feet couldn't find proper purchase. Luckily, the eloko only had eyes for N'Kota, so his awkward lumbering up the bamboo wasn't so vital.

When Ekko got halfway up, exhausted, he braved a glance over his shoulder. N'Kota was putting up a good fight, pulling ferns away from the eloko's back with his fangs. But for every one of his bites, he was clobbered with a bell against his body or a clawed hand across his torso.

N'Kota fought to protect his human side at all times, just as he did before when they fell through the bamboo. Was that his weakness? Did his hyena-demon side have some sort of strong hide like human warrior mystics sometimes had?

Durable skin or not, N'Kota wasn't going to keep up under the maelstrom of that bloodlusted beast. Ekko took in a deep breath through his nose and fashioned an image for N'Kota. If his magic didn't fail him, the half demon should've appeared invisible. But the eloko still kept coming like a little raging green ball of pure anger.

"Not gonna work!" N'Kota grunted. "It smells and listens more than it sees."

Okay, if visual illusions aren't going to do it, then what…

Ekko inhaled through his nose once more. This time he extinguished all sound from the clearing between the bamboo. The eloko stutter step for a moment, patting at its lupine ears.

That's all the time N'Kota needed.

With a lunge faster than Ekko could really see with his slow human eyes, N'Kota's hyena head clamped down on the eloko's neck. An amber sap-like substance oozed from the creature's ferned skin. The hyena would not let go, no matter how much the eloko shrieked or convulsed. It didn't even have the strength to fight back with its bell. It was all over. There was no breaking the bite of a hyena. Ekko had seen enough of their kills in the wild to know that.

A few moments passed as the last of the eloko's thrashing subsided, and with it, its life.

N'Kota let go of its neck and allowed the creature to fall in its own amber pool of sap blood.

"Would you believe me if I told you that's only a child," he called upward.

Another series of bells rang out through the bamboo forest. Ekko lifted his head to see three more slightly larger figures rampaging through the thicket with a force and speed that only told of one thing: savage rage.

"I think it's your turn to climb!" Ekko shouted.

"I think you're right!" N'Kota rushed up the bamboo stalk next to Ekko, climbing the same distance Ekko did within the space of two breaths.

Ekko's awkward climb renewed, and once he got to the top of his bamboo, the whole stalk rocked to one side. Shooting his chin down below, he saw three more eloko—three-feet tall instead of two—bashing the base of his stalk with their bells.

"Jump to another one!" N'Kota bellowed.

Ekko did as he said, making a clumsy jump just as his bamboo went crashing down. Unrelenting, the eloko started bashing again without missing a beat, the bells like a murderous chorus.

"I can't keep this up!" Ekko shouted. "Eventually I'm gonna fall, kijana."

"Hold on, I'm thinking, I'm thinking." N'Kota held tight, swaying back and forth smoothly as two more eloko came to bash into his own base.

"Do that little call you did again! The mating call." Ekko jumped to another bamboo but slipped a quarter of the way down. "On my count!"

"But all that did was get us pummeled!"

"Exactly! Just trust me."

There was only going to be one shot at this, but Ekko didn't have a choice except to try. It was that or die a very brutal death. It was moments like these that made it easy for Ekko to do the things he did, whether on a bloody deck at sea or in a crazy jungle zoo.

"Three. Two. One!" Ekko shouted.

N'Kota made his call and almost immediately the squawk of kongamatos rang out.

Over the tree line, the wide wingspan of the giant half birds, half reptilian creatures flapped against the bright morning sun. And just like before, they nosedived straight for N'Kota and Ekko.

Or so it seemed.

Ekko manifested the blue-and-red spotted feathers of a female kongamato, the spiky edges, the long talons, and yellow beak. He was terrible at creating portraits, but with the bamboo hiding his shoddy work, the image should've still sold—especially to lustful kongamatos.

The male kongamatos' dive cut sharp and low, aiming for the illusion of the female Ekko had projected. But instead of meeting a mate, their sharp beaks impacted against the attacking eloko. The ferned creatures went tumbling through the thicket just as Ekko and N'Kota had when they were hit by the kongamatos.

"Jump on their backs now!" Ekko ordered N'Kota as he let go of his bamboo stalk and landed on the nearest kongamato. The landing was rough and Ekko barely avoided one of the kongamato's spikes. Worse yet, the kongamato let out a loud screech.

"You're crazy, saabi! Crazy!" N'Kota called out through laughter. "I love it!"

He let go and jumped on the back of his own flying mount.

Ekko wrapped his arms around the neck of his beast, but it was doing all it could to unseat him. "I did my part! Now do yours, kijana!"

"On it!" N'Kota's eyes rotated into themselves and the kongamatos settled down. "Now, let's get out of here."

The beasts took flight and Ekko felt his stomach drop straight down and through his ass. The scream that scuttled from his mouth couldn't be helped—embarrassing as it was.

When they broke through the canopy of the tallest trees, Ekko heard a *thoo* brush by his ear. He turned his head over his shoulders to see several tiny figures around the great lake: al-Turabi's guards, all equipped with crossbows.

"They'll never hit us!" N'Kota called through the rush of wind. "We'll make it out without a—"

Again, the kongamatos thrashed and convulsed. Ekko's mount spun around and dived back down from where they came.

"N'Kotaaa!"

"Sorry, sorry, hard to handle two at once. Turabi's potion makes them afraid of leaving their home."

As though snagged on a line, like a fish to bait, the kongamato halted in the air, but it wouldn't fly up again. Two more bolts rushed by Ekko's head. The third one would've got him if he didn't duck under.

Ekko peered out across the landscape. In the distance where the steppe melded into desert, a dust cloud was forming. Ekko manifested another image of a female kongamato deep within the storm cloud to mask his second-rate illusion.

And it was enough.

The kongamato stopped hovering between the indecision of flight or dive and rushed for what it thought was a mate in the distance. And, finally, it flew far enough away where al-Turabi's estate and his monstrous zoo was a dot on the horizon.

Every so often, Ekko reformed his image to keep the kongamato going, and almost all at once his adrenaline went away like a fleeting wind and all the aches hit him one after the other like he was being stoned by the Gods themselves.

N'Kota flew up by his side, now back in his full human form. He cupped one hand over his mouth and shouted, "Great fucking work back there, saabi. Yeah, I'll make damn sure Vaziri finds that traitor girl of yours. What was her name again?"

CHAPTER 32
ZALA

"Zala, did you remember to get the dried fruit from the markets?" Fon asked, snapping her fingers next to Zala's ear. "Hey, I'm talking to you!" She waved her hands and one good wing to grab her friend's attention.

Zala raised her gaze from the recipe list in her hand. "I'm sorry, were you saying something?" She gestured to her ear. "It hasn't gotten any better."

The morning sun had barely broken over the Lowtown Borough, and Fon was already hounding her—as she had every morning since Zala started working the kitchens. Zala would've given anything to trade places with her. Fon was a natural at all that cooking stuff. No matter how many recipes and techniques Zala crammed into her head, she never seemed to really get it.

"Oh, right... your ear... my fault." Fon frowned and fiddled with the loose stitching in the tunic one of the children had lent to her. It was a dirty old thing, stains plastered all over it, but it was better than the bloody clothes Fon had been wearing after her wing was cut.

Zala didn't need her looking so downcast, though, so she put a hand to stop her friend's nervous picking. "What were you asking me?"

"Dried fruit. Did you get it?"

"Oh, yes. Yes."

"From the *coastal* markets?"

"Um… sure."

Fon snapped her hands to her hips. "I need a yes, Zala. Shaman el-Sayyed told us the coastal markets are the best because they soak their fruit in rum for moons. That's the only one that'll taste right. Are you sure you went to the man with the—"

"Lazy eye. Yes. I got it, Fon. Trust me."

"Sorry, I just worry sometimes. Mantu told me you burnt the last batch."

Zala smacked her lips and spoke in a thick island accent, "Mantu should mind his own."

"There's only a little over a week until the banquet, and you and Mantu haven't been picked. I just want to make sure—"

"Don't worry." Zala gave her ingredients list one more scan before placing it into her sash. "We'll get picked today. Mantu promised he has Chef Hadi under his finger."

"How?" Fon quirked an eyebrow. "He's not… being all sexy again, is he?"

Zala responded with a light chuckle before jogging off from their little makeshift shanty and between the group of children who were already starting up their favorite game of "chase the rats." When she got to her usual meeting spot with Mantu, just outside the district's shattered temple where two fallen pillars crossed into each other like an entrance gate, Mantu grumbled his usual annoyed hum at Zala's tardiness.

He was already dressed in his kitchen worker's attire, which was really just a bedsheet repurposed to what was barely passable as clothing. Zala's hand shot to her face to feel for the full head wrap that cloaked her features. She had often forgotten to wear her traditional Qibasi robes and made herself late running to retrieve them one too many times. Checking they were properly in place had become a bad habit that she really needed to kick.

"You got everything?" Mantu asked.

Zala lifted her bag of ingredients. "Got it all here."

"Including the coastal market fruits from —"

"The man with the lazy eye. Yeah, yeah, *Fon*, I got it." She rolled her eyes.

"And did you wish our little aziza a happy natal day?"

"Yes, I —" Zala heart dropped a little. "Oh, no I completely forgot. Give me a minute, I gotta tell her —"

"We're already late. You'll tell her when we get back. Make it up to her by getting picked by Chef Hadi today." Mantu led their walk up the steep hill to the palace.

"It's been a few days already," Zala said, following behind his giant body which blocked out the rising sun. "You said it would take only a couple. What's going on with Hadi? Is he picking us or not?"

"He's a tough nut to crack. But I know what I'm doing is working. Trust me, Zala. Today's the day."

Zala bumped into one of the many other workers heading into their morning shifts. "Apologies, sir."

"No it was my fault." The man helped her by the elbow before she lost her balance. "Excuse me for being nosy. Did I hear the name Zala?"

A slight pang of fear pickled at Zala's neck. She looked the man up and down properly this time, taking in his long dark hair of locs and golden eyes. He wasn't anyone she recognized… and she remembered faces, if not names.

"Who's asking?" she asked cautiously.

"You probably don't remember me." His smile was so bright, it nearly made Zala squint. "You used to run through the Seaborne all the time, didn't you? I used to chat you up. But I'm sure everyone did most nights, ya?"

Zala's little slice of thrill transformed into the awkward pit of embarrassment. She really couldn't remember the man's face, and his accent was strange. "I'm sorry… I don't —"

"Ah… I thought that was you." His tone lightened at her non-confirming confirmation. "I wouldn't have ever recognized you under all that. Did you go all religious? Wouldn't have ever pegged you for a Gods' girl. Or maybe I should've. The wild ones are always the first to turn over a new leaf, ya?"

"Come on." Mantu tugged at Zala's elbow, his tone just as cautious as Zala's. "We're going to be even more late."

The man gave them a slight bow. "Apologies, I didn't mean to keep you. Zala, if you're ever in Sycamore Square, find me in Harbor's Flask. Drinks on me. We should catch up. Name's N'Kota, in case you forgot!"

Despite Mantu's slight tugging, Zala felt the desire to rip away from him. She actually *wanted* to go along with the man for some reason. At the moment, it seemed like a great idea to leave her shift in the palace, which she knew full well she needed to be to get back to... to... what was his name? Jelani! Yes, Jelani, of course.

What in the Sapphire Hells? How could she forget his name, even for a moment?

"We'll take you up on that drink some other time, kijana," Mantu insisted. "We're already late as it is." This time Mantu tugged Zala along with a bit more force. And the moment they got a few paces away, Zala felt like herself again, like she had come out of a daydream.

Mantu laughed. "Ah, I see it now. There's a reason you haven't been able to pull in Chef Hadi."

"Huh? Why's that?" she asked as she rubbed the lightheadedness out of her mind.

"You attract a certain type. Tall, dark, and handsome. Jelani. That man back there. Not bad, chana. Not bad. Believe me, I get it better than any, heh." His smile faltered for a moment. "Ah, don't worry none. I ain't gonna tell Jelani you're blushin' right now."

That only made it worse. Zala felt the heat in her cheeks. Had she really been blushing? She couldn't remember the last time she looked at another man like that before. She wasn't even worried how Mantu might tease her when they got Jelani back, she was more flabbergasted at the whole run-in to begin with. Confused more than anything else.

Before she and Mantu turned the corner to Spine Street, she

looked over her shoulder for the man. The morning crowd was growing with the languid movements of folks who didn't want to be up so damn early...

But that man... the man she was looking for was no longer among them.

Zala had nearly forgotten her run-in with the mysterious man on the street by the time her and Mantu's shift had got into full swing. Between the morning rush, which saw four-hundred soldiers come through their mess hall, and the dozens and dozens of eggs she was required to boil, the only thing on her mind was if Officer Such-And-Such wanted salt or if Captain What's-Her-Name liked mint leaves with her roasted tomatoes.

By the time the lunch rush came around, Mantu had already started back in with Chef Hadi. Zala had watched him work the chef the past few days, but today was different. Mantu had ratcheted up his efforts a few levels, really laying into the chef like he was some doey-eyed academy girl. To Zala, it seemed a bit desperate, but Hadi seemed to be eating it up.

She had a little secret she hadn't told him when it came to her getting close with men. Whenever she actually made the effort or tried to swindle the men she encountered in taverns, it was only ever on the back of them being tipsy or outright drunk.

Though, it helped that those men were interested in women to begin with.

For a moment, it seemed Hadi's interest had moved onto Mantu's actual work as a slight silence fell between the two. Then, in a very exaggerated manner, Mantu started rubbing at his eyes and sniffling over his board of onions.

"People always cry when cutting onions," Chef Hadi said with a coy little smile. Then he leaned in close as though the words were for Mantu alone, but Zala could clearly hear him say, "The trick is to not form an emotional bond."

"Oh, I never heard of that one before," Mantu laughed at yet another of Hadi's terrible jokes. Zala could have gagged, nearly biting her lip off in irritation. That was damn near the same joke she had laughed at a week ago.

"Yeah, I should have been one of those jesters at the theater," Chef Hadi said dreamingly as he stared out the lone window of the kitchen.

Zala only noticed then that she had outright missed cutting the onions on her own board, too busy eavesdropping on Mantu and Hadi. Instead of cut little pieces in front of her, there were shallow scratches on her board where the onion should've been.

"Explain to me this recipe again," Mantu asked coyly. "I can never get this part right with the chickpeas." Hadi described the next step—something he never would have done if it was Zala who had asked him, but Mantu feigned that he couldn't hear over the racket in the kitchen of boiling pots and the *chop-chop-chop* of everyone else's knives. The head chef fell right for the bait, or perhaps welcomed it, touching Mantu's arm to show him how it was done, leaning into his ear to be more clear with light chuckling and all that.

Oh, Mantu. You're too good, Zala thought as she braved a look over her shoulder.

Mantu made it seem so casual. No effort. Sniffs would've been all kinds of jealous if he saw his man getting all cozy with the Chef.

When Zala turned back to her onions, she heard Mantu murmur to Chef Hadi. "Can I get a bit of a break? I wanna talk to you privately out in the corridor, if that's all right with you."

That was asking a bit much. Sure, Hadi definitely took an interest in Mantu, but he never gave anyone breaks under any circumstances. Zala hummed under her lips skeptically, waiting for the denial that would surely come. When Chef Hadi actually agreed to their private break, she nearly yelped and cut herself. Everyone gazed up at her, the cooks with red eyes and glistening brows, Chef Hadi with his beady little ones and damp turban.

"Apologies!" Zala let out. "I-I thought I saw a rat."

Chef Hadi grumbled. "And wasn't it you who was supposed to set the traps for them last night?"

"Yes, sir." She held her head low. "I'll reset them now after I get done."

"Good," Hadi huffed, then turned to Mantu to lead him out of the room. When Mantu and Zala made eye contact, Zala mouthed him a "good luck."

"So I got some good news and bad news," Mantu murmured a few moments later when he was sent back to finish his work.

"You know I want the bad news first," Zala said automatically, then corrected herself. That was something known between her and Fon, not Mantu. All this time with him got her confused. "I mean… yeah, just give me the bad news."

"I think you'll like the good news first." He flourished his knife in his hand. "I'm going to the banquet!"

"And I'm not?"

"You weren't supposed to guess the bad news."

"It wasn't exactly hard to guess, and I told you… bad news first."

"Well, it's not that he *didn't* select you. It's just that he hasn't *yet*…" Mantu sliced into his onion, dicing it up in ten seconds flat. "Just get that rum cake right today. No more burnin' it. And before you ask, I can't do that for you too. Bakin' ain't my thing. Too many measurements and all that nonsense."

Zala waved him off. "I got it, I got it."

Despite what she said, she didn't quite have it all together. Between her new duties of baking pita, and making sure she reset all the rat traps along the western corridor, it was difficult to check in with the rum cake's baking steps.

It was made all the more difficult because her station was right next to the little snot-nosed snitch of a kid, who was now chopping up garlic and onion beside her. And she couldn't exactly ask him to move or stop since rum cake wasn't exactly on the menu that day. If he caught wind of what she was up to, he wouldn't hesitate to out her. So she had to spend a few extra minutes to cover up her work under her station, whisking eggs and adding flour to her baking bowl little by little.

But after another hour, Zala's hopes lifted. She could smell the sweet butteriness of her cake wafting from the communal oven. The scent, however, was quickly replaced by the dreaded hint of burnt bread. And the moment she realized it, she was too late.

"Who's bread is this!?" Chef Hadi bellowed.

Where in the hells did he pop up from?

"It's mine, sir." Zala didn't hesitate to answer, knowing he had found her ruined cake. She didn't know why she couldn't keep track of it. She thought she had, checking on it every few minutes. There was no way it could've burnt like that.

"General Shadid was expecting his pita with his meals in a half hour!" Hadi bellowed.

Zala glanced down to Hadi's hands. In them was a bowl of burnt pita, not burnt cake. A wave of relief fell over Zala momentarily. At the very least it was just the pita.

"Discard these, now," he commanded. "And head over to the kitchens at the southern keep. The head chef there owes me a favor and he always has extra. Quickly, girl!"

Zala hid her face from Mantu and the other kitchen workers. Even if she was covered in a full head wrap, she didn't want to see any of their judging eyes.

Even if the rum cake came out perfectly now, it was unlikely Hadi would care or be all that impressed. That was probably the dozenth time he had yelled at her within a few days. At this point, the little kid was going to get picked over her.

The one benefit of being let loose in the palace, however, was that she could track more of its layout. She had to remind herself it didn't really matter though when she had pretty much guaranteed she'd never get picked for the banquet. Still, curiosity got the best of her, and after she got the extra pita, she stopped by a particular corridor that seemed to shine with the afternoon light spilling into the large stained-glass windows.

Each door was inlaid with all kinds of luxury, from rubies, to sapphires, and golds. At the far end of the hall, a pair of men and a woman spoke to one another, each one more fashionable than the last. The taller of the bunch wore a gentle lilac robe, the woman in fuchsia, and the last in black and gold.

Zala squinted. She thought she might've recognized the shorter one in black… If he'd just turn his head a little she might just be able to see. As though he read her thoughts, the man glanced over his shoulder.

It was Collector Vaziri!

She'd remember that sharply trimmed beard and head of curls anywhere.

He was right there, right in front of her. But she didn't have Mantu with her, there was no way she could get the Collector alone like she wanted to.

Vaziri turned back to his group and waved a farewell. "Well I should be off," he was saying. "I'm sorry to hear there was a break in at your estate, al-Turabi. I'll get my best on the job to see who was behind it. I hope this didn't soil your interest in my end of year banquet."

"Miss a party?" the tallest man, who was apparently al-Turabi, answered, aghast. "Who do I look like to you, Vaziri?"

"Good, I ordered some of Majida's finest just for you."

"Of course you did," the tall man was already making his way down the steps at the far end. "And I want one of your spies at my estate by the end of the day."

With his final words, Vaziri and the woman with him padded down the other end of the corridor toward Zala. Standing at attention, Zala retreated out of sight. But she couldn't just leave Vaziri unwatched. This was the whole point of cutting a hundred onions a day and getting shouted down by Chef Hadi. There was no way to keep track of him, however. The palace halls were too wide and too long. What she needed was a…

There! That'll do! Zala thought as she shuffled down the hall. Just to one side was a broom closet. She pushed its door inward and ducked in just as Vaziri and his fellow came pattering around the corner.

"You said you'd protect him, Vaziri," the woman hissed in a whisper.

"Al-Turabi? I never said anything like that."

"Not him. My son." Zala could hear them stop just a few feet from her closet. "The Seekers took him without any notice. You said he'd never—"

"Not here," Vaziri's whisper was like a curse. "I told you never in the palace. And I promised nothing. It's on you for not teaching the boy how to hide himself properly."

"We took the Draft of Dulagi like you told us too," the woman said in hissed anger. "Maji Arba will be hearing about this."

"Fine, tell her all you want. She won't treat you any differently than I am now. There's nothing that can be done for your boy. Now get back to the armory and leave this matter alone."

Zala could hear Vaziri trying to get away but it sounded like he was being pulled back by the woman, whose voice was laced with desperation. "I was careful. *We* were careful. There's no reason they should have found out about him. There's something going on, Vaziri. Someone's onto us. And not just in the slums. They'll come for someone like you too. I know you've heard the rumors about the Guardians of Àyá—those oni'baro all over the city, lurking in the shadows... they're popping up all over the slums... even that brothel woman has some under her thumb."

"Ugh, not in the corridor," he grunted again. "You never know who could be... Hang on a moment."

A shadow covered the light spilling below the closet door. Zala planted her back onto the wall and froze. Her heart pounded harshly against her chest.

"You see, there are always ears lurking in the—" The closet door swung inward. Zala's toes clenched tightly in her raggedy shoes. She had plastered her back where the door would swing, and thanks to her small frame, the door was only an inch from her nose. If she was even slightly bigger, it would've slammed her right in the face.

"Vaziri, you're just being paranoid," the woman finally told him.

The tax collector still didn't close the door. Zala could've sworn he was sniffing the air. She covered the pita basket she was holding in her arms with her hand.

"A healthy dose of paranoia has gotten me as far as I am now,"
Vaziri intoned darkly. "Something your son could've learned
from." He let the door close again, and Zala could let go of the
breath she was holding. Her inhale was met with a large intake of
must and mold, however. "Come, we'll speak about it at the
tavern. I've my crew to meet there."

Their footsteps receded down the grand corridor, but Zala
didn't leave from her closet until she was sure the coast was clear.
A few times she heard the rattling of armor pass by—likely
guards on their usual watch. And twice she heard whispered
conversations between scholars passing through—chit-chat about
this theory and that.

As she waited for the hall to fall silent for longer than a few
seconds, she thought about Vaziri and the woman. That was the
second time she had heard talk of Seekers. What had Mantu told
her about all that? Something about that in al-Anim... mystics
were regulated. Did that mean Vaziri was some unregistered
mystic, and he was apparently protecting others—or at least
making empty promises to others? That was something she could
work with. And those guardians... were they the same ones she
saw with the spiral necklaces at Madam Majida's brothel? She
could use that too. It at least gave her aimless planning a path to
follow. She'd just needed to talk it out with the others to figure out
what they should do next.

When the hall was quiet for a full five minutes, Zala decided
to grab one of the brooms and walk out with it in case anyone saw
her. When she opened the door to the much fresher air, she found
no one. So she put the broom back where she found it and made
her way back to the kitchens. Just before she rounded the corner,
a voice rang out from behind.

"Are you lost, young maiden?"

Zala gave a little jump and turned to find a palace guard with
broad shoulders. "Oh, no. I was just getting these back to Chef
Hadi." She lifted her basket of warm pita. "Well... I suppose I did
get turned around a bit."

"Chef Hadi is just down that way through the bridge and

down the spiral staircase." The large woman of a guard pointed. "I don't need to show you, do I?"

"No, ma'am." Zala hiked up her robes and made off before she got another series of questions.

At the very least, she had more information on Collector Vaziri—even if she wasn't getting an invite to the banquet.

CHAPTER 33
ZALA

"Well, you did your best," Zala told Mantu later as they packed up to go. "Today was on me."

Mantu assured her, "We still got time 'til the banquet. We can think somethin' up."

"Yeah, if I'm not given the boot first. But now we know where Vaziri does his business in the palace. He's just on the edge of the western keep where it meets the southern one. Even if I can't get back here you can peg him down. We just gotta figure out why he'd be cautious of the Seekers and the oni'baro guardians."

"Well it's obvious, ain't it?" Mantu said. "Vaziri is probably a mystic or something. And by the sounds of it, he's unregistered… and he got a network goin' with all the other illegals."

"That's exactly what I'm thinking. But we'll need more evidence against him."

"What do we need evidence against him for?"

"I've got a plan that'll stop a guy like him. Like I told Majida, just killing someone like that won't get the job done. We need to blackmail him, control him. I'll explain more later. The guards up there will hear us."

As she and Mantu turned the corner to get checked out by the guards for the day, Chef Hadi called out. "Girl!"

What was it now? She couldn't say she cared if she was kicked out. She was already thinking of ways to sneak into the palace at the end of the year. At least now she knew the whole western keep by heart—and a lot of the southern keep on top of that thanks to today. But getting into the palace was going to be much harder than breaking into the estates of the Sapphire Isles.

Despite her negative thoughts, she didn't need to ruffle the man's feathers before leaving. So she bowed. "I'll catch up with you later," she told Mantu, then faced the chef. "Yes, Head Chef?"

Mantu gave the Chef a little wink before he made his way out of the keep. Hadi returned it with a smirk of his own. Then he twisted a bitter expression on Zala, snorted, then spat into a bucket he held in hand. "There's this noble by the name of Talaat Malouf who's also going to that end of year banquet. You heard of him?"

At the moment, Zala was thankful her smirk was covered by her head wrap. With a shrug that feigned ignorance, she said, "I don't get involved with the noble types, sir. I keep my head down like a good cook."

"Well, you should know him… and his sister." Hadi spat again. "As you know, the end of year banquet is paying well. Really well." He glanced down at Zala's feet. "You could use some proper shoes, I reckon. Or maybe you got a husband down in the slums who needs something."

Perhaps Mantu did work his magic with Hadi. At least now the Head Chef didn't mistake Zala for Mantu's wife.

"Is there a reason I need to be acquainted with this… um… Malouf person? I was told my work in the palace was only kitchens. I'm not trying to do nothin' else."

"Oh, no nothing like that." Hadi set down his bucket and wiped the spittle from his beard. "I wouldn't dare ask a devotee such as yourself to do a thing like *that*. I was just wondering… I mean, I have a job that needs doing. The Malouf family got themselves a healthy craving for pastries and sweets. That rum cake you left out in the kitchens… That Mantu fellow says you've got a knack. I went ahead and sampled some and was thinkin' if you could do that again?"

AFTER SPENDING ANOTHER PAIR OF HOURS IN THE PALACE under Chef Hadi's watchful eye, Zala made him another rum cake, recalling everything she learned from Fon by memory. The moment she pulled out her creation in its simmering pan and served a piece to Chef Hadi, the man formally offered her a job at Collector Vaziri's end of year banquet, where she would head the deserts and help serve at the party.

It was all Zala could do not to skip down the palace halls — so she settled for a subtle little bounce as she checked out with the guards. Her feet felt lighter, all the weight of getting picked now free from her shoulders. No more need to cook up some new plan of breaking into the palace on some suicide mission.

When she was let out of the palace and back out into the city, the setting sun painted the sky a dusty orange that Zala usually didn't favor, but in that moment the sky's hue appeared more inviting.

Mantu stood waiting at the bottom of the hill leading to the palace, where the dual statues of the Emperor and Empress stood tall.

"Took you long enough, chana," he said in greeting. "He cut you loose or what?"

"I'm in!" Zala clapped and shook her hands in jubilation. "Fon's rum cake worked. I'll be leading deserts."

"Well I'll be…" Mantu smiled through his beard, then lifted a sack in his hand. "Now that we're all squared at the palace, I got some of Fon's favorites. Some Golah vendor was sellin' some *fufu* and peanut soup. Least I could do for the aziza's one-hundred-and-fiftieth." He pursed his lips. "What's that in human years anyhow?"

Zala snatched the sack out of his hand. "Mid-twenties. And these are *not* Fon's favorites. She favors fried plantain and red pea soup."

"Huh? That's Sapphire Isle stuff, that is. I thought she liked stuff closer to home."

"She *left* home, remember? She doesn't like anything that'll remind her of it." That had been one of the things she and Zala found in common during their earlier days of friendship. "Don't worry, Shomari will gobble this up."

Mantu yanked the sack back. "Nu-uh. If anything, I'm the one who's gonna be doin' the gobblin'."

Zala shook her head with a playful huff out her nose. Then she glanced back out toward the setting sun. "Speaking of Shomari, he said he wanted to do his little surprise for Fon at sundown, no?"

"Yeah, I think so."

"The best red peas are at the northern portion of al-Anim, and the best plantains are by the harbor."

"You got another thing comin' if you think I'm goin' way back north again. *I'll* get the plantains."

"Fine! I made you wait anyway. I'll head up to Agwe's and meet you back at Lowtown. Fair?"

Mantu was already taking steps into the afternoon crowd, well out of reach of Zala's potential objections. "You ain't got to tell me twice. See you in an hour! I'm lookin' forward to that plan you got for that Collector Vaziri."

Rain drizzled from above as Zala approached Mama Agwe's Little Slice of Zanzi. Rubbing warmth into her arms, she glanced down the street, which appeared much different from most of the others in al-Anim. Where many of the avenues had some form of Vaaji architecture of domes and arches bedecked with blood lily banners, Agwe's road felt like being on one of the Sapphire Isles. The buildings were square there, and no two flags which swung from the many storefronts were the same: from the black and gold of Zanziwala to the blue and yellow of Jultia.

"*Zala? Dat Zala?*" Mama Agwe called in Pakwan from her rustic nook. "*Come round an' get outta dat rain.*"

Zala had made it a habit of taking off her full head wrap once she was clear from the palace grounds. And visibility at the moment was already low, it didn't help to have her periphery compromised, especially in the lower districts where everyone was looking for an easy pocket to pick.

"Mama Agwe, wahgwan!" she called back as she snuck under the dry cover of Agwe's little hole in the wall. *"Mi just wanna some red pea soup today!"*

"Come right up now," the old woman said as she got to work on the order. The moment her red spices hit her pan, its fumes wafted into Zala's nose, making her stomach grumble.

Mama Agwe went on and on about the week's events, from rumors of pirates running the street—which Zala knew about all too well—to her granddaughter going around with some pakka near the harbor.

"Mi can't understand the attraction to dem big ol' cats."

Zala had come to understand this was the way of things with her. She always had a new story, even when Zala thought she heard them all already.

It was nice coming to visit her, not only because Mama Agwe reminded her of home, but because specifically she reminded Zala of Jelani and the villagers he used to be so fond of back on Kidogo. Once all this was done, and she had Jelani back, she'd be sure they'd visit Mama Agwe. He and her would really hit it off.

Zala drew her hand across her songstone around her neck and lifted it to her ear. The sun had just dipped below the horizon off the coast. Sometimes Jelani's hymn came just when the sun went down or a few hours later. That day, his gentle voice rang out just as the sun disappeared, a reminder he was still alive and what she was doing was still very much worth it all.

"All right, baby girl." Mama Agwe handed over a bowl of red-hot soup, speaking in accented Mother Tongue now. "You get back home safe, you hear? It gets dark fast this time of year."

"Of course, Mama Agwe. I'll see you next week."

"You know where to find me."

Zala waved and headed off into the dark alleys. It was just like being back on Kidogo. So long as she kept to the lit and busy corners, she would be fine. But with the sun already below the horizon, she needed to take a few shortcuts to get back to Fon and the others in time. So she dipped into a narrow path between an old theater and locksmith shop, which would've saved her a few minutes. No need to get Shomari angry for ruining his surprise for Fon.

But she realized her mistake the moment she stepped into the darkness of the alley.

A sliver of light spilled into the tight walkway from the main street, yet a slight shadow blocked it momentarily behind her. Without slowing her walk, Zala edged her chin over her shoulder. A small figure followed close at her rear. A little too close. Probably just a child, she wanted to think. But at this hour? Unlikely. No one walked down where Zala was. There was no other explanation besides someone who meant to track her. If she could just get out on the other end, she'd be back in the public eye, but she'd have to make a jog if that were a possibility.

Zala dipped her finger into the soup to test its heat. It was hot just like Mama Agwe always made it. Zala could even smell a hint of spice. That would do nicely.

Sorry, Fon...

In motion with her walk, Zala spun and threw out her soup at her purser. But the figure anticipated the move and lifted its arm —its very stoney arm in front of its face.

"Iokaja?" Zala gasped just as that stone arm reached out and grabbed her by the throat. She tried to speak again, but the grip was far too strong to break.

In the dark light, Zala could barely make out Iokaja's pale skin and freckles. The aziza's voice, however, was unmistakable.

"How you been, dikala? It's about time you come back to your crew."

"Io-Io..." Zala rasped.

Jelani's hymn still rang out from her songstone, which made Iokaja halt for a moment. The aziza peered down to the faint glowing stone around Zala's neck with a quirked eyebrow. "What is that? Is someone listening to us?"

Zala tried to cry out "no" but all she could do was squeak.

Iokaja snatched the songstone from Zala's neck and threw it on the floor. Before Zala could so much as struggle, Iokaja raised her stone fist and smashed it into pieces... and with it, Jelani's song.

Iokaja's stone grip compressed Zala's scream into nothing more than a whimper. Tears streamed down her eyes. That was her only connection to Jelani, the only way she knew he was still alive. Zala thrashed and thrashed. Strikes from Iokaja's elbows and knees silenced her every time.

"Stop your wiggling and come with me," the aziza seethed. "We've got a job for you, you bloody traitor."

CHAPTER 34
ZALA

IOKAJA'S GRIP WAS AS TIGHT AND UNRELENTING AS A HYENA'S
bite. But that didn't stop Zala trying her best to pull away
through shoves, kicks, and bites of her own.

Occasionally Zala's struggle earned the attention of passersby
—a concerned mother with her children or a citywatch guard.
Iokaja, who was disguised in Maji robes, didn't care, though,
either saying "this is Seeker business" or flashing some sort of
medallion anytime someone came to investigate. After one of the
guard encounters, Zala tried to signal for help, but Iokaja gave
her a quick jab to the ribs with her stone hand.

That shut Zala up. Or at least, left her in fits of coughs.

Eventually, as the rain storm grew all the stronger, they
arrived at a tavern near a lone sycamore tree in the middle of a
plaza lit by moonstone lanterns. Zala's mind raced back to Mantu,
who must've already been back at the Scars. Her heart pounded
against her chest as she realized that in another hour or two, her
crew would know she was missing and start looking.

There was no way to make her location known, however. She
wasn't in a forest where she could crack a few twigs or leave blood
on stones. Al-Anim was a huge city, perhaps even bigger than Port
Zanziwala. The moment Zala got lost in it, she'd be lost for good.

With these new and terrifying thoughts spiking through her head, she gritted her teeth and stretched against her bruised ribs to renew her energy. As Iokaja pulled the tavern door open, Zala lifted her legs and planted them against each side of the doorframe.

"Akbar!" Iokaja bellowed. "Go get the others. Tell 'em I found her!"

Through her thrashing, Zala caught glimpses inside the modest tavern. The innkeeper raced from behind his bar and up a set of stairs. A few of the patrons turned their heads to see the commotion, yet most of them casually returned to their drinks.

Great, it's one of those *taverns.*

After another set of shouts from Zala and calls of "Seeker business, mind your own" from Iokaja, Zala felt her legs being forcibly removed from the doorframe and pulled into the deceptively warm embrace of the tavern. Hanging lanterns overhead were all Zala could see, save for occasional glimpses of more patrons around tables, who deliberately weren't making eye contact with her.

Think, Zala. Think. Exits. Where are your exits?

She obviously wasn't wanted dead, or she'd have been left in that alley with a dagger in her back. The fact that she wasn't dead would be the Rovers' mistake. She just needed to find something, anything. She tried for another scream, but it came out more as a whimper through her aching ribs, which she was sure were broken.

She remembered with a stab of fear that the *Redtide* crew rarely just killed their enemies. They made them suffer. Brutally.

The creak of a door opening whipped by Zala's good ear, and she was thrown bodily into a small room. She cried out as she rolled over her ribs. She wanted to spring up and get into a defensive position, perhaps find a window she could jump from, but her aching body kept her solidly on the ground.

A pair of slender boots stomped toward her, the steps kept coming and coming until one of them came smashing into her nose. Zala's brain rattled against her skull as a steady ringing split through her ears. She rolled over onto her back to see, through blurry vision, the new captain of the *Redtide*.

"Hello there, Zala," Lishan leered. "Welcome to the Harbor's Flask."

The wicked grin Lishan was giving Zala would've made anyone's insides churn. But Lishan's evil expression was nothing compared to the others in the room: Iokaja, who massaged her stone arm and scowled with twisted lips, and Ouseni, the bow woman, whose grave frown was rivaled only by the deep creases through her forehead. Kwame stood in a dark corner of the room. Zala could barely see him, save for his intense glare that seemed to spit fire in the shadows.

"I can help you get Nubia out," Zala lied immediately. That's what the crew really wanted in the end. Not to see her dead, but to see their captain alive.

"Oh yes?" Lishan asked with a slight tone of amusement. "And where do you believe Nubia is?"

"In the palace dungeons probably, right? I've got access there."

The *Redtide* crew laughed, a laugh Zala was familiar with, though she had never been on the receiving end before. She did *not* like being on the other end.

"No," Lishan said. "You want to try for another guess?"

Zala didn't respond, instead gulping down a clump of blood welling in her mouth—which was entirely the wrong choice.

"No, our Captain is someplace else. The Vaaji have an 'important target' on that airship of theirs. And we'll have her back soon, thanks to what Ekko has done for us."

Almost on cue, a series of stomping boots thundered in the corridor outside the room. The door swung inward and slammed against the stone wall. Ekko and another tall man Zala thought she might've recognized peered through the threshold. An expression of total anger painted Ekko's face, while the dark, handsome man beamed and said, "Eastern entrance to the palace, huh?"

Iokaja nodded, then gave Zala a wicked slate stare of ice. "Just like you said."

"Did I tell you I've got the best ears in the city?" The tall man slapped Ekko across his arm, sauntered into the room, then crouched low for a better look at Zala. "Or did I tell *you* I've got the best ears in the city? Just two days. That's a record for me."

Then it dawned on Zala. She did know that man. The same one who "bumped" into her that morning. He was the one to blame here, the one who outed her to the Rovers. Who was he anyway? She never saw him on the *Redtide*. And he tracked her in the city? How? Zala had always kept her robes tight around head. No one knew her name, save for those in the kitchens...

Mantu and I didn't use monikers.

It wasn't exactly their fault. Ketifa had introduced them to the kitchen crew that first day by their real names. Though Zala would've preferred a byname, she didn't see how that would affect her negatively, especially when she kept to the western keep of the palace and always headed straight back to the shaman's district after her shifts.

As Zala's heart continued to thump against her chest harshly, she scanned the rest of the crew once more. There was one missing, one who might've taken her side if she hadn't...

"Marjani," she managed to get out softly.

The slow unsheathing of a large dagger scraped against Ekko's belt. He stepped forward with a stilted rhythm. "Captain, if I may?"

Iokaja intercepted Ekko swiftly with her stone hand. "What in the hells are you doing, kijana?"

"Slitting the dikala's throat. What's it look like?"

"Marjani..." Zala croaked again, her words garbled by blood. "She didn't... she didn't..." Tears welled in her eyes as the image of Marjani's wide eyes and beaded hair in that damn alley plastered to the front of her mind's eye. "Ekko, I didn't mean to... you have to know..."

"No more lies from you!" Ekko bellowed, pushing Iokaja aside. "No more!"

The tall man still crouched beside Zala cleared his throat. "Actually, she's not lying, friend. I sense that her remorse is true."

"You think I give a damn if she feels shitty about it or not?" Ekko lifted his dagger and grabbed Zala by the collar. Already the tip of his blade made a cut under her eye, and the harsh pinch made Zala whimper in pain.

"Stop," Lishan murmured, yet the command was stern, deliberate.

Ekko grinded his teeth and grunted. "All due respect, Captain. But I'm not leaving this room until this dikala gets what's coming to her."

"No, Captain," Iokaja spoke up. "We agreed to bring her in so she could make me stonesbane. The blight is already spreading from my arm."

Lishan stepped forward. Without a word, just like on the *Redtide*, everyone parted before her without protest. And like the tall man who had ratted her out, Lishan knelt down to look Zala eye to eye.

"Y-you can't kill me," Zala moaned again. "I'm part of the *Redtide* crew. I made the proclamation. You have to maroon me or bring me before a tide lord."

Lishan slapped Zala across the face. "You lost that right the moment you murdered Marjani." Zala opened her stinging mouth for another retort, but Lishan's raised hand halted her. Lishan knelt there for a moment, her jaw seemingly working through a thought. "The traitor will not leave this room without some justice."

"Captain—" Iokaja complained.

Lishan held up a fist. "But she will remain on the crew... as our very own brewmaster."

That's not so bad, Zala thought as she let her tight neck fall onto the dusty floor completely.

"Red tide?" Ouseni asked darkly from her shadowed corner.

"Yes, I think a red tide will do it." Lishan edged her chin over her shoulder. "Is that satisfactory for you?"

Ekko ran his tongue over his teeth in thought. "For now... yeah. How many?"

"As many dead as we have should do."

What's a red tide? Zala thought with dread.

"Leave her hands, will you?" Iokaja said, seemingly satisfied with her Captain's decision.

What's a damn red tide?

Captain Lishan lifted to her full height as she dusted herself off. "N'Kota, does the innkeeper have a tub? Something large enough for the woman here."

"I think so. Let me check for you right quick." The tall man raised up as well, his long locs swaying with him as he glided back out of the room.

"And find Arus," Lishan ordered again. "She's out back. Tell her we're making ready for a red tide. She'll know what she needs to bring."

Iokaja and Ekko yanked each of Zala's arms and pinned her to one of the room's dirty walls, stomach first. Zala didn't have the strength to fight them. She was still recovering from all the hurts she had already stacked up in just the past hour.

Just the past hour? she thought. *Maybe the rest will come after me. Taverns are the first place any of them would check. If they spotted just one of the Rovers lurking... maybe, just maybe.*

She was supposed to be with Fon sharing in some desserts and laughter. She was supposed to be with Shomari cracking jokes at Mantu's terrible singing voice. She wasn't supposed to be in a tiny room with its unwashed walls, grimey floors, and no windows, caught in some tavern in some unknown portion of al-Anim in the middle of a rain storm.

Thoughts of Jelani filled her mind, his singing voice echoing against her skull, the bits of songstone sprinkled on the ground of that alley. Without her, would the others even go after Jelani and save him? Or would they say "good riddance" and head back to the isles?

No, Fon would never do that. Neither would Shomari. Hells, none of them would. Not even Mantu.

Maybe.

She just needed to stay alive, she told herself. She just needed to hang on long enough until the Rovers slipped up, endure whatever it was they were going to do to her in the next few moments.

The squeak of the room's single door sounded behind Zala. Then came the loud thud of heavy wood slamming against the ground. Zala curled her feet against the great vibration that rolled through the ground.

"Thank you, N'Kota," Zala could hear Lishan say. "Appreciate you, Arus. All right, you can begin."

Searing pain lanced across Zala's spine. She hissed in pain, too much in shock to fully understand what had happened. Before she could let out her first scream, Ekko and Iokaja lifted her off her feet and dunked her into a pool of water. Whatever burn Zala thought she felt before didn't remotely compare to what the water did to her wound.

Ekko held her head underwater as her continued screams left her with a wide open mouth that took in lungfuls of salt water, brine, and blood. A fire burned in Zala's chest as the water searched for any hole it could fill: down her throat, up her nostrils, everywhere. Her hurts came in searing pairs, the drowning followed by the split in her back. And when she was just on the edge of blacking out, she was pulled out.

Two breaths of air filled her lungs, three, then four. Ekko grunted, and another horrible pain lined her back. This time she understood it. Ekko was slicing her back open cut by cut. "One for each of their dead" Lishan had said. Then the pirates dunked her into the salt water where her wounds burned against the brine. Time and time again.

Cut. Dunk. Near black out. Repeat.

On the dozenth or so round, the tall man named N'Kota clapped. "Holy shit! Seven minutes. How're you managing this, woman?"

"And look at her wounds," Zala thought she heard Lishan say. "It's like they're half healed already."

Before Zala could cry out for them to stop, she was already back in the water.

She had no clue how long it had been before it stopped, how many cuts she took, how many minutes her head was held underwater. But by the end of it, when Ekko's bloodlust was satiated — when Zala looked half dead — the wooden tub of sloshing salt water was as red as a goblet of wine.

A red tide, Zala thought weakly with her head slumped over the tub, snot and drool pouring from her nose and mouth. But just as that N'Kota man said, somehow through her stings and aches, she could feel her wounds sealing.

"I don't think I've ever seen a tub as red as that," Iokaja said as she gave Zala an inquisitive look. "She should be dead, honestly."

Ekko ignored the comment. Zala thought he was about to cut her again because of how "well" she was keeping up, but instead, through her dotted vision, Ekko tilted his head at the other end of the tub to say, "Marjani sends her regards. Welcome back to the crew, dikala." Then he spat a large wad of phlegm in her face. "You're tougher than your scrawny ass looks, but I'll be seein' you tomorrow morning. And the morning after that. And the morning after that. Sleep well, bitch."

CHAPTER 35
ZALA

Day one. Slow brew the honey and dawa root. Enchant with shavings of pure silver.

Day two. Burn aloe and stew from high noon until sundown. Aloe should have crisp edges. Never burn through.

Day three. At midnight, brew mazomba scales, stirring left fifteen rotations, and right for twenty. Finish with eye of tokoloshe only when brew reaches a hue of slate.

That's all Zala could think about—all she was allowed to think about—for the next week and a half. The crew of the *Redtide* were prepared. Mere hours after Ekko had tortured her, Iokaja came in with everything Zala needed to brew stonesbane. Not just the ingredients, but all the tools, the proper cauldrons, and the very specific enchanted baobab ladle that most forgot or neglected.

That second day had been the worst. After slow brewing the honey and dawa root, Zala hadn't realized how stiff her back had gotten with all her cuts. She could barely move her shoulder blades without earning a hiss from her lips or fumbling the tiny cauldrons she held in her hands.

It didn't help that right before she was allowed to go to the roof of the tavern for high noon stewing, Ekko paid her another visit to give her three more strikes and another round of the red tide. When she complained that she couldn't work under such conditions, he gave her two more strikes and held her underwater until she *actually* passed out. If N'Kota wasn't there to pull Ekxo off, Zala might've died then and there.

After her first successful brew—which hadn't been her best work for obvious reasons—she was made to concoct three stonesbane potions simultaneously.

"If your potions are only going to last a day," Iokaja had said when she brought more ingredients and more cauldrons, "then we'll work you thrice as hard."

When Zala finished her fifth and sixth potion, she lost all hope she'd be found. Her best bet was that first night. But even if she had left a trail of some kind for her crew to follow, it would've been long since lost to the rain. And without her songstone she had no means of communicating. Even if the magic in it was one way, having it would've got her through the agonizing nights. She had grown used to listening to Jelani's songs in the morning and before she went to sleep. Now his hymn would be heard by no one but the walls of whatever cell the Vaaji had him in.

By Zala's estimation—which had been deduced by Yem's nearly full moon when she was allowed on the roof—the end of year banquet was a few days away. She'd only been with the *Redtide* crew a little over a week, but rumor within their mess halls was that prisoners never ever escaped them.

Maybe it was because she was underfed, maybe it was because her wounds were turning and infecting her mind, but on what she thought was the tenth day of her captivity, her mind manifested Jelani in her room.

Or at least a version of Jelani.

His figure was one she knew from yesteryear: free of the stoneskin, free of that jaded tone in his voice he acquired after so many moons consorting with scoundrels and pirates.

"Jelani?" her voice came out in a husk, rough.

"Zee." He smiled. And that smile warmed her heart and brought a tear to her eye.

"I'm sorry, I failed…" She dipped her head low. "I couldn't find you, I couldn't get you back."

Jelani sat alongside her and rubbed his hand down her back.

Despite the cuts that couldn't quite heal all the way because they were reopened daily, hourly, his touch felt soft. "We knew what world we was steppin' into when we agreed to piracy. You knew it could end this way."

Zala kissed his right hand, his perfect, delicate hand. She'd forgotten how ruined they'd gotten when they started getting calloused from biweekly sword fights and savage raids. His left hand, of course, had been ruined by stone.

Ruined by stone? Just a moment ago it was free of it. But just before her eyes rocks and crags spidered up her Jelani's wrist.

"You're not real," Zala said, almost rejecting her husband's hand but stopping herself, instead laying her lips on it softly. "You're in some Vaaji cell. You're not… real."

"Does that matter?" He asked with a curious tilt of his head. "What matters is we are together. Always. No matter how far apart we are."

"No!" Zala drew away from him, hissing as she felt her back split open a little. "No, this isn't the same. We're meant to be together for *real*. I'm supposed to touch you, feel you, not make up versions of you that aren't flesh and bone."

Jelani's eyes went bright for a moment. Then he chuckled long and low. "Oh, Zee… Baba would've never believed who I bounded myself to if he was here."

"What's so funny?"

"You still don't know how to enjoy the moment. To let the magic just… be. But that's why I'm drawn to you, I reckon."

Zala rolled her eyes. "I can't talk to you—I shouldn't be talking to you. I need to think of a way to get out of here. When they let me up on the roof I could jump—"

"And break your leg."

"When Iokaja opens the door on a second-day cook I could throw the burning brew in her fucking—"

"They always post at least two to watch you. And if it ain't two it's one of them big boys."

"Then what, Jelani? What am I going to do?"

"Get up," he said plainly, then again, in a distorted way. "Get up!"

"Huh?" Zala quirked an eyebrow. "I'm already up. What are you talking about?"

"Get. Up!"

Swack!

A stoney slap cut across Zala's face, stirring her from her dreams. She was still in the room, still lying on the floor without bedding or pillow.

"When I tell you to get up, you do it," Iokaja grunted above her as she clenched her stone fist. "I know you better not have let those go bad." She pointed to the stonesbane Zala had brewing in the corner of the room. "Ekko's been looking for an excuse to give you more strikes. Which one is ready for me to take?"

Zala let out the start of an annoyed grunt. She was swiftly met with another rocky swipe, this time across her already chapped lips. Through a painful mumble, she told Iokaja where her next potion was.

"Speak clearly, I don't understand fucked-up."

Zala pointed to the corked bottle nearest to them. Iokaja followed the path of her finger and snagged up the potion, drank it, and set it back down with desperate speed.

"It... it hasn't grown since I've come here, right?" Zala mumbled through her burning lips. "How... how are you feelin'? Are you gettin' any spasms? Sometimes my husband got them, but if you take it with a bit of—"

Iokaja ignored her, spun on her heel, and headed back out toward the corridor. When she opened the door, the waft of falafel and mint tea filled the room momentarily. It must've been morning already.

When it came to conversation, Iokaja wasn't the most loquacious. Zala hadn't really considered herself a particularly social person when it came to small talk or chit chat. But sometimes she was left alone for hours at a time with no one to speak to. And every time someone came to change her chamber pot or give her some stale bread she always tried to strike up any bit of conversation. At first it was only a means to find a break in the crew, a weak link who would work with her to let her go. Then it just became a means to maintain her sanity—something she was apparently losing now that she was having fictitious conversations with her captive husband.

The only one who really spoke to her, ironically, was Ekko. However, those little chats came by way of insults and slanders between red tide sessions, not his desire to get to know her again.

"Who were you talking to?" a voice sounded from the other side of the door. It took Zala a moment to recognize the voice belonged to that man, N'Kota.

"I don't know what you're talking about," she answered as she examined the state of her in progress potions. A little blood came away at her cheek from Iokaja's slap.

"Ah," he said, then spoke in the Golah Tongue, *"Eti Eti must've stolen my ears then."*

"Only fools blame their plights on myths and legends," Zala threw back at him in his own tongue.

"And what is a fool when fiction becomes fact?" The man waited a beat. "You speak Golah, then?"

"I speak Golah." Zala added some silver shavings to one pot, and burned aloe in another. "What are you doing here anyway? Shouldn't you be running some errand for your 'boss man'? Thought you were his favorite, by the sounds of it."

"Favorites? That man doesn't know the meaning of the word." N'Kota yawned. "Or that's what I should've known. I'd been doing rather well over the past few moons under his employ. I mess up once, just *once* and he's got me relegated to guard duty—ah, no offense to you, saabi."

"You seem young. Why not find some honest work with someone else?"

"Honest work is a bore, and pays like shit."

"That it does." Zala agreed under her breath.

From what it seemed, N'Kota wasn't part of the *Redtide* crew exactly, which apparently meant he wasn't mandated to give Zala the silent treatment. She didn't think she'd get him to let her free or become her friend. Her suspicions were that he was some sort of empath. He had that unnatural aura about him when he was nearby. Even if she did try something, he'd know.

Well, at the very least she could get the chit chat she desired from him. "Whereabouts from Golah are you from?"

"The former Golah," he corrected. "And up until a year or two back... Bajok."

"Never heard of it."

"It's way way south. When I was there my father tried to put it back on the map. Had this whole thing cooked up with this princess from Ya-Set and some other saabi who used to be some famous pirate."

"Oh?" Zala took a seat near the door frame to hear N'Kota better. "Did this famous pirate have a name?"

"My clan—my brothers, I should say—called him Amana. Someone you know?"

Zala shook her head, then realized the man couldn't see her. "No, never heard of him. What made you leave your home?"

"Long story. The short of it though is that I wouldn't be welcome back there."

"You and me both."

"Oh? Do one of your tide lords have a price on your head or something?"

"The Isles aren't my home. Not my original one, at least."

"And what made *you* leave your home?"

"Long story," Zala echoed. "The short of it: I killed a man. An important man."

"Ooo," N'Kota cooed a little longer than he needed to and she could hear him turning his face to the door. Zala kind of figured he was a man for theatrics though. "Well, you're certainly more interesting than these other pirates who want to see you dead. Sure, I reckon they've all got high numbers where murdered folk are concerned. But they all have this... soulless way about them, ya know? Your words though... whoever that man you killed was... there's a loaded story there. Tell me about it."

Zala hadn't realized she was leaning back on the creaky old wall, which at that moment felt more like cool marble streaked with rich silk cascading down her back. "Please don't do that, empath."

"Perceptive." She could hear the smile in the man's voice. "Usually takes a bit longer for people to figure it out."

Zala moved away from the door and back to her potions. They didn't need any attending, but better on the far side of the room than next to an empath. "Maybe you're losing your touch, kijana. No wonder your boss demoted you."

N'Kota let out a loud chuckle, one that rung in Zala's good ear even from her distance. "Perhaps you're right, pirate. That's all well and good, though. I won't let that get me down. You shouldn't be down on yourself either… the way you was talkin' in your sleep like there was no hope. You're still breathing; I'm still breathing. We all got jobs to do in this world. That's all that matters in the end: a job, something to do, something to distract. I don't have much of a mind for plots and schemes, but I got the muscle and the charm to make 'em work for others. If you're gonna get out of your little funk, you'll need to make the most of what you got. Become the best brewmaster in Esowon… maybe then these crazy pirates might give you a bit more freedom. Might take a few years. But if they see value in you, you can do it. That or they'll kill you." He shrugged.

"Speaking of which…" His voice turned from the door and down the hall. "Ekko! Good morning to you. You and Lishan coming to tag me out?"

"Saved some falafel for you," Ekko answered on the other side. "She awake?"

"By Dulagi, you're sent from the heavens, saabi. My stomach thanks you. And yes, she's ready for her morning beating."

Zala tensed her body for the punishment she was about to endure, her back already stinging, wounds already set to be reopened when they were trying desperately to heal.

But N'Kota was right about one thing. Zala did have a job that needed to be done. And it sure as salt wasn't making stonesbane for the *Redtide* crew for the rest of her days.

CHAPTER 36
KARIM

Karim scribbled along the parchment in his hand. His marking joined a host of others clumped together. They weren't the neatest bits of writing, etched in haste as he tracked each man and woman that entered and exited the Harbor's Flask.

The latest mark-up was for a particularly tall and dark man with long hair down his back and a stick of falafel in hand. Issa had referred to him as N'Kota. As far as either of them could tell, he was just a frequent customer—and frequent customers weren't the type that Karim was concerning himself with today. Instead, he had his eye out for Vaziri, and those he employed to collect taxes. They usually wore dark turbans and darker expressions. Karim often spotted them out because of their neutral and near-dead expressions. But on that morning, none who came from the tavern wore such a face.

"What about that one?" Hajjar suddenly said at Karim's side —Karim had a hard time recognizing the young man in civilian clothing.

Karim followed the bushy-eyebrowed stare of Hajjar to find who he pointed out. "No, that's not one of them. That's just an elder who's spent too much time in the mines." And it was true. The old woman did indeed have that dead look, but there was a difference between her lumbering gait as opposed to Vaziri's crew, who walked almost mechanically.

"You didn't have to come with us today, Captain." Hajjar moved himself from the bench they sat on and stood away from Karim to not give them away as accomplices. "The gunner chief said we'd be fine today. Her man Akbar agreed to meet."

Karim ignored Hajjar's statements. It was true that the young officer and Issa didn't really need him. But even more true, Karim needed something to occupy himself besides toiling away with a prisoner who simply wouldn't talk.

"Where is Officer Akif, anyway?" Karim asked.

"She's meeting with that saabi al-Turabi out on the Steppes. Apparently he had some break-in not too long ago. He's plenty pissed." Hajjar pulled a wrapped skewer from his tunic and heated the meat on the wooden stick with his hands. Besides being a trusted confidant of Issa's when it came to jobs that didn't quite fit under official military business, he was a talented elemental. The best Karim had met, at any rate. He still couldn't believe how strong his wind magic had been on the airship all those weeks ago.

"A break-in?" Karim questioned. "And you're here with me instead of protecting her?"

"Her orders, sir," he said through a chew of some chicken. "She said not to worry about it."

"Why would any low-lives go way out there? What did they take?"

"A pair of kongamatos, apparently." Issa's voice came low behind them. "You two need to keep your voices down. I could hear you all the way from Spine Street."

Karim's wide eyes matched Hajjar's own as they turned to Issa, who stood with crossed arms in her own version of civilian clothing: a long dull gray dress with full head wrap.

Hajjar picked at his ear with his finished skewer. "Come again, Gunner Chief. Sounded like you said kongamatos?"

"Yes," she returned flatly.

"Those flying creatures died out, no?"

"Long story. I'll tell you about it later." Issa turned her glance to Karim. "The both of you. Anyway, did Akbar come in for his shift yet?"

Karim nodded. "About an hour ago. When were you going to tell me about al-Turabi?"

"I just did."

"No. I heard it from Officer Hajjar. What do you think you're doing going out to the Steppes alone?"

Issa scoffed. "This isn't the time right now."

Pride told Karim to press the issue, but he held his tongue. She was right. Getting angry about what she did on her own time in her own way wasn't going to do any good. She'd done all she had on her own up to this point.

"I just worry is all," is what Karim decided to say. "What is all this about."

A weight seemed to lift from Issa's shoulders as she took a seat next to Karim on his bench. Her voice came out low. "Today's the day we catch Vaziri in his little schemes. Did you guys mark that stout woman by the tavern?"

Karim glanced at the patrons around the tavern. Mostly morning workers who were chit-chatting before they went off to start their days. But there was one woman of short height and two chins who ambled past them, scanning the morning workers like she was sizing them up.

"I might have seen her a few times," Karim said. "But she didn't do anything suspicious. She hasn't even gone into the tavern."

"That's because she's guarding it," Issa explained. "She's an elemental like Hajjar. No one in the square recognized her, except for Akbar, who said she came in on the twenty-seventh day of the eleventh moon. You know what day that was, right?"

It took Karim a moment before a shockwave of revelation shot through him. "That's when reports of the *Redtide* came to the bay…"

"What?" Hajjar asked, joining them on the bench. "You saying the Rovers are holed up in there? What's that got to do with Vaziri?"

Issa leaned forward on her knees. "That's what I'm here to

find out. It seems the moment these Rovers started popping up, Vaziri's typical guard stopped paying visits to their usual stomping grounds. This new crew of his has been making rounds all over town, particularly around Shroud Street."

"What do you need from us, Gunner Chief?" Hajjar sat at attention.

"Wait five minutes, then follow me into the tavern."

KARIM SAT AT THE FAR END OF THE LOW-LIT BAR NEAR THE entrance—a cup of Vaaji's signature coffee brew cupped in his palm as he listened in on Issa's conversation with the Innkeeper, Akbar. Hajjar, who came in five minutes after him, took a seat at one of the beat up old tables near a set of stairs that must've led up to the rooms.

The Harbor's Flask wasn't a place Karim often frequented in adulthood. Not since Issa left al-Anim when they were children. Back then, he was locked away in the kitchens cleaning up just so he and Issa could watch the aziza singers that came at night. Karim wasn't even sure Akbar would recognize him, now that his face was hidden under a beard. Besides, recognition was seemingly far from the old man's mind now, with Issa holding him in intense conversation.

"Another one, sir?" one of the bartenders asked Karim. He, like N'Kota, was a tall and dark man with those same golden eyes—probably from the same foreign land. "Maybe something stronger for a long day, if that's your fancy?"

Karim waved his hand in the negative. "I'm good, thank you."

"If you need anything, holler."

The man wiped down the counter and moved to help another patron, who took a seat at the bar.

"When's your next break?" Issa asked Akbar innocently. "We haven't had a proper chat since I got back."

"Oh, you know I don't take breaks, m'lady."

Issa cocked her head. "Since when? Your wife finally whipped you into shape? When I used to work here you always passed work off to me so you could have your time with some hash out back." She smacked him lightly on the hand. "What's wrong? You don't want to talk to me anymore?"

Karim had been watching the conversation out the corner of his eye, his head angled toward the Vaaji Imperial banners that hung from the walls. But at the mention of Akbar being nothing more than an excessively lazy old man, he shifted his gaze to the bar.

The man wasn't quite meeting Issa's eyes as he spoke. And Akbar was the type of person who stared into one's soul, maintaining eye contact to an almost uncomfortable degree. Now he was acting as though Issa's eyes spat poison.

In the darkness of the tavern, two bespeckles of light caught Karim's eye. The bartenders who were assisting Akbar were cleaning together, each of their eyes alighting hazel. Karim could've sworn their irises were a slow drifting pattern, cascading down and down like an amber waterfall. And the way they rubbed the goblets they were cleaning seemed offhand, an afterthought, even when some of them were caked in coffee dregs.

Karim's gaze darted between them and Akbar, who looked near to passing out. Lifting out of his seat, Karim passed by Issa and tapped her twice on the back. Then he moved to one of the tables, where he pretended to set up a game of King's Way for himself. A few minutes later, Issa excused herself from the bar where she "inspected" a wanted poster for a black pakka mere feet away from Karim.

"There's something up with Akbar's help," Karim murmured without looking at her. "I think they're —"

"Empaths," Issa finished for him. "Yeah, I pegged them a few moments into talking with Akbar. They're N'Kota's relatives, I believe. He tried that trick on me not too long ago. Did you notice the moment I started asking about the goings-on, Akbar just shut down?"

"Yeah. So what's the play? Come back with the citywatch and bring them in for questioning?"

"Maybe... I just don't want to cause too much of —"

Issa stopped talking suddenly. Karim waited a moment in case she was just pausing because someone was eavesdropping. When the moment lasted longer than mere discretion, he glanced up to see her staring down someone who had just entered the tavern. A woman with a pale and freckled face. Though she was wrapped in Qibasi robes, there was no denying the lump at her back hiding her wings, or the strange clump at the side of her face under her head wrap hiding her pointed ears.

It was the aziza from the airship. The same one who frosted an entire corridor.

"Hajjar!" Karim shouted. "Stop her!"

CHAPTER 37

ISSA

THIS IS WHY ISSA DID THINGS ALONE. KARIM WAS GREAT IN A fight, relentless, unforgiving, effective. But when it came to espionage...

He was complete shit.

She didn't have time to throw him a scowl or an outcry of anger. What she needed to do was duck out of the way of the ice blast shooting from Hajjar's hand. A torrent of icicles sliced at her side, then impacted against an ice wall manifested by the short woman who had just entered the tavern.

The whole of the inn came alive in an instant. The languid morning crowd sprung with renewed energy as they fled for the nearest cover in the form of overturned tables and chairs. The whole bar's sudden movement seemed practiced to almost drilled precision—a tavern intimately familiar with high-stakes barside brawls.

Issa tackled Karim and flung him out of the path of the elemental fight, which turned from a chilled duel of ice that splintered through wooden panels to a heated battle of fire that set the air alight with a burnt scent. Issa shielded her eyes from the bright orange blaze.

One of Hajjar's fire blasts singed the other elemental's head wrap, revealing red hair and the pointed ears of an aziza. The female flicked her wrist and a sleet of ice formed below Hajjar's feet, forcing him to slip and fall.

"You two, get out of here!" The aziza commanded as the two dark men with the golden eyes shot up from behind their cover at the bar. "Tell your boss to send some help! And get Arus' ass in here."

The two men vaulted over the bar as Hajjar renewed another attack, this time with wind instead of fire or ice. The long hair of the men swayed as they ducked under each of the blasts, until they finally shouldered through the entrance and out into Sycamore Square.

Karim bolted from the overturned table he and Issa were behind, then called over his shoulder, "I'm going after them. Keep up with that aziza."

"Wait!" Issa shouted over another loud blast of wind. "You're by yourself!"

"The citywatch will be here any minute. Have some confidence." Karim withdrew his short sword from his hidden sheath and twirled it around in hand as though in answer to her doubt. Then he was gone before she could get out another word.

Turning back to the elemental brawl, Issa watched as the aziza mixed ice and wind to cover the room in a dense fog. Then, slipping her cloak to free her wings, she flew into the gust and disappeared.

The room fell silent for a moment. Then, a shuffling of wood against stone rumbled across the bar. The patrons who had been trapped in the tavern made their way out, some at full sprints, others hobbling with icicles pierced through thighs, and still more who were nursing burnt limbs and singed cloaks.

"Hajjar!" Issa called in the dissipating fog.

She crouch walked through the mist, bumping into a few inert bodies. Thankfully, each one she checked was still breathing. She knew she'd get chewed out by the Admiralty later, but that didn't matter now. So long as she brought in at least one of the Rovers, it would all be forgiven. At least, that was the hope she clung to.

"Issa," grumbled a voice behind the bar. Akbar slumped over a set of goblets that clattered on the ground. "Issa, those men… they… had me… in a spell. Damn empaths."

"I know, I know," Issa said softly, shifting over to the bar. "Just lie down and take it easy. The citywatch will sort it out."

With a dizzy rock of his head that she thought was meant as a nod, the man lay his head against the bar.

"Hajjar!" Issa called out again, turning to where he fell.

A nasty fear cut through her. The carnage of the airship all those weeks ago flashed in her mind and the iron scent of blood attacked her nose. For each chair she moved aside, every slumped form on the floor she checked, her heart dropped with the fear she had found Hajjar's body, his corpse.

A grunt sounded at her side.

"Hajjar!" She knelt down to the figure, turned it over, and Hajjar looked up at her with anger as he rubbed the back of his head.

"Should've known she'd go for my feet," he grunted. "I had her pressured. Messing with my balance was her only play."

Tears in her eyes, it took everything Issa had not to embrace him, professionalism be damned. She was just glad another of her comrades hadn't gone down to the pirates. Instead of a hug, she asked, "Can you walk?"

"Of course, Chief." He sprang up. "Just hit my head a little, nothing major." The line of blood coming down from beneath his head wrap disagreed.

"She couldn't have gone far." Issa nodded. "There's only one place to go, since she didn't go out the front."

Hajjar clapped his hands together and swiped them outward to magically remove the rest of the manifested fog. "You know this place better than me. I'll follow your lead."

Issa gave him another swift nod and jogged toward the back of the tavern, where a set of stairs led up to the floor for lodging. "Keep your ears open."

It wasn't long until they came upon a long, shadowed hallway of dark wood and tattered rugs. Only a single door into one of the rooms was left ajar.

"She sold us out!" bellowed a man's voice.

"How? She's been in her room the whole time," the elemental retorted in anger. "Put that dagger down, dikala!"

Issa picked up the pace and rushed down the corridor along with Hajjar as the man replied, "She's smart. She's playing us, just like she played us before."

Nodding over her shoulder, Issa gave Hajjar a hand signal of attack, which he returned in affirmation. Hajjar pushed a hand out and a burst of wind lashed out, slamming into the door, and blowing it off its hinges.

Inside the room, a large pale man with curly hair stood over a thin, small woman with dark skin. He was wielding a large dagger, but his wrist was halted by the aziza, who's entire arm was covered in stone.

"Help me!" The thin woman said. "They've taken me against my will. I'm just a kitchen worker!"

A flash of frost filled the room and blocks of ice rooted the attackers to the floor. Hajjar's brow twisted in concentration. "Don't try it, aziza. You know I'm more powerful than you."

"I don't need magic," she seethed as she pounded her stone arm into the ice. The ice around her ankle cracked quickly.

The thin woman didn't wait for the aziza to free herself and rushed to Issa and Hajjar for protection. "Thank you, thank you, thank you," she exhaled hysterically. "I've been locked up in this room for days." She held Hajjar tight like she were a child clinging to her father.

"What's happening? Where'd they go?" Hajjar asked, looking over the woman's shoulder.

Issa followed his gaze into what now looked like an empty room.

"The man's an illusionist," the thin woman said, pulling away from Hajjar and retreating into the corridor. "Careful. He'll play games with your eyes."

"Show yourself, pirate!" Hajjar raged. "Stop your tricks, or I'll flame this whole room."

Issa braced for Hajjar's next attack as his hands alighted with balls of flame. "Step back, civilian," she said. "This'll get heated."

But when Issa turned, the woman was already bolting for the window at the end of the hall, where she slammed through the glass and out into Sycamore Square.

CHAPTER 38
ZALA

IF ZALA HADN'T LISTENED TO SHOMARI ALL THOSE TIMES ON the *Titan*, she might've broken her legs at the end of her jump. But she remembered to tuck and roll out of her vault instead of letting all the force push into her legs where bones were liable to break. Shomari explained it had to do with kinetic energy or something. All Zala cared about was whether she could keep running. And as she came out of her roll, surprisingly, her calves kept her going, and her thighs, though strained, kept her standing tall.

But she was in the middle of a downright skirmish.

All around her, the citywatch were in battle with Rovers and others Zala didn't recognize. Pristine sabers clashed against weathered swords. Elemental blasts thudded against storefronts and impacted against the cobblestone roads in fireworks of fire and ice.

Most shocking of all, however, were the two brothers with the long locs, who apparently were some strange form of shapeshifters—half men and half hyena. At least three or four of the Vaaji authorities had to take them on just to keep up with a form of acrobatics that would've rivaled Shomari's own.

The fact that Zala had just crashed-landed out of the tavern was the least of anyone's worry, save for the woman who stared down from the broken glass at the tavern's second floor. Behind her, flashes of orange and blue painted the corridor, where Zala assumed the fight between that other elemental and Iokaja set off.

Not caring to wait to see if that woman could brace her own jump, Zala pushed into the growing crowd who were trying to get a better look of the skirmish. She wasn't sure what a normal day in al-Anim looked like, but over the past moon or so, she was sure the citizens of the city were having quite an eventful few weeks.

Zala put the distracting thought of the al-Animites aside in favor of her destination: her crew. That's all that mattered then and there. Not the fact that the fresh air filling her lungs were a welcome change to the stale room she spent days in. Not the fact that her legs were already growing tired, aching from inactivity. Pushing forward and onward was all she had as she dipped between roadways and alleys she only vaguely recognized.

And then she met a dead end.

Doesn't matter, Zala thought. *Just turn around and try again.*

But when she did so she was met with the sharp tip of a saber. And at its end was the woman from the tavern.

Zala had met her once before, though briefly. Both that day and on the airship, she hadn't gotten a good look at her face—only flashes. The woman had thick eyebrows and a slightly large nose over olive skin. Despite the menace of the blade held in her hand, however, her face was neutral, placid. The only deviation from her stoic expression was her slightly parted lips as she caught her breath.

Had Zala really let her catch up? Was she so slowed by her injuries?

"Who are you?" the woman asked. "And don't tell me you're a kitchen worker."

"I'm not the one you want." Zala lifted her hands in genuine forfeit. She didn't have anywhere near the energy to fight or run. And calling out for help would do nothing. She looked like a drifter with her tattered and bloody clothes, and the woman's weapon was clearly military grade. Anyone decent would side with the woman.

"You're after the Rovers," Zala asked, "right?"

"That wasn't my question, pirate."

"Captain Nubia," Zala blurted. The slight irritation that was working its way into the woman's thick brows curved into a look of curiosity. "Captain Nubia... they're after her. They've come back for her. They're working with some person in your ranks to make that happen." Zala glanced at the woman's sword hand, hoping to see it slack. It didn't. "And they're after that sky ship."

The woman held fast but Zala could tell her mind was working. "Turn around. You and your answers are coming with me."

"I'm not your enemy, chana. Just listen—"

"Turn around."

Zala sighed heavily and made the slow turn that was demanded of her when another voice came from the end of the alley. "No, you turn around, dikala."

A pair of swords unsheathed and Zala's heart jumped when she recognized the deep, gruff voice.

"Old Man Ode?" Zala gasped.

"Good to see you again, Captain."

Zala turned again and peered over the woman's shoulder to see not only the old man, who still had his peg leg, but the young and thin Rishaad as well, who held his sword forward in a shaky hand. They had made it; they had survived! The load on Zala's heart lightened a little.

"We ain't got to hurt you," Ode grunted. "Just drop that there weapon and let our Captain go."

"Do what he says, Sister," Rishaad added.

"Don't call me sister, traitor," the woman spat as she dropped her blade defiantly.

Swiftly, Zala snagged it up and leveled it against her would-be captor. "Now I've got a question for you. Where are you keeping my husband?"

"Husband? You'll need to be more specific." The woman raised her hands peacefully and pressed her back against the alley wall.

Zala pressed the saber into the woman's cheek. Her grip was so weak, but she couldn't betray her fatigue. "I was on the sky ship. You had a bag over his head. Answer the question or I'll gut you right here. Cry for help, and I'll cut out your tongue."

"I can't tell you that, pirate." The woman's face remained placid, a military woman's composure.

"Then you're coming with us."

"Uh, Captain," Ode cut in. "We can't bring her with us with that crowd out there. We'll get spotted easy."

Rishaad drew in closer to them, speaking to the woman directly. "You're fighting on the wrong side, Sister."

"And *you're* on the right one?" the woman slung back with slitted eyes, her indifferent brows finally caving into a scowl.

"We have to take her with us," Zala said. "She's my way back to Jelani."

"Jelani?" Revelation dawned over the woman's face. "Hang on… that was *you* on the airship. And that illusionist back at the tavern, he was there too, wasn't he—"

Zala pressed the saber deeper into the woman's cheek. "Where is he, dikala? He's sick. He needs me. You don't understand!"

"I do…" The woman's soft tone caught Zala completely off guard.

Ode tugged at Zala's arm. "Time to go, Captain. We ain't come all this way just to get you caught again. Their citywatch's gonna sweep through here real real soon."

Zala couldn't bring herself to move away from the woman. Twice now she'd crossed paths with the man and woman she knew for a fact had Jelani within their grips. It was worth the risk to get information out of her now. She'd only need a few minutes, or however long it would take to cut off a finger or two.

But her grip on the saber was already failing her, her head was throbbing with dehydration. And what if this woman was strong enough to resist her?

Better to live another day for Jelani than to die trying to get information.

"Let's go," Zala seethed as she left the woman with a light cut across the cheek. "Keep looking over your shoulder, dikala. We'll be back for you."

In anger, Zala jogged away before she changed her mind. Ode hobbled behind her, and Rishaad hustled along her side.

"We thought one of you lot would make trouble at one point

or another," the young man chuckled. "Betted on it, in fact. How you been, Captain?"

"Not now, Rishaad." Zala sighed, trying to take the sting from her terseness with a weary grimace. "Just lead us back to the old temple by the harbor. Lowtown."

"Yeah, I'm doing pretty shitty too."

They continued through more roads and hidden paths as Zala reminded herself of the new rules Shomari and Mantu requested of her. Following behind Rishaad and Ode, she finally said, "Thank you. Both of you. I owe you for this."

The men turned to each other with expressions of shock. Then glanced over their shoulders to say simultaneously, "Don't mention it, Captain."

CHAPTER 39

KARIM

WARNING BELLS CHIMED THROUGHOUT THE CITY, STARTING from Sycamore Square and all throughout the surrounding districts. The plaza they fought in was modest, but it still felt too small to contain the bout with all the onlookers bunched around the central tree.

It seemed Issa was right about the pirates being holed up in the Harbor's Flask. What Karim hadn't anticipated was how well prepared they would be. Perhaps he should've expected it, considering the group that raided their airship a mere few weeks ago. Then they had elementals, aziza, pakkami, and illusionists. Karim was alone with his meager crew then and they had managed it somehow; now, fighting along with the citywatch who counted in the dozens, outnumbering the three scoundrels they fought, he couldn't understand why they were losing.

The pirates' momentum was funneled primarily through their morbid shapeshifters, whose hyena maws stuck from the back of their heads instead of transforming completely.

"You four, flank that one's right!" Karim ordered the citywatch with his saber brandished. "You two, dead center. Form a shield."

They heeded his words, but their opponents were outclassing them—too fast by way of the shapeshifters, too crafty and powerful by way of the elemental. The beasts jumped and pounced like real hyenas in the wild before the citywatch could get close. And anytime the monsters faltered, even for a moment, the elemental was there to protect them with spellwinds and lightning strikes.

And soon, the square was painted with Vaaji blood.

The men and women who fought with Karim weren't as well trained as the naval officers alongside which he usually fought, but where they lacked in skill, they made up for it in sheer numbers and superior weaponry.

Above, bowmen lined the roofs enclosing Sycamore Square with crossbows in hand. Karim caught sight of them just before they took their aim. "Watchmen, pull back," he called out to the ones fighting in the square. "Bolts in the sky!"

Those who were still able to move drew back and out of the way of the volley of bolts that rained down.

"Citizens, get back, get back!" Karim shouted at the still growing crowd.

Bolts wisped passed Karim's ears as each one found their marks true. The shapeshifters slowed with each bolt that impacted them through the torso and limbs of their human sides. Anything that found their animal hides simply thwacked away like brittle sticks. The sole human elemental, however, went down quickly.

"Captain el-Sayyed!" Hajjar's voice called out from the entrance of the tavern, just behind the enemy.

Karim pointed toward the shapeshifters. "Ice them!"

"Mernaz! Taali!" one of the citywatch captains bellowed. "Assist! Assist!"

Two of her own pushed forward, a chilling fog manifesting around their fists. Hajjar worked with them, and together they pinned the shapeshifters between a triangle formation. From each corner a concentration of ice shavings formed from their fingertips and solidified around the beasts, who stood on all fours.

"Keep it up!" Karim and the Captain shouted in unison.

"Captain, we've more elementals across the square!" another watchman shouted.

"You there!" the Captain commanded, shouting across the plaza. "Surround and contain!"

From that point it was all over. With a little more than a half dozen elementals working together, the shapeshifters were locked in place in a prism of ice. The sounds of battle died down, replaced by the rumbling of the crowd that braved closer into the square, and the outcries of comrades finding their cohorts among the dead. From Karim's count, the ratio of the dead to living was a dozen of their own to the one pirate, who lied motionless in her own blood—the pirate with the double-chin Karim identified a mere half hour prior.

Guilt slithered through Karim's chest. The whole thing was a mess, and Karim was surely going to be the one who took the blame. They weren't exactly supposed to be there investigating how the pirates were connected to Vaziri. An operation like that was supposed to be left to the citywatch or the spymasters employed in the palace. But he couldn't just let them get away, couldn't let Vaziri get away with whatever it was he was up to.

Like on the *Viper*, it was his fault this happened, and his insides ate away at him.

The only way to win back any favor was to pin the whole fiasco on Vaziri by way of his captured minions. Karim stepped up to the ice block lodged near the sole tree in the square. He tapped on its hard surface and gritted his teeth. "This blood is on Vaziri's hands," he told the shapeshifters, convincing himself more than them. "Mark my words, you'll give him up."

"Captain…" Hajjar huffed out through a strained breath. "Captain… where's the Chief?"

"She's not with you?"

Hajjar shook his head. "She went after one of the runners."

"I'm fine!" Issa called out. Karim and Hajjar whipped to see the Gunnery Chief shouldering through the crowd and shouting to them that she was military. When she got close, Karim could see a line of blood trickling down her cheek. Through a labored breath, she huffed, "We have a problem."

alleyway near the central districts, the pirates that ambushed her, and how a female pirate knew Jelani's name—a pirate that Issa said was the latter's wife.

Issa had brought them over to a storefront where other wounded were being attended to. Shop owners brought out water to douse the simmering embers at the edges of imperial banners strewn about the square, while others chipped away with hammers and pickaxes where their entrance doors were frosted shut.

"Skies and stars! How many bloody pirates are crawling around our city?" Hajjar asked after Issa got them settled. He curled a fist and pounded it into his hand. "I almost had that illusionist and the aziza. I should've just burnt them out of the room, but I wanted to bring them in alive."

"The pirates I encountered in the alley said they *weren't* working for Vaziri, though," Issa said as she held a poultice of dawa root to her cheek cut. "At least that's what that woman told me. But I'm still certain the Rovers in the tavern were working with him. There's something we're missing. We're close, Karim. I know we are."

Karim had sat and listened quietly, never interrupting Issa once during her retelling. The only answer he could think of was, *That's piracy for you. No loyalty among those sorts.* But he assured her by saying, "We'll get our answers soon." He nudged his chin over to the shapeshifters who were just then being carted away to the palace dungeons. "Apparently they come all the way from the former Golah Empire. One of the watchwomen said they're some sort of demon. She called them 'kishi.'"

Issa shrugged. "Never heard of those. Are they Twice Blessed? Those are the two who were influencing Akbar, right?—Gods! Akbar! Is he okay?"

Hajjar set a hand on her shoulder. "He's fine. A little woozy. But he's good."

Karim snapped his fingers suddenly. "Two different crews!" Issa and Hajjar stared at each other, clearly indicating Karim needed to explain himself further, so he did. "You said those pirates in the alley called the woman their Captain, yes?"

"Yeah, but I figured she was the one who took over for Nubia…" Issa smacked her hand against her forehead. "That's right, Akbar described the *Redtide* Captain to me."

"The woman with the long braided hair," Hajjar added.

Karim nodded, glad they were following along. "And the one you ran into had short hair."

Issa bit her lip. "It's possible. It's also possible she cut her hair when she came to the city."

"True enough." Karim rubbed his temples. "The answers will come. We'll just have to wait for them from Vaziri's men."

"You gonna interrogate those pirates yourself, sir?" Hajjar asked proudly.

"No, he will not," an elderly voice said from the square. They all looked up to see Vice Admiral Shamoun, who had a flat line plastered across his face. "You three have a lot to explain."

Issa was the first to come out of the Vice Admiral's office an hour later. Her flushed red ears clashed with her simple grey dress, and they could be seen even in the dark administration corridor of the western keep.

"How bad?" Karim asked, exchanging a sidelong glance with Hajjar who sat alongside him on a stone bench.

"I'm not exactly sure yet," Issa said.

Hajjar sat forward. "What does that mean?"

"It depends on how much valuable information we get from our two shapeshifting captives. If it's good, he can protect us, sweep it under the rug. If we get nothing… I believe his words were 'a punishment suitable for our little fiasco.'" Though her skin reddened even farther, she gave Karim an encouraging smile. "Whatever happens either way, we should be good. The banquet's in a few days. We'll get Vaziri then. Too many pieces are falling into place for us not to."

Hajjar let out a long sigh and stood up. "I should've said no when you invited me into all this. It's easier taking orders. This is why I didn't go into citywatch work." He took a few steps toward Shamoun's office.

"Where are you going?" Issa asked.

"It's my turn to get chewed out, right?"

Issa shook her head then turned to Karim. "No. He wants to see our Captain next."

<hr>

"Thank you very much for giving me even more paperwork than I already have, Captain," Shamoun intoned a few moments later. Karim couldn't quite tell how serious or playful his tone was.

Shamoun's office was as mundane as his fashion. Not unlike Umar Jad's quarters on the *Viper*, everything was immaculate and orderly, everything, that is, save for his desk. Ledgers and parchment piles were stacked so high a few of them were on the precipice of spilling over the sides. Some of the tome towers cast shadows over Shamoun that rivaled the ones developing under his eyes.

There wasn't much Karim could think of to say in response, so he stayed silent.

Shamoun cleared his throat. "What is your title under our Navy, el-Sayyed?"

There was no denying the earnestness of the question then, and it felt a whole lot like a trap.

"Captain... Sir," Karim said flatly.

"Captain of what?"

"Captain of the *Viper*, of the First Air Fleet."

"And is Sycamore Square the *Viper*?"

Karim swallowed long and hard. "I don't know what you mean, Vice Admiral."

"Can Sycamore Square sprout wings and fly? It's a simple question. No tricks."

"No, sir. It cannot—"

"So why then did you think it was your job to pursue criminals in a district that was not yours to oversee? Your domain is the sky, Karim, not the taverns of the central districts." Shamoun said all this while barely moving. All force came through his words; he sat as still as a night owl — an owl on the hunt.

"Well, if I may, sir." Karim adjusted his collar uncomfortably. His hand came away with a bit of blood and he tried to hide it. "The pirates we pursued today may be connected to a plot *against* the *Viper*."

Shamoun made the first significant movement since Karim had arrived, leaning forward ever so slightly. "Pray tell."

"I can't do that right now, sir." Karim wondered how much Issa had told the Vice Admiral, then chided himself privately for not asking her.

"Oh? Why is that?"

"Right now, anything I say could be considered slander without more solid evidence."

Shamoun pointed outside his office. "By evidence, you mean the testimony of those two beasts you brought in."

"Yes, sir."

Shamoun scratched at the stubble on his chin that was usually clean shaven. It was a small move, but Karim could tell it was one of irritation. If anything, the gesture was a testament to how much respect the man had for Karim. There were officers who were demoted, cast out, and never heard of again for less.

Quietly, the Vice Admiral pushed his chair back, moved to the arched window sill behind him, and stared out of it. "You know, I stopped by your office this morning and I found a few interesting items there. If I didn't know it was your office, I'd say I came upon the desk of a student scholar who didn't know what they wanted to specialize in. There were medical books, law books, even tomes detailing the operation of the human mind. Where the first and latter is concerned, I understand. But the law book piqued my interest the most. From the chapter I found open, it would seem you were looking for technicalities in the law to land someone in the palace dungeons." Shamoun turned to look to Karim with a somber expression. "You need not mince words with me, el-Sayyed. How is Collector Vaziri these days?"

Karim dug his nails into his palm. If Shamoun knew what he was up to, he could shut it down straight away.

"He's…" Karim trailed off. "Doing well."

Much better than he should be, he thought.

Shamoun tapped his fingers along the window pane in thought before continuing. "Officer Akif didn't divulge much, sharp as she is. But I've heard rumors about the Collector and some of what he's doing in the Old Temple Ward. Your father lives within one of them, does he not?"

Perhaps it was time to be forthright. Shamoun watched Karim for a long moment, and Karim let himself be watched, allowing the awkwardness of it all to fall on him in its totality. He wasn't sure how much Shamoun knew, perhaps all of it, more likely a little. But his next words weren't what Karim was expecting.

Taking his seat once more, reestablishing his stone face, the Vice Admiral asked, "Have you ever considered the expression 'in over your head' before? Do you know where the phrase originated?"

"No, sir."

"It was a phrase written by the former merfolk: *chi na té.*" Shamoun signed the expression with his hands. "Our ancient ancestors knew it as a warning. It implies swimming somewhere where one's feet can't reach the bottom, and where one is not strong enough a swimmer to handle it."

Karim didn't respond right away. Perhaps he *was* in over his head, but he couldn't let Vaziri get away with it.

"I won't stop, Vice Admiral," he said, making his words clear but inserting as much respect as he could.

"Ah, and I probably don't expect you to. But Vaziri is a slippery one. There are several individuals who have crossed him. I only fear you do not have the fins to swim in waters like his to survive. What's more, you have a sea speaker you're supposed to be attending to. From what I know, little progress has been made there... am I wrong?"

Karim stayed silent, that nagging failure biting at the back of his neck.

"Do not let what's happening with your district affect your

work for the Empire," Shamoun went on. "We need you locked in on that sea speaker. I need you locked in." He set a hand on one of his stacks of papers and removed the top sheet. "This is a message from the East. General Najjar is making her final push to Mount Junga with little to no resistance. After she secures the mountain, Their Majesties will turn their eyes to Kidogo and your sea speaker; to you… and to me."

He let that message settle for Karim, and then he melted back in his chair. "Now, be completely honest with me. Why is Collector Mahir Vaziri of such importance to you? And do not give me this business about your desire not to slander him. Lay it all on me, rumors and all."

Karim sat trying to think of a lie he could tell, but each one he ran through sounded half baked at best. More than that, he couldn't think of why he needed to lie to Shamoun at all. The man had always had his back before. Perhaps honesty was the best route, not just because the Vice Admiral demanded it, but because it was the right thing to do.

Karim sighed.

He told it all plain and true, from how he, Karim, was essentially sponsoring not only his father but the entirety of those who dwelled in the Old Temple Ward, to his conflict with Vaziri, to how deep the conspiracy around the Collector seemed to go.

"Most of all though, sir," Karim said as he finished up, "all of this, whatever it is Vaziri needs all that extra coin for… it's connected to the airship." He leveled his eyes on Shamoun, never looking away to illustrate how serious he took all this. "He's making a play for it, of this I'm certain. I don't know how he'll do it or who exactly he's doing it with, but you said it yourself. He's a slippery one. He could pull it off."

Shamoun hummed under his lips, interlocked his fingers, and sat his elbows on his table. Whatever he was considering in that brilliant mind of his must've been troublesome. The valleys in his creased forehead were deeper than Karim had ever seen on anyone. But his mind was built for battle, for tactics out at sea. The game Vaziri was playing was something else entirely. The rules he played by simply didn't translate.

"Have you spoken with your father about converting?" Shamoun asked, to Karim's shock. What he had expected was some sort of plan of action against Vaziri, not... conversion.

Was that truly Karim's answer? For his father to convert and everything else would go away? Was Vaziri so fearsome a schemer that there was absolutely no other option but to bow down?

"That's a hard thing to ask, sir, if I'm being forthright." Karim humored Shamoun. "You can't ask a man to break his traditions so easily."

"Too true." Shamoun stroked his stubble again. "Did I ever tell you the reason I came into the light?"

"No, sir."

"It wasn't when I was as young as you. Much of my military career, I held to my familial traditions, prayed to the Old Gods under the Old Way. It was my failure with the Andala Inquisition that set me on the pious path I am on now. You see... I wanted to take my life then. For moons, I made excuses to stop at this outpost and that just so I wouldn't have to see my comrades back at home. Yes, I fought well, but I was being entirely stubborn. And part of me wanted to go down in combat so I wouldn't have to face the Admiralty. So many of its members then told me I was a fool for trying to hold out a defense so long, that I would get a lot of my crew killed, which, of course, I did. And it never helped how hard I prayed, or how many Gods I made sacrifices to. It wasn't until I found the strength within myself, the strength given to us by Shati'ala that I found a way back to some semblance of victory. I still hate myself for not realizing it sooner. Perhaps then I could have retaken Andala altogether instead of being lauded for an impeccable defense—really an extended retreat, if you ask me."

"Sir? You're not a mystic, though."

"That I am not. That's not the only thing Shati'ala gave to us, Karim. What truly separated us from the ancient beasts all those ages ago was not our ability to throw illusions or self healing our wounds... It was our higher function of thinking. The kind of thinking that has manifested the airship you captain now, the kind of thinking that has driven the invention of our medicines, the kind of thinking," he pointed behind Karim, "that will help you break that sea speaker."

The words the man said were not new to Karim. Hell, he had just been saying them to the sea speaker Jelani a week ago. But at that moment, the meaning was different coming from the Vice Admiral's mouth, for it was not backed by theory and lofty spirituality but by a practical story the man lived through.

"But we cannot move forward," Shamoun went on, "*you* cannot move forward until you shave the weight. Your focus must be singular at this time. We cannot put stock in a multitude of dead gods, but in our own minds. And your mind should be set on the one task given to you, or I feel you will sink. You understand? Now, I know you will need time to let that stew, but promise me at least that you'll think on it."

"I'll think on it… but, sir, Vaziri can't just be left to his own devices."

Shamoun lifted a finger. "Just think on it, el-Sayyed. *Think* before you act, whatever it is you decide."

Karim sighed and licked his lips to wipe away the response he really wanted to say. "Yes, sir, I'll think on it."

"Good. Now get out of here and bring me some results. I want to get through these stacks by the end of this century."

CHAPTER 40
ZALA

THE SIGHT OF THE TWIN FALLEN PILLARS WAS A WELCOME ONE as Rishaad and Ode carried Zala around their last street corner of the Lowtown district. Now that all adrenaline had retreated from her veins, her limp had grown more severe.

Maybe I didn't learn that roll from Shomari well enough, Zala thought.

But the strain in her legs barely registered as familiar faces passed her along the cracked and broken streets, city dwellers who likely didn't recognize her because she always covered her face, but individuals she had come to know—at least in passing.

"Just right through those two fallen pillars." Zala nodded ahead. "That old temple just to the left. We'll find the others there."

The moment they passed the threshold and into the stale air of the old temple, a great fit of excited shouts assaulted Zala's ears.

"Zala! Zala!" a red-eyed Fon cried out. The aziza was sat cross legged and leaned against a crumbled statue with cloth and embroidery in hand. With utter jubilation she cast her project aside, leapt up and around Zala's torso, and planted a huge kiss on Zala's cheek.

"Ouch!" Zala hissed. "Sorry, a little tender."

Fon let go immediately, then covered her mouth. "Sorry, sorry,

sorry." Her huge, forest-green eyes flitted to the men holding Zala up. "Wait... Old Man Ode? Rishaad—is that you under that beard?"

"Yeah, we're just as surprised I could grow one too," Rishaad chuckled as a rush of children surrounded them.

"Zala! We thought you were dead!"

"Nu uh, I told you she was just hiding."

"Look at all her cuts and how pale she is. She looks half dead as it is."

"That's rude, Aron."

"Your breath is rude!"

Fon did her best to quiet the children. The most she could do was get their raucous outcries down to a modest form of yammering. It wasn't until some of the children's parents came over when Ode could actually get his first words in.

"Only you and Zala made it out of that shitstorm with the Rovers?" he asked. Zala could feel him starting to strain under her weight. Maybe someone could help him with his peg leg here...

"No, no, Mantu and Shomari are with us too. They're just out looking for—" Fon covered her mouth again. "Ugara's Spear! Katya, can you go out with some of the other children and get them back here. Tell them Zala's back!"

Katya, whose skin was caked with dirt and arm lodged in a sling, bounced up from behind the dozens of children ahead of her. "Which way they go, ma'am?"

"Out near Arba's theater, sweeping through the hiller districts."

"All the way up there?" Katya whined.

Fon snapped her fingers. "You better change that tone right now, young woman."

The young Katya slumped her shoulders, then shouted, "Come on, Cobra Squad! We got a job to do."

Half the group of children fell in line as Katya led them out into the city streets.

"Well, you definitely have them in order," Zala said, impressed. "Almost sounded like I was back home as a girl—ow!"

Zala winced as one of the straggling children bumped against her leg as they passed.

Fon examined Zala up and down, her eyes crossing over each one of her friend's cuts, both deep and shallow. "Right, let's get you to the shaman."

Elation brightened Shaman Ismail's sunbaked face once he opened the door to his small home.

"The Gods are good." He smiled as he ushered everyone inside.

"The Gods are always good," Fon repeated. "Do you need me to get the dawa root spread ready for the cot?"

"Yes, if you would."

Fon went to work in the corner of the room, where she gathered together what looked like an enormous bird's nest. She said some sort of chant and the bunched sticks caught alight. Flames plumed in a hue of blessed purple fire. There was no heat, the magic instead feeling more like a cool breeze.

"On the fire you go." The shaman nodded to the others. "If you will, gentlemen. Please undress her before she goes on."

They did as they were asked, Zala helping them to strip off her clothing, some of which stuck to her old wounds and ripped away bits of flesh, forcing a whimper from her lips. Then, with a pair of heaving breaths, Ode and Rishaad settled Zala onto the fire as gently as they could. The moment the first flames licked at her back, she was instantly soothed.

"This is old magic," Shaman Ismail explained. "It will take the rest of the day and most of the night before you can get up from the flames. As strong as the magic is, though… you will still scar."

"What am I lying on?" Zala breathed easy. The flames not only purged and cleaned her wounds but her lungs as well, apparently.

"Enchanted dawa root." Fon perked up. "Shaman Ismail knows all sorts of old magic. It's almost like being back home for me. He spends weeks prepping and gathering all his reagents together. I've learned all sorts of things with him while you and Mantu were in the kitchens and well... when you... What happened out there? The Rovers?"

Zala's entire body shivered at the name of the pirate crew. She felt Iokaja's cold, rough hand around her neck, felt every strike Ekko gave her each morning. When she explained everything to Fon and the others, there were moments where her voice hitched and her eyes welled with tears. She didn't think she'd be so broken by the ordeal. All the time she was imprisoned she'd felt dead more than anything else.

Thankfully, or perhaps because she was exceedingly compassionate, Fon stopped Zala when she got into the details, instead of asking for more information. The aziza changed the subject to what she had been up to. Ode and Rishaad came in too, explaining how they hid out near the harbor until they heard rumors of pirates showing up in the lower and central districts. Fon was in the middle of explaining the different kinds of shifts they had all been going on to search for Zala when Shomari barged into the small room. Like the cat he was, he bounced atop Zala's wooden cot—disregarding the purple flames—and slapped a hand against her leg with a triumphant laugh.

"Ouch, ouch!" Zala complained.

"Let her rest!" Shaman Ismail shouted from his corner where he prepared more dawa root bedding.

Shomari vaulted back from Zala's cot just as fast as he jumped on. "Apologies, Captain. But I told Mantu you'd be fine!"

"Where's the big guy?" Fon asked.

Shomari fluttered his fingers. "You know how difficult it is carrying around all that weight of his. He will be catching up in another year or so!" He grinned. "I came the moment the little ones found us—wait, wait, wait." His gaze found the other two pirates sitting in the room. "I underestimated you two, it seems."

"What? You thought we got captured?" Rishaad asked.

"No, killed."

Ode chuckled. "Not yet, cat. Not yet."

After a little bit of catching up, a great thunder rumbled throughout the little shanty before Mantu came storming in. Like

Shomari, he made a beeline for Zala, though unlike the cat, the giant of man grabbed Zala out of her cot and clutched her in what she assumed was his version of a warm embrace—sweaty and crushing as it was against her naked chest.

"Ooouch!" Zala cried out for the third time in the past half hour. "I thought it was the Rovers I had to worry about."

"Sorry, my fault." Mantu put her down, his face flushed a reddish-purple.

"Okay that's it!" the shaman cut in again. "If any more of you pirates comes in here and disturbs your Captain, she'll end up needing the fires for another two days."

As painful as all the squeezing was, Zala couldn't help but feel warm inside. She had grown close to her crew, true, yet she never expected everyone would miss her like they apparently had, least of all Mantu, who only a moon ago was debating if he should kill her or not.

"Woah, Mantu," Fon giggled. "I didn't think you were a hugger."

The big guy gave her a look, which did absolutely nothing to halt Fon's giggling. "You fools are still alive too then, huh?" He jutted his chin to Ode and Rishaad.

"Alive and kicking." Ode threw out his peg leg. "Well, kinda. You know where I was gettin' at."

"I filled in Fon." Zala fell back into the comfort of her cot and the dawa root spread that was sewn there. Once she regained her breath again, she reexplained what had happened to her the past few days of her absence.

"So the Rovers are making another play for the sky ship, then." Shomari stroked his furry beard. "I can't for the life of me understand why they would be keeping Nubia on the ship instead of a dungeon, though."

"The woman you mentioned," Mantu cut in. "The one in the alley. Was she fairly tall? Thick eyebrows. Lightish brown eyes?"

"Yeah, I think so..." Zala trailed off, trying to recall the woman's features.

Mantu snapped his fingers. "That's the same chana that did

Ajola in. I'd bet my sword on it. She must be trackin' the Rovers. You think she has us pegged too?"

Zala shook her head. "I don't think so. Not that I can tell, anyway. She thought I was working *with* the Rovers and whoever their new boss is. I couldn't figure out who exactly they were working with, but it's someone likely on the inside of that Vaaji palace, or close to it. So long as we can bring down that Collector, Majida will tell us everything we need to know. We'll find our crew and the sky ship. Everything is leading there."

"Speaking of which," Mantu said. "The last time I saw you, you were going to explain your little plan with Vaziri and that Seeker business."

"Oh right…" Zala had almost forgotten. Nearly dying tended to do that to a person, she supposed. "I definitely want to use the Seekers against Vaziri. Once we get him alone in the banquet, we can let him know we know his secret."

"Seekers?" Ismail lifted from his workstation. "What do you want with the Seekers?"

"*I* don't want anything with them. I just want to use them against Vaziri. They seem to have him spooked."

The shaman spat on the ground. "Those bastards came through here while you were away…" He trailed off, anger in his eyes.

Fon grabbed one of his fingers, stroked the back of his hand, and finished for him. "They took little Jaali."

"The sewer speaker?" Zala asked, remembering the first day she saw the children chasing after the rats. "When?"

"When the rains stopped," Shomari said with his head low.

"Everything might be okay though," Shaman Ismail said as he finally got his voice to stop hitching from half cries. "Arba might be able to get him out."

"Arba?" Zala asked. "They mentioned that name in the palace. Vaziri and that other woman. Who is that?"

"Arba is a friend of the unregistered in the city. She and Vaziri are quite close, from what I remember… though it's been a while since I've gone down to her theater. It's way up on the hills and these knees can't make that trip too often."

"So... what?" Old Man Ode asked from the side, still nursing his peg leg. "This Collector fella some mystic or something?"

"Not that I know," the shaman answered. "It's unlikely. Noble types get more scrutiny. Only reason we can hide our children so long is because those government officials stay clear of us folk if they can help it, or in times of peace. When they need new recruits for their armies though..."

"We'll find out for sure once we get to that banquet," Zala said. "We just got to get him alone and figure all this out. I've a feeling a lot of these players will be there... speaking of the banquet..."

"Don't worry yourself none," Mantu assured her. "We got you covered. By the way, when we go back tomorrow, your grandmother Zhanda passed away, if anyone asks."

Zala threw up an eyebrow. "Zhanda? Really?"

"That one was actually my idea," Shomari confessed sheepishly.

"We haven't had the best plans while you were away." Fon blushed.

"Zhanda is fine..." Zala said. "It's just, you know, a little..." She wanted to say cliché, but instead she peered at all of them: Fon's wide eyes, Shomari's casual lean, Mantu's giant physique paired with a blushing expression. "It's all good. Really. I'm glad you came up with something."

"Apparently the Vaaji take death in the family as seriously as we do on the islands." Mantu sat himself on a crate full of incense sticks. "'Cept for the week-long festivals and parties we got and all that, of course. Fon's been makin' daily rum cakes that I bring to Chef Hadi so he doesn't get too pissed. So we all good there."

"It's time to change out those roots you got," Shaman Ismail said. Zala had barely noticed the flames had died down to half their original size. "Just lift up a little for me."

Zala did as he asked—as painful as it was. The moment between the switch made her realize how much pain she was truly in without the soothing flames.

The shaman hissed, voicing the pain Zala felt. "Damn, they got you good, girl."

"It's only half as bad as it looks." Zala sucked in a sharp breath as the shaman pulled away dawa root that had embedded in some of her wounds. "I got to find out firsthand where they got the 'red tide' name from. Upside is, I got a lot of practice with stonesbane over the last week or so."

"How is Iokaja?" Fon asked, her eyes genuinely curious.

"Pissed. Very pissed. But... good. I don't know if she got out of that fight with the citywatch though. But with her wings, she should be fine." Zala tucked a strand of Fon's hair behind her ear. It was a complete mess, and Zala made a note to rebraid it later. "Sorry I missed your natal day, Fon. I owe you some of Agwe's red pea soup I threw in Iokaja's face—well, tried to throw in her face anyway."

Fon gave her a weak smile. "Don't you go worrying about that. I'll have plenty more of those, and now so will you." She bit her lip, then laughed. "I wouldn't say no to something nice from that banquet though."

CHAPTER 41
ISSA

Surgeon Abadi's proper caring chamber at the Hammadi Hospice was a lot different than the tight confines of his space on the *Viper*.

For one, it appeared a lot cleaner—with bright sandstones that had been cleaned twice since Issa came in—once for each patient Abadi saw before her. Second, it was at least three times as large, with enough space to fit in four cots and an entire section filled with medical instruments. And third, Abadi's usual bitter mood was traded for a mildly tart one thanks to him being back home and comfortable again.

"You should have come to me straight away," he said as he examined Issa's exposed side. "You could've avoided all this bruising."

She winced each time he pressed along her ribcage, which she hadn't realized was as sore as it was until she left Karim back at the palace.

"May I ask what you were doing that was so important that you neglected to come to me sooner?"

"You heard about what happened at Sycamore Square, yes?"

Abadi adjusted his monocle and peered to the far side of the room, where his top shelf had recently acquired a new set of bottles filled with a curious set of potions. "Ah, I supposed that's why those were brought to me. I was in the middle of verifying them before I was told you were checking in. The first two I could decipher were Draft of Dulagi." He pointed to the phials filled with a purple hue of sludge. "And that last one there is stonesbane. And a decent sample of the concoction, I might add."

"Yeah, there was a big fight at the Flask. I got this off a blade," she pointed to her cheek which had mostly already started to heal thanks to the dawa root she had taken, "and this beautiful collage of purple must've come from the fall I took when I chased down one of the pirates." She gestured to her side. "Oh, and did I mention that it was the same pirates who attacked us on the *Viper* who were holed up there in the tavern."

"Oh, my. Did you take any of them in?"

"A handful got away. One killed. Two taken in for questioning. Why?"

"I would like to speak to the one who made the bane. The potion is obviously amateurish and its effects would only last a handful of days but there is talent in the brew." Abadi plucked a few pieces of hash from a jar, shoved the buds into a pipe and offered it to Issa. "Blow. This will take some of the pain away. I'll need to work some of my magic so you don't walk around with a canted slump when you get to be my age."

Issa did as requested, sucking in the pipe until the smoke burned her throat.

"So, let me guess," Abadi said as he took the pipe away. "The one who made the potion was one of the ones who got away?"

Issa winced again as the surgeon started work on her ribs once more, but the pain had subsided a little. "Yeah, she did get away. With the help of a few of her friends…"

Issa wouldn't soon forget the woman and that fire in her eyes, nor could she ignore the words of the young man who came to save her. "*You're fighting for the wrong side, Sister,*" he had said, and the earnestness in his voice disturbed her. Her response of traitor against him had merely been habit, someone else's words.

Still… they might not have been her truest thoughts, but siding with pirates was still a path to be denounced.

"It's a shame about that pirate," Abadi mused as he took a drag from the pipe himself.

"Why's that?"

"I was hoping my old cohort in the academy would be in the city," he explained. "Al-Dima. I mentioned her to you and Captain el-Sayyed on the ship."

Issa recalled their conversation. That was when they had first found out that the pirate Jelani had stoneskin, when they thought he was marked for death. Well, he still was, but thanks to Abadi they knew it could at least be delayed.

"Well," Abadi sat down in a chair next to Issa, "I was hoping I could catch her, but she's already with General Najjar out East. You'll remember she's the only one I know who has any real familiarity with stonesbane. Ever since we returned I've been trying to figure out how to make it properly myself. But that there," he edged his chin to the stonesbane on his shelf, "that there would do. I was actually going to send a bird up to the palace about having it sent to that pirate prisoner of ours."

Issa wondered for a moment if that's why that female pirate was in a room full of stonesbane to begin with. Was she preparing enough for when she'd steal back her husband? No, she was being held by that other pirate faction. And that aziza had an arm full of stone. Perhaps then she was only made to brew for them by force. Issa could only assume her, at least "amateurish" skill, was thanks to having learned the potion's creation process for...

"Abadi, did you already send for that messenger bird?"

"Not, yet. Why do you ask?"

"Fix me up as fast as you can, please. I think I'll be delivering that stonesbane for you."

THEY HAD PUT THE PIRATE JELANI IN A SPACE WITH NO windows and no real sense of light, save for a single lantern near a cot. She understood why. He was a high-risk target and it took a lot for Karim to get him his special accommodations, but Issa wondered how the seclusion might've affected his psyche. How long had it been since they captured him? It felt so long ago in Issa's mind.

"Has he given up, then?" the pirate Jelani asked as Issa continued her silent assessment of the room. He sat with his back to the wall, cross legged, chains binding him to the far wall.

"What do you mean?" Her response was off-handed, her eyes still examining the chamber.

"Your Captain never has no one else come talk to me. But I ain't seen him in a little while. Maybe he thinks you can sway me to 'open up'."

"No, he's not given up, he's just... preoccupied." Issa's gaze caught the edge of a loose board beneath the pirate's single cot. "But it does seem he's neglected you for some time."

She pressed the toe of her boot onto the board, making it groan. Lifting her head, she could see the pirate wasn't quite meeting her eyes. Clearly he had something to do with the slightly uplifted flooring. The edges around the boards were slightly jagged, leaving the faintest of gaps. Presumably so no one would notice.

Then, searching more of the room, Issa ran her hand over the pirate's pillow where she felt the smallest impression of an iron needle. She pulled the object from the pillow's lining and lifted it in front of her nose.

"And where's this from?" she asked the pirate.

He didn't answer.

Issa tucked the needle into her belt sash, then set the stones-bane bottle on the floor, just out of reach of the chained pirate. "Well, I was going to offer you this for good behavior, but I don't think escape attempts fall under that branch, do they?"

Jelani stared intently down the bottle, and Issa could've sworn she could hear the muscles under his stoneskin creaking. He didn't look much different from when she first saw him on his ship out at sea. But come a few weeks from now, maybe even a couple of moons, there would be little left of his deep brown skin to speak of.

"How'd you know 'bout the boards and that tool?" he decided to say after a while.

Issa smirked a bit and sat cross legged across from the pirate before saying, "I had my fair share of escapes in my youth."

"With Captain el-Sayyed?"

The question halted Issa for a moment, but she didn't let it show on her face. What had Karim been doing with the pirate all this time? Had he divulged some of his own past as a ploy to garner the pirate's trust? Instead of meeting his question head on she ignored it and asked a question of her own. "That bane there." She gestured to the bottle. "It was brewed by someone you are familiar with. Would you like to know who?"

Jelani shifted in his position, and a slight change came to his breathing. Where before it was steady, normal. Now it came long and slow.

He knew who she was talking about.

"I can tell you where she is," Issa said, "if you can give me something on the cove. Anything at all."

"No you can't. If you knew that, she'd be captured already."

"What makes you think she isn't?"

"'Cause you woulda started with that and been done."

"Would that work?" Issa lifted an eyebrow and settled in her cross legged sit a bit more comfortably. "If we had your friend, would you tell us about the cove then?"

Jelani's head fell back in a heavy sigh. *"Shi 'av un'nu fyah,* Ugara."* Then he sucked his teeth, though the lip smack was less one of irritation—as Issa had come to know it from the pirates— and more of a lighthearted chiding. "I've already told your Captain el-Sayyed. I ain't know nothin' 'bout the cove. Nothin' that could help you Vaaji anyway."

"Well, what *can* you tell us?"

"What it means to my people. Ain't nothin' you'd be interested in."

"So you truly *are* Jo'baran?" Issa asked.

"Yes. Been tryin' to figure out your Captain on that. He was one too, from what I could gather."

Karim *really* laid it all out for the pirate, then. Was he really so desperate? What's more, it seemed he got absolutely nowhere where the pirate was concerned.

"I don't think that would be appropriate conversation," she said, "between captor and captive."

"Yeah, I thought the same. Your Captain's methods are real different. Funny really, most of our chats stem around his musings of the Old Way."

"Karim? Talking about the Old Way? How did you manage that?"

Jelani canted his head a little, and his face fell into a sliver of brilliant light cast by the lantern near his cot. "I didn't 'manage' nothin', just spoke to him, was all."

"I find that hard to believe." The last time she and Karim properly spoke about the Old Way without it turning into a tension-filled debate was when they were children.

"Well, I reckon he was just tryin' to get me to talkin'. But like I say, I ain't got nothin' to say. Your Navy killed all the shamans and oni'baro that could open the cove."

Issa shook her head. "That story isn't going to play with me. The Captain might have forgotten the Old Way, but I know it well." She peered down at Jelani's wrist, where she knew his oni'baro marking was. "You've been marked. And that means you know how to open the cove. It's not that complicated. We just need access to what's inside Mount Kidogo, is all. We'll get in eventually, it's just a matter of time."

"Then I reckon y'all have to go spending that extra time then..."

A silence hung heavy between them. Issa didn't expect she'd really get anything out of the pirate, at least not that day. Karim needed the help with everything he was dealing with, though, she just hoped she could help chip away *some* of the rock-solid devotion the pirate clung to—where his home island was concerned. As she sat there trying to think up some new tack, perhaps leveraging the bane instead of the man's wife, she was surprised to find it was the pirate who spoke up first.

"Your Captain chatted up what's goin' on in your slum," he said. "All that escapin' you did with your Captain got me to thinkin' y'all know each other, ya? He's always venting 'bout some tax man in the city who keeps houndin' your old district. I'm curious how you feel on that."

"Why does that matter here?" Issa asked, perhaps a hair too defensively.

The pirate raised his chained hands and made a long circle—no, a spiral—in the shape of Àyá's Grace, the same symbol on his wrist. "It's all connected," he said gently, "A child of the Old Way like yourself should know that—oh, excuse me, you *do* follow the Old Way, don't you?"

"You're perceptive," she challenged, "you tell me."

The pirate hummed under his lips a little, then dipped his head back into shadow. "If this city treats the old and sacred like shit, what's gonna happen from this point on? How far will your hungry Navy go? If, or when, y'all do get into that cove and have access to all of Ula's Skyglass, what then?"

Issa didn't respond right away, even if she should have. The pirate was speaking words she only gave voice to in the deepest recesses of her mind. Hearing them spoken out loud brought a haunting truth she didn't quite want to face. As though still working to keep those thoughts buried, she replied harshly, mechanically, "If you're trying to get me to tell you imperial secrets, you are sorely mistaken, pirate."

"I could give a damn 'bout what your Empire's got goin' on with its airships or Gods know what else. What I'm talkin' 'bout is what's gonna happen to Kidogo's cove itself."

"What do you mean?"

"You got a holy city on these lands, ya? A place called Akeem? From the sounds of it, it's less than holy these days. Limited pilgrimages. Sages traded for miners."

The pirate paused, as though waiting for Issa's rebuttal or denial, but Issa had nothing for him. Is this what happened when Karim spoke with this pirate? Did the conversations always flow away from what the intended topic was supposed to be?

"Your Captain said he was lucky to make his pilgrimage before all of that happened," the pirate went on. "But I wonder… if your own holy city is being defiled by irresponsible mining, how you figure Kidogo will be left in the end?"

Issa swallowed hard and she hoped the lantern wasn't bright enough for the pirate to see the lump at her neck.

"I ain't gotta tell you what rests in Kidogo, do I?"

"I thought that was a myth," Issa finally spoke, curiosity betraying her previous grit.

"It's not." Jelani leaned forward again to show his stone face. "I saw the Great Ula there personally, and I don't know what will happen if she's disturbed. That's why me and the other oni'baro defended it with our lives." There was a change in his tone then as he continued to lean forward. He was… trying to convince Issa. But *she* was supposed to be convincing *him*. Drawing forward as far as his chains would allow, Jelani continued, "Help me get out of here. You know I don't deserve to be here."

The way he said those last words cut through Issa as deep as a spear tip. It was completely honest, completely genuine. The pirate wasn't trying to play tricks, not trying to save his own skin. He didn't have the same forced facade, that same rehearsed voice or false smile that she so often dealt with among those she met throughout al-Anim. This was a man of his word, a man of honor.

A child of the Old Way.

Yet still, something pickled at the back of Issa's mind, pulled at her like a band of merfolk forcing their enemies to drown at the ocean's depth: The truth she could not allow herself to see.

"Drink your stonesbane, pirate," she said coldly, kicking the bottle forward where it dropped, rolled, and landed against the pirate's crossed legs. "We need you alive and kicking."

CHAPTER 42
LISHAN

WHEN LISHAN RETURNED WITH OUSENI AND KWAME FROM their latest job for Collector Vaziri at night, she was expecting to return to a nice brew of Akbar's Andalan Reds. She never expected to round the corner onto Sycamore Square to find it flooded with al-Anim's citywatch.

She couldn't comprehend the scene before her: broken glass, scorch marks, and her crew nowhere to be found.

"What's going on here?" she asked one of the vendors who was closing up shop.

The wiley old lady got all giddy and went on a tear about the greatest battle she had ever seen, how the citywatch took on an elemental and two strange shapeshifters. "And then them bowmen came on in and killed the one shootin' out the fire. Then these other ones, the citywatch, I mean, froze them beasts in an ice block and cut them off."

"The one shooting fire… was she an aziza?"

"No, not an aziza. She was kinda, you know, on the chunkier side."

Arus… Lishan thought, and her heart started to ache. She was supposed to find her twin sister Sura in this place and now… perhaps it would be a mercy if they were both dead at this point.

"Damn, not Arus… not her…" Lishan could hear Kwame say

at her back. She knew the two of them were close. But, like always, Ouseni didn't voice what she felt, stoic as ever.

"How many did they take in in the end?" Lishan asked the vendor, keeping a strong tone.

"Just them shifters, like I say."

The old lady kept going on with a second retelling of the events, but Lishan left her talking to nothing but the night winds.

As she stomped through the streets of al-Anim, up and up toward the hiller districts with one destination in mind, her thoughts growing hot.

That Collector Vaziri had promised her that her crew would be protected, that the tavern wouldn't have eyes on it. Now she had another crew member dead and others missing.

"At least Ekko and Iokaja are still out there," Kwame said at her back, doing his best to keep up alongside Ouseni. "Just sounds like them kishi brothers got snagged up."

Like with the vendor before, Lishan let Kwame babble away at theory after theory, ignoring him as the buildings turned from blacksmiths and tailors to opulent villas and estates. Soon, a very specific estate, modest among the others but with a wall cast from obsidian and inlaid with streaks of silver, revealed itself around a corner. Lishan made a straight line for it, stomping straight for the gate guard who stood at attention with a pike in hand and a helmet over his eyes.

"Tell your boss I got the number of the damned cell he wanted," Lishan shouted at the gatekeeper. "The kadal at the base in the desert, right? I got it's cell block and number. If your boss wants it, I demand to know where my crew—"

The guard held up a hand. "Keep your voice low. You'll wake the master's neighbors."

Lishan looked down the road both ways. The closest estate was at least a fair few yards away, like all the grand dwellings in the area. She gave the guard a look of utter derision. "Don't play games with me, dikala."

The guard simply smiled and opened the gate with the grace of a servant. "He's waiting for you in his sitting room. Your remaining crew is with him."

Lishan didn't waste another moment to stomp through the gates with Ouseni and Kwame trailing behind. She barely noticed the topiaries of the nude male and female figures that seemed to watch her as she went along the cobbled path to the sprawling estate of domes and white sandstone, a perfect contrast to the black wall that surrounded it.

Barging through the front, Lishan immediately found Vaziri's sitting room and before she could as much as open her mouth —

"Captain Lishan!" Vaziri exclaimed with one leg crossed over the other in his golden framed chair. "I'm glad to see you, Ouseni, and Kwame are still among us."

The room was small but the high ceiling and the great arches that flanked it made it seem larger. Among those sitting in their own golden frame chairs were N'Kota, who for once didn't wear his signature smile, Iokaja, who had a few burns about her ears and cheek, and Ekko, whose typically pale face was completely flushed with a red hue.

"What in the Sapphire Hells happened today?" Lishan belted. "You said my crew would be safe. You said —"

"These things do happen in our line of work. You of all people should understand that. I lost more than you did today, Captain."

"No. *You* got two of your own captured. One of mine was killed. Arus can't come back from that. You've probably already got it worked out how to free your men. If you can't assure me our safety, how in the name of the Gods am I supposed to trust in this plan you have, huh?"

"Losing the brothers was a setback. And while it would've been nice to hold onto the likes of Arus, there are others like her. However, with your elemental aziza," he waved a hand to Iokaja, "your illusionist," a hand to Ekko, "and my empath," a final gesture to N'Kota, "we'll have more than enough for our plans in a few days' time. Don't worry, Captain. We'll get everyone back that we can. My men will be mine again. Your captain will be yours. And that airship will still be ours."

CHAPTER 43
ZALA

Zala had become familiar with Collector Vaziri's reputation over the course of her time in Jasmiin Towers. She'd been told he was a man of theatre, with a taste for the dramatic. But what he had done with the mess hall was entirely unexpected.

Foremost, the flooring had been entirely replaced. Whereas before a drab collection of stone lined the floor, now it was covered by a plane of glass over clear blue water which housed all sorts of fish from the Sapphire Seas. When Zala walked the surface, it was like floating on water. Whenever she could, she stuck to the few marble platforms that covered the illusion of the water walkway to keep herself from having a very odd sense of vertigo.

The walls, which had been made up of nondescript sandstone and covered by imperial banners attempting to hide their mundanity, were now quartered by spiralling pillars bedecked with assortments of flowers. Each flower matched the hues of the bright fish below; coral, cerulean, and gold.

Between the newly decorated walls and redesigned floor stood dozens of tables spaced out around an elevated stage at the grand room's center, which was spotlighted by the shaded mesh windows that let in the morning light. At either end of the hall were more elevated platforms that traveled between large structures that looked like rock faces—rock faces that funneled waterfalls into the pool of water that flowed beneath.

It was like a lush, cliffside forest had been cut from the wilderness and dropped into the palace chambers.

The Vaaji pay their tax collectors very well, apparently, Zala thought
as she gaped at the space around her. *Hells, the Golden Lord himself
would have a hard time matching something like this.*

Mantu whistled. "Makes you feel a little underdressed,
don't it?"

"We've been given these robes to blend in and disappear, not
to stand out," Zala murmured back, though she too felt her plain
clothing was indeed overshadowed by the space. It was a step up
from their usual: less a bedsheet, and more like a simple off-white
cotton robe with blood lilies stitched at the breast.

"Where are those damn workers from the Whispers?" A very
fashionable woman decked in flowing silks bellowed at another
group across the hall. "They were supposed to be here by sunrise.
And where's that aziza?"

Her assistant—Zala assumed as much—bowed several times
over. "Apologies, Mistress. I'll send for a messenger right away.
And the aziza just got in. She's preparing her vocal cords now, so
she said."

Zala smacked her hand against her head. "We're idiots. We
could've got Fon that job. She sings better than anyone we know."

Mantu shrugged. "How were we supposed to know? We've
been in the kitchens all this time. Speaking of which… here comes
Hadi now." He lifted his chin and waved with a wide smile. "May
Shati'ala's Will be yours, Head Chef."

"The both of you are late." Chef Hadi stomped toward them
between the labyrinth of tables, anger coloring his cheeks. "Get in
the kitchens right away." Despite the favor Mantu had garnered
with the man, it did not seem to win out over the stress of the big
banquet bearing down on the Head Chef that night. "And you, get
started on the rum cake. We'll need a fair few more than anticipated. Don't just stand there gawking at me. Get to it!"

Zala and Mantu scurried toward the kitchens, still in awe of everything around them. If Zala hadn't known it was all for a banquet, she would've assumed the Prince himself was going to have a wedding. And she couldn't begin to understand what Hadi was bothered about. The feast wasn't supposed to begin for another few hours. Getting rum cakes and dishes in order was one thing. If anyone had the right to be at her wit's end, it was Zala.

After all, she was the one who needed to pull off a ruse that would get her one step closer to her husband, and the sky ship. She just needed to make sure it didn't land *her* in a dungeon.

When Zala got done with all her prep work, Hadi informed her—in another spittled outcry—that all the tables were set up incorrectly and needed to be readjusted immediately.

In the mess hall, the platforms that disappeared between the rock structures served as walkways for beautiful men and women who flaunted all sorts of different fashions, from long sweeping robes to gold-studded tunics. They were still only rehearsing, but that didn't stop Zala from gawking.

Despite the high fashion, the walkable lake, the floral pillars, the overall decor... Zala still felt like something was missing from the picture. She had been to her fair share of feasts before; they were extravagant things on Kidogo, in their own way. There were always dancers and drums, rum and food, guests who frolicked like they didn't have any sense, and party crashers who were even more ridiculous. What she participated in now could never be deemed as a banquet by her people on the Isles. Sure, there was more money and effort put into the grand hall, but for Zala it seemed to lack... spirit.

The musicians, who were also already rehearsing, played music that could've helped Zala fall asleep. And the food she stole from this platter or that was without the kick of spices that she was used to.

Nobles take the bite out of everything, she thought as she started to struggle with the table Hadi wanted her to move.

"Hey, you're that woman who replaced Ketifa, aren't you?" came a voice from her side.

Zala turned to a man wearing kitchen tunics who was even shorter and smaller than she was. "Who's asking?"

"Name's Na'im." He came over to help Zala with the table. "I'm the one who set up Ketifa with her husband-to-be. I work in the northern kitchens." He whistled and gazed all around. "This little banquet turned into something else, didn't it? I wasn't even supposed to be here. So glad when I got the word to come in... They promised ten silvers!"

Zala couldn't bring herself to tell him he was being ripped off. She and the others had been promised gold, not silver. When this was all done she'd need to slip him a few.

"So," Na'im asked excitedly, "do you think we'll be serving the Emperor and Empress themselves today?"

"Unlikely..." Zala started, but took another glance at the extreme decadence. "I take that back. Who knows. Looks like every noble on the hill is about to be packed in here."

"Well, at least it's someone besides regular soldiers. They never talk about anything interesting. Maybe one of these officers that comes through will have an open position for me." Na'im dropped his side of the table, then shook his very, very thin wrists.

Ismail had been right about most of the cooks. Many of them were from the slums with aspirations of being chosen by a military official. She could only hope Na'im was planning on becoming an engineer or something. He wouldn't last five minutes on a front line.

Neither could you, Zala thought. *And look where you are, pirate.*

Zala had come to understand that Ketifa's famous cousin Karim, whoever he was, was recruited at the tail end of the Andala Inquisition. But just before he was shipped out, the Vaaji had officially surrendered. After that, many other prospects, not unlike Na'im, had tried to follow his lead.

"You, girl!" Chef Hadi shouted at Zala. "They're almost here! Get yourself ready!"

"Right away, Chef." Zala bowed meekly, then murmured to Na'im, "See you around."

She found her place against the ornate wall where Mantu stood at attention, a platter of figs in his hand. They gave each other a brief nod before turning their attention back to the mess hall.

"Did you cut the onions like our little friend told you to?" he asked in a whisper.

"I don't see the need to cut them in little squares when all they'll do is stew," Zala snorted, keeping her eyes forward.

Mantu sighed. "At least you got the rum cake right."

The first in attendance was Collector Vaziri with his retinue of armor-clad guards. He had brought at least a dozen with him. They lined the walls in perfect form as the Collector inspected each corner of the room.

"Very nice, very nice," he was saying each time he approved of a place setting or decoration.

He wore an all-cream outfit, the chest and shoulders embroidered with a floral design sewn with gold. The perfect complement of a burgundy patterned silk shawl was draped over his shoulder like a cape. He didn't wear a headscarf like most nobles did, instead letting the curls of his dark hair rest on his delicate shoulders.

Next to show up was another noble, by the looks of him. He came with only one bodyguard, a giant of a man with tree-trunk arms. After that, a few officers Zala hadn't recognized shuffled into the room, all of them taken by the pure majesty of it all. Zala tried not to stare too hard as she attempted to distinguish their features. Some of them could've been a part of that sky ship crew.

"Recognize anyone?" Zala whispered to Mantu as they began serving water to the guests. Within minutes, the hall was already a quarter-full, filling with people and the murmur of early party chit chat.

"Just our tax collector." Mantu shook his head as he doled out hot tea. "You still got Fon's potion with you, ya?"

"Right here." Zala tapped at the hidden phial strapped to her belt sash. "Once Sir Collector drinks this, we'll have a half hour, and then he'll go running to relieve himself."

"I'm still not sure about those guards of his. There's too many of them. And they stick close on his ass."

"Which is why I'll slip into the bathrooms beforehand. Just stick to the plan, follow my lead, and we'll be out before sundown."

"Oh, Captain, you're early! I'll take your robe for you!" An attendant said at the entrance.

One of the last officers to enter was a man with an unforgettable face. And latched around his arm was that same woman from the alley.

Zala gripped her water jug tightly. There they were again, side by side like the first time Zala saw them. They almost didn't look like themselves. Weeks ago, on the sky ship, blood and grime caked their faces. Now, their cheeks were rosy, their hair was slicked back and out of their faces, instead of spilling out of sweaty head wraps.

The woman wore a delicate blue dress. Nothing special, except for the silver scarf she wore around her neck, instead of her head. Unlike the other noblewomen they had come across, this one wore her hair down around her shoulders in beautiful brown curls. Her scarf and hair were almost as eye-catching as Vaziri's. The man wore blue as well, a loose-fitting tunic with no real sense of style or flair, save for a silver medallion on his chest.

Zala caught Mantu's attention again, gesturing a pirate signal under her jug of water. Mantu gestured back, tracing his finger from eye to lip, confirming the man's scar. Thankfully, as always, Zala was covered up head to toe in her traditional Qibasi head wrap. But the woman still might recognize her eyes, so she turned away from them slightly as they were directed to their seats.

At first Zala thought her focus was too tied to the new guests' presence in the hall—and her signaling with Mantu—but then she realized that Hadi had been shouting on her left side.

"Girl! Girl!" Chef Hadi shouted a whisper in Zala's ear. "Girl, serve the bread and oil. Are you deaf as well as dumb?"

"Sorry, Hadi, I'll be right on it."

"That's *Chef* Hadi to you," the man gritted. He almost sounded like the late Captain Kobi.

Zala made sure to roll her eyes when she was out of his view. Then she grabbed a platter of bread and olive oil, which she quickly served to each man and woman in attendance.

By the time she was done with her first round, the room filled out with even more military officers. They all wore immaculate uniforms denoting different positions in the military—of which Zala was vaguely familiar with—to other non-military ranks, that Zala was entirely unfamiliar with.

When Zala finished serving her third and fourth round of bread and oil, she headed back to the kitchens to prep the rest of the meal. Na'im was there at her side, practically skipping.

"Did you see him?" he asked with glee as Zala prepared an assorted salad.

"Vaziri?" Zala asked. "Yeah, him and all his guards. What's the need for that many at a private banquet?"

"No, not him." Na'im shook his hand in front of his face. "Ketifa's cousin Karim! Karim el-Sayyed. I didn't know he'd be invited to something like this. He didn't tell us he was made a captain, either. That medallion looks nice on his uniform. He's come so far."

Zala must've been putting on some kind of face, she expected a scowl, but Na'im seemed to take it for confusion, saying, "He's the one with the scar down his face."

"Yeah, yeah, I know… Did you say el-Sayyed?"

"That's the one."

"As in, he's Shaman Ismail's son?"

"Yup! I've known him a while. You know, he's had that scar since we've been kids. The slums are rough." Na'im shrugged. "If they let us talk to them, I'll introduce you. It probably won't happen though. He didn't even look at me. Well, it has been years since we've spoken to each other... I've seen him come through the slums, but only to give his father coin. He probably doesn't remember me."

"I'll take you up on that introduction," Zala replied offhand-edly as she worked out in her mind how this all affected her plans.

She wouldn't let either the Captain or his partner get away again this time.

Chef Hadi barged into the kitchens. "What are you all doing in here? Hurry, hurry, they've almost finished with the starters." He waved them back into the mess hall. Before Zala grabbed her platter, she turned close to Mantu.

"I didn't think the Sky Captain and the Collector would be here together. We might not need Vaziri at all, at this point. I'm thinking we could split up. You on the taxman, and me on the Captain."

"How? There's at least ten guards out there *just* for Vaziri. And you said to follow your damn plan..."

"Okay, then let's just switch targets then. We'll try and get the Captain in the bathroom instead of Vaziri."

"Shomari might've found somethin' already." Mantu shook his head as he pulled out a steaming grill of halloumi from a fire pit. Zala almost forgot Shomari was roaming the palace halls, doing his own scoping of the palace to clear them an exit when they needed to run off eventually.

Mantu turned back to her and murmured, "We should at least wait until the cat's got some —"

"You, girl. And you, too." Chef Hadi's face turned red as he pointed his meaty finger in their faces. *Where did he even come from?* "Sweet nothings aren't going to work today. Get your asses out here now and serve the damned guests!"

Zala and Mantu swooped up their platters and marched to the tables. Zala made sure to serve Karim first. When she approached, the Sky Captain had been speaking to Vaziri in the Mother Tongue, but when the man sensed Zala's presence with a sidelong glance he switched to High Vaaji.

"I'm surprised Empress al-Nasir and her financial representatives allowed for the expense this all must've cost," the Sky Captain Karim spoke through his fingers as he chewed through the halloumi Zala had served him.

She moved to Vaziri next, serving him a plate of dates as he responded, *"Oh, I'm sure they would be too if I asked them. Oh, no this whole endeavor was out of pocket, I'm afraid."*

The men's cups were already more than half full, yet Zala filled them to the brim to stay in earshot. Thankfully none of them looked up at her. She was as invisible as she intended to be. It couldn't be helped that she found their conversation particularly interesting. So much so, that she'd forgotten to slip Karim the potion she was supposed to.

For whatever reason, the Sky Captain was trying to catch Vaziri out on something. Did he know about the Collector and what he was doing in the slums too? Clearly this whole banquet was for the benefit of the many nobles present. And apparently, Karim had close ties with the old districts.

"How's the halloumi, by the way, Captain el-Sayyed?" Vaziri asked casually. Zala didn't register Karim's response, too caught up in the revelation. The implications were enormous and made the backs of Zala's hand chill over. It was obvious that they had a common enemy in Vaziri. Both of them were trying to bring him down, and both at the same time.

Who cares, Zala told herself. *Karim's the direct path to Jelani. Focus on getting the damn potion in his damn drink.*

But as she passed her hand over her sash she caught the eye of Karim's partner, the woman from the alley. Through her big curly hair covering half her face, a curious expression crossed her brow. And it was directed at Zala.

Fear shot through Zala, but she pretended she didn't notice the exchange at all and moved farther down the table to fill more cups—though she stayed within earshot.

 Karim was saying behind her.

Besides extortion, Zala thought. She realized too late that what was meant to be an internal musing had manifested as a light chuckle in reality.

"Is something funny?" a mean-looking woman sneered in Zala's direction. A few of the others looked up at her as well.

"Nothing at all, ma'am, apologies." Zala bowed meekly and continued on before she could be ridiculed some more.

Not too many would've noticed her anyway. All the other guests at the table were leaning in toward the head, where Karim and the Collector continued on about business ventures. Hells, even she was putting out her good ear to hear if there were some sort of insider secrets; when she got Jelani back, she had no intention of continuing the pirate's life. But she'd still need coin all the same.

"*You know, that's an age-old question isn't it?*" Vaziri was saying. "*If everyone knew the answer, we'd all be swimming in gold. Ah, but I do think I know a good one for you. Catering is all the craze right now, especially with all the nobles and officials we have up here in the hills. That's something you can try for, saabi.*" He slurped up a bit of his lentil soup. "*As I know it, you're already acquainted with people in the service industry, am I wrong?*"

Zala could see how Karim's shoulders were clenching. She could guess at a few choice words he probably had for Vaziri, with him throwing his past in his face like that. Zala couldn't blame him. She hated those types of people too, the kind that would subtly insult you all with a smile.

As Zala finished her rounds, instead of going back into the kitchens, she made her way back to the head of the table while the hall filled with light applause. Up on stage at the room's center, the aziza singer had finally arrived. After the polite clapping died out, she began her song, a slightly reflective tune that apparently brought in the new year in Vaaji culture. A few of the guests sang along.

The sight of the aziza, with her translucent wings and perfect skin reminded Zala of Fon, and the little phial that was tucked away in her sash.

Zala, focus. Potion in the cup. That's all you should be thinking right now.

Making her way to the far end of the table again was easier now that everyone's eyes were looking up at the stage. Zala noticed that the Collector ate only with his right hand, his left was tucked under his shawl at all times. Was it a nervous tick, she wondered? Karim seemed to notice too, his gaze falling often to the shawl.

"You've come into quite a few additional guards since I was away," Karim said when the aziza's song was finished. He kept eyeing each armored man and woman who stood around the table.

Vaziri snapped his fingers. *"Perhaps that is an industry you can get into. I can't tell you how much coin I have to pay for all those I employ. The sellswords take more than the Empress' new income tax. What's more, you know how dangerous things can get in al-Anim."*

"Outside the walls of our palace, perhaps. But not so much within."

"Well I'm paying them, so I might as well use them, right?" Vaziri laughed through a cup full of wine. Still, his left hand stayed tucked under his burgundy shawl.

"You heard about my first tour out to the islands, didn't you?" Karim asked, adjusting himself in his seat. The movement gave Zala an opening. As she filled his cup, she fingered for the phial in her sash.

"Of course," Vaziri replied. *"We were all privy to that… failure. Is it true it was a kubahari that took down most of your ships?"*

Karim ignored that last question. *"Grand Admiral Awad told me and the former captains of those fleets to be wary. Apparently the 'failure' wasn't the case for some of the crew. Some of the Gods' Glass we got our hands on, the Glass that was supposed to be sent to the Admiralty fell into other hands. He says that—"* Karim turned to Zala, who had finally freed the phial from her sash. Her heart dropped as she did her best to hide it again. "Can you understand me?" Karim asked in the Mother Tongue. Zala's eye's went wide. Then she realized she had given herself away when she should've played dumb.

"How do you know the tongue of the nobles?" Karim asked. Zala looked over her shoulders twice, as though Karim was talking to one of the models up on the platforms. He didn't buy it. "Answer me."

"I'm so, so sorry, Captain el-Sayyed." Chef Hadi shuffled over, sensing trouble like a hare sniffing out a wolf. "She will not disturb you again." Hadi pinched Zala's back end—and it took all Zala had not to slap the stout man out of pure spite. "She should be back in the kitchens preparing the dessert! Isn't that right, girl?" Hadi gave her another pinch.

"Right," Zala spoke in the Mother Tongue through clenched teeth. "I'm sorry if I disturbed your meal, Captain." Zala gave him a low curtsy. When she brought her head back up she didn't meet his gaze, or the gaze of the woman next to him, who decided then to speak up.

"Hang on," she said in a very light and airy tone, much different than her voice in the alley. "Have we met before?"

Zala clenched tightly against her nerves. At the corner of her eye she could see Mantu at another table, where he withdrew a steak knife held between his fingers. She shook her head subtly and Mantu placed the knife back on the table. As she thought up a proper response, it was Chef Hadi who spoke for her. "Of course not, Officer Akif. None of my workers are meant to leave the kitchens. I'll take care of her. Please, enjoy your meal. Is your soup too cold?"

A few moments later, Hadi clutched at Zala's elbow and threw her into the kitchens. "You stay here for the rest of the feast. You're done after today, you hear me? Do not come back. I don't care how good your cakes are."

Hadi stomped back into the hall and slammed the door behind him with such force, it made Zala's bones rattle.

This isn't part of the plan, she thought as she stared down at the potion still in her hand. *Well, fuck...*

CHAPTER 44
ZALA

ZALA CLENCHED HER TEETH AND BALLED A FIST. SHE WAS SO close. How could she have been so obvious? It was lucky Hadi stepped in when he did. Who knows what Karim or the woman would've done—or what she herself would've done—if they pressed her.

Then it dawned on Zala that she was alone. Finally alone.

Sure, her plan was to get one of those men isolated, but perhaps now she could figure out Jelani's location on her own with so many of the palace offices and their occupants emptied out into the banquet now.

All the other cooks and servers were under the thumb of Chef Hadi in the mess hall, but she had been left to sulk and consider her actions against the Empire—as if understanding their tongue was some major offense. It was true that if Zala was playing her role correctly, she shouldn't have understood a language designated for the nobles. She couldn't help it though—that's how she was raised.

With no time to think, she needed to figure a way out, and fast. The kitchen was relatively large, but the most distinguished part of it was the slit of an open window that sat at its back. It was used for letting out the hot air and the smoke. Mantu had thought it was the perfect place for them to slip out of, but it was impossible when they were so heavily guarded and watched. And it would take time for Zala to fit through such a small hole.

Without Hadi hounding her—or any other cooks to snitch—Zala could take her time squeezing through the slit properly. But she had to be fast. There was no way of knowing when Hadi and the others would be back.

Taking in a deep breath, she stood atop a stool, vaulted into the slit, then started the long and painful process of squeezing through. She held her breath, sucking in her already tiny stomach so that she could fit. It was an uncomfortable affair. She felt her bones crunch against her abdomen; her shoulders were the most difficult parts to get through, but bit by bit she did it.

The kitchen window faced the eastern cliffs of al-Anim, rather than the rest of the city, so she knew she was safe from being caught by anyone passing by. Thankfully her cream robes camouflaged against the palace's bright sandstone, which was then being painted by the sunset's hue.

She clung to a stone outcropping. A few paces to her right was a balcony. As she shuffled along the side of the structure, she couldn't help looking below to another balcony. It wasn't a far drop if she were to fall, but just below were a pair of soldiers with long, pointed spears in their hands. If she jumped, she would, at best, knock them over and make them angry, and at worst, impale herself on their spears.

Neither were good options.

The ledge was just big enough for her small feet though. If she kept her balance she could shimmy herself across the ledge onto the balcony beside her, which was connected to an open door. Inch by inch she shifted across the ledge, holding close to the wall. Her breathing kicked up the more she shimmied, her calves a quivering mess.

Don't you dare fail me now, legs.

After a few near slips, Zala made it to the next balcony with a small jump that could've easily left her crippled if she missed it. The balcony rested next to an open door, which led into what she assumed were sleeping quarters, perhaps Hadi's and the other military officials that stayed overnight.

Zala dashed across the room with its simple cots and bed trunks to the door at the far end. She pushed against it with a light touch, opening it to an empty corridor. She had to be somewhere near the main compound judging by the darker, more compressed hallway.

And just as she expected, the halls were ghostly quiet. The only hints of sound came from around the corner where the banquet continued.

With light feet, she continued down the corridor, opening doors as she went, giving each room a quick once-over. At first, she only managed to find more sleeping quarters and what looked like instruction rooms. But after a few minutes she came across one of the armories. With a quickness that could only be fueled by adrenaline, she armed herself with a small dagger, something she could keep hidden if someone caught—

"You, there." A booming voice echoed off the walls. Zala closed her eyes as she shifted the dagger further down her trousers. "What are you doing here?" Zala turned around to find one of the guards, a woman who towered over Zala with broad shoulders.

"Chef Hadi sent me out to replenish our supply of flour," Zala lied.

"Oh, yes," the guard said. "You were the one he dismissed. You do know you're going the wrong way, don't you?"

"To be honest, I'm new here. I'm not sure where I'm going. It's easy to get turned around in this big place."

"This area is nowhere near the kitchen." The soldier raised a questioning eyebrow as she pointed over her shoulder. "The surplus is that way near the livestock. Ground level."

"Oh, right. Like I said... I've no clue how I got turned around." Zala tried her best to play the part of a dumb servant who was out of her element. But she was never very good at playing dumb. It just didn't suit her.

Slowly, she moved her hand to her dagger. She couldn't afford to go back.

"What's that you have there?" the guard pulled at the saber in her scabbard. "Turn around!"

Zala froze in place. She had just got her hand around the dagger's hilt. But without the element of surprise she wasn't sure she could face off against the soldier.

"Show me your hands," the large woman demanded. "Now! Or I'll cut you where you stand." She withdrew her saber fully.

Zala measured her choices, but then decided her best option was to forfeit her weapon. She dropped the dagger at her feet and lifted her open-palmed hands at her sides.

"You'll be whipped for this, street rat." The guard pressed her saber against Zala's neck. "Turn around and walk. Something tells me you know your way back. I thought I might have recognized your voice from a little while ago. That 'I'm new here' shit wasn't gonna play this time."

Zala turned around slowly—as not to be cut by the saber. She shuffled down the corridor she had come from reluctantly, thinking of how she could slip the guard and make a run for it. A little voice told her she could probably outrun the woman, especially with her seeming so top-heavy, but after a dozen or so strides the stiff steel at Zala's back went limp. Then she heard the sound of metal hitting the floor.

"I really hope saving your neck doesn't need to become a regular occurrence today," purred a familiar voice.

"Shomari!" Zala turned with a grin to find the guard knocked out at the pakka's feet. "How did you find me?"

"I could smell you a league away." The pakka wiggled his nose as he dusted his hands off casually. "When is the last time you have been having a bath, Captain?"

"Oh, hush," Zala said. "You haven't bathed since we've been here."

"When have you ever seen me bathe?" Shomari licked the back of his furry hand.

"Fair point."

"Did you not trust I could get the job done on my own? I'll have you know I've been in this place a half day without being caught. How long have you been snooping around? A few moments?"

"I just didn't want you taking all the glory, was all." Zala smiled, then gestured for Shomari to help her with the unconscious body at their feet. "There's no time for me to get back. Any minute now Chef Hadi or the others will notice I've gone. Let's get this body hidden. What have you found?"

"Well, for one, I'm fairly certain there's no sky ship here. This side of the palace is strictly for training the soldiers and general military education. The rest of the palace is locked down pretty tight. But, I did find us a route out once we've got Vaziri under our thumb.

"Some of the officers live here—I have been coming across a few of their offices. A few commanders stay near the western end of the fortress, an admiral lives a few floors up… 'Shamoun' or something… one of the other offices belongs to someone who just got promoted. Some kijana named el-Sayyed, just like Ismail's family name."

Zala dropped her end of the unconscious soldier, whose head thunked on the ground.

Shomari sucked air through his teeth, one eye pinched as though he felt the soldier's pain. "Well if she wasn't knocked out before she certainly is—"

"What was that name you just said?"

"El-Sayyed. His first name was something with a 'K.' Oh, what was it? It rhymed with one of my favorite deserts."

"Karim."

"That's it! Karim."

"Help me drag this body out of sight," Zala said. "Then show me to this man's office. Now."

CHAPTER 45

KARIM

"The fashioners tell me this will be a bright new year for al-Anim satin. See that man just there?" Vaziri pointed to one of the performers on the over decorated platform. "I funded the threading apparatus that produced that tunic he's wearing. Come next season, everyone on the hills will be wearing them."

"And I can't thank you enough for the fund!" a very drunk guest slurred with a lifted goblet at the end of the table.

Everyone seated seemed primed for others to leave their spots so they could take them themselves, getting closer and closer to the head of the central table, where Vaziri lazed back in his plush seat. Karim was shocked to see his assigned chair was only one away from Vaziri; then he realized it was likely at Issa's behest that they got there, as she sat just at the Collector's left, and Karim at her's.

"Of course!" Vaziri lifted his goblet to the drunk several seats down. "Anything for you, Merchant Sani. Oh! Which reminds me... I'm working with a few investors to design swim clothes." He nudged his chin down to the swimmers under the glass floor, who glided along with the fish. "We still have issues with dampness, but come the dry season in a few moons we should be ready to—"

Karim cleared his throat before Vaziri could go on. "With all due respect, Collector. You didn't answer me earlier about the Gods' Glass that's been unaccounted f—"

"Oh, enough with the questions, Captain el-Sayyed!" Vaziri silenced him with a grin. "This dinner is for pleasure, not business. Have a drink. Loosen up a bit. You always look so stiff!"

Loosen up? How could he, with his father and his duty and so much else hanging like weights around his neck?

A brief pang of guilt spiked through Karim. It had been more than a week since he'd actually seen his father; he had been too busy with his investigation of Vaziri and his nightly meetings with Issa. His father had not sent him any new letters however, and Karim knew that meant whoever his father was in league with now was probably staving off the Collector for the time being. Somehow, that didn't make Karim feel any better about the whole situation.

A grimace crossed Karim's lips as Vaziri turned his back and moved away, making jokes with High Priestess Fayad without a care in the world. What was the man playing at? This feast had to be more than an excuse to strengthen Vaziri's social circle. The crowd here was too diverse for that. He had invited engineers and religious heads, military leaders and market socialites. The only person here who might have run with the tax collector on any normal day was Umar Jad, the former purser of the *Viper*.

Karim leaned on his chair's armrest and nudged his foot against Issa.

"What's he doing?" he murmured behind his goblet of cider.

Issa didn't turn her head, her attention fully committed to the exaggerated war story from a general farther down the table. At least on the surface, anyway.

She spoke from the corner of her mouth, her tone playful. "Simmer down, el-Sayyed. Engage, don't enrage."

Karim bit back his scowl and forced a crooked smile across his face. He pretended to be completely enraptured by Vaziri's latest, and very poor, joke.

"So, Sister Fayad." Vaziri gestured to the Priestess, the jewels in his robes sleeves clinking together softly. "I hear you are making the trip to Akeem, soon. Correct me if I'm wrong, but you have already made the pilgrimage, have you not?"

The portly woman sat up straighter in her chair, her cheeks flushed. What could Vaziri want her for? Issa had mentioned something about him getting a travel pass, but what would he stand to gain from a visit to the Holy City?

"Yes, I took *saa'fa ala* many years ago now," she said. "I am to take our newest disciples with me, those I've brought here with me today." Fayad gestured to the group seated at her sides. Unlike the collection of bright blues and vivid reds adorning the Priestess, her cohorts all wore the same simple, flowing gray robes with matching head wraps.

"Our thanks for having us, Collector Vaziri," the young man sitting closest to Fayad said.

Vaziri dipped his head low, the loose curls he had decided to style his hair in tonight falling atop the table. "But of course, Young Priest. I have been neglecting my duties to the Good Word of al-Qiba and the Supreme One far too long. My father always taught me, 'You are the company that you keep.'"

"I'm sorry to hear that, Brother." Fayad nodded. "You must join me at the temple sometime. I am always available to those who wish to learn more of Her Will. There is so much Shati'ala can teach us all."

"I think I shall take you up on that." Vaziri took a casual bite of bread. "I have never made the pilgrimage myself, but I hear High Priest Mufti is quite the speaker."

"Oh, yes. No one knows the word as well as Tollah."

"I saw him during my pilgrimage," Karim cut in. He needed to get involved in the conversation. He stole a brief sidelong glance at Issa before saying, "His speeches were… moving."

Fayad tilted her head toward Karim, her ornate necklace dropping to one side. "I did not know you had made the trip, Young Captain."

"I did, right after I enlisted. I used the whole of my first payment to set out on the pilgrimage."

"And was it enlightening?" Her words always seemed to have an edge of sweet malice, her eyes always looking down her long-stretched nose. Even after all the time he spent with her on the *Viper,* he still managed to find a new reason to dislike her. It was like Malouf's old council meetings all over again.

"'Enlightening?'" Karim took a moment to feign thought to cover his disgust. "Very much so. I've never been among so many brothers and sisters before. The energy was…"

"Tangible," she finished for him.

"Yes." Karim nodded. "But I had trouble with the High Priest's words. Al-Qiba states that no intoxicants that alter the mind should enter the body while in the Holy City. Yet on the final night of the pilgrimage he offered a few of us a milky spirit. I denied, of course, but many of them, including the High Priest, partook."

Disgust and disbelief carved a scowl across Fayad's lips. "What? Never. You lie. Tollah knows better. How could you slander his name?"

"I didn't mean to—it's just something I didn't understand," Karim tried for a lighter tone. "We are denied the pleasures of rum and wine during *saa'fa ala,* are we not?"

"Yes, of course. The fifteenth verse of the Great Book is very clear."

Vaziri cut in. "I'm sure the Young Captain is mistaken—"

"I remember it very clearly. The High Priest—" Karim asserted, but he stopped himself when Issa pinched his thigh. "Maybe I mistook the smell of alcohol for sour milk."

Fayad didn't change her twisted expression, but she let the matter go as a server with a thick beard came to refill her goblet of cider. Karim settled back in his seat, embarrassment heating his ears as he fiddled with his uneaten bread. He just couldn't help throwing the counterfeit piety Fayad and her cohorts so often peddled back at them whenever he could.

To avoid the scolding eyes of the mistress, he glanced up at the aziza singing on the center stage. He had to admit, despite the decor being completely overdone, there were moments he forgot he was in the mess hall instead of some strange aquatic jungle setting. Still, all the setting really did in the end was serve to stir the ire he had for Vaziri. Each outfit worn by the platform performers, or the fish that swam underfoot was probably procured off the back of one of his old neighbors having their coin stolen from them.

"Do you know High Priest Mufti well?" Vaziri asked Fayad with a light tone that seemed to settle her nerves.

"Yes, he was the priest who brought me into the Sisterhood."

Karim thought of starting up a new conversation, but decided to join the others and listen to the Priestess and the Collector. He and Issa had decided to split their attention to each side of the table. She was working her magic like usual; it was time for Karim to step up his game as well.

Engage, don't enrage, he reminded himself.

Vaziri gracefully dipped a piece of bread into a saucer of olive oil as he addressed the High Priestess again. "Do you visit him often during these trips to Akeem?"

Focus, Karim. What's he after? Listen between the words.

"Oh, yes," Fayad squeaked. "I always try to stay with him. Anytime I can get him talking to my students is always a treat."

"Correct me if I'm wrong, but he is the one who takes those of the Faith into the Great Cavern, yes?"

"Yes. Well, him or any of his other trusted priests."

Karim finally chewed into his first piece of bread, considering why Vaziri needed to know any of this. The only thing in the Great Cavern of note was a bunch of worshipping Qibasi. What would a tax collector need them for? Or was he interested in something that was hidden away in the cavern itself?

"I think it's overdue that I do the same. It's time I undertook *saa'fa ala*. Is there room in your caravan for another? I'd like to meet this man, and to see the Great Site. Is it true that Shati'ala rests there?"

"Yes it is. And I'd love to have you along. But what about your duties in the capital?"

"As you can see, I have plenty of those who can take my place." Vaziri gestured to the guards who lined the walls. Karim's eyes drifted automatically to the hand Vaziri had tucked under his audacious shawl.

"So you'll be taking a leave of absence, then?" Karim asked. "I would have thought the Empress' tax would have been your number one priority."

"Karim," Issa hissed under her breath. "Excuse him, Collector. He's just very... *passionate* about the imperial economy."

"Officer Akif." Vaziri nodded then smiled, his eyes drifting from her face to her body. "I may have mentioned this already but... that dress suits you *well*."

She dipped her head respectfully, her blue dress seeming to shimmer like the Sapphire Seas themselves. "Thank you. And it's only the second time you've paid the compliment, Collector."

"A shade revealing, however," Fayad interjected with a sneer. "The color is nice enough, but the material is too translucent. It looks like something the women of the Silks might wear."

"I think it looks very nice," Vaziri said with a look Karim didn't like at all.

"Lovely enough in the privacy of Akif's home." Fayad turned up her nose. "But too much for a gathering such as this, I think. The text is clear on modesty for those of marrying age. And no, I don't mean just the women. Look at you, Collector Vaziri. Your tunic is very nice and covers all that it should. No excessive shaping to draw the eye."

Karim suspected her disapproval came more from jealousy than adherence to faith. She might've been attractive once, fifteen or twenty years ago. She might've even been pretty now, if she didn't pinch her face into lines all the time. Karim could only wonder what she would've said if Issa had worn the first dress she showed him a few weeks ago.

Issa, in her usual way, gave no reaction, almost as though she didn't hear the Priestess altogether, holding to that fixed smile she had perfected. Karim wondered if his own looked genuine enough at that moment.

"The more reason we should take those private lessons from you, Priestess Fayad," Vaziri said. "We can all learn more about the proper modesties."

Fayad settled in her seat again as Issa flipped her hair, revealing her bare neck and shoulder to the woman. The sight brought a renewed scowl to the High Priestess' face. Karim's smile was now most assuredly an honest one.

"How about you, al-Kindi?" Vaziri cast his attention farther down the table. "I heard your newest project is working with *flying* colors. Your breakthrough with that invention will be great for us all."

"Thank you. It has. The Captain had a lot to do with that," Al-Kindi said through a thick and curly beard as he gestured a wrinkled hand to Karim.

Karim returned his acknowledgment with a short nod. It was a kind gesture. But he and the man both knew that Karim had very little to do with the *Viper's* technical success. He didn't know much of anything about the mysticism and science that powered it, and without great minds like al-Kindi's, the airship would've never taken flight to begin with.

Despite al-Kindi's praise, Vaziri ignored the compliment. "I've heard you've had troubles with funding though. Your first project is very small, yes?"

"It could certainly use some more breathing room, but it is a prototype. I understand the sacrifices that needed to be made," al-Kindi answered through a soft voice.

"If you ever needed any extra funding, I could supply you. As I was saying, the satin market will see its day very soon. In fact, that's why I've invited Umar Jad here today. We both believe we can speed along this most important project."

"That would be appreciated." Al-Kindi nodded, his odd spectacles sliding down his nose. "With the Grand Admiral's approval, of course."

"Yes, with his approval, of course." Vaziri said through a snake's smile.

Karim definitely caught the hint of distaste in the Collector's tone. It seemed as though the only one not under Vaziri's thumb was the Grand Admiral. In fact, neither he nor the Vice Admiral were in attendance. Though perhaps that was more to do with their busy schedules rather than any active animosity. Whatever the case, Karim was glad to know that the final piece to whatever it was that Vaziri was planning was being apparently slowed by a non-compliant Grand Admiral Awad.

"Awad provides enough funds for us as it is," Karim said defiantly. "The Empress has her reasons for the budget."

"I'm sure she does," Vaziri returned. "But neither she nor the Grand Admiral are known for their management of coin. Hence, the reason they appoint someone like me."

"And do they know you are holding private dinners with their trusted advisors? You said this was a casual affair yet you've only spoken about—"

"I think the Captain just needs to get some fresh air," Issa cut in.

Karim knew that Shamoun, Awad, and of course, Issa, wanted him to be more diplomatic, but it was easier said than done. He simply could not keep up with the facade of the conversation. There was only so much that bit lips and curled fists could hold back.

"No, I don't," Karim said sternly. "The only thing I need is for our 'Righteous Collector' to stop taking what isn't his." Karim stood. A few heads turned, guests and servers alike. "If you don't stop messing around with the slums you'll hear from me."

"You and what influence, Captain?" Vaziri leered. "You've no power here. Go back to your ship and do some good for the Empire, won't you?"

"What would you know about the good of the Empire?" Karim asked, feeling heat rise in his face as his heart pounded in his ears. He didn't have to look to know everyone at the table was staring at him.

Vaziri gave him a smug grin. "I've got a few years over you, Young Captain. You were still a street rat when I was graduating from the academy."

"You wouldn't last a day where I come from."

Though no one spoke up, it was clear by the clearing of throats and the fiddling with silverware that the rest of the guests were getting very uncomfortable.

"Is that so?" Vaziri dropped his cocky smile at last. Then, very slowly and deliberately he placed his spoon on the table and folded his hands over his napkin. "And how about you? I've been told that scar on your face didn't come from your time in the military. What happened? Did one of the other street rats fight you over a piece of cheese?"

Karim punched Vaziri across the face, and the Tax Collector went down hard. Karim's knuckles bled, but he shook life back into them. It had been a very long time since he'd punched someone.

He was far too out of practice.

Everything stopped. The chatter about the room, the shuffling of the servers, even the singing aziza stopped her song and floated in the air to get a better look.

Before Karim knew it, two pairs of arms came around him as a few of the guests gasped. Vaziri touched his lip gingerly. When he pulled it away there was only a hint of blood about his fingertips. Karim cursed at himself internally. He did more harm to his own hand than to Vaziri's chin.

"Take him away." Vaziri grunted to the guards at Karim's side, his hand covering his mouth. Karim could see the hint of a smirk peaking through. "You can take the man out of the slums, but you can't take the slums out of the man."

Karim surged forward, but the strength of the guards was too much. The pair easily moved him between the tables, past the aziza, through the platforms and the models atop it, until they made it to the hall's entrance, where they shoved him back into the corridor. Compared to the lively colors in the transformed mess hall, the corridor looked almost completely devoid of color—drab, lifeless, and cold.

In only a moment, the music started back up, now muffled on the other side of the door.

Karim knew he'd hear about it later. He wondered if it'd be Awad or another commander who would reprimand him. He'd probably lose his title as the *Viper's* captain. At the moment it didn't matter very much. Punching Vaziri was worth it.

"What in the stars' name was that?" Issa said as she poked her head out of the mess hall. She closed the door behind her and fixed Karim with a look. Her face was colored with scorn, her arms crossed and her brows furrowed.

"I couldn't keep up that charade," Karim said. "The man is so—"

"You just got *promoted*, Karim. You can't just—"

"Don't you think I know that?" He stepped to her with fire in his eyes. Issa stood still. "Sorry. I didn't mean to—look, I don't want a pick-me-up conversation right now if that's all right with you."

Silence hung between them for a moment, a silence that was becoming far too familiar between the pair of them. Karim didn't like it, but he didn't want to break it either. As was often the case, it was Issa who made the first move.

Slowly, she grabbed Karim's hands and examined his swollen knuckles. "You've neglected your hand-to-hand, I see."

"I've been at sea and in the air the past few years, what do you expect?" A small smirk betrayed Karim's lips.

"So, can I assume Vaziri is using Gods' Glass as we expected?" she asked as she massaged his knuckles.

"I think so. When you return, take a look at his left hand. It never leaves his pocket. Even after I punched him. He's probably soothing the others. That's why he's been running around with those foreigners at the Harbor's Flask tavern. They could've been training him."

"I'll keep an eye on his hand. And I'll try and talk to the Vice Admiral—help him understand the situation."

"He already knows the situation. Don't worry, I'll deal with him. Whatever I get, I deserve. He told me I was in over my head already." Karim put a hand to Issa's own to stop her massaging. "And something else isn't right. Those people in there, the ones he invited… he's definitely wanting an airship of his own."

"I know, I'm just trying to work out how he plans on doing it. Don't worry, I'll figure it out."

"Thank you, Issa."

"If Deh'ala's passage is clear, it should all be okay."

Karim bit his tongue. He didn't need to argue the merits of the Old Gods with her, at least not now. Instead he gave her a stilted grin. Issa turned away and back into the banquet, her blue dressed trailing behind her.

It was a stupid decision. Karim had no business getting violent with Vaziri. He should've settled down and used his own card of blackmail. He suspected that Vaziri had something he was hiding. He just needed to get back to his office and figure it all out. Perhaps he could put it to a letter.

But a letter felt so fake to him, so indirect. Where he came from things were settled face to face, not through pen and paper.

It felt like snitching. And there was a saying for snitches in al-Anim. But Vaziri had forced Karim's hand. Karim's only choice was to play the hand that all nobles were dealt in the capital.

So, he stomped down the corridor and made his way up the flight of stairs to his office.

CHAPTER 46
ZALA

It did not take long for Shomari to show Zala to Karim's office. It was a simple room decorated with rows of scrolls atop desks and maps against the wall. A single window set at its back, the late afternoon orange shining down onto a lone wooden desk.

"You take the left and I'll take the right," Zala ordered.

Shomari nodded, shuffling to the left side of the room filled with the rows of scrolls. Zala moved to the right, examining the maps. Most of them were depictions of Esowon, stretching from the former Golah Empire in the southwest to the Sapphire Isles and the rest to the east. Nothing looked out of the ordinary. The maps held no annotations or clues, so Zala shifted her attention to the lone wardrobe in the room, which held a keyhole in its center. As she fiddled for the picks hidden away in her robes, Shomari asked, "Need help, chana?"

"I got it." She waved him off, keeping to her digging.

"Oh, really? Because that lock you're about to be picking doesn't need it. Just tug on the door."

Zala grabbed the wardrobe handle and pulled. Sure enough, it opened without any need to pick the lock. With shock, Zala looked back to Shomari who was smiling and searching the walls for hidden crevices.

"How did you know?" she asked.

Shomari pointed his paw to his yellow slits. "Cat's eye. I could tell from here the door on that thing was slightly ajar. Our Sky Captain must've left it open in a hurry. I would be doing this too with how long it took us to pick the door to his office itself."

Always so astute, this one, Zala thought.

The first object she came across was an open-faced scroll, an ink bottle at its side. She glanced over the writing, which was inked in High Vaaji. If this Karim el-Sayyed had been writing the letter, he did not finish. Several crumpled pieces of papers bedecked the edges of the wardrobe's bottom, all discarded attempts.

> *To His Majesty's Council,*
>
> *As the council knows, the first attack on Kidogo was a minor success. Though we were forced to retreat, our team extracted enough samples of the skyglass to move forward with a follow-up attack plan. We also discovered a handful of Glass of Dulagi among the collection. Some were larger than a fist while others were nearly spent, only the size of a marble. Though all of our deposits were given over to Their Majesties — including the Glass not suited for our airships, it is my belief that some of the crew have taken some of the Glass for themselves. And there may be those who have sold their share to nobles and commoners alike within Al-Anim.* ~~*I believe Collector Mahir Vaziri might be chief in this black-market trade.*~~
>
> *We have returned from the testing of the Viper. We made contact with one of the pirate ships that frequent the area. After disabling their ships with resounding success, we captured an individual who may have been responsible for our initial defeat at Kidogo. I suggest that we keep this individual...*

The letter ended there. The last stroke of the ink suggested Karim had to leave before finishing, or forgot about it altogether to write another letter. Zala lifted her head and told Shomari what she had found.

"So they did get some of the Glass, then?" Shomari snatched

the scroll from Zala, his face distorting in an uncharacteristic scowl. "That's from our home!"

"You remember that first attack on Kidogo, right?" she asked. She had never seen him so flustered.

"I lost a friend to it," he growled through clenched teeth. "And we lost most of the sea speakers too."

"All except Jelani." Zala nodded. "Read the passage again. He refers to an 'individual.'"

Shomari pulled the scroll close to his nose. "I understand some of this, but other words read a bit…"

"Oh right, it's in High Vaaji, I'm sorry." Zala pointed to the last line of the letter. "You see there, the line with the swoop? In High Vaaji it means roughly 'lone person.'"

Shomari scanned it over again, then turned to Zala with curious eyes. "You are thinking this is Jelani?"

"Who else could it be?" Zala bit her lip. She would jump at any crumb of information that could lead to her husband, but if Shomari agreed, perhaps there was more to it than her own bias.

Shomari stroked his furry face in thought. His eyes scanned the rest of the document. "It is possible. But what about this line here? It means Glass, ya? Does it say some of the nobles in this city are using the Glass of the Gods? Isn't that being regulated here? In fact, since we've been here I've not seen many mystics. Who do you think is peddling the stuff without going unnoticed?"

"You know how this part of the palace has far more guards than it needs, right?"

"Correct."

"And the guards tend to cluster around certain parts of the palace, like today's banquet." Zala brushed her hand over the desk for more documents. "And guess who brought the biggest retinue?"

"Vaziri." Shomari's eyes lit up. "You are not thinking he is an illusionist, are you?"

"I don't know for sure but it would make sense. I just haven't seen any one illusionist produce so many copies, not even Ekko. And Vaziri's seem solid. We'll have to capture or question one of the guards to be sure."

"And I should be able to sniff them out."

"It would have helped if Fon were here. She'd sense them."

"What about this?" Shomari lifted another half-written letter from the corner of the wardrobe. Zala squinted her eyes to read.

"It's a proposal," she said, then read it out loud:

Official request to move forward with the second attack on Kidogo. Even without the pirate's compliance, we could possibly move on with force. If the council allows it, I hope to lead this second attack. With the target in our possession, the island will be unprotected. Perhaps then we can buy the Golden Lord of the pirate islands off as we have before...

"But it stops there," she said. "It just ends."

"Does this dikala finish any of his letters?" Shomari brushed his hand along the bottom shelf where several pieces of paper were balled up.

"Ketifa and one of the cooks told me this Karim was just promoted." Zala stroked her chin in thought. "He's just measuring his words, drafting."

Shomari shook his head. "I can't believe we have been spending time with this dikala's father the whole time." He lifted the parchment in his hand once more, re-reading what he could. "Who would've thought the Vaaji would have the balls? I know we've been chasing after them for moons, but it's still surprising all the same. I suppose I would have the courage too, with a flying boat like that." Shomari moved back to the scrolls resting on the room's single desk. After a while he pulled out a manifest. "This one wasn't written by that Sky Captain."

Zala walked to Shomari and examined the new document. "Doesn't even look like he opened it yet." Zala broke the seal and read it.

"Anything special?" Shomari asked.

"Nothing." Zala rolled the scroll back up, but just before she rolled it all the way something caught her eye. "Wait. There's something here. It says someone was brought in recently to the palace dungeons, a few weeks ago. It's an unnamed man: Large with a big nose. Always catching colds. Proceed with caution."

"Sniffs!" Shomari exclaimed. "He's here! Mantu will be happy to hear it... So where are the dungeons?"

"I assume down below. I just don't know where at, exactly."

"How do you not know? What kind of recon work were you all doing all this time?" Shomari asked with a raised brow.

"We told you, we couldn't get out of the kitchens. This is only the second time I've been away, and it's likely our only chance. The only reason you found me is because I got kicked out."

"Did you at least slip the potion to our kijana?" Shomari questioned. Zala's silence was answer enough. "Oh, come on, chana! How are we supposed to be making any of this work without—"

Shomari stopped himself short and started to sniff the air.

"What is it?" Zala asked.

The cat held up a finger just as his ears started to twitch and flail like sails in the wind. "Someone's coming," he whispered.

The door behind them cracked open. Instinctively, Zala and Shomari pressed their backs against the wall behind the door. When the door opened fully, Shomari was on the interloper faster than a fleeting shadow, grabbing the person with an intricate cat hold. When Shomari finally pulled the person into the window light, Zala could make out the distinct scar on the man's face.

"Wait, Shomari." Zala lifted a hand to Shomari's, which already held a dagger to the man's neck.

Now that Zala could look Captain Karim el-Sayyed in the eye directly, she saw now that he looked a bit gaunt around the cheeks and thin in the neck. The shadows under his eyes made his light brown eyes pop, and his beard was slightly wispy at its ends. It took a little longer than she would've liked to get her words out, but she reminded herself that the man was simply an obstacle to get over.

"Hold that thought, Shomari," she repeated, taking off her head wrap so Karim could see who he was dealing with. "We should show the Sky Captain some respect."

CHAPTER 47
KARIM

Despite being caught off guard, Karim's heart did not race. He learned to put his fear away in light of dangerous, life-threatening situations during his first year of training at the military academy. At times he got himself in trouble for not showing emotion at all, as though he was sleepwalking through his regimes. But it was the only way he knew how to control his emotions.

It was all or nothing.

He didn't recognize the woman, but he couldn't forget the yellow eyes of the pakka—the same one he faced on the *Viper*. And even now, he thought he recognized the shape of the woman's face, not only from that iced corridor on the airship, but from Madam Majida's only a handful of weeks ago.

"I told you we'd meet again," the cat said with a menacing smile, teeth and fangs stark white against dark fur. He barricaded the door with a nearby chest.

"Bind him," the woman ordered the pakka, who wrapped Karim up to his office chair before she started her questions. She was a small woman, with cheekbones showing through her skin, short hair, and nondescript brown eyes.

"You are making a mistake," Karim said coolly. "You will not hold me for long."

"I don't need to hold you indefinitely." The woman dropped down to her knees, getting level with Karim. "The quicker you answer me, the faster we'll be done with you."

"I have no intention to speak if all you plan to do is kill me afterward." Karim looked askance toward the cat. The pakka seemed keen to kill him the last time they met, and he wasn't confident he'd changed his mind.

"Who was saying anything about killing you, kijana?" the cat crossed his arms.

"Isn't that your way? The way of pirates."

"Depends on the pirate you're dealing with," the woman answered for the cat. "Some of us are reasonable, decent even." The light through his window revealed her left ear, which looked as though something had chewed its way through it.

"If I call for help, my guards will be here in moments," Karim said, though he had no intention of doing so, and had no personal guard to speak of. Most of the guards were still at the banquet and many of them were Vaziri's.

The woman only shrugged her shoulders. "It wouldn't come to that."

"Why's that?"

She nodded toward her cohort. The pakka withdrew his rapier and cut the tip of a candlestick atop Karim's desk in one fluid motion. Though Karim had seen the speed with which the pakka fought, the strike slammed a small bit of fear into his heart.

"You see, if you do not cooperate, my friend here will give you another scar on your face," the woman said darkly.

Karim did his best to keep his face still, though the strike had nearly made him flinch. He hoped his expression wasn't too stilted, too guarded. That was almost as bad of a giveaway as exaggerated reactions.

"Do we have an understanding?" the woman asked, a finality in her tone.

"I guess we do." Karim turned to her. Something warm slid down his face. Out of the corner of his eye he could see a red line dripping down his cheek. The cat had nicked him. The woman's mouth parted when she caught sight of the blood. When Karim met her gaze she tightened her lips.

So, this one has sympathy, Karim thought.

"Where's my husband?" she asked directly, her face hardening.

"You'll need to be more specific. There are many husbands in al-Anim."

"You know who she's talking about, dikala." The pakka uncrossed his arms, his yellow eyes pinching a menacing stare. "You've already made us as pirates. You know who we are coming for."

"Ah, the pirates from Kidogo, then?" Karim turned to the woman. "You must be the survivors." Now that he examined it more closely, the scar on her ear didn't look like it was chewed; it looked as though it were nearly blown off.

"I'm sorry to say we killed all the rest," he lied, leaning back in his chair as though that was the end of the conversation.

The pakka stepped forward. "What about Sniffs?"

"What's a Sniffs?" Karim scrunched his face.

"We saw the manifest. We know you have one of ours in one of your cells."

"This is not my compound. I don't know anything about a 'Sniffs' or whoever it is you're looking for." Karim relaxed his shoulders. It was always easier to withhold information when he truly didn't know the answers.

"He's right, Shomari." The woman lifted from her crouch and whispered to the cat, turning her back to Karim. The one called Shomari had an interesting name for a pakka... almost human.

Karim gave a small tug at his bindings. They were tight, too tight to escape from. He had had enough of these pirates. There was a signal in the room he could activate—a torch that he could alight to let it be known that his room had been breached. But he couldn't get to it with his hands bound.

The woman continued to whisper. "We broke the seal on that manifest. He might not know about Sniffs yet. But he knows where we can find the cell." The woman turned to Karim, raising her voice. "Don't you?"

Karim stilled himself, hoping they didn't notice him working at his bindings.

He bit down on his tongue, giving no words. He didn't know who they were looking for but he did know where the cells were. The one called Shomari withdrew his rapier again with menace.

"Go ahead and kill me," Karim bluffed. "That won't help you find your friend."

"No, but it might make me feel better." Shomari's eyes darkened. "Your people are the reason my family is dying now."

"You refer to those who opposed us with the Gods' Glass?" Karim turned to Shomari. "It was a fool's action. We will have Kidogo one way or another. You all have only delayed what's to come. Those *things* should have submitted to us."

Shomari bore down on Karim faster than the woman could react. In an instant, the cat's blade was on Karim, just under his chin. Shomari bared his fangs a breadth from Karim's throat. "Now, tell me, Vaaji. Have you heard how painful it is to be eaten alive?"

"Shomari, stop." The woman outstretched a hand. It was clear she wanted Karim alive, uneaten.

"Listen to her. She's your captain, isn't she?" Karim let himself smirk. He had only guessed she was a captain. At first she seemed too green, too unseasoned for the role. But Karim and the others had decimated her crew. With so many dead, perhaps she was next in line. Plus, the cat had done everything he did at her request.

Growling, his breath hot on Karim's neck, the pakka finally let him go and stepped away with a scowl.

"You have a few minutes more, Zala. This man doesn't deserve to breathe for what he's done," Shomari said. "We will be finding the dungeons on our own. Jelani will be there too."

Jelani? Zala? Karim thought, his heart fluttering. Then he remembered what Issa had told them after the skirmish at the Harbor's Flask. She had described a woman like the one before him asking about her husband, asking about the pirate Jelani.

Yes, this was something he could certainly work with...

"I can help you if you'll allow me to walk over to my scrolls there." Karim interrupted them as he nodded to the scroll shelf besides Shomari.

"I don't trust you enough for that," the woman named Zala chuckled, and Karim knew then she was the same woman from the airship, Majida's brothel, and the banquet. "You stay put, kijana"

"Would you let me if I told you about... Jelani?"

The change on Zala's face was unmistakable, going from slight amusement to a paling flush. Her body visibly tensed as though she were bound by a spell. She could barely get out her next words. "W-what... did you say?"

"Jelani. The one who was infected by the stoneskin. Your husband." Karim gestured to the scrolls again. "If you'll allow me, I can get the papers necessary—"

"You mean this?" Zala rushed over to the wardrobe, slammed her hand into it, snatched out an unfinished letter, and she lifted it in front of Karim's face.

"No, not that." Karim shook his head, barely looking at the document. "It's about his condition. But the scroll is bonded by a blood seal—*my* blood seal. I'd need to give it willingly to open it without ruining it."

"Show me," Zala snapped.

"We shouldn't let the rat out his hole," Shomari growled.

"What's the worst he can do? He's already seen how fast you are with a sword."

The pakka took a deep, guttural breath, almost a purr. But he walked to Karim's side, unbinding his hands. "Any sudden movements and I will be running you through, you feel me?"

"Crystal." Karim nodded as he approached the shelfs of scrolls. He rummaged through the mountain of documents. "It's difficult for me to find it. Would you allow me a candle to see better?"

"So you can burn us with the wax?" the cat sneered.

"If a pakka and his captain can be taken down by wax, then I would question how they infiltrated a palace such as this to begin with."

"Just let 'im get his candle," Zala said.

Karim nodded, moving to the window where five candlesticks sat. To signal the guards, he needed to light every other one. He lit the first one straight away but hovered over the second.

"Light that one too, kijana," the female pirate gritted. "All five. Then bring one with you to do your search."

Karim made a slow turn to the woman and they locked eyes knowingly. This pirate was certainly above the usual. She really had done her homework, then. She nodded forward, crossing her arms impatiently. Without any fallback, Karim complied, lighting all five candles and taking one to his shelves to find the scroll he needed, but his search was slow.

"What's taking so long?" Zala asked.

"You've been through my things. I had them organized by date and subject. It'll take me some time to sort through the mess."

"He could be bluffing," Shomari said, "buying time."

Zala didn't pull her eyes from Karim. "To what end? He seemed to come alone. There shouldn't be any guards for at least—"

"Here it is!" Karim withdrew a scroll from the shelf. "I didn't understand the infection you husband had at first, so I did some digging."

Zala read over the documents in her hand, and Karim watched for her expression, her reaction.

"I don't understand," she said. "This isn't telling me anything I didn't already know. He'll die within the year. What does this have to do with anything?"

"Keep reading," Karim said. "A few lines down."

Zala's eyes scanned the document again. When her brow caved in a V-shape, Karim knew she had found it.

"What does it say, Zala?" the cat asked, head snapping between her and Karim.

"It says the stoneskin infection can spread if under duress."

"It seems the pirate life has taken its toll," Karim said, trying his best to lay in a sympathetic tone. "He told me he was a priest once. I thought it interesting to find him among pirates. But it makes sense now. The both of you have been trying to stave off the infection, haven't you? Perhaps it was your fault he was in such poor condition—"

"*Keeba yuh mout, ðikala.*" Zala pointed a quivering finger between Karim's eyes.

Karim ignored the threatening gesture. "When we found him, the damage was done. He had welts up and down his skin. I tried to get my surgeon to brew him some stonesbane to stop the spread—"

"Are you telling me he's dead?" Her eyes went deadpan, her mouth still.

Karim measured his response. He could let the cat run him through with its blade. Or he could tell her the truth, and figure out another plan. In one scenario he ensured his value, in the other he did not.

"No, he's not dead."

The woman's eyes glistened, though her expression remained still, a single tear bordered the bottom of her eyelid.

"Where is he?" her voice cracked. "Here in this palace?"

"No. He couldn't be kept here. It was too close to the coastline."

"Then where is he, dikala?"

Karim sighed, looking both pirates in the eye. It would not be advantageous to lie now. "He's on the airship."

"You'll take us to that ship, then. Now," the woman's voice was stern, her energy completely changed. Karim could feel the anticipation coming off of her like a tangible thing.

"You know I'd die before I'd do that," Karim said.

The cat withdrew his rapier again. "That can be arranged."

Karim measured his options. Again, he could die there, or he would play along with their little game. He knew he had the woman on her heels—all he needed to do was mention her husband. His value was too great if he was the gatekeeper between her and her reunion with him. She wouldn't kill him, even if she wanted to. But the same couldn't be said for the pakka.

"How about this," Zala started darkly. "You tell us what we want to know, and I can assure you that a certain shaman in the

Scars remains whole. We've a few of our crew back there who could make it happen with a simple message."

This time it was Karim's turn to freeze up, and he was almost certain the color in his face had left him. There was nothing that could be done for it, no amount of training that could prepare him for information like this to be revealed. The pirates really *had* been tracking him... So much so that they knew about the whereabouts of his father, likely overwatching him for a moment just like the one they were in then.

With a large gulp, Karim said very slowly, "I can show you the way to where your husband is being kept, but it's heavily guarded. I won't be able to get you inside."

"I have a way of getting through heavily guarded situations," Zala challenged.

"And I am having a way with cutting through said situations," the cat added.

"Well, then," Karim said dryly, concerned thoughts still on his father and the image of a pirate lurking in the shadows behind him. "Will I lead or should I follow one of you?"

CHAPTER 48

KARIM

ALL KARIM NEEDED WAS A SET OF GUARDS HE COULD TRUST, and he'd be out of this situation. The gate leading out of the palace would be his best play; he only needed to give the guards the signal and they could take out the woman and the pakka who held him captive. But that plan would be difficult to enact. The pakka, who was now dressed in full Qibasi servant robes like a devotee, held a knife to his back. And knowing how fast the cat was, any sense of betrayal could be fatal for Karim. The woman named Zala had disguised herself in a full soldier's garb after they made their way past an armory.

As they approached the grand doors that led out of the west wing of the palace, four guards stood tall, each brandishing a saber and shield. Karim glanced at the platinum rose sigil that attached their breastplates to their pauldrons. They were Vaziri's crew.

"Halt," the largest of the men said in a flat tone. "State your business."

"What's the need?" Karim asked. "I can come and go as I please."

"Collector's orders. The Head Chef said one of his cooks went missing."

Karim could feel the woman and the pakka looking to one

another behind him. "Well," Karim went on, "I don't see what that has to do with me. I need to report back to the Vice Admiral on military business."

Karim took a forceful step forward, asserting an air of authority. The guard pushed him away with his shield. "Everyone is to stay in this wing of the palace until the matter is settled."

Karim stammered "Well... I—"

"You need to be thinking of something quickly, *Captain*," the cat's whisper was sharp in his ear.

"But the Admiral says it's vital." Zala stepped to Vaziri's guards in Karim's stead. Her perfect Vaaji accent impressed Karim. "You wouldn't want him coming down on the Collector, would you? Vice Admiral Shamoun doesn't like delays."

The man turned a lazy look on Zala. "And who are you?"

"I—I am the new guard to the Captain." She straightened up.

"Everyone is to stay in this wing of the palace until the matter is settled," the man repeated in the same tone as he did before. Karim lifted an eyebrow. Were all of Vaziri's guards so lifeless... so rote?

Despite the man's deadpan, Zala didn't quit. "We understand that and appreciate your protection. However, we have an appointment that cannot be missed. I'm sure Collector Vaziri will understand." Zala pushed forward but the man's shield stopped her just as easily.

Karim noticed a small change in the man's face, something in his eyes. It was quick and subtle, but he was certain there was a change.

"Captain el-Sayyed," the man said—this time his voice had a more natural inflection. "What brings you here?"

"We've already told you..." Karim answered. "We have a meeting with the Vice Admiral."

The guard's eyes were misty. "Oh, yes. My apologies. My mind wanders sometimes."

"Something's not right about that one," the cat whispered again.

Karim thought the same. Something was definitely off.

"I told you back in the office," Zala murmured to her cohort, "mystic work."

But Karim didn't feel the influence of an empath. The guards weren't trying to soothe or persuade them from what he could tell. So what kind of mystic work were the pirates referring to?

The guard stood up straight with a confident upturn of his lips. "I'm sorry to say no one is to leave the premises until the assassin is found."

Karim quirked an eyebrow. "What assassin? I thought we were just dealing with a missing cook?"

"One of Chef Hadi's cooks went missing. And my guards found one of the soldiers knocked out near the armory."

"Who was it?" Zala asked, though Karim suspected she already knew something about it.

"One of the fortress guards. Not one of ours. Her name is Fatima."

"Oh, no." Zala lifted her hand to her helmet's mouth plate. "I was stationed with her a few days ago. Is the whole of the palace secure? Was the assassin meant for Their Majesties?"

Karim had to admit the pirate woman was good. She sunk deeply into her role as a guardswoman, and even *he* almost believed he had hired her.

"Their Majesties don't need to know," the guard said casually, "so long as the issue is resolved."

Karim had been thinking of giving the other two up, but everything about the guards before them seemed odd. And for them not to inform Their Majesties of a potential assassin within the walls of the palace was a blood-red flag of "up-to-no-good" shenanigans.

They needed to get out of this situation. And fast.

Karim held his hand over his heart in a courteous salutation. "I think that'll be all, then. There doesn't seem to be anything else we can do. We'll head back to my office and wait out the ordeal."

"One question," the guard said. "I've not seen this woman before in your guard. Why's she dressed in full armor? Is there a siege we don't know about?"

Karim gave Zala a sidelong glance. He hadn't paid her getup

much mind. But indeed, she *had* put on a full plate, with thick helmet, heavy pauldrons, and strong chainmail. Most of the guards just wore light leathers with perhaps a standard chainmail at most.

"Well... I took the advice of your boss," Karim replied cautiously. "Al-Anim has become ever more dangerous. I thought it'd be smart to employ a soldier as a guard for my private travel. And you can never be too well-armed, right?"

"I see..." The guard's gaze shifted to Shomari. "And the woman here in the robes... I'd like to see her face."

The cat rocked on his heels, and Karim knew he already had his hand at the ready to draw that signature rapier of his. In that moment, Karim thought it might not be so bad for them to get in a little fight. He hadn't forgotten his bout with the cat. It was unlikely Vaziri's guards would be his match. Still, considering all the tricks the Collector had up his sleeve, there was no real need to test the waters, esteemed pakka fighter or not at his side.

"She's very modest." Karim held a hand out to Shomari, then bowed. "She's taken an oath to the Supreme One."

"That might be so, but we have an intruder. I want to take account of all those in this wing."

Shomari stuck the dagger deeper into Karim's back, hissing. "Do. Something."

"I insist, there is no need for—"

"Captain el-Sayyed, there you are!" a voice echoed down the corridor. It was Issa, still dressed in her flowing blue dress. "My apologies," she called to the guards, "I meant to find him before he met one of you guards." She turned her voice to Karim. "The whole palace is on lock down."

"So we've discovered," Karim said.

Issa craned her neck to the guards. "I'll take them back to the barracks."

"That's fine, just stay inside until everything has been resolved." The guards' eyes changed again. His shoulders seemed to slump and his gaze turned back to a stoic expression.

What was wrong with him?

Before Karim could get a proper second look at the other

guards, Issa pulled him away and led them back down the corridor.

"We are heading the wrong way," Shomari whispered at Karim's back, though his words were mostly for Issa.

"And what way are we supposed to be headed?" Issa replied, "You're pretty hairy for an oathkeeper." She jabbed her chin at Shomari's robes, which indeed were bursting with his furs near his backside.

"We should be headed where *we* want, chana," Zala said as they turned their first corner.

For the first time, Issa seemed to get a proper look of Shomari and the hint of a dagger at Karim's back as he walked nearly shoulder to shoulder with the cat.

"Lovely 'friends' you have here, Karim," Issa said sarcastically as she drew her hand to her side.

Zala clicked her tongue. "Nu uh, get your hand from your waist, or I'll run you through."

"Do as she says, Issa. And the cat is right, we can't go this way if there will be more of Vaziri's guards. That said," he twisted his neck slowly to Zala, "I would like to have my spine free of a blade."

Zala nodded and murmured, "Weapon away, Shomari. The kijana could've sold us out back at that checkpoint."

Reluctantly, Shomari withdrew his dagger, to Karim's pleasure. He hadn't realized how tight the pressure had been on his back.

"Where did you go?" Issa asked Karim as they passed over a small courtyard where some of the banquet guests had corralled, and a half dozen guards to protect them — or more likely to watch them.

Karim nodded to the pirates. "I met some new friends.".

Issa turned to the pirates with a curious expression. "Considering you're not bleeding out, can I assume they are the good kind of friends?"

"We're still working that out," he replied with a coy smile.

"If it helps any," Shomari said, still hovering his dagger close to Karim's back, "we are no lovers of that Collector either."

"Mildly," Issa said. "I'd feel a bit better if you weren't holding my Captain hostage."

That cat fluttered his fingers. "It is what needs to be done, chana."

"I never properly thanked you before," Zala said to Issa. "Back at the tavern. You really did save me. Sorry about the alley though, I couldn't let you take me in."

Issa brushed her hand along her cheek, a faint scar healed with dawa root barely visible. "*This* was a bit excessive."

"Don't play that game, you would've done the same." Zala furrowed her brow in a deep frown.

"Everyone calm down, calm down," Karim said as they crossed from the open view of the courtyard and onto a bridge blanketed by the early evening moonslight. "I'm the only one in any physical danger here and I'd like to keep this a bloodless affair. Let's not point any fingers and assign blame right now, can we agree to that at least for the next few minutes? We all have the same problem of dealing with Vaziri's guards."

Issa lowered her voice. "Yeah, about that. Vaziri is definitely using Glass. And he must be plenty strong to be influencing all these guards of his."

"Influence?" Zala's helmet canted inquisitively. "You mean his copies, right? Your Vaziri's an illusionist, not some soother."

Karim stopped walking at the end of the bridge, whipping to Zala with sharp eyes. "How do you know about Vaziri?"

"That's sort of the reason we're here. And we figured he was an illusionist. He was channeling himself through that guard, couldn't you tell?"

"Of course..." Karim said, almost to himself.

"How did I miss it..." Issa trailed off, and Karim knew she was beating herself up internally, especially when some pirate figured it out before them. Before she betrayed her thoughts through her face, however, she stood straight and went on to say, "And that's not all, Captain. Vaziri's making a play for the airship *sooner*, not later."

Zala rubbed her head through her helmet. "The Rovers who

held me captive said as much. They never mention their boss's name, but I reckon it's Vaziri who hired them, ya?"

"Makes sense," Karim said, "considering they made a play for the airship once. We'll need to get Vaziri alone."

"Well…" Shomari, finally, took at least a single step away from Karim. "It was our Captain here who was giving them the idea to bring down your ship to begin with. Seems like they are just following through now."

"Think about all the people Vaziri's been meeting with," Issa said. "He's never been interested in the engineers until now—"

"And this is the first time I've seen him speak directly to the Priestess," Karim finished for her. "He's trying to make a play for the Skyglass at Akeem on top of it all."

"What are we going to do about it? We have no proof. We're alone on this."

Karim turned to his two captors. "Didn't you say there was someone you wanted from within our cells?"

CHAPTER 49
ZALA

Z ALA DIDN'T TRUST K ARIM OR THE WOMAN WITH THE BLUE
dress, but if the guards were to be believed, they couldn't get out
of the palace without their help—without all of them helping one
another, that is.

"Listen, I know you've only just met me. But the only way
we're getting out of this thing is by getting past those guards,"
Karim said for the third time in a pair of minutes. "And here I
thought it'd be you pirates trying to convince *us*."

"The only way past them is *through* Mahir, though," the other
woman in the blue dress said.

"If he wants that airship, he's a problem for us both," Karim
added.

"So, how do we get Sniffs out of his cell?" Zala asked, leaning
on the threshold leading out to the palace bridge.

Shomari stroked his cat's beard through his head wrap, never
moving more than a few feet from Karim, his dagger still in hand.
"And don't forget about Mantu. He's probably still in the
kitchens."

Zala pushed away from the wide threshold. "Can we get both
of them out?"

"That shouldn't be a problem," the woman said. "The kitchens
are on the way to the cells."

"I never got your name," Zala said to the woman.

"I never got yours," the woman answered back darkly.

Zala sighed. "Listen, you want to stop Vaziri... so do we. We don't have to like each other, but I'd rather call you something other than chana. Unless you prefer being called chana. I could also use 'dikala who stole my husband.'"

The woman turned to Karim, who gave her a short nod. "Issa will do fine, pirate. And you?"

"Zala. Nice to meet you without having a sword at my face or my husband in your imminent custody."

"Likewise."

"All right, then we'll all head to the kitchens first." Karim clapped his hands together. "What a way to bring in the new year..."

With the imperials leading the way, navigating the palace was much easier than before. They went from wide corridors to open studies, cutting through sections of the palace Zala hadn't realized were shortcuts before. Zala never took her eyes off either of them, watching for any move of escape or a lunge of attack. Shomari held his shoulders tight, his eyes never leaving the pair either.

The woman named Issa whispered to Karim in High Vaaji. "*Is there anything I should know? Do we need to slip this pair?*"

"She can understand you," Karim said, then looked over his shoulder. "She was eavesdropping earlier at the banquet. The server giving us water, remember."

With a raised eyebrow, Issa turned to Zala. "How do you know the high tongue?"

"I know a fair bit more than that." Zala gave her a wry smile. "And as your Captain knows, my cohort here is quite lethal. Try anything, and he'll silence you. And we'll find another way out of this place ourselves."

"What fun, but unlikely, pirate —"

"Zala"

Issa sighed. "Fine, *Zala*. What is it you and your partner here want with Mahir?"

"We've got a job to stop him taking taxes. But right now we're more interested in a certain sky ship."

"You told them?" Issa said to Karim with a hint of shock.

"They're the ones we attacked," Karim said, an air of defensiveness in his tone. He pointed to Shomari. "This is the pakka who tried to assassinate Malouf."

Shomari pulled back his head coverings, flashing a smile at Issa. "I would be calling it more of a standard gutting than an assassination. That fool is not exactly worth the word, yes?"

"Well…" Issa said with caution. "We have a common enemy in Mahir, but the airship… you must be out of your minds if you think we'd hand it over to you pirates. We could never—"

Karim held up a hand to Issa. "We have her husband. She won't release either of us until she has him." There was a change in his voice, as though he were conveying a message to the other imperial.

"Oh," Issa said. "Oh, I understand."

"What was that?" Zala stepped between them as they climbed a spiral staircase. "What did you just signal to her?"

Karim's face bunched in confusion. "I don't know what you mean."

"What are you two playing at? Planning to sell us out to another set of guards?"

"I've done everything you asked. Aren't we on our way to release one of your people now?"

Zala eyed the man and woman, looking for a break in their faces. Maybe she had been reading too much in Karim's tone. Perhaps he was only trying to reassure his partner, rather than plan something behind her back.

"Whether we make it to the airship or not," Karim said, "we'll need to bring down Mahir to do it. Right now neither of us has much of a choice."

Issa added, "And we've been tracking Mahir since our return to al-Anim. We knew he was up to something. You can trust that we want to stop him as well. You said it yourself. My Captain could've given you up back there."

Issa and Karim stopped walking at the top of the steps. Zala hadn't noticed that they had arrived at the kitchens already. This was the first test. They could either sell Zala and Shomari out to

Chef Hadi and the potential guards inside, or they could prove they truly did have a common enemy.

"Will you allow us to enter the kitchens?" Karim asked Zala, breaking the moment of silence.

"Yes, but we will remain at your side."

"Very well." Karim led the way into the mess hall.

It was empty, free of the guests, the cooks, and performers. All that was left were the platters of half-eaten food and goblets of wine. Some of them were overturned, as though the guests had left in a hurry before the lockdown went into effect. Zala never thought she would cause such a commotion. Vaziri must've been hiding something valuable if he went through all this trouble.

There was an eerie quiet to the room... the only sound breaking the silence was the splashing of the artificial waterfalls that fed the pool under the glass platform—that and their own footsteps as they padded across the hall.

Karim pointed to the door at the far end. "The cooks are probably locked away in the kitchens."

Zala nodded, allowing Karim to lead the way to the wide doors. She hoped her face was well hidden under her soldier's helmet. If Chef Hadi was in there, he might recognize her. But she couldn't risk letting Karim or Issa out of her sight.

Karim opened the door to the kitchen. All the workers from the banquet were squeezed into the small space, boredom or anxiety etched on each of their faces. Some of them were horror stricken to see Karim and his retinue. Perhaps they had thought the worst. If one of the cooks was a supposed assassin then they knew they would be questioned, even tortured, Zala knew. Mantu recognized Zala instantly, a coy smirk stretched across his face.

"We need to question one of your cooks," Issa commanded in an authoritarian tone.

"That one there, with the beard." Zala pointed to Mantu, disguising her voice with extra bass.

Out the corner of her eye she spotted Na'im, whose face shone with acknowledgement. Zala had been so concerned with Chef Hadi that she forgot she could be recognized by others. Where had the man's loyalties lied, she wondered. Sure, Shaman Ismail and Cousin Ketifa might've told him why she and Mantu were really there, but didn't he have a desire to join the ranks of the Vaaji military?

Uncovering the "assassin" would be the perfect introduction.

"Oh, yes. This man should know something," Chef Hadi snapped his fingers. "He and that woman joined my kitchen at the same time. Don't hold back on this one."

Hadi stomped to Mantu and grabbed the much larger man's arm forcibly. His hand looked like a child's around Mantu's forearm. The Chef must've realized he had been played. After all, it was Mantu who suggested Zala be picked for the banquet in the first place.

Mantu grunted when Hadi tried to pull him to the group. When Mantu didn't budge, Hadi let go of him promptly. "Well... y-you... heard them," Hadi said, his voice weak, stammering. "T-they say you're wanted for q-questioning."

"I heard 'em fine," Mantu said, taking his time to walk out of the kitchens with the group.

Zala eyed Na'im again, who visibly struggled to keep his mouth shut. Zala pleaded with the little man as best she could through the helmet and scarf that covered her mouth. But would it be enough?

"Chef Hadi," Na'im said as Mantu continued his dramatic, lumbering walk.

Zala's heart stopped cold; her fingers hovered over the hilt of her saber.

"What is it, street rat?" Hadi spat. "Can't you see we're dealing with something?"

Na'im opened his mouth to reply, his eyes flitting between Zala and the Head Chef. But it seemed that Hadi's words had quieted his response. "N-nevermind, sir. It can wait."

Zala let out a private sigh, then made eye contact with Na'im again, giving him a short nod.

The moment Mantu was several strides away—or in other words, out of reach—the Chef spoke again, his confidence apparently returned in full. "It's just like I said. He's your man! Don't hold back. Give him—" The last of his words were cut off by Mantu slamming the kitchen door shut as they left.

Mantu turned to Zala. "I thought you were dead."

"Not yet." She smiled.

"So what's the *new* plan?"

"These people know where Duma is being kept. He's here in their dungeons."

"Really?" Mantu's face lit up, an expression Zala hadn't seen on the man in a long while. It was the same one she must've had when she realized Jelani was still out there somewhere.

Karim stepped forward between two fallen tables with spilt cider at its edges. "Yes, he's just through the door that leads to the main courtyard. We keep our dungeons below the soldier's barracks."

"Wait a minute." Mantu stopped the group with a raised hand. "This one… correct me if I'm wrong but ain't this the one who attacked us and sunk our ship?"

"We know," Shomari spoke from beneath his disguise. "But for now, we are all agreed to being friends. Isn't that right, everybody?"

"Shomari?" Mantu tilted his head to the figure in dark robes. "You got a thing for women's clothing, don'tcha?"

"What can I say? They favor my waistline very well, no?" he said with a hand on his hip.

"Not to interrupt your little reunion," Issa cut in. "But Vaziri *will* eventually discover what we're doing if we're not quick about all this."

"Right," Zala said. "Lead the way."

AGAIN, THE GROUP FOLLOWED THE IMPERIALS OUT OF THE MESS hall and through the palace. Shomari took the lead ahead of the pirates, still looking ready to pounce if Karim or Issa tried anything. Zala was a bit more comfortable with them now. They could've sold them out to Hadi, but they didn't. They didn't even tip him off, it seemed. For now, it looked as though their goals were indeed aligned. More than that though, their little group was now four to two — Zala always counted Shomari twice, even if he still might've been getting over his near-miss with death.

Still, Zala made sure Mantu was just as vigilant. "I don't trust these imperials. Keep your eyes open. They may really want to bring the Collector down like they say, but expect something — *anything.*"

Mantu smiled. "Good. I was gonna tell ya you're trustin' these dikala too much. You're becoming a pretty good pirate, Zala."

<hr>

THE ENTIRE WESTERN KEEP WAS ON HIGH ALERT.

At every turn they found a new set of guards, all of them belonging to Collector Vaziri. Yet the imperials stayed true to their word, finding another route or doubling back to avoid confrontation whenever they ran into the armored sentries.

Once they made their way into the open courtyard leading to the barracks and the cells, Zala could see that every battlement and tower was manned by a guard. Though many of them watched for what was outside the walls, many more were looking inward for the interloper — for *her.*

"Mahir's smart," Issa said as they avoided another patrol. "Not all these guards are illusions. He's only supplementing his real guard with his copies."

"Oh, good," Zala replied, keeping pace with the taller woman. "So he might only have a score of copies instead of a hundred."

"How you tell the difference anyhow?" Mantu asked from their rear.

"It's hard to see at first glance but..." Issa pressed her back to a wall as another patrol went up a flight of stairs at the end of the courtyard. "Look at their features. Whether man or woman, they all look very similar —"

"To Vaziri..." Zala finished, trailing off. She noticed a glint of pride in Issa's expression, as though she were back on top for figuring something out before Zala did.

But the woman was right, Zala had to admit. Whether the copy was a man with a sharp beard or a woman with delicate skin, they all had the same nose, mouth, and jawline. And their mannerisms were all the same too.

Mantu rubbed the back of his head in confusion. "I don't know how you see it."

Zala and Issa shared a light look of bemusement. Zala suspected if they were better acquaintances their smiles wouldn't have been so stiff, but considering the circumstances neither of them was willing to entirely break down their guards around the other. Not so easily.

The group ducked behind separate arched pillars, cloaked in shadow. Each of them had an eye on the guards that paced in front of a squared structure. The palace's western cells were well hidden to those who wouldn't know where to look. The dungeon was, apparently, disconnected from the main keep, adjacent to the armory from which they had come.

Zala turned to Karim. "So where are these cells *exactly*?"

"We keep the prisoners as far away from the nobility as possible," Karim whispered from the pillar he hid behind.

"So the southeast edge?"

"Yes."

"I *told* you it was the southeast edge," Mantu shout-murmured to Zala, who rolled her eyes. "We walk by here all the time. Who'd've thought Duma was just under us?"

"There are only two guards, but we'll have to be careful," Karim murmured. "The dungeon watch are usually mystics or sindisi."

"Si-what?" Mantu asked.

"That's what the Vaaji call the guards assigned to protect their mystics," Zala explained. "Native to your tongue, I believe it's *m'shet*."

"Ah, noted." Even in shadow, Zala could see Mantu's anticipation engraved on his fierce gaze and carved in his tense shoulders.

"We'll rush the pair of them and hope for the best. We have them outnumbered."

"There's no need to," Issa said, sharing a hiding place with Karim. "We can just request the one you're looking for."

"Well then, get on with it," Shomari said sharply from his own pillar.

"We would, but look." Karim gestured his head to the guards. Zala didn't notice anything wrong, though, the guards paced back and forth like normal.

"They are only walking," Shomari finally said after taking two looks of his own.

"Look at their faces," Issa said.

Zala squinted, taking in a better measure of the guards. Below their helmets were the same expressions she had seen from all the others.

"What? All you hairless are looking the same to me," Shomari explained.

"Those are Vaziri's illusions..." Zala trailed off. "They won't give us Sniffs, even if these two go up there and make the request. Vaziri will likely take over and—"

"Know something is up," Karim finished for her. "It's too risky. Issa and I shouldn't be here. If they can link us to—"

"So you'll give us up then?" Shomari snorted, unfurling his claws from his paws menacingly.

Karim raised his hands, gesturing for Shomari to keep his voice down. "I didn't say that, did I? We just can't walk up there, is all."

"Well, what *can* you do then?" Mantu asked harshly, whipping his head from the group to the guards and back again, his fists clenched tight.

"How about the Lord of Records?" Issa said over her shoulder.

Karim's face lit up. "All we'd need to do is make an outside claim for the prisoner. Perhaps a transfer. It would get their man in the open, at least. It would just take a scroll to do it. We'd just need some parchment and my seal."

"Your office isn't far from here," Zala said, following the thought pattern Karim was going on.

"So you agree?"

"Yeah, I think I do." Zala met his eye. She'd never thought she'd find herself an ally to a Vaaji officer, but Karim was different than most — from what she could tell.

CHAPTER 50

ZALA

"We're here," Karim said with a scroll bound by his personal seal tight in hand. He stood before a grand door etched with passages from al-Qiba.

"Your people know how to make anything look beautiful," Zala gawked.

She expected something more dark and dim, not an ornate door flanked by grand windows that let in the bright glow of the rising moons. There was an awkward silence as the group stared at one another.

"So… what are we waiting for?" Zala glanced between the two imperials.

"We can't go in there," Issa said first, as though it were obvious.

"Why not?" Shomari purred darkly.

"If Mahir is told either of us was trying to move a prisoner, he'll grow suspicious. But if one of you go in and request the change…"

"You mean we have to pretend to be imperials?" Mantu asked, giving Zala a side eye.

She knew he didn't like the idea, but she followed Karim's logic. They just needed to sell the lie well. She couldn't expect the imperials to put their neck on the lines for some pirates they barely knew, no matter if they were being forced or not. Still, she would've liked some warning. Neither of them had said any of this before they arrived.

"That sounds like a quick way to land us in a dungeon of our own," Zala said. "You two would like that, wouldn't you?"

"It's not the best circumstance, I know," Karim explained cautiously, "but it's the best chance you've got."

His words sounded genuine to Zala. She chewed at the thought, going over the scenario in her head.

Mantu must've noticed her increasingly agreeable disposition, because he stepped into the conversation. "We can't just go in there pretending to be imperials."

"You did well enough pretending to be kitchen workers until now," Karim returned.

"That was different, dikala," Shomari purred from the side. "Playing the kitchen servant is an easy act compared to some poncy officer type. Mantu is still in his kitchen getup and he does not have the class."

Mantu bristled a little at that, but he didn't argue the point.

"Well, *you* have the high tongue learned well enough." Karim pointed to Zala. "It's indistinguishable from any other noble I know. And there is a new noble—her family name is al-Sulayhi— your Captain here looks a little like her, at a squint. It could work."

There was a brief silence as Shomari and Mantu turned to Zala.

"You speak High Vaaji?" Mantu asked. "That why those nobles was lookin' at you back at the banquet? You didn't think tellin' me somethin' like that coulda help us while we in *al-Anim* of all places?"

"I learned long before you met me."

"Why ain't you tell us? A skill like that woulda been useful at port."

Zala shrugged. "I wanted the crew to accept me, not use me as a tool."

Mantu put his large hand on Zala's tiny shoulder. "You did do a good job of persuading the Rovers back on the Ibabi Isles, and then that stuff with Madam Majida, and everything we been up to in the kitchens. Oh, and let's not forget how you got up and out of the Rover situation in that tavern almost all by yourself. You have a knack for putting on a face."

"No, I'm with what you said before." Zala shook her head. "It'd be suicide. If they suspect me, even a little, they'll capture us. I'd have to be perfect."

Issa cleared her throat. "You don't have to be perfect, just good enough. The record keeper's work is a dull affair. No one in there'll give you a second glance so long as you've got confidence."

Shomari tilted his head and shrugged a lazy shoulder. "It's simple, chana. Just pretend you are having the same spear up your ass ol' Lishan seems to struggle with so much."

"Right..." Issa said.

Zala turned back to the imperials. "All right, we'll go with this plan of yours. What will you be doing while I'm freeing our man?"

"We'll be dealing with Vaziri," Karim explained. "I'll need to compromise his office somehow so that you and your crew can take him down and create an exit for us."

"One of his windows might do the trick," Issa suggested.

"But I thought those were all enchanted?" Zala questioned. "Won't the mystic guards know if there's a break-in?"

Issa lifted a finger. "Not if you open one from the inside."

"All right, I'll try to get a window open." Karim turned to Zala. "I'll try for the northwest window. It's the one inscribed with the first verse of the third chapter of al-Qiba. Do you know it?"

Zala nodded. "I know *of* it. But what am I supposed to do about freeing our man? I'm dressed as a guard, not some official."

"Just take that helmet and armor off. The tunic underneath should be enough. And use your sash to wrap your hair."

Zala did as he said, dropping the armor and fashioning a head wrap. She had never worn armor before—at least nothing so protective, and now she felt naked without it.

"How do I look?" Zala asked with outstretched hands.

Issa looked unconvinced; Karim raised a single eyebrow.

"If they question what you're wearing, just say you came from saber practice," Karim finally said. "We're all required to attend it at least twice a week."

"You know no one actually does that, right?" Issa turned to Karim. "When was the last time you saw Mahir trading blows with one of the blademasters?"

Karim thought it over for a moment, hand over his mouth. "You're right. But al-Sulayhi is new. There's no reason why the pirate couldn't play that up." Karim turned his eyes to Zala with a reassuring voice. "Just tell them that your Duma person needs to be moved for questioning. That way he'll be in the open. Then you can free him."

"I think we can handle that."

"All right, we'll be off now..." Karim started down the corridor.

"Not so fast." Zala said. "Shomari will accompany you to make sure you open that window for us."

"Right... right, of course." Karim cleared his throat. "The cat can come with us."

Shomari gave a low growl before turning away. "Good luck, chana. I know you can do it. But if you don't—"

"You told me so," Zala finished.

"Right." He snapped his fingers, then turned on his heels to accompany the imperials.

Zala watched as they jogged around the corner, nerves already building from her gut and up to her mouth. She clenched her throat to keep the bile down, and twisted to Mantu. "You wait out here for me. Try and move my armor if you can. I don't want to have to explain what you're doing here as well as selling the lie of this al-Sulayhi."

"Fine by me. Holler if you need anything."

"So that you can get a head start on your escape?"

Mantu gave her a sly smile. "Wouldn't dream of it."

ZALA TOOK A VERY, VERY DEEP BREATH.

For a moment she wondered what was more nerve-racking: jumping from the crow's nest of a pirate ship or impersonating an imperial official. Both could have easily ended in her demise but somehow she felt acting under such circumstances was far more terrifying. What if she screwed up like she did during her speech on the *Titan*? What if the administrator set an alarm? There would be no way to escape, even if they could run. One of Vaziri's guards would catch up to them, or surprise them from some dark corner.

There was no other option, she thought. She had to be perfect.

Zala closed her eyes, searching her mind for the voice of a noble woman. What made them sound different from the slummers? They had a confidence, an entitlement that they belong at the top of the class system. They talked down to others like they were children. That couldn't be so hard, could it?

The latch on the door felt cold to her touch, but she knew it was only her imagination. She put the thought aside, pushing the door open with the boldness of a Vaaji official.

The room was just as beautiful as all the others. Two arched windows at the back let in a soft light that perfectly illuminated the single wooden desk at the center. The woman who sat at the desk was backlit, the wisps of her tarha highlighted by the shine, almost like a moons-lit halo. The contrast on her face could not be more stark, however; the woman's face was withered, aged by experience, and it wasn't encouraging that she wore a cruel frown before Zala had even stepped foot in the room.

Zala forced herself not to gape at the majestic balance of the room. Then she reminded herself... that wouldn't be the expression a noble would have at all.

"I need a prisoner transferred," Zala said immediately, getting straight to business.

"No hello? No Grace of Shati'ala? Just straight to it, then?" the old woman shook her head with a grumble.

"This transfer is very urgent." Zala remained curt, holding her poise firm.

"State your name and the prisoner," the old woman said,

pulling a new piece of parchment in front of her with the lazy routine of a scribe.

"Al-Sulayhi. And the prisoner's name is Sniffs—Duma, I believe."

"That's your family name, what's your given name?"

Zala's heart dropped for a moment. Karim had never given her a first name. "My given name?"

"Yes?" The old woman stared at Zala with a low brow set over dead eyes.

"I'm just not used to giving out my birth name. Everyone always addresses me by my family name."

There was a brief silence before the woman spoke again, this time with a raised note. "I still need your given name, girl."

Zala wanted to cave, to leave the room and just make a break for it. But she held herself like stone. She had fallen overboard and now it was sink or swim.

Or be eaten, Zala thought, wincing internally at the woman's deadpan stare.

She let none of her fear show. "Don't take that tone with me, scribe," she gritted. "I gave you a simple directive. I need a prisoner transfer: given name, Duma. Family name, not given. He's to be relocated from the southwest barracks to the offices of Vice Admiral Shamoun for questioning. You may read this manifest from Captain el-Sayyed if you need assurance. And if I have to ask one more time, I will make sure the Council knows that you were the cause of any delays." Zala held out the scroll Karim had given her, unwavering in her facade.

She measured the woman's response, but it was hard to tell what she was thinking at any given time. Her expression was too stoic. But then the woman shook her head, closing her eyes.

"I don't know what the Empire is coming to." She took the scroll from Zala, mumbling to herself. She barely glanced at it before she started writing on her new piece of parchment. "Back in my day you youngsters gave elders respect. Now you think you can just rule the world without wisdom." She sucked her teeth. "Such a shame, such a shame."

Zala cleared her throat, snapping her fingers for the documents. "Enough, scribe. Thank you for your assistance."

The woman snorted and waved Zala away. Zala turned on her heel, doing all she could not to break face or smile with glee.

She did it. She actually did it.

"Oh, one more thing," the woman called out. Zala's heart sank. "Are you sure it's this 'Duma' person you're transferring? I see here Collector Vaziri has a different prisoner scheduled to be transferred. This one was actually brought in with your Duma person. You'll oversee that transfer as well, young one." It was a demand, not a request. "I know the keep is still on lockdown, but you should be able to get through. This person is going to the south western block, just on your way."

Zala gulped, her heart hammering before asking the question, "And who might this other prisoner be?"

CHAPTER 51

LISHAN

LISHAN HAD DECIDED THAT SHE ABSOLUTELY *HATED* FLYING. She'd take the sea any day: typhoons, monsoons, whatever "soons". It was better than having her stomach roiling and guts bouncing like it was at that moment.

As she clung to Ekko's back atop a kongamato that rocked up and down with each flap of its wings, she felt like she wanted to hurl up her breakfast. Though Iokaja could've flown alongside them, she too sat mounted at Lishan's back, her stoneskin enough to hold her upright without clinging to Lishan's waist.

"When are we getting there?" she yelled over the high winds. The clouds were already changing from white to orange with the dying sun, and N'Kota had said the trip wouldn't take long.

Ekko chuckled. "Few more minutes. Don't worry, I'm just as queasy. Gettin' off this thing is priority number one."

"You two all right over there?" N'Kota called out over the breaking winds, Ouseni wrapped around his middle, and Kwame around hers atop a kongamato of their own.

Lishan signaled a rude pirate gesture in N'Kota's direction as she held back yet another bite of bile threatening to rise to her mouth. Skepticism had riddled her mind ever since Vaziri had told them that six was all they needed for the operation, so long as they had an empath in N'Kota and another illusionist in Ekko. It would be a lie if she said she didn't have her doubts about Vaziri and his care for her crew—or even his own, but getting this done would see her reunited with Nubia.

Getting this done would see her taking the Vaaji's airship as her own.

The clouds broke ahead to reveal rocky structures that started as sporadic dots on the horizon but quickly grew more frequent, eventually melding into one another until they fed into an enormous desert bluff that nearly rose into the clouds themselves. Vaziri had told them this is where the Sky Navy hid their base, at the peak of what was known simply as the "Great Rise." And just as Vaziri said, an unnatural collection of cyan-hued clouds spiraled at the top of the rock structure. Within it, Lishan knew, lay the Vaaji's airship.

"Ekko, you're up," N'Kota bellowed, slowing his kongamato's flight ahead. "Cloak us in the sky. That's the base just down there on the bluff."

"On it!" Ekko returned, then edged his chin over his shoulder to Lishan. "You got the Collector's Glass, ya?"

Lishan dug into the satchel at her side. It held several glowing orbs of various pulsating hues, no larger than an apple or an orange.

Gods' Glass.

One for each of the crew, save for Kwame who was the only non-mystic among them. Lishan carried three for herself, Ekko, and Iokaja. Ouseni, on the other kongamato, had been given her own.

It probably would've been smarter to sell the glass off and hire her own army to storm the Vaaji military base that approached below them. The stuff was dangerous. That's what her father had always told her, what all her maji trainers had always said. Too many warriors, soldiers, fighters, criminals, whoever, used it in excess and went mad, or were careless enough to spend the whole of the Glass and get cursed with stoneskin.

Lishan frowned when her eyes passed over Iokaja's stone grip around one of the kongamato's spikes. She couldn't ask her to use the Glass again. Not when she had already paid its price. She didn't want Ekko using it either. Losing his wife—and the woman responsible for her death—made him a liability in Lishan's eyes. Yet nothing he did all night really warranted caution on her part. If anything, it was he who reassured her more often than not.

"Captain?" he asked again. "Everything okay?"

"No." She came out of her reverie. "You don't have to use the Glass. You'd only need to hold your illusion for a little while as we come down, right?"

"We've been through this, Captain. I can't guarantee I can cloak two flying creatures going as fast as they are. You saw how I struggled in that alley back in the city. We can't risk it, not when we're so close to gettin' Nubia back. I *have* to use the Glass."

Lishan turned to Iokaja behind her. "I can't convince you to help me out here, right?"

The aziza flexed her stone fingers, making them scrape, like rubbing two rocks together. "The Glass Vaziri gave us aren't nearly as spent as the one I had before. Everything should be fine." Her tone was without any real bite, the kind they Rovers were known for. She, like the rest of them, simply went through the motions with rote stoicism.

They had lost so much in so short a time.

Digging her hand into her bag, she held out the Gods' Glass assigned to Ekko, a purple-tinted orb Vaziri referred to as Glass of Dulagi. "Be quick about it. The moment we get down there, this goes straight back in my bag."

"Of course, ma'am." Ekko grabbed the ball and his eyes flared white.

Lishan didn't understand the magic behind his illusions, nor could she say she truly felt his power when he used it. But with the Glass working through his fingers and coloring him in that amethyst glow, she could almost sense the false picture he conjured about them. It was like her own a'bara—which dealt in flashes of the future, not images of deception—somehow recognized the language of Ekko's own. Like the faint memory of something long lost yet eerily familiar.

The sudden nosedive of their kongamato completely cut off that sensation for her, however.

It took all she had not to let out a screeching scream as her braids whipped behind her. Her stomach left her somewhere several feet above. She clutched to Ekko's waist ever tighter, hoping to the Gods the dive would finish soon.

As though jolted back by some invisible force, Lishan fell back into Iokaja's outstretched stone hand as the kongamato flapped its wings wide to slow their descent.

"You all right there, Captain?" the aziza asked with the tiniest hint of humor.

Lishan measured her surroundings. They had landed on the top of the bluff, just outside the bank of the unnatural fog. Were it not for Ekko's illusion, they would've been blasted away by fireballs and cannons from the moored airship and surrounding base defenses. Lishan was just thankful she could finally jump down and settle herself back on solid ground.

"Much, much, better now." She stuck out her hand to Ekko. "Give that thing here."

"No go, Captain." Ekko said, still mounted, and still white-eyed. "Not until you're all on board."

"Fine." Lishan relented, then addressed her little crew. "Focus up, Rovers—and... guest." She gestured to N'Kota who dismounted his kongamato along with Ouseni and Kwame. "The operation is simple. Vaziri said there'll only be a skeleton crew. And with his little banquet, most eyes won't be watching out this way. Ekko and N'Kota, get down into the base," she pointed down below her feet, "Get us that kadal. We're not going anywhere without a proper pilot. Everyone else... on me. Let's clear this place out like we should have done the first time."

"Aye, aye," they all echoed in earnest.

"Can't forget our ticket out of here," N'Kota said jokingly. The only one of them who could still find whimsy in the job.

Lishan gave them a short nod and unsheathed her sword. She turned to the eerie fog she knew housed their new airship, and, with commanding resolve, shouted, "For Captain Nubia!"

CHAPTER 52

KARIM

KARIM DIDN'T ENJOY THE RETURN OF THE DAGGER TO HIS back. Now that the pakka was alone with him—without Zala to rein him in—he obviously didn't mind pressing his knife deeper into Karim's tunic.

"I've been doing as you ask," Karim said over his shoulder. "What have I done to deserve such hostility from you?"

"I must just not like you, Vaaji," Shomari leered. "I got a good feeling about this one though." He tilted his head to Issa.

"Should I be flattered?" Karim wasn't sure if Issa was asking him or the cat.

They walked the length of the corridor, turning a corner to a high ceilinged room belonging to the chamber of the financiers. Near the end and to the right stood six guards outside a door with a platinum rose sigil at its center.

"Is that his office?" Shomari's eyes narrowed. "Looks more like the entrance to a throne room."

"He's been here a while," Issa said. "He does seem to overcompensate a bit, doesn't he?"

Karim was the first to step forward. Before he could speak, one of the guards interrupted him. "Everyone is to remain in their quarters until this situation is abated."

"I'm here to apologize to the Collector," Karim said. "Is he here?"

"Collector Vaziri says he wants no visitors until this conflict has been abated," the guard repeated, monotone. Karim looked him up and down. He'd never seen an illusion before—at least not knowingly. But now that he looked more closely he noticed that they always seemed to be looking slightly off from Karim's eye line... and their skin was almost too perfect.

"I am not the assassin he's looking for, though I'm sure he would say otherwise." Karim forced a laugh. Humor was lost on the illusion, however. "Tell him that I was wrong. That I see reason now. I shouldn't have hit—just tell him Captain el-Sayyed's here to make amends."

"Collector Vaziri says he wants no visitors until this conflict has been abated," the guard droned again.

Issa cleared her throat. "What Captain el-Sayyed is trying to say is that he did not see the wisdom of the Collector. He wishes to clear the air. He was only apprehensive that he was not invited to the banquet, that he wasn't a part of Vaziri's inner circle. And when he tried to speak to the other guests he felt as though no one was listening."

Like the guard from before, the man changed, his eyes flitting into themselves in an inhuman way. "Is this true, el-Sayyed?" the guard smiled, the first change of expression he had since they arrived.

Karim nodded, keeping his head low as he spoke. "It is."

The guard looked Karim directly in the eye with a strange smile that sent a chill down Karim's neck. "The Collector will see you now."

Karim, Issa, and Shomari stepped forward as the guards opened the door. But Issa and Shomari were stopped by the shaft of one of their spears. "The Collector will only see the Captain. You two must stay here."

It wasn't lost on Karim that the guard shouldn't've known what Vaziri wanted without a direct order.

"Are you going to be all right in there?" Issa asked as she took a step away.

"I'll be fine."

"Just don't forget to keep your hands to yourself. Engage, don't—"

"Enrage," he cut her off. "I'll try. But I can't make any promises."

"And do not go forgetting what you're supposed to be doing, kijana," Shomari purred in his ear.

"Of course," Karim gave the pakka a small scowl, then walked into the room, leaving the others behind.

Vaziri's office was changed from what Karim saw a mere week ago. Where before it was almost minimalist, now it was as opulent as the man's current outfit of pure cream satin. All the windows were adorned with fancy lavender silks. Each corner of the room had a statue of the more celebrated monarchs, including the current ones, the al-Nasirs, whose likenesses sat nearest Vaziri's grand desk. And the floor was finished with marble, though most of it was covered in an ornate rug that stretched the length of the room. Had the man really been so lucrative in only a few days for such a makeover, or had he set up his office in such a way to impress whoever he conned to join him here from the banquet?

The only thing that seemed the same from before was the bookshelf that lined the back wall, along with his paintings, which Karim had to admit, now that they were done, looked more real than even the twinkling cityscape outside the windows.

"You have a lot of courage to show your face here." Vaziri's tone was playful. "You know I could have you kicked out of the military for what you did—if not executed altogether."

He sat behind his desk on a chair Karim could only describe as overindulgent. To say the least, it was made entirely of pure gold.

"I made a mistake. I thought I was taking initiative by being a part of the conversation, but I can see now that I should have deferred to you first. You were our host. It was not my place to challenge that... certainly not... physically."

For a moment Vaziri sat in silence, staring at Karim as he stroked his perfectly trimmed beard. He looked halfway bemused at the words Karim had chosen to open with, but didn't comment further on it. "Take a seat."

Karim obeyed, sitting across from Vaziri. His desk was neat and tidy like everything else about him. There were a set of goblets on one side of the table with a single piece of parchment at its center. Vaziri moved the parchment when Karim's eyes lingered too long.

"I must ask." The Collector pressed his fingers into his lips. "Why was it so important that you be at my little banquet?"

"I was heeding the counsel of the Vice and Grand Admirals. They said I needed to be more... friendly with the nobles of the capital."

"You still have a ways to go with that lesson then, I'd say." Vaziri leered. Karim held his eyes low, submissive. Vaziri's grin only grew the farther Karim tilted his head down. "Do you know why I meet with so many of the nobles myself?"

"To maintain a good rapport with them?"

"That. And to know who my true friends are, and who my enemies might be." Vaziri's eyes pierced Karim's with his last words. "That's why I didn't have you killed on the spot. You showed me your true colors at the dinner. Now I know what to expect from you."

"Is that something you really could do?"

"Oh, you'd be surprised what I could do, Young Captain."

Karim leaned forward in an attempt to make his "genuine" feelings known. "You don't understand... that was a mistake."

Vaziri held up a hand, basking in the control he maintained. "You came to apologize because you want something from me, yes?" Karim remained silent. "Now, I wonder what that some-thing might be — I'm sure it has very little to do with your father and the others. We've been through that dance already."

"Look, I'm no fool," Karim said. "I know you're planning something big."

"Is that so?"

Karim raised his hands in defense. "And I don't mean to chal-lenge that, not at all. The reason I wanted to come to the dinner is because I wanted in, not as one of the leaders, I've never been cut out for it, as you saw firsthand."

Play to his hubris, Karim thought.

"I'm better when I follow orders. But I am more than a fair pilot, the only real pilot the Empire has. If you needed a man who could fill that role for whatever it is you're planning… I could be a candidate, a front runner even."

"I've people of my own." Vaziri gave Karim a short nod, pushing his lips out in an overly affected frown. "The others speak about you often, though. But they are hesitant about your loyalties. We all know you give support to your father. Support that wouldn't exactly be smiled on by the Empire."

"Do you think the Empire would smile on the kind of support you give to the slums?" Karim couldn't help the jab. Vaziri didn't take offense, however. Instead, the Collector stood up from his chair and moved to a store behind his desk.

"Would you like a drink?" Vaziri asked as he pulled out two rose gold goblets.

"Yes, please," Karim accepted, only to be polite.

"Do you know where this is from?" Vaziri tapped a barrel marked with a language Karim couldn't understand. "This palm wine is from the former Golah Empire. Do you know what happened to them?"

Karim tried to recall the history lessons about the former Great Nation. But he could only remember one thing. "Something about in-fighting. They broke up into smaller cities—villages, really."

"Yes, it was due to in-fighting, but do you know the cause of that fight." Vaziri poured wine into the goblets with a single hand. Still, his free hand remained hidden under his shawl. For a moment, Karim watched the milky liquid drop.

The wine was a forbidden drink on the eve of a new year within al-Qiba. But as he thought about it, he wasn't entirely sure what faith the Collector kept to. During the banquet it was he who said he could do better, didn't he? Was that a true sentiment or was he only saving face?

"Territorial disputes," Karim answered. "Something about

farming locations. They feuded about which plot of land they could hold claim over."

"More or less." Vaziri set a goblet in front of Karim, then moved to retrieve his own. He still only used one hand. "What really happened was that some of the farmers butted heads about which of their Gods favored their harvest."

"But my father always said Jo'bara is tolerant of other beliefs. Some of the provinces up north have different Gods, but my father says they're all the same." Genuine curiosity colored Karim's tone.

"That could be true for individuals, but we're talking about nations here, el-Sayyed. It's a bigger game than that. What a man says in his home isn't the same as what he says to his district, or his village, or his city, or his nation. There are too many moving pieces, too many people to please. And if a problem gets big enough... we have to set that blame somewhere. Why not on religion?"

Karim gave a slow nod. Now that Vaziri brought it up, he *did* recall something about the Golah Empire falling because of a smaller dispute among zealot farmers.

"And let's not forget the Great and Powerful Aktah. There was once a time when they ruled over most of the known world. Yet now they are only a shadow of their former glory. Can you guess what happened to them?"

This one Karim remembered. Aktah was much closer to Vaaj than Golah. It had been one of the first nations conquered in Vaaj's initial campaigns all those years ago. Conquering them had been an easy affair. When Vaaj brought al-Qiba, the people of Aktah accepted the faith with open arms. This had mostly been due to the torments of their previous civil war. Most of the powers within knew they needed a nation like Vaaj to shepherd them from their dark ages.

"It was something to do with their Sun God, right?"

"Correct. They all had their own ways of worshipping and they squabbled about the importance of the Sun and River Gods." Mahir took a sip from his goblet. Karim mirrored him, though he did not swallow the forbidden drink. "You see, the belief of multiple Gods has caused rifts within Esowon, divides of preference. Sun God. Tree God. Warrior God. Harvest God. Too many to count or manage. It's what brought the fall of the people of Golah and the people of Aktah. It's what was happening to Vaaj before The Great Uniter brought us through our own dark times. People need black and white. They need right and wrong. They need a chief to follow, a captain to lead them, a monarchy to govern their cities. The same is true of their Gods. Shati'ala offers that. It is by Her will that we humans were given our own powers. Many attribute our success to the powers we were given, our abilities to move mountains or control animals."

Or create illusions, Karim thought, eyeing Vaziri's hand, which was still tucked within his cream silks.

"But it's this." Vaziri pointed to his forehead. A shiver ran down Karim. It was almost the same gesture and conversation he had had with Shamoun, the conversation he had with the pirate Jelani. He'd never think the Vice Admiral and Collector would share in their philosophies from two entirely different paths. "This is what makes us great," Vaziri went on, "that's what sets us apart."

"It is by Her Will that we are made in the Gods' image. It is by Her Sacrifice that we will endure." Karim recited the opening lines of al-Qiba. "I've tried to tell them..." Karim almost spoke to himself. "That the Old Way will die. It's time for us to set ourselves apart."

Vaziri lifted himself from his chair. He moved closer to Karim, sitting at the edge of his desk. "And that's why we must observe only Shati'ala. The others are extraneous..."

"Irrelevant," Karim finished for him. He'd been saying it time and time again, but he never thought of it on a grander scale. He'd always only considered it all from an individualist approach. He supposed it all made sense though. From the example of the individual, the model of society could manifest.

Vaziri nodded. "Irrelevant they are. And the Empire will be the vanguard for Her Will."

"If only they could understand that..." Karim tilted his head to the window, which looked over al-Anim from the noble plateaus and down to the port markets. Karim lifted himself from his own chair and moved to the window. "Do you mind if I open this?"

Vaziri shrugged, taking another sip from his goblet.

Karim turned to the latch on the window. If he left it open, he'd let in the pirates. But after his conversation with Vaziri he wasn't so sure that was the best course of action. He had never taken the time to speak with the man one-on-one with a genuine open mind. He hadn't realized how much their own opinions aligned. Yet the man was despicable, with no loyalties to either the Empire, his faith, or the people they protected. Vaziri's only regard was for Vaziri.

Yet even a fool could make sense at least some of the time. Karim hadn't related the fall of the Great Nations to the foundation of faith, or the importance of singular rule. How could Vaaj reclaim their dignity when they were divided?

He gazed out to his old district near the harbor, and his next words did not frighten him as he thought they would. "Al-Anim must be made to convert. To save them. We cannot be united if we hold to different beliefs."

His fingers hovered over the latch, still deciding.

Vaziri walked up to his side, opening the window. The young night's wind wafted into the room, blowing back Karim's keffiyeh and Vaziri's curly hair.

"I know you come from the slums," the Collector said. "I know your ties for your family are strong, as they should be. But it doesn't have to be this way. You must convince them to become proper citizens of the Empire."

So Vaziri was a true man of the Faith, at least in part, at least for the function of unity.

Karim's eyes hovered over the fallen temple that was his family's home. From this distance it was only a small speck, but a whole childhood spent with its rubble allowed him to see the details. Could it really be that simple to ask? His father was so stubborn. He'd never convert. But funding his stubborn lifestyle would cost too much and he couldn't keep it up forever.

Karim shook the notion away again.

Vaziri didn't care about the Empire or its rule. He was planning his own coup or whatever it was he had in mind. He didn't care for progress, he was advocating for his own personal gain. That was no different than the nations he criticized. And if all the citizens were to convert this time tomorrow, the extra coin that funded his banquet, funded the very office they stood in now would all go away.

He was just placating, speaking the words Karim wanted to hear, no matter if there was a truth in them or not.

"Let's get this window closed, shall we?" Vaziri requested. "Night will settle properly soon and I can feel its cold breath already."

"Of course, Collector." Karim nodded.

Vaziri turned back to his desk. Karim closed the window but he let his fingers rest on the latch. Funny how the simplest of actions could change great outcomes. Should he follow the path of Vaziri, join his little band of nobles and carve out an empire he saw fit despite how fake it all was? An empire who did not let their military officials rise up simply because they had the right resources like Old Captain Malouf. Or could he let the pirates have their way, save his family from a corrupt man, only to be left in the same position he was in now. Back to a family who had no desire for progress, but was comfortable remaining stagnant in their old ways?

Or... he could choose an entirely new path of his own...

"I must say, I enjoyed our conversation, el-Sayyed," Vaziri said. "I feel like we have finally got to know one another for once."

"Same." Karim rested his hand on the latch another moment before he turned back to Vaziri, just on the edge of whispering the counter enchantment to lift the protections on the window.

They had small talk for another few minutes before Vaziri finally dismissed Karim. Holding his hand over his heart, Karim thanked the Collector for his hospitality and then took his leave.

When he crossed the threshold into the corridor, Issa's face lit with anticipation, Karim could even feel the anxiousness from the pakka, even under its layers of robes.

"It's done," Karim finally told them as they walked out of

earshot. "You should get to your people now before he notices something."

"You're not done yet," Shomari said. "You're coming with me."

"But we've done all you asked."

"And you're the only one who knows how to get to that airship. You've only done half the job."

Karim sighed. "Fine, but we can't be seen by Vaziri."

"Then disguise yourselves in some of that steel you've got in the armory. What's the problem?"

Karim thought back to the window's latch. "Nothing." He gave Issa a sidelong glance. "Nothing at all."

CHAPTER 53

LISHAN

L ishan's sword tip sunk deep into the back of one of the few remaining naval officers of the Vaaji's skeleton crew. Before he fell onto the airship's upper deck, he groaned to his surviving comrade, "Nabila, go! Warn the Captain."

Silhouettes against the unnatural fog billowing around them, Iokaja did battle with another officer dressed in rags. No, Lishan couldn't call it battle. The officer had no fighting skill whatsoever, hiding behind the tall shield she held in front of her. When she heard the call from her fallen comrade, she threw the shield awkwardly at Iokaja. The aziza didn't miss a beat, using her wind magic to cast the shield aside harmlessly. But it was only a distraction.

Before Iokaja could shoot forward with a second attack, the officer in rags changed from human form to that of a gull and flew into the surrounding fog, out into the desert's night sky.

"Iokaja!" Lishan ordered. "After her."

The aziza gave a short nod and flapped away after the shapeshifter. Through the sheet of mist, orange flares blossomed from what Lishan could only assume was Iokaja's fire magic chasing after the gull.

"Is it going to be a problem if she can't catch that one?"

Ouseni asked as she ambled down the weather deck, cleaning blood from her saber.

Lishan shook her head. "Doesn't matter. By the time she tells anyone in the city, we'll be long gone. Where's Kwame? We need one of these dikala alive."

"Right here, Captain." Kwame dragged a bloodied and bruised officer from below deck. The man was bone-thin and almost unnaturally tall. Falling to his knees, he lifted his chin up to Lishan with a quivering lip.

"P-please, p-please… don't," he blubbered.

Without anyone manning the engine room, the cloak of the fabricated fog was already dissipating, letting in the moonslight glow. Taking a piece of loose cloth from one of the dead officers, Lishan wiped away the blood from the young man's face, as gentle as a mother's touch. "Shhh, shhh. Stop your tears and die like a man of Vaaj." His body rocked with shivers at her last words. "What I can offer you now is a quick death. That is my mercy. But only if you cooperate. So, I will ask you plainly and you will answer me plainly. You feel me?"

The officer nodded his head with a new set of sobs. "Y-you don't understand. M-most of us are just covering for other—"

Lishan slapped him across the face. "Now, now. That's not how this is going to work. Next time I won't hit you with my hand. Next time it'll be the true edge of my sword. Got it?"

The officer nodded vigorously again. This time he kept his mouth shut, just as Lishan liked it.

"Good," she said. "My question is very simple. Where are you keeping Captain Nubia?"

"C-C-Captain who, ma'am?"

"Captain Nubia."

"I-I-I don't know who that is, ma'am." Lishan raised her sword. "Honest! I-I-I don't know anyone by that name on this ship."

"Lishan, you up there?" came Ekko's voice from an open pipe nearby. "N'Kota's got our kijana. Meet us at their… whatever they call it. The place they keep their helm."

Lishan turned a wicked glare on the officer, deciphering

whether or not he was acting or being genuine. But no one could fake that slobber running down his chin.

"Bring him with us," Lishan ordered the other two as she climbed down the ladder toward the helm's room.

The compartment that held the airship's helm was a strange one, lined with wood paneling, piping, and apparatuses she didn't know the names of. The far end of the room was completely covered by glass, which gave a view to the edge of the cliffside outside.

N'Kota stood tall, his back to them as they entered the new space. But the image of him seemed strange against the low glow of the moonstones lighting the cabin. It was like he had four arms instead of two, both sets working one of the strange devices that appeared to be a set of pulleys and a helm at his side.

"Oh, there you are!" he said as he turned, and the illusion was broken.

Behind him sat a very long, very tall human-like figure with orange and red scales wearing a threadbare robe which must've been white at one time. It flipped its head over its shoulder, its partially elongated neck accommodating the reptilian movement. The faint lantern light above revealed a long snout, a split tongue, and yellow-orange crocodile eyes.

"With haste every one, with haste," it said with a hissing accent Lishan had never heard before. "Time now to be gone from here. Look lively!"

"Doesn't seem like *he* needed any convincing." Kwame murmured at Lishan's side, still holding onto their captive officer.

"Convincing?" N'Kota laughed and patted the creature on its shoulder. "It was hard enough keeping up with him. You ever seen a kadal running on all fours before? Had to stay in my kishi form just to match him."

Lishan stepped forward around the chairs and tools that dotted the room to get a better look at their new guest. Whatever or whoever it was didn't have an odor, and despite N'Kota saying there was a run to freedom involved, the creature had no sweat dripping down its oddly shaped head. Though cautious and a little apprehensive to ask the question, Lishan said, "You didn't want to know who we are, erm…"

"This one V'sshan. And knowing who you are, irrelevant to escaping." He took a moment to halt his spindly fingers working their way over his panel and levers to look Lishan up and down very quickly. It was bizarre, not because his movements were so erratic, but because they were so very inhuman. At least pakka and aziza moved fluidly like she or any other human would. This kadal, this… thing was something else. And as that reptilian eye looked her up and down it didn't even move its head, just flipped the eyelid to look out its side.

"Though judging by crude weaponry and dower expressions," it continued. "You are pirates. Stealing Vaaji's aeronautical vessel, yes?"

"I think they're just calling it an airship these days," Ekko explained.

"Hmm, airship. Simple. Effective. One thing Vaaji get right. Everyone, please sit still as this one gets airship working. Do we have engineer?"

"Um… engineer?" Lishan glanced between each face of her crew, who all shared in hesitant shrugs. "Um… We were told you would have everything covered."

It was true. All Vaziri had said was to come at the airship from above, as all the defenses were at the bottom of the base. He also said they didn't have a chance of getting off the bluff without crashing the airship if they didn't have a certain pilot, this V'sshan apparently, who was being held in a prison within the rocky compound.

"This one shall guess," V'sshan sighed—well, it was more of a hissing flick of his split tongue. "None left functioning after your attack. Small minds did not think to keep one engineer to use later? Hmm, maybe that one there?" Again, he didn't move his head, only shot his eyes back in their bizarre domic way. "You in the behind, what function do you serve on-vessel?"

The officer, whose eyes were still wet, and whose arms were still locked in tight by Kwame, stammered, "I-I'm just a guard, s-sir. Erm… m-m-ma'am?"

"Sir is good. This one likes sir." The kadal seemed to tilt its head at that. If he were human, Lishan thought, he might've had a satisfied smile.

"S-sir. I've never actually flown in this thing before. Like I was telling her, I-I-I'm only covering for—"

"Ugh, of course." V'sshan sprang up from his chair and showed everyone his true height, which had to be at least over seven feet as he craned his neck not to hit the low ceiling. "One's genius is one's curse. Everyone assumes this one will do everything by self. Out of way. Need to start up engine before this one can do anything here."

"How much time you need?" N'Kota asked, following him out of the helm's room, "an hour or something? We took out the guards in your cell block but someone will find them at some—"

"Five. Shall be sky flying, in five minutes. You will see. You," he pointed his long finger at Ouseni, "follow with N'Kota. This one needs extra hands."

Ouseni gave Lishan a look, checking for permission. Lishan nodded and Ouseni fell in line.

"Remind me," Lishan asked N'Kota's back as he moved to leave the room, "who or what is this creature we trusted our lives to?"

"V'sshan, the kadal," N'Kota replied, halting at the door. "Rare but highly intelligent creatures. The Vaaji have been forcing him to work for them for quite some time now. He's the one who designed this thing. Be nice to him, please."

That left Kwame, Ekko, and Lishan alone with the Vaaji officer. The room was oddly quiet without the rattling of V'sshan's fingers pulling and pressing at the controls. Murmuring to herself, Lishan said, "This airship better be worth it."

Then she reminded herself the airship was really only for Vaziri's benefit. What she really came for was still onboard somewhere. She just needed to continue prying it out of the red-eyed man before her.

"So, where were we?" Lishan asked him again, pulling out her dagger. "Oh yes. Where is Captain Nubia?"

The young officer raised his hands in defense. Kwame immediately threw them down. "I have no idea who this Nubia person is! Do you mean the pirate?"

"Yes, the pirate." Lishan's heart fluttered. He did know who she was, then. Maybe they just didn't tell him the name to keep her identity a secret. "Where is she?"

"She?" The officer furrowed his brow in confusion. "T-the only pirate we have on board is a man... a man with the skin of stone. G-goes by the name of Jelani."

"Jelani?" Ekko asked. "Ain't that Zala's husband?"

Yes, if Lishan recalled it correctly, that was the name of the one Zala had said she was fighting for. But that still left one very important question. Where in Sapphire Hells was Captain Nubia?

CHAPTER 54
NUBIA

Nubia still hadn't decided what was worse, the darkness or the cold. She'd heard many tales of dungeons and jails, of course; when she had been Captain to soldiers she had put many there herself. She had never seen one personally though. And she had braved the seas as a pirate for so *many* years now, she thought herself immune to capture.

Now she knew the dark and cold as intimately as a lover. And it had only taken a few weeks.

Her visitors were few, outside of that first week, when the Vaaji Emperor and Empress came to verify it was actually her. But after that, for whatever reason, she had been left alone, likely because she was going to be used as a bargaining chip in some future political play between nations. It was just a matter of which ones... her homeland that she had forsaken, or the pirate islands that saw her as a nuisance. She'd find out eventually. But until then, she was trapped, locked at the far end of a craggy corridor that led to nothing but blackness.

The only reason she knew she wasn't alone was from the intermittent coughing of other prisoners—in particular the constant sniffing of the one who called himself Duma three cells down.

She didn't attempt conversing with any of the other prisoners, she didn't see the point—or maybe, in truth, she was just being prideful. The whispers of the others carried in a place like this. And without anything to distract her but the abyss, all she could ever do was listen.

They spoke of how she had fallen, how she had been fooled. And in the end it was her own fault. She had put faith in someone she barely knew, a captain she had never even heard of before. But the greed she had fostered among her people was too much when she saw that that sky ship was indeed real. She still dreamed about what could've happened if she had managed to take it as her own—and she reminded herself it was a dangerous delusion.

A rattling of keys echoed through the cells.

It couldn't have been meal time. Nubia's stomach pains hadn't started up yet—and meals usually came several hours after that. With a slow turn of her head on the flat sack her captors called a pillow, she peered into the darkness.

"Step back," a man's voice called out. "Pirate, step back."

"Me a-go, me a-go, calm yourself." This second voice belonged to the one called Duma.

"Turn around. Hands behind your back. Belly to the wall."

"Yeah, yeah. Me know how it go."

The sounds of his slow lumbering shuffled to the back of his cell. Then came the high-pitched squeaking as his cell door swung open.

"You too, pirate." A female voice came just outside Nubia's cell.

Nubia stirred a little. She hadn't even seen the guard that was mere inches from her.

"Hurry up," the guard droned. "Officer al-Sulayhi is waiting."

So today was her reckoning. She hoped it was the Ya-Seti she was being bargained away to. She had far more of a chance with her own people.

Clearing her parched throat and lifting to her feet, she said. "Belly to wall, ya?"

"Belly to the wall," the guard echoed.

Zala and Mantu walked down the long corridor to the barracks. Now that she was back in armor, Zala felt more comfortable. Even if someone was coming after them, or her story didn't sell, at least she was hidden beneath chainmail, a helmet, and a scarf that covered most of her face. Mantu was still in his cooking uniform, though a dagger was hidden in his tunic. That could sell her lie all the better.

After all, Mantu was *supposed* to be transferred for questioning.

"Do you remember everything I told you?" Zala asked as they turned a tight corner into one of Karim's shortcuts.

"Wait for the guards to bring Duma into the corridor and then kick their asses," Mantu said.

"Yes. But you have to be quick about it. And they can't see you. I'll be leading them, so I can't help you. If Vaziri takes control of the guards and they see your face he'll know something is up."

"I don't get it. Won't he know somethin' is off if two of his guards are suddenly killed?"

"He will, but if he can't see what killed them or how it happened, he'd only be making a guess. He already knows we're sneaking around, this'll just heighten his paranoia. Ekko told me back on the *Redtide* that illusionists can feel when their copies are destroyed, but unless he's directly controlling them he won't know what else is going on."

"All right, all right, I got it. Kill them before they know what's going on. Easy."

"Take this." Zala handed him the saber at her hip. "A saber and a dagger for each guard."

"But how do you know they'll follow you? Maybe they'll just release Sniffs and that'll be the end of it."

Zala shook her head. "Not Vaziri and his guards. They'll want to know everything that's going on in this place. You heard the imperials, they haven't even informed their leaders. He's trying to keep this all hushed up."

Mantu put a gentle hand to her shoulder when their tight corridor finally led into the courtyard. "All right. Yem be with you, Zala. May Her waves be merciful."

"And with you, friend—er—I mean, may Her waves be merciful."

Mantu chuckled. "You'll get the hang of it eventually."

Zala walked from the corridor into the courtyard alone, now in plain view of the three guards stationed at the central barracks. She strutted across the courtyard with a confidence that could only have been gained by the sealed scroll clutched between her fingers.

"Shati'ala be with you, Brothers, Sister," Zala greeted, but her salutation was not returned. "I have an order to release one of your prisoners for questioning." She stuck out her hand, scroll pointed at the guards. Their expressions changed after that.

"Let's see then," the female to the right said, examining the scroll. "Give me a moment." The guard walked into the barracks, gesturing for another of the men to join her.

Zala turned to the lone guard left, wondering if Vaziri was listening in.

"Nice afternoon we're having, aren't we?" Zala attempted to break the silence. The guard did not answer her, nor did he even make eye contact. But she resolved not to break the gaze she initiated. Perhaps she could distract the guard by staring at him. Yet he never turned, he never even blinked.

"Any news about that assassin?" she asked slowly.

Zala was used to using distraction through small talk, but perhaps it didn't matter when the guard wasn't entirely human. For a moment she wondered if illusions were considered human at all.

She was still thinking on her conversational lessons back in the academies when one of the male guards came back with Sniffs. Even in captivity, the man looked like a great beast, despite the shadows under his eyes or his slightly skinnier figure. Instead of his usual rows of braids along his head, his hair came undone in a huge mass of hair. Zala owed it to him to rebraid his hair when all this was done. He and Fon both.

When Sniffs finally looked up to Zala there was only a flicker of recognition. Did he even realize it was her? The guard held him with a rope around the large man's wrists, tugging him along.

"We will escort you for his questioning," the guard said, a request Zala expected.

Then the female guard came up from the shadows of the barracks and tugged along her own prisoner. Zala steeled in anticipation. The administrator had told her Captain Nubia was the prisoner who was to be transported as well, but the woman who squinted at the lantern at the head of the barracks didn't look like the Great Captain she knew.

Her skin was pale, her locs a bird's nest, her cheeks completely sallow and gaunt. But the eyes—the eyes were the same. Fierce and unrelenting. Unlike Sniffs, there was no recognition at all, however, she barely even looked at Zala. The moment the realization came, Zala wasn't sure what her reaction would be.

"Very well." Zala bowed her head. "I'll take them both." Turning on her heel, she led the two guards back into the main keep.

She didn't get five steps into the adjoining courtyard corridor, out of sight of the lone guard that stayed at the barracks, before she heard two thuds on the ground. She whipped on her heels to find the soldiers fallen over, dead. Slowly their bodies vanished like sands, leaving only their empty armor and helmets, with dagger and saber protruding from where their backs had been.

Zala lifted her head to Sniffs and Mantu, who held each other tight—well, more accurately, Mantu held Sniffs tight since he was still bound at the wrist. Mantu held Sniff's face in his arms, tears welling in his eyes, locked in a passionate gaze.

They kissed. A long, sensual, soft kiss, one where each lover savored the other longingly. Zala felt her own spirits lift. The joy on the mens' face brought her heart up a beat. Though she couldn't help feeling a pang of jealousy. What she would give to hold Jelani in her arms just as they were with each other in that moment. But to do that, she had to take care of Vaziri and his guards first.

Zala cleared her throat. "I know the two of you haven't seen each other for a long while, but Vaziri will know his guards are dead. We need to move now before he sends more."

"Right, of course, my bad," Mantu said, though his eyes didn't leave Sniffs'.

Zala went to retrieve her sword on the ground, handing Mantu his dagger back.

"Wait. Where they go?" Sniffs looked down to the floor, finally realizing the guards had vanished.

"The Vaaji have an illusionist," Nubia croaked. They all turned to her. She appeared dazed and a little confused.

"Them weren't no illusions. Them was holdin' me tight."

"They're technically not illusions." Nubia stretched down to the keys that had also fallen from their belts. "They're corporeal. Um... may I?" Her question was directed to Zala.

"Ka-pour-ree-what?" Sniffs asked, clearing his nose. Zala chuckled under her breath. She gave Mantu a sidelong glance. He too was smiling.

Ignoring Sniffs for the moment, Zala bent down to Nubia. "No. Let me, Captain." She took up the keys and freed the woman from her chains.

"My crew... where are they?" she asked immediately and hoarsely.

Zala was already ready with her half lie. "They're in the city, waiting for their Captain."

She knew full well what they were after. Lishan had told her back at that tavern that they thought Nubia was on the sky ship. Obviously she was not.

"You're a good woman, Captain Zala." Nubia gave her signature expression between a grin and a grimace. "Never expected to see your face again."

"Uh… yeah… thanks. Don't mention it."

Then it hit Zala.

If Nubia wasn't the "special individual" on the sky ship… that could only mean… Jelani really *was* on that sky ship. And he was likely on it alone. It made sense. With his powers to speak to sea creatures, they'd want to keep him far away from the ocean. No better place than up in the clouds, Gods know where. The thought of Jelani floating up somewhere over Vaaj didn't calm her though. If anything, it made the task of finding him all the more impossible.

This just meant she had to get in good with the Rovers again. Saving their Captain would earn her some points, wouldn't it?

The wounds that snaked up to her hands reminded her that probably *wouldn't* be the case.

When Nubia got all the information of what happened while she was away, it was unlikely she'd be jumping for joy.

A problem for another time, Zala thought.

Right now Vaziri was the focus. The Rovers and what to do with Nubia would come later.

"The man we're after has Gods' Glass in his possession, so his illusions are stronger," Zala explained to Sniffs. "Right now he's powerful enough to make his copies solid, so they can actually hold us and do us harm."

"We'll explain everything on the way," Mantu reminded Zala as he looked over his shoulder. "To the both of you."

"Right, follow me." Zala said. "And don't forget to pick up their weapons and armor."

Sniffs scratched his nappy hair. "But you say the bodies is fake."

"Most illusionists use as much real materials as they can," Nubia explained as she took the woman's armor. As she hefted the weapon, it looked like she never missed a day with a hilt in her hand—a warrior through and through. "Whoever your illusionist is is smart, or they're maintaining more illusions than they can handle. C'mon, I don't want to get recaptured. Who of my crew is in the city?"

"Um…" Mantu gave Zala a side-eye. "A few."

"Last ones I saw were Ekko and Iokaja," Zala said. "They were… well. Lishan was with them too and a few others. Let's figure out getting out of here first though, ya?"

With lovers and pirate captain in tow, Zala rushed through the palace's shortcuts once more. Nubia was fully decked out in Vaaji guard armor of light leathers, whereas Sniffs and Mantu split between armor pieces, with the former in helmet, and the latter in chainmail. In a few moments, her group had approached the courtyard outside and below Vaziri's office. Besides the occasional patrols, they were alone in the corridors.

Zala held a hand up once they had reached their destination, just outside Vaziri's office with its high arched windows and bamboo inlaids along the side of the sandstone.

"Scaling these arches shouldn't be too difficult, even for you, Sniffs," Zala said as they waited for Karim and the others. "Nubia, if you want to sit this one out, you can wait for us just here. Just watch out for the patrols."

"No, a good fight's the best way to get some life back in me." The woman could have been lying, but the grip around that saber was unmistakably steady.

"Do you know which window we need to break into?" Mantu asked, gazing up.

"The one with the inscription Karim told us. I just can't tell between these three." Zala pointed along the arch windows above. "The symbols look very similar. High Vaaji is difficult to read."

As Zala pondered which window was the right one, Shomari came bounding through the courtyard door from the side, pulling off his robes as he went. His fur was matted with sweat and it puffed out all over. Karim and Issa followed him, now dressed in full armor, their faces covered in helmets like Zala, Nubia, and Sniffs.

"It's like a desert under that thing," Shomari huffed. "How do those devotees wear that year round?"

"They're actually quite nice in this weather," Issa said, her voice muffled by her full helmet. "They're just not designed for mattes of fur like yours."

Shomari waved a dismissive hand.

Karim did a double take, his eyes just beyond Zala's shoulder. "Who is... I never said anything about breaking *her* out."

Zala turned round to see Nubia crouched beside her. "Yeah, well, she was being transferred to Vaziri's office anyway. We might as well drop her off, ya?"

Though his face could barely be seen, Zala could tell he was furrowing his brow heavily. "Having Captain Nubia is one of the only reasons I'm holding onto my position now—"

"And now she's going to help you hold onto it a little longer," Zala cut in. "The more we have the better the chances we have against Vaziri and his illusions. Or do you want me to march her back to the dungeons and tell them Vaziri didn't want to see her?"

Issa hummed under her lips, looked up to Vaziri's office windows, and then back down to Nubia. "Karim, what we really should be asking is what Vaziri wants with Nubia to begin with. If he's using her old crew to take the airship or whatever he's got planned, maybe it's something we should consider."

It was true, Zala thought. An idle thought had passed in her mind about why Vaziri would need Nubia. And there was only one answer... to use her as a bargaining chip to make sure the pirates handed over the sky ship when they got their hands on it —if that was even possible. Zala had tried it once, and it didn't go too well.

"Some Vaaji is using *my* crew?" Nubia hunched up, that familiar malice Zala had come to know returning to her eyes.

"Didn't you tell her?" Issa asked Zala.

Zala whipped between the women and their very opposite expressions, Issa's confusion and Nubia's rising anger. "I told her they are in the city… but we don't have the time to catch her up on everything." She cleared her throat awkwardly. "I didn't think we'd meet you all again so soon. Karim, do you remember which window you opened?"

Karim lifted his head toward the office's outer wall. "I—I believe it was that one." He pointed to the third one from their right.

"You had one job, kijana." Mantu stepped forward with a clenched fist. "What you mean 'I believe'?"

Zala couldn't make out Karim's expression through his helmet, but his voice continued to stammer. "H-his office is large. I can't recall which one it was… it could have been that one." He pointed to another window, two from the left.

Zala turned to Shomari. "Were you there when he spoke with the Collector?"

"I was not able." The cat thumbed between himself and Issa. "The guards wouldn't let either of us in."

Zala kept her eyes on Karim as she spoke. "Do you trust Karim has done what he said he would do?"

"You can trust him," Issa interjected for Shomari. "If he says he compromised Vaziri's office, then he did it. He doesn't break his word."

Zala crossed her arms. "That might work for you, chana, but none of us know this man. And we hardly know *you* any better."

"Then what about your husband, then? Jelani, right?"

Zala felt herself empty a bit at her husband's name. It was one thing to hear from those she knew, Fon, Shomari. Yet to hear it from someone she knew had him in her custody was another thing. It nearly sent her reeling.

"What do you know about him?" Zala's tone was ice.

"We've spoken to him a few times," she gave Karim a sidelong glance. "*I've* spoken to him. He's a man of honor, a good man on the wrong side of all this. Were he here he'd put trust in Karim."

"If he were here, none of us would be in this situation to begin with—"

"Then go ahead and be done with us," Karim gritted, the confidence in his voice returned. "You question our integrity but we've done nothing to break good faith." He struck a finger toward Vaziri's office, his voice rising with what seemed to be genuine anger. "If you can't place your trust in us after what I've done for you, then slit our throats now like the pirates you are."

Issa glanced between Zala and Karim, her armor squeaking as she turned her head. Mantu and Sniffs stood with raised eyebrows, anticipating Zala's response. Shomari crossed his arms, his hand resting on the pommel of his sword. Nubia's expression was etched with utter confusion. Who would she side with if this turned to a fight in the end, Zala wondered.

"Shomari..." Zala finally said. Without hesitation, the pakka drew his sword. Zala whipped her head to him. "What are you doing?"

"You want me to kill them, right?" he spoke with *far* too much enthusiasm.

"No," Zala said with exasperation. Then she sighed. Shomari's nerves must've really been frayed if he was that keen to be rid of their latest complications. "I want you and Karim to be the first to climb. If the Captain is telling us the truth, then we attack Vaziri together. If he's holding something back —"

"Then I slit his throat and drop him over the battlements?" Shomari leered.

Zala sighed again. "Yes, then that." She turned to Karim. "Fair enough?"

"Do I have a choice?"

"Well, it's like you said. The Collector is a common enemy, is he not?" Zala directed her gaze to Shomari and pointed to the windows she suspected were the right ones. "It's one of those three."

Shomari scaled the courtyard's pillars to the balcony above without effort. Karim followed, though with far less finesse. Issa took his rear and the remaining trio followed her. It was a good thing Vaaji architecture was so lavishly detailed with its wealthiest buildings, Zala mused as they went. They might've had a harder time with the climb otherwise.

When they all got to the terrace, Zala pressed her hand into her chin. "These two expressions make mention of Shati'ala's Will, but these two speak to humility. I just don't know which combination is right."

Zala looked into the window closest to her. She could make out the outline of Vaziri near his desk. The man was examining something in his library, his back turned to them. To Zala, his office looked more like a ballroom or an art gallery than a workplace.

Shomari started pushing on each of the windows.

"What are you doing?" Zala whispered loudly with wide eyes. "If you break the seal, the enchantments protecting this place will sound off."

"My delicate fingers will not be breaking the glass, do not fret," Shomari responded with a cavalier tone.

"Wait for Karim's order. He should remember which one is opened by now."

Karim squatted, resting his hands on his knees, his sword scraping the ground. "It's the last one right here. I'm sure of it."

"I hope you're right… for your sake," Zala said.

"This plan of yours seems less-than-baked," Nubia croaked again from the side.

Mantu gave her a light chuckle. "Welcome to our fucked-up crew. Now you know why you found us stranded on the Ibabi Isles. But… we manage."

At the last window, there was a give as Shomari pushed. Then he pulled. "I think I am finding our winner."

Zala shook her head, smiling. "Good work. Does everyone know what needs to be done?"

"Get 'round the tax man," Sniffs said. "Cut him from his Glass."

Shomari crouched close to the terrace. "I'll get the door. He had six men just outside it."

"Nubia can watch for any tricks," Mantu added, clutching his saber tightly.

"That, I can do." Nubia moved her locs from her eyes.

"Good," Zala said. "We can do this, people. Just keep your wits about you. This should be over in a few seconds. He has no one with him and we have surprise on our side. Ready?"

"Ready," they all said, save for Karim and Issa. But Zala knew the crew was eager to be done with all this business.

Zala threw up three fingers, then two, then one...

"Wait," Karim said. "We can't go in there."

"Ugh! He ruined the count!" Shomari snorted. "You know... we can kill him now. Once we're done with Vaziri we can escape without his help."

"But what about the sky ship?" Zala asked. "We need him for that part."

Karim ignored the pakka. "Look, we've gotten you this far, but we can't take direct action against the Collector. Why don't we support you from the rear. Issa and I can deal with the guards at the door."

"That's not a bad thought, Zala," Mantu said. "He's right. If he wanted to betray us he could've already. And I'd rather not get trapped in the office if we can help it. We'll need an exit route."

Zala didn't like it. There was something amiss about Karim but she couldn't see how or why he would betray them now. He opened the window, which meant he wanted Vaziri dealt with. What else could he do to prove himself? "Fine. The imperials will cover the door from the outside. When we take out Vaziri there may be more guards that show up but they'll ward them off."

"Thank you, Zala." Karim nodded.

"But we'll be taking those sabers from you." Mantu gestured with his hand. Karim traded a look with Issa. "Don't look at her. Give me your weapon."

"And how do you think we'll be able to defend ourselves?" Karim spat back.

"You was just talkin' 'bout not wanting to kill anyone. I'm sure you'll think of somethin'." Mantu crouch walked to Karim, forcibly taking his saber from his scabbard. "You see, that weren't so hard."

Mantu turned fierce eyes on Issa. With a full helmet, Zala couldn't see the imperials' expression, but she knew they were frowning.

"Go on," Karim ordered her. She was reluctant, but she gave her saber to Mantu.

"All right then, off with you two!" Zala shooed them away. Karim and Issa climbed back down before Zala turned back to her crew. "Okay, let's go."

"Awww, no countdown?" Shomari asked playfully.

"Just go," Zala said, irritated.

Shomari shrugged, then opened the window silently. When the window's door was wide enough to fit through, he rushed into the room, securing the entrance door at the far end. Mantu, Sniffs, and Nubia went for Vaziri, their feet lumbering. The tax collector turned on his heel with an "oh shit" expression, color drained from his face. For the first time since Zala had seen him, she saw his true face, one of complete and utter cowardice.

Tripping over himself, he retreated, stumbling to the book shelf that lined the back of room, where he started pulling at books like a mad man. One of them gave way and the whole shelf started to push inward, letting in a chill air into the room from the small sliver opening.

"Guards! Guards!" Vaziri cried out in horror. "The assassins are here!"

The grand wooden doors started to open but Shomari over-turned a bookcase in front of it. The guards started shouting, then slammed their hands against the door like thunder.

"That was easy," Shomari said, dusting his hands.

Vaziri was completely surrounded by the points of their swords and sabers. Now, there was nowhere for him to go.

CHAPTER 56
KARIM

Jogging, Karim and Issa made their way back to the financial corridor.

"What are we going to do without weapons?" Issa questioned as they rounded a corner to another open courtyard.

"We just need to distract them, that's all. We'll wait for the pirates to secure the office and—" Karim stopped short at the bizarre sight before him. Within the central fountain of the court-yard, a gull flapped in the shallow pools. Orange embers peppered the edges of its wings, but they quickly vanished under the water. "Wait... is that?"

It had only occurred to him then that the shortcut he and Issa had used was just outside his own office. The bird in that fountain could only be one person, one *human* person. But what would Nabila be doing here? And why was she on fire? Karim barely registered the oddness of it all. She was supposed to be watching over the...

An uncomfortable heat rushed through Karim and he almost felt sick.

Vaziri wasn't planning on taking the airship on some future date.

He's making his play right here and now, Karim thought bitterly.

Rushing to the fountain, Karim urged a very confused Issa to follow him. When he approached Nabila, who was breathing rapidly in her gull form, he cradled her in his hands and spoke softly. "Nabila... Nabila... what happened?"

Nabila opened and closed her beak, but no sound came from it.

"Did... did she fall from the sky?" Issa asked, then looked up to the lone tree that hung over the fountain. And indeed a few of its branches were bent, retelling the crash-landing Nabila underwent.

A little squeak left Nabila's beak at last, and her human mouth started to take form.

"No, wait," Issa said suddenly. "You shouldn't change until we look at your injuries."

It was true. It was already a nasty business changing and unchanging under regular circumstances for any shapeshifter. But with burns and injuries, Nabila could've done permanent damage to herself. Yet still, she continued to shift, her body staying the same, but her head growing slightly larger.

"Don't strain yourself, Nabila. Issa is right."

Still, she did not listen. She did not stop until her beak was mostly lips. And then, with an odd rasp that wasn't quite human she said three words: "Pirates. Airship. Taken."

Karim froze in place. He did this because if he didn't root himself in apathy he might've clenched Nabila tightly in his hand. He couldn't believe he could be so foolish, couldn't believe he went along with it all. Trust in pirates? What was he thinking? Composing himself, he made the slow turn to Issa, whose shock was apparent on her face, the utter gravity of what this meant as crippling to her as it was to him.

"Forget the office for now," Karim gritted. "I've another plan."

CHAPTER 57
ZALA

T̲HE SLAMMING AT V̲AZIRI'S OFFICE DOORS CEASED IN EERIE unison.

Zala and her crew jerked their heads to it. They were all thinking the same thing. What in the Sapphire Hells happened to all the guards outside? They couldn't have been taken down by Issa and Karim that quickly. Not all at once like that.

Vaziri's bark of laughter pierced the silence despite the deadly weapons pointed at his neck. The pirates turned their heads to him, watching as he tucked his hand below his shawl.

"Stop him!" Zala shouted.

She bounded for Vaziri—as did everyone else—but before any of the pirates could make their first vaults, a trio of illusions stopped them. Zala craned her head to Vaziri, who manifested another trio of illusions around him, and then three more, and then three more. Vaziri tried to manifest a thirteenth but it fizzled out like fleeting sands in the wind. Twelve must've been his limit for solid copies, his energy spent, even with the Dulagi Glass in his possession.

Shomari traded blows with the illusions who surrounded him on the other end of the office near the entrance door. Zala engaged one of the closest illusions to her with rapid stabs and thrusts while Sniffs and Mantu fought back-to-back, protecting

476

one another like a duo of Aktarian soldiers. Nubia sprang into a flurry of blade strikes Zala realized she had never seen before from the woman, a masterclass of fencing maneuvers that didn't seem to be diminished in her weakened state.

The illusions were easy to fight. From what little Zala knew of illusionary magic, the copies were only as good as their host, and Vaziri was clearly not a fighter. He had all the tells of an inexperienced fencer: no sense of timing, erratic, over exaggerated swings, and a palpable fear. Each of his illusions attempted to swing as quickly as possible, instead of swinging at the right times, making Zala look like a champion swordswoman. All she needed to do was take a brief side step or give a light parry before stabbing each through padded chests or cutting across their wrists.

And not only were Vaziri and his copies terrible fighters, but Vaziri was an even worse illusionist. He had the tools but the wrong execution, like a novice blacksmith working on his first forge. He worked hard, not smart, replacing his solid copies with no respite, no finesse. Master illusionists knew to supplement solid copies with incorporeal ones to throw their opponent off, yet Vaziri kept coming with one force, only using solid illusions.

That said, though Vaziri's skill was rudimentary, the illusions were many and Zala's crew were few, even with Nubia. While none of the copies could fight worth a damn, they just kept coming. Shomari took out five guards, but five more replaced them. Mantu and Sniffs teamed against another four, but another four replaced them. And the pair Nubia took on went down blow after blow—and kept coming back blow after blow.

Zala did her best to take out one every dozenth stroke or so, doing the worst of the bunch, but still, another copy replaced the ones she defeated.

They couldn't win this fight through pure bladework. They'd eventually tire. And that was exactly Vaziri's play. It would've been Zala's play if she were in the Collector's position.

"Shomari, we can't keep fighting them," Zala shouted across the room. "You have to get to Vaziri. Separate him from his Glass."

"That's what I've been trying, woman!"

Zala grinded her teeth. Shomari was right. He had no way to move from his position. Each time he tried to scale a wall or bound between Vaziri's easeled paintings to get closer to Vaziri, a new group of illusions converged on his position like a band of angry wasps protecting their queen. The Collector clearly knew that the pakka was the best fighter of the pirates, and he was making it his mission to do away with Shomari first before applying his attention to the rest of them.

Zala ducked under another wide swing from an illusion when she glanced to Mantu and Sniffs. They were closer to Vaziri than she was, and their paired fighting was perhaps even better than Shomari on his own as they called out to each other for this attack or that, like seasoned soldiers on a battlefield. But if they started moving toward the illusionist, she knew he would just send more of his guards at them. And now that the fight had gone on a few minutes, Nubia's weeks and weeks of doing nothing but wasting in a dungeon were starting to show, her strikes growing more and more sluggish with each push forward.

Zala was the only one who could slip his attention—not as flashy as Shomari, or as strong as Mantu or Sniffs, or as experienced as Nubia. But how could she do it? The group was at a deadlock.

Zala watched as Shomari took out two illusions by ducking under one of Vaziri's paintings and shooting back up with two quick moves. Zala whipped her head to Vaziri, who seemed to wince with the destruction of each illusion, his movements staggered. Shomari moved a step closer but Vaziri recovered, manifesting another pair to face off against the pakka.

That was it! Zala thought.

They just needed to hurt enough of them at the same time to stop Vaziri. Then Zala could make a break for him. Slipping his illusions would be easy enough if he was hunched over trying to recover from the residual pain.

There were many mystics who trained in the academies where Zala was raised, but she never knew an illusionist personally until Ekko, and Ekko had only been able to create landscapes effectively, not copies of people. Even with her limited knowledge,

Vaziri's lack of skill was telling. He might not have been a *total* novice but he certainly hadn't excelled past intermediate. Controlling the pain of one's copies was a mark of mastery.

"Shomari, stop killing them!" Zala shouted across the room.

"Are you mad, chana?" he growled back as he blocked three blows at once.

"Mantu. Sniffs. Nubia. You too."

"Killing them is what's keeping us alive," Mantu panted as he destroyed another illusion.

Nubia curled on her back foot, more defensive than she was at the start of the fight. "There ain't no way I'm letting 'em tag me."

"No time to explain," Zala grunted. "Trust me."

Zala ducked under the daggers of her two opponents, then ran to the far side of the room, where Vaziri had his back implanted to his wide bookshelves. The illusions gave chase, leaving a gap between the others and Vaziri. Now all Zala needed to do was find an opening that wouldn't be blocked by the other guards. If she killed the ones she fought, Vaziri would just get tipped off. If she kept them alive and just ran for it, however, maybe... just maybe.

"All right now! Kill as many as you can!" Zala ordered as she traded blows with her opponents.

Shomari took out three, one after the other. Mantu and Sniffs took out one a piece, though one caught Sniffs across his unprotected hip; he fell back to a knee, clutching at his side. Nubia couldn't get a true strike in but thrusted a kick against one of the illusions' stomachs. Zala evaded the next two strikes from her opponents, then used her agility to cut between them—straight for Vaziri.

"Master! Master! Master!" the illusions said in echoed unison.

Vaziri turned his head as Zala bolted for him, the tip of her sword leading her charge. He twisted his body around so fast, the cloth he wore over his shoulder flew off, revealing the purple hue of the Dulagi Glass in his hand, which was only the size of a small kiwi now.

Zala's eyes zipped to the Glass like a predator to prey.

Touch and rip, Zala thought.

She set the edge of her sword against Vaziri's wrist, then with-drew the blade, splitting his skin open.

Vaziri gave out a great cry, collapsing to both his knees.

But Zala felt a sharp pain at her back as steel seared through her skin.

"Zala!" Shomari shouted as she fell to the ground next to Vaziri.

Above her stood one of the guards, its dagger wet with her blood. It raised its hand over its head, ready to stab down, but then it vanished like sand in a storm. Zala moved her eyes to the marble floor, where the Collector's Glass rolled to the far end of the room, its purple glow dissipating with each revolution.

CHAPTER 58
ZALA

"Zala, are you all right?" Mantu was the first one to her side, holding her head up.

"The Glass..." she uttered, pointing to the marbled ball. Her lifted arm strained with the cut on her back and she seethed through her teeth. But somehow her body hadn't felt the pain in full and Zala wondered if all that time getting red tides from Ekko had something to do with it.

"Nubia, could you?" Mantu nodded toward the retreating Glass.

"I'm on it," she said, still clutching her thigh. She jogged with a limp to the other end of the room.

Mantu turned Zala over, examining her wound. "It doesn't look so deep. Your pads took most of it. Don't worry, those imperials should have a healer in here somewhere," Mantu said, smirking. "That was a hell of a move, chana."

Zala tried to turn herself back over, but she felt like her skin was splitting apart, a sensation she wanted to forget about.

"Take it easy. We got him," Shomari huffed, his mouth parted and his tongue lulled like a lion after a hunt.

Zala smirked up at him. "You're getting old, cat."

"Hey, hey, I was the one taking on five at a time."

"Is it over?" Sniffs looked around his shoulders as if another illusion could manifest from behind Vaziri's desk. His turns came slow though as he grabbed at his bleeding side.

Nubia came back with the Glass, and Sniffs snatched it from her in fear.

"Don't touch that!" Mantu exclaimed. "Cover it with somethin', or put it in your shirt." Sniffs did as he said. "The fool's gone and used it all up. Anymore and he woulda got the stoneskin."

The crew turned to Vaziri, who grunted as he lay on the ground, clutching at his cut wrist. The blood ran free under his cream robes.

"He might try to conjure some new illusions but they won't be as powerful as before," Zala said, trying to lift herself up. "We have him."

"Good—if you will allow me, I would like to be killing him," Shomari lifted his sword to Vaziri's throat.

"Wait!" Zala said as Mantu got her to her feet. Though her back was pained she still found strength in her voice. More strength then she thought she had.

Zala lifted her hand to Shomari's blade. "Remember what I told you before this day started. He's no use to us dead. His value comes from him being alive."

"Yes, listen to the woman. She speaks sense," Vaziri said through tears.

Zala slapped him across the face despite the pain it caused her.

"You're not getting off that easy, dikala." Zala pushed Shomari's sword away. "I'd gladly kill you, but you and I both know you'll be replaced the next day. But if I control you, then we could work something out."

Vaziri spat blood on the wooden floor. "Yes... yes I'll do whatever you want."

"Oh, yes you will. Because I know how to speak your language," Zala said. "No, not High Vaaji. I know what it is you *fear*. Sure we could rough you up, make you squeal some more, but that'll only get us so far. What you truly fear is what your Empire would do to you if they knew."

Vaziri went ghost quiet, even his whimpering ceased for a time.

"On our isle we can use the Gods' Glass as we please, though no one does," Zala spoke in the Vaaji Tongue so Vaziri would know the gravity of her words. *"On our isle they are sacred, only used in times of great need. Here in al-Anim, Gods' Glass is strictly regulated much like on our isle, but for a different reason. Since your Emperor and Empress came into power, Gods' Glass has been heavily controlled. And not because of the sanctity of the stone, but because your leader has uses for it, correct?"*

"How do you know this?" Vaziri asked, his face colored with shock.

"I've spent weeks infiltrating this palace, and I had a little help piecing it together from some others," Zala said, thinking back to the Rovers who often spoke of making specific shifts to avoid mystic hunters. *"But today I found a document that would really do you in. And I'm sure you know which document I'm speaking of. In this particular article it says all discoveries of Gods' Glass is to be turned over to the Monarchy at once. I've also come to understand that mystics are supposed to come forward with their gifts. Something tells me your higher-ups don't know that you're an illusionist—and better yet—that you possess Glass of Dulagi. What would happen if someone were to find this information out, I wonder? It wouldn't take much, just a letter to one of the Royal Family's advisors. We could plant our own supply of Glass in a hole somewhere, say that it's one of your hiding places. We know there are other nobles who know of your ability. They'd have to confess."*

"He'd never take a letter from you—"

"Then one of your contemporaries. I know you have at least one rival in Captain el-Sayyed, no?" Zala said. *"We wouldn't even need anything solid, we would just need to slip the rumor out there. And then the next day you'd have a shaman or a Seeker at the door commanding you to submit for a moonsbeam ritual. And once that happens, your secret would be revealed. The fact you have Gods' Glass is just a bonus. I've seen what your Empire does to those who don't pay their taxes. I can only imagine what they'll do to a traitor."*

Vaziri didn't move at first. He parted his lips a few times as though to speak, but stopped himself each time.

"I know right now you're thinking of the ways you can get out of this

situation. You might have some more Glass stored away somewhere, lots more. You think you might have a way to tail us. Let me stop you right there." Zala's voice shot daggers. "*There is nothing you can do. Have you noticed how easy it was for us to get here? If you step out of line once, just once, we'll frame you. If you so much as take an extra bronze from those you collect in the slums, we'll frame you. If you generate even one more illusion, in any context, we'll frame you.*

"*And I know what you're thinking right now... How can we know you're doing any of this? We have eyes everywhere, Vaziri. I know you've heard the rumors about the oni'baro guardians. We're only the foot soldiers in that organization. Imagine what will happen if our leaders caught wind of a noble who is stepping out of line?*"

There was a long pause before Vaziri answered. "*What is it that you want?*"

"Our terms are simple," Zala returned to the Mother Tongue so her crew could understand her. "In fact, I would say they are quite generous. Usually my friends and I would have you point us to your riches, we'd rob you blind, and we'd be on our way."

"We're not doing those things...?" Shomari asked.

Zala shot up a hand, silencing him. "We're feeling charitable today. We just want one thing."

"What's that?" Vaziri looked between Zala and the others.

"Stop taking the extra taxes from the slums," Zala said simply, matter-of-factly. "That's all."

"That's it? You're not even going to ask me to stop taking taxes all together?"

Zala shook her head. "No, Vaziri. And you know why."

"If you stop takin' them taxes, the Emperor will look to you," Mantu added, "and wonder why you ain't doin' your job."

"And we don't want eyes on you." Zala nodded. "We want you to hold your position here in the capital."

"I-I-I can do that..." Vaziri said, almost to himself, as though he were thinking over the scenario in his mind. What sort of machinations was he concocting? He must've had some new plan for climbing the ranks of his Empire, even with this setback.

"And that goes for the local businesses as well. No more," Zala ordered.

"Whatever you people say." Vaziri shot his hand up, still clutching his bloody wrist.

"Good. Now that we have an understanding, we need more information," Zala said. "Tell me, what do you know about these sky ships?"

"Y-you mean… the *air*ship?"

"Shomari."

Shomari lifted his sword and cut just above Vaziri's knee. Blood spread under his silky robe.

"Don't be smart with me," Zala said darkly. "I don't have any plans to kill you, but I've no issue leaving you disfigured. You've a pretty face and you seem to know it. What would you do if I gave you a few cuts."

"No need for that! I've been reasonable," Vaziri pleaded. "I mean—I could be reasonable."

"I don't know." Zala started cutting the edge of his lips with her blade. "Your illusions cut us up pretty good. It's only fair we return the gesture."

"No please, not my face," Vaziri cried.

"Then don't play coy with me." Zala's voice cut sharp. "Tell me about this *sky* ship."

"Well, if all goes to plan…" Vaziri said through gritted teeth. "It should be in my possession. Your little friends should be flying it back now for me."

Nubia stepped forward quickly despite her labored breathing. "What are you talking about? Are you talking about my crew?"

Vaziri laughed for the first time since he went down. "That's what tonight was all about, you see. It was all a ruse to take the airship. In a way we are all getting what we want, yes?"

Zala couldn't be sure, but she thought she could see the start of a proud smirk form on Nubia's lips at the information that it was her Rovers who took the airship. Then Zala considered the Collector's words a little while. Perhaps that wasn't such a bad thing. With the airship out of the Navy's hand and into a wannabe pirate like Vaziri, this all could work out for the better, Karim and that other woman be damned.

But that still left Jelani… alone with the Rovers.

I have Nubia with me, she'll vouch, Zala thought, *but first...*

"One last request, Collector," Zala said. "You are going to walk us out of this palace."

"I'm *what!?*" The color in Vaziri's face drained, and his laughter with it.

"All of you government officials must be knowing the secret passages out of here," Shomari said. "And I am knowing someone like you knows of at least one of them."

Vaziri's mouth went dry, constantly eyeing each of the pirates and back to his book shelves like they would save him. Zala grew tired of waiting for his response. She took her knife and split Vaziri from lip to cheek. "I told you I'd cut you if you didn't heed us."

Vaziri weeped, clutching the side of his face, his beard line highlighted by red.

"That gave me chills," Shomari purred, then smiled. "Remind me not to ever be messing around with you in the future, ya?"

"I gotta say... I agree," Nubia parroted. She too wore an impressed face, a genuine one.

Zala shrugged. "I told him it was fair. Look at you all, look at me." Zala showed them the cuts on her arms. "He got off easy." She turned to the crying man. "That was only a test. We already have a man on the inside who can get us out of here. Speaking of which... can we make sure they're not dead." Zala turned to Sniffs, thumbing a finger to the door.

When Sniffs was halfway to the door, hobbling and nursing the wound at his side, there was a knock.

"By the order of Emperor and Empress al-Nasir, you will open this door," a booming voice bellowed.

Sniffs stopped dead in his tracks, looking over his shoulder for direction.

"Wait." Zala lifted a hand quietly. "Wait."

There was another voice that came through the door, a voice they were all too familiar with "Pirates, put your weapons down. I have a score of twenty soldiers ready to raid this office."

It was Karim.

"Dikala, he only wanted us to defeat the illusionist," Zala seethed, mostly to herself.

"You have a count of ten before we blast through this door." Karim started his count. "Ten."

"What are we going to do?" Mantu asked, gripping his bloody saber.

"What about the window we came in through?" Zala asked, pointing.

"Nine."

"No good. There are guards there waiting," Nubia said, peering through the window.

"Eight."

"There has to be another way out." Zala said turning from left to right, pain searing through her back. She wouldn't have the strength for another fight.

"Seven."

Zala turned to Vaziri. "You, there has to be a tunnel out of here or something… where?"

"Six."

But Vaziri didn't have to tell her. He had been looking to his bookshelf the entire time he was being questioned. When they first got there he was pulling at something… something that… He was pulling for a lever!

"Five."

"Everyone to the bookshelf. No time to look for levers just push the whole damn thing," Zala ordered.

The crew pushed against the shelves as hard as they could, but it didn't budge. Zala did the best she could but she was too hurt to help much.

"Four."

"Push harder, dikala, push harder!" Zala shouted. "You too, Vaziri! If we go down, you do too. Your secret would be done."

"Three."

The crew put their full weight into the shelf, but it just wouldn't give. Zala, Nubia, and Sniffs were injured. Shomari and Mantu were exhausted. But if they were caught, the whole day, the whole past moon, would have been for nothing.

And still, Vaziri just stood there, transfixed.

"Two."

They had to push through, they had to. Zala bit down on her tongue, forcing herself through the pain as she pushed. She drove through the agony, drove through all the hurts.

If she was going to be a leader, she had to lead.

"One."

Silence. There was one, long terrible silence. And then…

"Hajjar," came Karim's cruel voice. "Blast down this door."

Zala, Karim, & Jelani

A NOTE FROM THE AUTHOR

Thank you for reading the second novel
in the *Sky Pirate Chronicles*.

Originally, I outlined and wrote the story as a duology between
Zala and Karim. But when I started drafting it, it was apparent
that their stories were far too connected to divide them into two
separate stories.

This second book was a huge undertaking
and it is my longest book to date.

If you enjoyed *Of Ruin & Silk*, please leave a review on your
favorite retailer or social media (and don't forget to tag me).

THE CHRONICLES CONTINUE

Read the next book in the series!
The Sky Pirate Chronicles: For Code & Honor

Lines have been draw. Allies become enemies.
And an airship hangs in the balance.

Visit this link to get notified:
antoinebandele.com/stay-in-touch

ALSO BY ANTOINE BANDELE

TJ & THE ORISHAS

The Gatekeeper's Staff

The Windweaver's Storm

The Hero's Equinox

ORISHAS AMONG MORTALS

Will of the Mischief Maker

When the Wind Speaks

An Axe for a Hammer

TALES FROM ESOWON

The Kishi

THE SKY PIRATE CHRONICLES

By Sea & Sky

Of Ruin & Silk

LOST TALES FROM ESOWON

Last of My Kind

Stoneskin

ANTHOLOGIES

Orishas Among Mortals

Demons, Monks, & Lovers

Tales from the Otherworlds

The Chronicles of Underrealm

ABOUT THE AUTHOR

Antoine lives in Los Angeles, CA with his life partner and cat.
He is a YouTuber, producing work for his own channel, which
mostly covers *Avatar: The Last Airbender*.
He is also an audiobook engineer.

Whenever he has the time, he's writing books inspired by African
folklore, mythology, and history.

antoinebandele.com

To my beta readers:

Kristina Collins, Lukas Gibson,
Calvin Klontz, and Andrea S.U.

Thank you for your time and dedication to this project.
The story wouldn't be what it is without you marvelous marauders.

To my editors:

Fiona for giving the characters heart,
Callan for bringing the prose and dialogue to life,
and Seth for tying it all together.

I couldn't've picked a better
bunch of buccaneers.

GLOSSARY

Terms and Locations from Esowon

- **A'bara:** The word for "magic" in the Old Tongue.
- **Agal:** an accessory worn by Vaaji to keep their head wraps secure on their heads.
- **Ajowan:** The southern most island of the Sapphire Isles.
- **Akeem:** One of the Great Cities which holds one of the most sacred religious sites.
- **Aktah:** One of the Great Nations, just north of Ya-Seti. Known for it's ancient history and large pyramids.
- **Andala:** One of the Great Nations north of the Midland Seas.
- **Anjunjun:** *Mysterious creatures with elongated tongues that look like tails in silhouette.*
- **al-Anim:** The capital of Vaaj.
- **al-Qiba:** The monotheistic religion of Vaaj. It holds Shati'ala, the Goddess of Free Will and Magic, as its Supreme One.
- **Asiya Bay:** The inlet sea between the borders of Aktah to the west, and Vaaj to the east.
- **Àyá:** The Goddess of the Rivers and the Little Moon.

- **Aziza:** A fae species originating from the jungles of Kunda, though many half-breed offspring can be found throughout Esowon.
- **Chana:** Slang used for female pirates of the Sapphire Isles.
- **Darkstone:** A spent Glass of God, a stone that, when touched, can infect a person with the stoneskin disease.
- **Dawa:** A common root used as an all-purpose healing salve and poultice.
- **Deh'ala:** The God of Gates and Thresholds.
- **Dikala:** An insulting word used mostly among the peoples of the Sapphire Isles and the Esterlands.
- **Eloko:** A kind of dwarf-like creature that lives in the Kunda jungles. They are believed to be the spirits of ancestors of the ancient little people who once lived there.
- **Eti Eti:** The God of Hearing, namely of deafness.
- **Foglands:** A persistent and mysterious fog region at the southern tip of the world.
- **Genizebi:** The God of Wealth.
- **Golah:** The former empire which stretched from Bajok in the south to Imtubo in the north.
- **Golden Lord:** The ruler of the Pirate Nation of the Sapphire Isles.
- **Grootslang:** A creature known colloquially as an elephant snake residing in large caves near the Fog Lands, though scholars have spotted them within Kunda Jungle as well.
- **Ibabi Isles:** A collection of uninhabited islands north of the Sapphire Isles and south of Asiya Bay.
- **Illopa:** The Goddess of Love.
- **Impundulu:** One mystical bird native to the Fog Lands at the southern tip of Esowon. Their wings and talons are said to summon thunder and lightning which make the Fog Lands uninhabitable. Legend states these creatures were the direct creation of the God of Lightning and Storms, M'Bani.

- **Imtubo:** One of the Great Cities which holds three of the most prestigious academies in literature and arts, science and mathematics, and theology.
- **Injera:** A spongy flatbread from Jultia which serves as a replacement to utensils. It is foundational to all Jultian meals.
- **Janbiya:** A curved dagger used by the people of Vaaj, both military officers and common folk.
- **Jasmiin Towers:** The central palace of al-Anim, the heart of the Vaaji Empire.
- **Jo'bara:** The Old Way. An old religion that gives praise to all the old gods without putting any one above another.
- **Julti:** The language and tongue of Jultia.
- **Jultia:** One of the Great Nations, just south of Ya-Seti. Known for its unique religious fervor and sweeping palaces. Some claim it to be a pioneer of Esowon's future infrastructure.
- **Khopesh:** The military capital of Aktah. Also the favored sidearm weapon of the Aktarian military.
- **Kidogo:** The northern most island of the Sapphire Isles.
- **Kijana:** Slang used for male pirates of the Sapphire Isles.
- **Kongamato:** A flying creature with leathery skin, bat-like wings, and beak filled with razor-sharp teeth. Also known as a "boat-breaker" among the river people near Kunda Jungle.
- **Kor:** The primary ruler of Ya-Set.
- **Kor'de:** Spouse to the ruler of Ya-Set.
- **Kubahari:** A giant sea creature of legend. One of the most ancient beings of Esowon noted for their large and magical twin-horns.
- **Kunda:** The largest unbroken rainforest in the world. Home to many of the ancient creatures and mystical beasts of the Old Times.
- **Maji:** A master of a mystical art discipline.

- **Mazomba:** A giant fish of mystery whose scales can often be found near the Ibabi Isles.
- **Merfolk:** The sea people who once lived in the Lost City, north of the Sapphire Isles.
- **Mero-Set:** The language and tongue of Ya-Set. It is unique in that its formal speech and dialect is paired with many hand gestures.
- **Moharam the Uniter:** The leader who united the former tribes of what is now the Vaaji Empire.
- **Nene Kato:** A small fishing village on the northern coast of Ya-Set.
- **Ogó'ala:** The Supreme God. Also known as the King God.
- **Oni'baro:** Religious devotees and leaders of the old spirit-religion, Jo'bara.
- **Pakka:** Cat-men from the forests of Daji and the jungle of Kunda, though their kind can be found all throughout Esowon.
- **Pyrus:** The commercial capital of Aktah.
- **Riqq:** A type of tambourine used as a traditional instrument in Vaaji music.
- **Saabi:** A casual term used to refer to friends and acquaintances within Vaaj.
- **Saa'fa ala:** *The Vaaji phrase for the pilgrimage taken to the Holy City of Akeem, translated, it means "God's Path."*
- **Sapphire Isles:** Seven Islands that cut between the nations of Aktah, Ya-Seti, Jultia, to the west, and Vaaj, to the east.
- **Shati'ala:** The Goddess of Free Will and Magic.
- **Sindisi:** The military title given to the mystguards of Vaaj. They are tasked with the protection of the nation's active-combat mystics.
- **Sonamancer:** A mystic who can manipulate and alter sound waves.
- **Stonesbane:** The temporary remedy to stoneskin. Slows growth, but does not remove affliction.

- **Suhul Steppes:** The northern outskirts of al-Anim proper, known for its one landmark—al-Turabi's grand estate, once a holy site of the Old Way.
- **Tarha:** A tight head wrap typically worn by Vaaji females.
- **Tokoloshe:** A gremlin creature from the swamps of the Kunda Jungles and its outskirts. Child-size bodies, gauged eyes, and a hole in their heads. Though originating from Kunda, these mischievous bunch of creatures can often be found wreaking havoc on local villages.
- **Ugara:** The God of War.
- **Ula:** The Goddess of the Cosmos and Foretelling.
- **Uqapele:** The God of Discretion.
- **Wageni:** A non-human.
- **Wazantsi:** The most southern region of the Esowon continent, pressed up a mysterious foglands that no one ever enters.
- **Ya-Set:** One of the Great Nations. Known for their skilled archers and lavish palaces.
- **Yem:** The Goddess of the Oceans and the Big Moon.
- **Yemàyá:** The Twin Goddesses of the Oceans, Rivers, and Moons. Also an expression used at the turn of the new moons.
- **Vaaj:** One of the Great Nations, just east of the Sapphire Isles.
- **Vitumbua:** A small flat cake, often thin and round, prepared from starch-based batter containing coconut milk, almond extract, and brown sugar.
- **Zanziwala:** Also knows as the "Big Isle." This island is the central location of the Sapphire Isles and the hub of all commercial activity in the Sapphire Seas. Home to the Golden Lord and his wealthy merchant court.
- **Zizah'r:** The native language and tongue of the aziza.